PERESTROIKA

An Eye for an Eye, a Tooth for a Tooth

JOÃO CERQUEIRA

8TH HOUSE PUBLISHING

8th House Publishing
Montreal, Canada

First Edition

Cover Design by 8th House Publishing

ISBN 978-1-926716-77-0

www.8thHousePublishing.com
Set in Garamond, Raleway & Grobold.

LIBRARY AND ARCHIVES CANADA CATALOGUING IN PUBLICATION

A CIP data block is recorded at the National Library of Canada.

PERESTROIKA

An Eye for an Eye, a Tooth for a Tooth

João Cerqueira

CONTENTS

INTRODUCTION

SLAVIA is a country with an area of 40,000 square kilometers, situated between Poland, the German Democratic Republic, the Federal Republic of Germany, Czechoslovakia, and Austria. Its capital is Tiersk. It has four million inhabitants, and its main resources are natural gas, copper, and timber. Founded in the thirteenth century, it was ruled by a succession of monarchs until 1940, when it was invaded by the Nazis. After its liberation in 1945, Slavia became part of the Eastern Bloc dominated by the Soviet Union.

Since 1950, on the death of the former president, Alfred Ionescu has governed Slavia. His most important cabinet ministers are Pietr Schwartz, the Chief of the Secret Police, Igor Olin, the People's Commissar for the Economy, Zut Zdanhov, the People's Commissar for Culture and Propaganda, and Helena Yava, the People's Commissar for Education.

The regime controls the economy, the courts, and the forces of law and order. It uses mass media, the cinema, theatre, art and sport as tools of propaganda and for the indoctrination of its citizens. The regime banned religion and closed the churches. Elections are not free, and neither freedom of expression nor any individual initiative is permitted, nor even the publication of books and newspapers unless they have been approved by a committee of censors. Citizens receive ration cards with which they can purchase goods in the shops, and they need a visa for permission to leave the country. Dissidents are persecuted and sent to labor camps for re-education, where they are turned into slaves.

CHARACTERS

Alfred Ionescu – President of Slavia
Igor Olin – People's Commissar for the Economy
Zut Zdanhov – People's Commissar for Culture and Propaganda
Helena Yava – People's Commissar for Education
Pietr Schwartz – Chief of the Secret Police
Luda Schwartz – Chemical Engineer and Pietr's wife
Stanislau Yovic – Concentration Camp Commandant
Pietr Huss – Chief Guard at the Concentration Camp
Chef Kristoff – Cook
Marius – Concentration Camp Prisoner
Koba or Ivan Fiorov – Boss of organized crime cartel that controls Slavia
Adam Jacek – Leader of the resistance movement, Solidarity
Rufus and Zacko – Members of Solidarity
Leonidas Vall – Dissident in Solidarity
Cornelius and Rado – Leonidas' companions
Silvia Lenka – Student of Art History
Albert Remus – Writer and dramatist
Ludwig Kirchner – Painter
Maria Kirchner – Kirchner's wife
Lia Kirchner – Daughter of the couple
Aliocha – Olin's son, who suffers from cerebral palsy
Hans Ross – Police Inspector
Ruth Meyer – Orphanage Director
Elias Roth – Child living in the orphanage
Tobias Munt – Child living in the orphanage
Guro Nuria – Travelling salesman
Ivo Karlovic – Priest
Markus Richter – Secret Police Agent
Dr Max Steiner – Ionescu's Physician
Joseph – Ionescu's Chauffeur
Matieux Foucault – the French Consul
Hector Lott – Painter
Ana Kull – Journalist
Szut – Fiorov's Bodyguard
Jacob Levi – Art Collector
Isaac Miron – Russian Businessman
Jan – Neo-Nazi Ideologue
Stefan – Martial Arts Fighter

What is truth? Pilate asked Jesus.

John 18:38

I
PARADISE ON EARTH
♛ 1978 ♛

IT WAS the day of the grand opening of the Palace of the Arts, whose purpose was to celebrate the regime's aesthetic achievements, or, as it had been advertised, 'the great deeds of the People's Republic of Slavia in the fields of painting, sculpture and photography.' The building was neoclassical in style, fifteen meters tall and 2,000 square meters in area. The marble façade had a triangular pediment and a sculpted frieze depicting the triumphs of the revolution, supported by four Doric columns. A staircase with twenty granite steps led to the entrance. Inside was a corridor with a red carpet which led to three salons where works of art were exhibited. The floor was wooden and the walls and ceilings were white. Since there were no windows, crystal chandeliers provided the lighting. A central heating system with radiators maintained a constant temperature of twenty-two degrees Celsius. The exhibition hall on the right held works of sculpture, the one on the left displayed paintings, and the central hall was for photography and posters.

Eighty regime officials had been invited, along with diplomats from the countries that had relations with Slavia. In all, a hundred and sixty people were present. Forty-five liveried attendants had the task of serving them with vodka, champagne, and French wine, as well as caviar, lobsters, and smoked salmon. Twelve young women aged between twenty and twenty-six, chosen for their physical attractions, were charged with entertaining the diplomats, furnishing them with information on the country and the works of art, and in the event of any of them showing an inclination, accompanying them afterwards. Among these hostesses, the most solicitous and ever-smiling was Silvia Lenka.

In the hall devoted to painting, Pietr Schwartz, the Chief of the Secret Police, with Zut Zdanhov, the People's Commissar for Culture and Propaganda, and Albert Remus, one of the regime's official writers, were contemplating a picture that was four meters wide and two tall. It was a painting of an industrial complex that manufactured fertilizers, and it showed workers entering the main building, and smoking chimneys. The factory was painted brown, the smoke was black, and the human figures wore grey uniforms. In the background was a yellowish plain that seemed to dissolve in a dusky horizon. The contrast between the gigantic building and the smallness of the workers made them look insignificant beside the factory, indeed gave the impression that they were tiny creatures entering the mouth of a monster.

Zut Zdanhov was fat, of average height, with brown hair and eyes. Without looking away from the picture, as if he were talking to himself, he began to critique it.

'This is a good example of how a work of art can be modern and at the same time accessible to the public. The way the light is depicted, along with the power of the color and the aerial perspective are notable features of the vanguard, and yet anyone can understand the theme. In contrast to the art of some modernists, which is nothing but rubbish fit for children, this work expresses the truth. Our workers will feel proud of this picture.'

Schwartz was a short, thin man, bald, with a black beard and blue eyes.

'I visited the factory last year and I can assure you it's excellent. It produces high quality fertilizers that not only enable us to increase our own agricultural production, but also to supply a surplus for export. Working conditions are superb and the workers are highly motivated. They're so dedicated that they volunteer to work on Saturdays and Sundays without pay. Where could that possibly happen in capitalist countries?'

'Yes,' said Zdanhov, 'the devotion of our workers proves that capitalism is doomed. In America the worker is an alienated being who has no relationship with the company. He works for whoever pays him most; all he cares about is his wages. Even so, he's unhappy because he knows he's serving a boss who exploits him and a system in which he occupies the lowest position. That's why America has the highest rate of suicide in the world.'

Albert Remus interrupted the conversation. Tall and thin, with fair hair and green eyes, he struck a contrast with the other two men.

'Isn't it Sweden? It seems it has something to do with the lack of sunlight…'

'I said America!'

Remus lowered his head:

'Yes, you're right. In America people commit suicide whenever the prices of stocks fall.'

'And which artist painted this picture?' asked Schwartz.

'Ludwig Kirchner,' said Zdanhov.

'But he was arrested and is in a re-education camp. Shouldn't they withdraw his works from the exhibition? Couldn't there be some subversive element here, disguised? We must be careful…'

'Comrade Schwartz, as you can see for yourself, everything is clear in this picture. The factory, the workers, and nature are in perfect harmony, nothing else. Besides, the work of art is independent of its creator. Once it's exhibited, it no longer belongs to him. In that situation, it has become the property of the people. As for the painter, he's just a poor devil.'

'He was denounced as a counter-revolutionary.'

'Right, but as you know, at times denunciations are motivated by personal revenge.'

'That doesn't make the slightest difference. He was denounced and he's in custody. Our system has a fist of iron for its enemies, but it allows them to defend themselves because it's also fair and impartial. In the event of an excess of zeal, the accused only has to prove his innocence and his problems are over. But let's change the subject, there are other interesting works of art to see.'

In the hall showing photography and posters, Igor Olin, the People's Commissar for the Economy, and Helena Yava, the People's Commissar for Education, were contemplating a photograph of Pioneers that was a meter long and sixty centimeters wide. A squad of forty boys and girls between the ages of twelve and fifteen, wearing blue trousers and skirts, white shirts and red scarves round their necks, in four ranks, were saluting as if they were in a military parade. Sunlight struck them diagonally, illuminating the left side of their faces but leaving the right side in shadow. In the second row, in the third place, stiff and serious, was young Roman Schwartz, the son of the Chief of Secret Police.

Helena Yava gave her impression of the photograph:

'How strong and healthy our youth are. Just look at those arms and legs. Look at those faces: what character, what determination! When I see these boys and girls marching, so disciplined and obedient, loyal to the fatherland and ready to take up arms in its defense, I feel great pride in our work. They are the cast iron guarantee that the revolution will triumph and the future will belong to us. Can you imagine what this generation will be achieving ten or twenty years from now?'

Igor Olin shook his head with a smile.

'My nephew has been made the leader of a brigade of Pioneers. This past weekend they visited a farm and helped to pick half a ton of tomatoes. A group of enemies of the people were also there, being re-educated through labor, and they were humiliated. They couldn't pick even half the tomatoes that our lads did.'

Helena Yava turned to him:

'What do you expect of such miserable riffraff? They want the people to starve. It's the most perfidious form of sabotage. I'll tell you, that group should be sent to a re-education camp where they have to chop wood. We're far too soft on the enemies of the people. Picking tomatoes never worried anyone.'

'You're right, but let's not waste time on such scum. Instead let's talk about our Pioneers, our young men and women we're so proud of. In the whole of world history no project has ever been so noble or so ambitious. They really will transform the world. We need to devise contests between them to induce them to exceed themselves and become better still, we need to...'

Helena Yava raised her right hand:

'Comrade Olin, you don't have to teach me my job. Our Commissariat works incessantly to raise the cultural, physical and patriotic standards of our youth. Are you aware that at the last international meeting of Pioneers, ours beat the Soviets? They are going to be the most perfect revolutionaries humanity has ever produced. I don't have the slightest doubt that their generation will deliver the final blow to the capitalist system.'

Just then, at the entrance to the exhibition halls, an agitated murmur of voices was heard, resembling the buzzing of a swarm of bees. But just as suddenly, as if they had found an exit and escaped at once, the hubbub ceased. The guests halted their conversations, girls held their hands behind their backs, and the waiters did not dare to take a step. In the Palace of the Arts the people in attendance were as silent as the figures in the photographs and paintings and as still as the stone and metal statues. A word or gesture out of place might subject the body of the careless person to painful stings.

Alfred Ionescu had arrived.

♚

Maria

MARIA Kirchner had been in the queue for food at the grocery in her quarter of the city since dawn. She had been up at five and dragged her tired legs up the steep streets of Tiersk to the shop, which only opened at half past eight. She was wearing a grey jacket, a white polo-neck sweater, a red cap, and the only pair of boots she possessed. Night was beginning to fade in violet tones and the snow on the roofs struck a contrast with the grey façades. The yellow light of the few streetlamps that worked seemed to shrivel with cold. The city would only thaw around noon. But at that hour men and women were already rushing to factories and government offices, setting in motion a transport system consisting of trains, buses, and a few private cars.

When Maria arrived there were ninety-six people in front of her, all with cross faces, shivering with cold and with breath steaming from their nostrils, none of them uttering a word of greeting to whoever joined them. She took her place without greeting anyone either, treating the others as enemies who meant to rob her of the bread and milk she needed to feed Lia, her thirteen-year-old daughter. The line of hungry citizens awaiting their turn to be fed by the Party restrained the urge to pillage the store and the desire to steal the food ration cards from the nearest citizen. The prospect of a sentence in a labor camp dissuaded everyone.

In front of her was a tall man with a bent back who never stopped coughing. *He must be a widower or have no sisters,* thought Maria, since men did not do women's tasks, especially when it was a question of waiting in the cold for hours for food that might not be what you expected, and might be in insufficient amounts. Maria's ration cards gave her the right to a bottle of milk and a kilo of bread, but before now she had had to return home with nothing but a bag of flour or a rancid sausage. Sabotage – that was the answer you invariably heard when the food distribution system was not working.

Who is this man and what is he hoping to get?

This was one of the ways she whiled away the time to put up with the wait and cheat the cold; she tried to guess what kind of person was in front of her and what kind of food the Party allowed him. Usually she concluded that it was someone like herself: a civil servant whom the Party provided with a basic food basket, and who probably did not have a spouse under arrest – which meant fewer rations. Sometimes, though, she decided that she was in the presence of a woman even more miserable than herself, someone who had fallen into disfavor because of a denunciation by an envious neighbor – she did not believe that genuine conspirators could ever be in that queue – and who, following the appropriate re-education, recovered their freedom, but were deprived of a portion of the rations they had formerly enjoyed. Occasionally she imagined that the person in front of her was a privileged person, someone with a more important post than usual, or the lover of a Party official, or someone who had carried out an important denunciation, and so had the right to more food, as well as fresh fruit and butter. Noticing the quality of the clothes and the boots the man wore, she decided he had found some way of improving his lot, by riding on the backs of those unluckier than himself. If she detested everyone in the queue, for that kind of person she felt real hatred.

Parasite, scum, I hope you are denounced.

Maria was silently insulting the man when he turned abruptly and stared at her for several seconds. Maria trembled, believing for a moment that he had divined her thoughts. However, instead of showing hostility, a sad smile played upon on his purple lips.

'I used to work with your husband. He's a good man. Everything will be fine, don't worry.' No sooner had he spoken than he turned his back as if he had no more to say to her.

Maria was terrified. The man had to be in the secret police and was tormenting her; or else the message meant that they would soon shoot him or he was already dead. In the hell which her life had become, such words pronounced by a stranger, or even a friend, could only be interpreted as a prediction or confirmation of a calamity. Good news never came from the re-education camps; the best you could hope for was no news at all, not a single message, perfect silence. And suddenly, with as little warning as he had vanished, the convict would come home, re-educated by work, cold, hunger, and daily beatings. The method was nearly always infallible. Once re-educated, the former troublemaker became a model citizen who followed Party rules to the letter. For instance, he would never again give an opinion on anything, even the weather, unless it had first been expressed by Party leaders or had appeared in the official newspaper, *Unity*. When in doubt, he resorted to silence, or if his interlocutor insisted, withdrew, making some excuse. Besides, the re-educated person no longer practiced solitary hobbies such as fishing or walking in public gardens, but preferred to dedicate his free time to activities organized by the Party, which he attended as assiduously as before the revolution saintly women had attended church. All the same, the best way for a re-educated person to prove his loyalty to the Party was denouncing others, guilty or innocent, it mattered little, and making them suffer the same horrors he himself had undergone. The Party truly appreciated this attitude, especially when the informer accused members of his own family. To be responsible for sending one's parents or a brother to a re-education camp, to show more love for the Party than for the family, to break the ties of blood for the sake of Party doctrine, was considered a proof of complete rehabilitation, and naturally was rewarded by a more ample basket of groceries.

So it was that Maria neither answered him, nor asked him anything. Pretending that it had nothing to do with her, pretending to be deaf, playing dead as if one were under attack by a bear, was the best defense from such provocations. And that was the sole advantage of the cold: the shivering of a terror-stricken soul was no different from that of a frozen body.

She was just wondering if she could give up her place in the queue to get away from the man, swapping her place for that of someone behind her, when she heard shouts:

'Thief, you stole my ration cards,' the older woman yelled.

'Get off me, you loony,' shouted the other.

The younger woman was tall and pretty while the other was squat, with lumpy features. Both had glaring eyes, snarling lips and throats dilated by blue veins. Maria thought the first was a student or a secretary, while she categorized the second as a factory worker or cleaner. Such scenes she had witnessed many times, involving women of all ages and walks of life, sometimes because of a real theft and sometimes simply as a pretext for taking someone's food.

The younger women grabbed the older one's hair and yanked it; the older one got her hands around the other's neck and started to strangle her; their faces reddened and the howls of the two enraged beasts split the air; the two bodies began to merge, so that the torso of one seemed to have the head of the other, and their limbs entwined like snakes; now the two were one, a single frantic creature that flailed in all directions, disrupting the queue; then they lost their balance, fell and rolled in the snow, and the older woman managed to get her right arm free, opened her calloused claw, curved her fingers and flung the yellow nails at her opponent's face; the crone's nails pierced the apple-like face of the young woman and tore her flesh down to her jaw; the victim bellowed as smoking blood ran down her cheek and soaked her clothes; the older woman let out a triumphant roar, stood up, snatched the shopping bag of the other and ran off. The younger stayed shaking on the ground, disfigured, but no one helped her. A police car arrived and out got two officers who grabbed her, forced her into the vehicle and took her away.

A white molehill with red stains was all that was left of the incident.

Not long afterwards, a woman called Ruth joined the queue, who lived in the same street as Maria. Although they were not friends, they knew one another and greeted one another when they met in public places, but there, in that situation where the instinct for survival was uppermost, neither acknowledged the other. The neighbor positioned herself just two meters behind her and put her empty bag on the pavement.

At last, an hour later, it was Maria's turn to be served. The grocery was a dark place that smelled of flour and soap. Instead of a door, there was a lobby with a greasy floor and a cracked marble counter behind which two assistants with grey uniforms and surly faces inspected the ration cards and handed over the corresponding items of food. With her head held low, Maria slowly approached the assistant who had called her. The citizens' veneration for these workers was similar to that they held for police officers or judges, since, if for any reason the assistants became annoyed with anyone, they could supply them with less food, or spoiled food, or even pretend that the requested item was sold out. And any protests would only worsen the situation.

'Bread and milk, please,' said Maria.

The assistant was a middle-aged man with sleepy eyes. He

turned his back on her and headed for the inside of the store. Presently he returned with two loaves under his arm but no milk. Maria gave him a pleading look, in the hope of an explanation which was not offered.

'The milk, the milk's missing,' Maria murmured.

The assistant bit his lip and sighed. 'There's no milk.'

'How come there's no milk? Just two days ago there was.'

'Sabotage. Enemy agents have managed to sabotage the agricultural production. Didn't you know?' He raised his voice as he asked.

Maria lowered her gaze and swallowed. 'Yes, I knew, of course I did...'

'Then why did you ask? Are you making an insinuation about the Party's competence?'

'No, not at all. Sorry.'

'Next!' shouted the assistant.

Maria grabbed her loaves, shoved them in her bag and left. As she passed the queue, tears ran down her face. A few people looked as if they felt sorry for her, while others stared at her with scorn, but most ignored her.

Maria began her journey home. The sun was starting to warm the city, but its rays did not warm her body. Her feet were frozen and her paces dragged. Her boots scraped the cement of the pavements as if they wanted to act as brakes. The other pedestrians moved fast and ended up bumping into her to get the nuisance out of their way; one or two passers-by cursed or insulted her. Maria did not even see them, or hear them. Her eyes registered the crowd around her, the buildings and the cars in the streets, the simmering noises of the city and the coarse remarks directed at her reached her ears, and her nose smelled the bodies and machines. However, all this sensory information collided against a wall she had raised in order to concentrate on her problem: how to explain to Lia that she had not brought the promised milk.

It would not be the first time that she came home nearly empty-handed. Lia was used to disappointment, she had already begun to understand what sort of society she lived in, she did not even complain, but even so, every time it happened, an earthquake of guilt, shame and disgust tore Maria apart. Now she was trying to rebuild herself from the rubble so that she could reason clearly. Unfortunately, as the problem she was trying to solve was the cause of her desolation, the more she thought about it the worse she felt. The few possibilities she had of fixing it failed to encourage her: stealing, prostituting herself, or becoming the lover of a Party official—each of these made her feel like vomiting all the milk in the world. Even so, for the sake of Lia, maybe she had no alternative left but to choke on her own vomit. Plenty of women as respectable as her had done it, and one friend who was a convert to the new laws of survival told her that it was only hard the first time, then you got used to it, after a while it became normal, a routine like any other, and sometimes, when the comrade for whom you opened your legs was nice, you even ended up liking it.

Maria leant against a wall, opened her mouth and let her gastric juices fall.

When she got home, she found Lia at the kitchen table, doing her homework. She had eaten a crust of bread from the previous day and drunk a cup of tea. Lia raised her head and no sooner did she see her mother's face than she understood everything. As usual, she tried to lessen her pain and save her from embarrassment.

'Never mind, mum, today I don't even feel like drinking milk.'

Maria tried to smile but her lips would not obey and, instead of describing an upward curve, rumpled and twisted. Then her breathing was disrupted by sobs and at last tears fell. Lia got up and hugged her.

'Don't cry, mum. It's not your fault. The saboteurs are destroying our economy to delay the revolution. We were just talking about that in school yesterday. Our teacher said we must be prepared to make sacrifices. But victory is certain.'

Maria stopped crying, disengaged herself gently from her daughter, and looked at her again. Would she ever be able to speak to her without fear? Would she ever be able to tell her what was going on without exposing her to the danger of reprisals? She had told her that her father had been sent by the Party to do important work in another city, and she did not know when he would be back, but she had never thought that Lia believed it. What might they have told her about the matter in school, if they had told her anything?

She was thinking about this when she heard a knock on the door. *It's the old man from the grocery queue who's come to arrest me.* He must have heard her complaints about the milk shortage and informed his colleagues in the police. They had probably been following her for some time and just waiting for a slip from her so that they could send her to a re-education camp. A lot of public projects were underway and they needed new hands to finish the work. And what about Lia? What would happen to her if they took Maria? Doubtless they would put her in an orphanage, where she would suffer even more hunger and maltreatment. Maria had heard rumors of girls being forced to prostitute themselves with foreign diplomats or commissars of the people; and worse still, some had preferred suicide. Maria looked everywhere quickly, as if there might be a secret passage in her kitchen from which she could escape, or for some hideaway where they might be safe, a magical place where they could live.

The blows on the door redoubled in force, impatient now.

Maria resigned herself to her fate. She would go wherever they sent her, do whatever they ordered her, confess whatever they wanted her to say, and swear eternal love for the Party if that could help her lessen the suffering of her daughter. She had heard that the children of criminals who behaved well got special treatment. Some even finished their university studies and became Party officials. Maybe Lia would escape unharmed, she was so brave and strong.

She hugged her daughter once more and, like a person under sentence who has made his confession and heads without fear for the scaffold, she moved into the entrance hallway. For the third time she listened to the knocking, which was softer now, but she knew the kind of mind games they played to confuse their victims, to give them an illusion that they were safe so that prison would prove even more painful. Before she opened the door she glanced at one of her husband's paintings – a street scene in vivid colors, which foregrounded two women and a child in a hat. It might be the last time she would see it. Only then did she raise her hand to the door handle.

Her mouth gaped in astonishment. She wanted to speak but she could not utter a syllable.

Ruth said nothing either, as if no appropriate words existed for the occasion. Nor did her grey eyes express any emotion. On the other hand her breathing seemed to have sucked all the air around her. Then she raised her right arm, handed over the shopping bag and turned her back. Maria stood and watched her leave, beating down the snow with her energetic steps, and only when her neighbor had turned the corner was Maria capable of looking into her bag. Her eyes widened, her hands shook, and laughter and tears came simultaneously.

Inside the bag was a bottle of milk.

Kirchner

LUDWIG Kirchner had been arrested in his studio, where he had been working with other artists on a painting that was five meters wide and three high, and supposed to depict the triumphs of the revolution. The central figure was President Ionescu, portrayed as a mythical Greek hero in a military uniform who trod underfoot his defeated enemies. His face was younger and more handsome than in reality, he radiated serenity and strength, and his fictitious green eyes gazed at the horizon, where the rising sun was glowing. His physique was as athletic as a gymnast's, quite unlike his real flaccid, stooping body. On Ionescu's left side, accompanying his triumphant march, were equally athletic but smaller figures, who symbolized the various professions: the peasant in brown trousers and white shirt, a hoe angled over his shoulder, a worker in blue overalls with a hammer in his right hand, a fisherman in black trousers rolled up to his knees and a green shirt, with a net slung over his back, a civil servant in a grey suit holding a pen in his right hand, and an intellectual with thick glasses, black trousers and a red shirt, who held a book in his left hand. To his right, following Ionescu too, was a group of five beautiful women in grey uniforms and four smiling children in the red and white garb of the Pioneers. Over the heads of the people, in a grey sky which was incompatible with the rising sun, fluttered flocks of white doves.

Kirchner had a different vision for the composition of the canvas, and considered the work he was creating ridiculous, a pastiche of Liberty Leading the People by Delacroix, but Zdanhov had imposed his own will. That was why Kirchner had been sent to the re-education camp: he had confided in one of his colleagues, Hector Lott, his disagreement with the realist aesthetic of the picture. Although Lott agreed with Kirchner, he realized that he could use his words to his own advantage, and informed Zdanhov that Kircher was an artist who deliberately tried to ridicule the great leader Ionescu.

The People's Commissar for Culture saw a double opportunity: to show his zeal to Ionescu and at the same time embarrass Schwartz, whose police should have detected the subversive tendencies of the painter. He filed a charge based on the denunciation, and an hour later Kirchner was under arrest. That same day they began to interrogate him. After a night of being deprived of sleep, and after his first session of beatings, with a pierced eardrum, a broken nose and three teeth missing, Kirchner confessed to the charge of sabotaging the President's portrait and to having received payment from capitalist forces. A shaky signature with three drops of blood on a sheet of paper with a text he could not read was enough to make the beatings stop.

Without any trial, the next day he was sent to the Akha Re-Education Camp in the far north of the country, where the average winter temperature was fifteen Celsius below freezing, and sometimes reached thirty below at night. Handcuffed and blindfolded, he travelled for six hours in a closed van, without food or water.

Because no other painters were available who could paint high quality propaganda pictures, Zdanhov made Lott responsible for finishing the painting. Lott painted as if he had a pistol pointed at his head, faithfully carrying out all his instructions, and the work underwent no changes.

Ionescu liked it so much that, besides wanting to meet Lott, he decided to hang it in his palace, and not allow it to be shown anywhere else. More than the heroic triumph and the apotheosis of the revolution, whose scenes of delirium frankly had begun to bore him, what stunned him in the picture was how lifelike his rejuvenation was. Although no portrait from his youth showed him so perfect, Ionescu convinced himself that long ago he really had been that splendid athlete. First he thought he would hang the picture in a room where he received diplomats and leaders of other countries, in order to inspire their respect and admiration, but then it struck him that such a work of art could have a use far superior to any political ploy.

THE re-education camp was a complex a hundred meters long by sixty wide. It had four wooden barracks to shelter two hundred prisoners, a hut used as a kitchen, a two-storey building reserved for the thirty guards, a house for the commandant and four watch towers. An electrified barbed wire fence three meters high surrounded it and there was only one entrance gate. Inmates included political prisoners, thieves, murderers, and rapists. This mixture was partly owing to reasons of economy, but also to terrify opponents of the regime even more. These were often assaulted by other inmates. Violence was not punished, even when it resulted in death. To the contrary, killing a political prisoner in a brawl might be worth better rations and a new pair of boots. The inmates' work consisted of felling trees to supply the country with the timber it needed for industry, for heating homes, and export.

At night, wolves surrounded the camp and howled until dawn.

The camp commandant was Stanislau Yoric, a man of forty with grey hair and dark eyes. This post was a punishment for having mediocre achievements as a manager of a newly established farming co-operative years earlier. He had evaded the charge of sabotage, but had still been exiled to the camp. More than preventing escapes, the main duty the Party had charged him with was managing to ensure that political prisoners died of natural causes. His right-hand man was Pietr Huss, the chief guard, who, during the Second World War, at the age of ten, was supposed to have set fire to a haystack in which three Nazi soldiers were hiding, burning them alive. He was a tall, strong man with grey hair and yellow eyes. The Party trusted him more than they trusted the commandant.

On arrival at the camp, inmates' personal effects and clothes were confiscated, their hair was shaved off and they had to use a brown uniform of a single size. They were given two blankets and had to sleep in wooden bunks with no mattress. The latrines were a ditch which they had to clean daily, carrying the feces out. There was a single nurse whose job was to treat wounds that prevented inmates from working. No prisoner managed to avoid infestation by lice and scabies, or dysentery. The weaker ones succumbed to tuberculosis or typhus and died shortly. Rats and cockroaches infested the barracks, but guaranteed a rich supply of extra protein.

From Monday to Saturday, the inmates woke at five, were counted, ate hot porridge and a crust of black bread, and left the camp to work. At noon they had a soup of potatoes and bacon and rested for fifteen minutes. At five in the afternoon they came back to the camp, ate the same soup and a crust of bread, and were locked in the barracks. The camp rules imposed a strict adherence to this routine, and disobedience to the guards might be punished by beatings, deprivation of food for two days, or, in the most serious cases, the most feared penalty: to be hosed down with water at night and left in the open air until dawn, which meant freezing to death. The guards called this sentence 'the snowman'.

Kirchner arrived at the camp at seven in the evening. After the usual procedures for new arrivals, he was given water and a crust of bread and two guards led him to one of the barracks. A guard switched on an outside light and the other opened the door. Kirchner smelled the rank smell of sweat. Inside, dozens of men uniformed alike stared at him in silence. The floorboards squeaked as he and the guards tramped between the bunks. Some inmates sat on the bunks while others peeped out from under the blankets like frightened mice. When they reached the far end of the barrack, one of the guards shoved him towards an empty bunk and then left him. As soon as the door closed and the light went out again, he felt that someone was approaching him. By the moonlight entering through a barred window, he made out a shape.

'What's your name?' murmured the inmate.

'Kirchner.'

'My name's Marius. Why are you in here?'

'I don't know…'

'You don't know? That means you were conspiring against the Party.'

'They accused me of sabotage.'

'They accused me of murdering my wife. What did you use to do before they arrested you?'

'I was a painter.'

'A painter? I suppose you didn't have much work, then. The building industry has been paralyzed.'

'I…'

'Listen. If you want to survive in here, you've got to know the rules of the camp. Out there the guards rule, but in here Koba rules.'

'Who's Koba?'

'Koba's the leading criminal in the country, although in his view he's a businessman.'

'I didn't know such people existed.'

'Because you don't have the money to make deals with him.'

'What kind of business does he do?'

'Smuggling, illicit drugs, hit jobs, just about anything that's profitable. He won't be in custody long because he supplies the Party leaders.'

'What with?'

'Banned capitalist products and other luxury goods. Koba brags that he's decorated the homes of several Party commissars, and supplied their wives with their wardrobes.'

'But they arrested him all the same.'

'Yes, from time to time the Party has to show who's in control. But as he bribes the commandant and the guards, they let him do what he likes, as long as he doesn't try to escape. It's a good deal for both parties because apart from the money they get, the guards charge him with watching the political prisoners. If anyone talks about politics, Koba's men thrash him. So keep your trap shut. The punishment for theft is a finger cut off, and informers are killed. Got it?'

'Yes.'

'If you need anything, tell me and I'll talk to Koba.'

'Do you work for Koba?'

'Everyone works for Koba. He can arrange anything, as long as you pay for it. Food, medicine, women.'

'Women? Women visit here?'

'Of course. Koba talks to the guards and they fetch the women from another re-education camp. But just for a single night.'

'And do the women get anything in return?'

'They get a good hiding if they make a fuss.'

'That's not right. That's sex slavery. Such things shouldn't happen in our country.'

Marius laughed. 'Listen, Kirchner, I don't know where you've come from or what you've been doing, but that's exactly what your country is. Some give orders, others obey, whoever plays the wise guy gets it in the smacker, ends up here, or is killed. Now go to sleep because tomorrow you've got a lot of work to do.'

Despite the cold, the hardness of the bed, and the snores of the other inmates, Kirchner fell asleep quickly.

At dawn, Huss, the chief guard, put him in a work company of fifty men that included Marius – and Kirchner saw that the latter was a thin man with white hair, prematurely aged. The company's task was to go to a part of the forest where pines, firs and spruces grew, fell as many as possible, strip the trunks, load them on carts and transport them to a railway depot warehouse. The inmates were given saws and axes, with the usual warning that they would be killed if they attempted to use these tools against the guards. Because he had no experience with saws, Kircher got an enormous axe – which he had no more experience with.

It was still dark when the gate opened for the inmates to leave and march out for half an hour until they reached the felling area. The carts were reserved for the guards and only a few privileged prisoners were allowed to stow their tools inside. To the east, a coppery light tinged the sky, illuminating the silhouette of a snowy mountain. Resisting the advance of the light, the white spot of the planet Venus also seemed to be made of ice. From the north, a glacial wind spread the message that people were entering lands hostile to life. The frozen ground confirmed the truth of the warning. Nonetheless, a few birds defied death with melodious song. It was these creatures, these angels fallen into an icy hell, far more than the light from a vanquished sun, that helped the prisoners bear their punishment.

Kirchner stamped his boots on the ground, but instead of warmth, needles pierced his feet. Beating his arms across his chest had no effect either, except to tire him and make him cough. Now and then he touched his ears to make sure they were still there. Marius warned him that when he pissed he should not expose his member too long to the cold or it would get gangrenous. However, the will to survive so that he could see Maria and Lia again burned like a furnace within him.

On entering the forest, after making their way through bushes and undergrowth, they came across the big trees. Most were more than ten meters tall and a meter thick. Snow-capped their tops. Just a few meters to the west was a clear-cut for several kilometers.

The prisoners had to fell the trees in the other direction. The guards stopped the carts and ordered the prisoners to pick up their tools and start felling. Kirchner expected instructions on where to start and how to proceed, but Marius moved away and no one told him anything. Following the usual routine, the prisoners spread out through the forest, and singly, or in pairs, attacked the trees. The sound of steel cutting wood filled the forest.

Standing before the pine with the huge axe in his hands, Kirchner felt as if he were about to commit an act as grotesque as attempting to paint a picture with a broom. Worse still, the idea of embedding the blade of the axe in that trunk until he had chopped it down struck him as an absurd act of violence. The shout of a nearby guard – a boy of twenty – showed him the value of delicacy in such a place. He stroked the bark of the pine as if he wished to ask its forgiveness for the act he was about to commit, then grabbed the handle of the axe, hefted it over his head and struck with all his strength. The blade was blunt and the handle flew out of his hands. The axe ended up beneath another tree, and Kirchner gaped at it, open-mouthed. Two prisoners burst out laughing, but the guard did not see the joke: he came over to Kirchner, kicked him, and made him pick up the tool.

After an hour's work, Kirchner had still failed to cut down a single tree, although other prisoners had already felled two or three. He was hungry and dizzy. His hands were nearly raw and the rhythm of his axe strokes was ever slower. He winced with the pain, and each time the blade struck the tree, moans escaped his lips. After a while he could not bear any more and he let go of the axe. His hands burned as if he had been holding hot coals. He knelt and blew on them in an attempt to extinguish those invisible flames. The young guard saw him and advanced on him, yelling. Kirchner lowered his head, expecting more kicks. Prisoners stopped working to enjoy the spectacle of the thrashing of the new convict, one of the rare diversions they could expect during the day. Kirchner heard the rustling of the boots in the foliage, but continued to blow on his hands, indifferent to the fate of the rest of his body.

All of a sudden another voice rang out and the boots stopped. Kirchner raised his head and saw Huss signaling him to come closer. For a moment, the undefeated tree, the frozen earth, and his hands in flames all span in dizzying vision. Then the sounds of the axes and the saws moved inside his head. He rose with difficulty, took two stumbling paces, and fell. On the orders of the head guard, two prisoners picked him up, carried him to a cart, and laid him down beside the felled trees.

'You're lucky that the director feels sorry for you,' said a guard as he held a canteen of water to Kirchner's lips.

'Hold your hands up so I can bind them,' said another guard.

'If it were up to me, I'd chop them off with an axe,' said a third, spitting to the side.

As soon as his hands were treated, the guards left Kirchner on the cart as if he were another length of wood. Marius came over with a frown.

'Who are you, anyway? A spy?'

Kirchner opened his mouth but was unable to reply.

'Speak. Who are you working for? Who's protecting you?'

'Nobody. I told you, I'm a painter.'

'All right, I can see you're someone important and don't want to reveal your identity. It doesn't matter. But don't forget that I was the only one to help you. Don't forget that I was your friend.' Marius waved goodbye and left.

Exhausted, Kirchner watched him move away, and kept glancing behind himself as if he feared some danger. To manage to understand the rules of the camp appeared even harder than mastering the art of chopping down trees. With trees, at least, you could gauge the quality of the wood without any worry about surprises from within. When Marius had told him, during their first conversation, that his country was exactly that, he had taught him something which was just starting to make sense.

In the pine he had been unable to cut down, a yellow bird was singing. Kirchner raised his head. The song passed through the rattle of the axe-blows like a ray of sunlight that penetrates muddy water and illuminates a pebble. Kirchner seemed to be the only one listening to it, and he heard nothing else. Presently the bird beat its wings and vanished into the sky. The painter smiled. At that moment the fire in his hands was doused.

On the way back to the camp the guards let him stay in the cart. Beside those men who stared at him with scorn, he entertained himself by looking for the first stars in the dusk. When he had assembled enough of the luminous material, he began to join the dots to draw Lia's face on the dark canvas.

BACK at the camp, a guard told him that the director wished to see him, and ordered him to follow. Kirchner was no longer surprised. The guard took him to his superior's house, opened a door which gave onto an empty space and knocked another door. Kirchner heard a voice bid him enter, and the guard opened the door. With some anxiety, Kirchner approached. The commandant's office had wooden walls, a wooden floor, a desk, two cabinets, and a portrait of Alfred Ionescu. There was a ceiling lamp and a fireplace with a burning fire. The commandant was on his feet. He wore a black suit, new boots, and a hat. Smiling, he approached the painter and carefully shook the fingertips of the bandaged hand. Kirchner smelled alcohol on his breath.

'A man like you shouldn't be ruining his hands in a place like this. Work of this kind is for animals and scum like those out there. If it were up to me, artists and intellectuals would be re-educated through their own work, in very different places. Talent should never be wasted.'

'I didn't do anything against the Party.'

'Mr. Kirchner, I have studied your trial. You confessed to trying to sabotage a picture of the president. That's a very serious crime. If it had been anyone else, he would probably have been shot already. But let's change the subject. I'm a great admirer of your expressionist painting: the girls, the nude women, the landscapes, the self-portraits. The way you express the complexity of the human being through intense color and the strength of line is remarkable. There's something disturbing about your characters, even when they're smiling. A hidden menace we can't quite make out. Only they know what is tormenting them. But sadly the Party doesn't appreciate this style. If you had called them enemies of the people or something, they might have had a different opinion.'

'They call it degenerate art.'

'Yes, but that will change. One day your talent will be recognized. One day your work will be shown in all the galleries of the world, believe me. Listen, did you know that I'm an artist too? I've done some drawings of the camp. Would you like to see them?'

'Yes. I'd be very happy to take a look...'

The commandant went back to his desk, opened a drawer, found a box inside and took from it a bundle of thick sheets of paper. Then, with a charming smile, he began to display his drawings. They were scenes of camp life, showing the inmates talking to each other, sitting in the sun, enjoying games; their faces seemed almost happy and their bodies indicated neither sickness nor thinness. If not for the uniforms and the barbed wire fence, they could have been mistaken for ordinary citizens relaxing in a park, as no guards ever appeared. Other scenes showed the local flora and fauna: trees, birds, wolves, rabbits, and snakes. Their quality was average for anyone who only aspired to be a portrait painter.

The commandant's eyes gleamed. Kirchner bit his lips.

'What do you think?'

'Very interesting, very interesting...'

'I'm just an amateur, but if I had studied fine arts I know I could have gone far. You could say that I have talent, right?'

'Indeed, a great talent...'

The commandant clasped his hands behind his back and gazed out of the window as he spoke. 'My dream was to have exhibitions in Paris and New York. Unfortunately circumstances have brought me to this camp where I have to put up with the cold and being away from my family. You have no idea how sick

I am of this frightful place. Sometimes I feel like grabbing an axe and chopping down trees too, but I can't trust the prisoners or the guards either. In the end, I'm a victim too. You know, Kirchner, we artists shouldn't be here. Society doesn't understand us. But one day this will change; yes, one day they will recognize our worth. Maybe one day we'll even work together.'

Kirchner stared at the floor, and when Yovic turned around he took the painter's pose as a sign of respect. Satisfied, he slapped Kirchner's shoulder and sent him away.

When Kirchner got back to the barrack, Marius came up to him. He approached him in the same humble manner that he approached the guards.

'I kept your food and didn't let anyone touch it. They've given you milk and fruit.'

'Thanks.'

'Two new inmates have arrived,' Marius said, pointing at a bunk on the left. 'Their names are Rufus and Zacko and they're enemies of the people. It seems they were distributing a subversive newspaper that called for a revolution against the Party, and they were sentenced to twenty years forced labor. In other words they'll only leave here in coffins. They're dangerous and they have nothing to lose. Keep away from them.'

'What if they approach me? I can't turn my back on them, can I?'

'You're the commandant's protégé, but you shouldn't push your luck. Things change really fast here and anyone can fall into disfavor, just like that. Did you know that the last commandant was denounced by someone important and is in another re-education camp?'

'No, I didn't…'

'Like I said, follow the rules and you won't have any trouble. Oh, I forgot the most important thing. Koba wants to talk to you tomorrow. As you've been excused from cutting timber, you'll have lunch with him. Naturally, he doesn't work either.'

'At last I'll meet this Koba. Where's the lunch?'

'In his barrack. Someone will come to fetch you.'

The next morning in the small hours Kirchner was awoken with the other prisoners. He observed Rufus and Zacko. They were both young, tall and thin. Rufus was fair, with blue eyes, whereas Zacko had brown hair and eyes. Both limped and had faces bruised and cut from their interrogations. While the other prisoners looked resigned, reconciled to their fates, rage throbbed in the faces of the newcomers. Nearly two thirds of the inmates had been sentenced for political crimes, charged with conspiracy, sabotage or treason – accusations which in most cases were unfounded, the result of neighbors or relatives informing on them, or of the excessive zeal of public servants who wished to please their superiors. However, this was not the case with Rufus and Zacko. They were journalists who belonged to a dissident group called Solidarity.

Formed by Adam Jacek, Solidarity had a hundred and forty members, including intellectuals, civil servants, and workers, and its objective was to bring down the dictatorship and install democracy. Its members promised to fight the regime peacefully, through subversive activities like distributing newspapers and pamphlets that condemned the citizens' subjection, the violence of the police and the corruption of the politicians. They also pledged to carry out particular measures meant to awaken the political awareness of workers and students, as well as pass information to foreign diplomats, and take part in acts of civil disobedience such as unauthorized meetings, protest marches, and hunger strikes, if they were incarcerated. However, a faction led by Leonidas Vall supported acts of violence, like the placing of bombs in factories, and the assassination of regime leaders. It was a minority group, with no experience of armed struggle, and few financial resources, so few people in Solidarity took them seriously.

When they were captured, Rufus and Zacko had been in possession of dozens of leaflets they had prepared to distribute in a Department of Economics. Through graphs, charts and statistics, these leaflets compared Slavia's standard of living with other European countries. Nothing else. Rufus and Zacko believed that the mere presentation of the information, without any commentary or call for revolution, would be enough to awaken the political awareness of the students and disturb the professors. It was also enough to get them arrested. They had not resisted arrest, but had admitted they were opponents of the regime and demanded to be treated in accordance with the international conventions for human rights – which gave the guards a good laugh.

After being counted with the others outside, Kirchner was not put in a work group. Even so, he was not allowed to return to his bunk either. Left alone in the camp, he began to tramp over the frozen ground, looking at the leaden sky and keeping away from the guards. He thought that Lia and Maria would still be asleep and tried to convince himself that they would have a normal day, just as when they had all been together. He made an effort to believe they were fine, with the support of the neighbors or even the Party, and that soon they would be a normal family once more. That was how he kindled his beacon of hope and consolation, as the freezing air lacerated his body.

Huss's hoarse voice chilled him further: 'Come with me. You thought you were going to spend all day doing nothing? The commandant has you under his wing, but he doesn't want you to become useless. Today you're going to help in the kitchen, under the orders of our chef,' he said with a laugh.

The barrack that served as a kitchen had six wood stoves piled with the pots in which the prisoners' rations were cooked, three tables for preparing food, a sink for washing the dishes and other tableware, and a cupboard. The wooden floor was always wet and covered in potato peel. Grease and spots of mold-stained the walls. A sour smell of rancid bacon and rotten vegetables infested the air. Whenever the men left, mice, cockroaches and centipedes took over the kitchen.

Kirchner gagged as he went in. A short, stocky man with red hair and blue eyes came up to him. He wore an apron over a white uniform. Hands behind his back, he looked over Kirchner with suspicion.

'Who's this? You know I don't allow just anyone to come here. I have a reputation to keep up,' he told Huss.

'The commandant sent him. Treat him well.'

The cook shut his eyes and took a deep breath. Huss muttered something and left. Kirchner glanced at the exit door. The cook picked up a rolling pan and smacked it down on a table so hard that it made a plate jump up.

'You can call me Chef Kristoff. Understand that I'm the most important man in the camp. Without me, no one eats, not even the commandant. I have the right to increase or diminish anyone's ration. Besides, everyone's afraid of me because they know that any time I like, I can poison the food. A slow death, agonizing pain, and in the end even the animals don't want the corpse. Do you see now who you're talking to?'

'Yes, sir… Chef Kristoff.'

The cook seemed satisfied. 'I'm not a prisoner. I was conscripted from the place I was working at to serve the Party. This camp needs the best professionals. I can leave whenever I feel like it, unlike those bastards,' he said, pointing with the rolling pin at four lads peeling potatoes. 'They're thieves and they're being re-educated through cooking. They only open their mouths when I allow them to, but you can speak. What do you want to know?'

Kirchner searched for a relevant question but could not find one. To his relief, the cook turned his back on him and headed for the larder, his boots splashing through the puddles. He was inside for a while, and emerged with a leg of bacon on his shoulder, which he flung on to the table. The fat was yellowish and the rancid smell was overpowering. Kirchner held his breath.

'This is too good for them, but hell, I can't let them die of hunger,' said the cook as he began to slice the bacon.

'Do we eat bacon every day?' Kirchner said in a low voice.

The cook's eyes goggled. 'Course not. This isn't a hotel. Spuds, sure, you'll eat them every day.'

He continued cutting the bacon into tiny strips, and as Kircher said nothing, the two kept quiet. Kirchner admired the cook's precise technique; the angle of his slicing and the symmetry of the pieces was the work of an artist. The yellowish tone of the carcass no longer struck him as revolting, but as an unusual hue he could use in the depiction of tormented faces. For the first time since his arrest he had the urge to paint; a self-portrait against a backdrop of barbed wire, or maybe the forest, in the brown uniform, with an emaciated body and bleeding hands, and his face the color of that rancid bacon.

Presently the cook revived the conversation. 'I'll tell you a secret. Promise you won't tell anyone?'

'Sure… I promise.'

'Listen: all wars start because of food. This,' he said, pointing at the strips of bacon, 'is humanity's tragedy. It's no accident that the Jews don't eat pork. The Nazis knew what they were doing. If cooks ruled the world, it would be very different. The trouble with the Party is that it has no idea how to manage food. The people are hungry? They are, but it's because the Party doesn't know how to look after the available food resources. That's why a man like me is indispensable. Sooner or later, the president will call me. He has no alternative, really, does he?'

'No… yes…'

'Now you can peel some potatoes. You're capable of that, aren't you?'

'Yes, I can do that.'

Kirchner took him over to the four silent assistants, none of whom greeted him or even glanced at him. They were beardless boys with sad faces, who looked as if they were missing their mothers, but they seemed better fed than the other prisoners. Their delicate hands worked like components of a machine designed to peel potatoes with maximum efficiency. The peel was so finely cut that the light shone through it. Kirchner noticed that all the lads had scars on their skulls, and understood that such perfectionism had been imposed thanks to the cook's rolling pin. The latter pulled up a stool and handed a knife to the painter.

'Do you know what happens to a man who spends his life

eating potatoes?'

'No…'

'Of course you don't. No one does. I'm the only person who's studied the subject. I've got dozens of notes, but I don't show them to anyone. I'm keeping them safe for when the president summons me. If anybody tries to steal them from me, I'll kill him.'

No sooner had he spoken than he slapped one of the assistants. 'Don't try to cheat me, you swine.'

AROUND noon, Huss came back and told Kirchner to accompany him again. Kirchner tried to say goodbye to Kristoff the cook, but the latter was stirring a steaming pot and made a sign for him to leave as if he were swatting a fly. When Kirchner got outside and the stench of the kitchen gave way to the pure air of the forest, he filled his lungs with air. The sun was white and frozen. He crossed the camp and went into an empty barrack. The interior was cleaner than his, and to his surprise, he found that towards one end of the building, a curtain marked off a sort of private area. Huss drew it: inside was a bed, a stove, and a table with a cloth and a bottle of wine. A tall, well-built man, bald, with black eyes, held out his hand.

'Welcome, Kirchner.'

'Thank you for inviting me, sir…'

'My name's Ivan Fiorov, but everyone calls me Koba. They say ugly things about me, but I'm simply a businessman who was born in the wrong country. This country is broke and the leaders need people like me. I bring in everything they want but don't dare import through legal channels. Household goods from West Germany, Japanese cameras, American calculators, French wine, Swiss chocolate, Italian shoes and clothes, plenty of stuff, in fact. I play this dirty role for their satisfaction. As you know, the higher you rise in the Party hierarchy, the more access to consumer goods you have. Until, at a certain point, the communist leader is living like a true capitalist. Do you get it?'

'I think so.'

'Now if the Party officials don't lead by example, if they don't believe in the virtues of their ideology, and in fact embrace their enemy's, how can it have any future? Communism won't last more than fifteen years, and what's going to defeat it is not tanks and missiles, but human nature. Because the people want the same as them. They want the high life, a good standard of living, money…'

Kirchner scratched his head. 'Maybe, but some values you can't buy.'

Koba let out a belly-laugh. 'Why do you think capitalism is successful? Because of freedom and democracy? No, it's because of the wealth. Capitalism only guarantees a bare minimum of freedom to the citizen, but it allows him to grow rich. Now our system doesn't offer one thing or the other. Do you think our kids want to keep living this way? Has it ever occurred to you that the day the Chinese leaders realize they can use their billion inhabitants on low salaries to compete with the capitalist system, they'll be able to dominate the world?'

'It's a complex subject, I wouldn't like to risk making a prediction about the future.'

'Ever tried Coca-Cola, Kirchner?'

'No.'

'It's a water with additives of petrol and cocaine that the Americans invented and the world's youth is getting addicted to it. Coca-Cola is the face of capitalist success. It's no good for anything, just good shit – juice from our oranges is much better – but they've managed to turn it into a symbol of success and happiness. A bottle of Coca-Cola annihilates all the theories of Marx and Engels. As soon as Coca-Cola and their music enter the country, it will be the beginning of the end for communism. Naturally, I expect to represent the brand here.'

Kirchner pulled a face. 'That sounds terrible to me. Are you saying that art will become a consumer good like Coca-Cola? Paintings will leave the museums and go into the homes of millionaire collectors? Will the market decide what's good art, and what's bad? Will the artist become a mercenary? Will it reach the point where he paints pictures of Coca-Cola bottles instead of still lives? I don't want to live in that world.'

'You prefer to be a prisoner in this camp?'

'No, but you can't go from one extreme to the other…'

'When communism collapses, you can be sure we'll adopt the opposite system. The change will be brutal and no one will have the power to stop it. After the earthquake you'll have the tsunami.'

'I don't know what you're talking about.'

'Could you drink salt water?'

'Of course not.'

'You're wrong, if you were a shipwreck survivor and you'd been drifting for days in a boat with no drinking water, you wouldn't be able to resist drinking seawater.'

'What point are you making?'

'Like I said, our people has been deprived of so much that when they have the chance to get their hands on the goods, they'll jump on them with no thought for the consequences. The abundance of capitalism will bring plenty of salt water in its wake, and hardly anyone will have the discernment to avoid swallowing it.'

'I'm with you now.'

'But the problems of some will be opportunities for others.'

'I suppose you'll make some great deals then.'

'Sure I will, but I was thinking of the short-term. Like now.'

'I don't get it.'

'You will. Let's speak about art again, since that was why I invited you to have lunch with me. As you know, you're under my protection. The commandant will make sure that the guards don't mistreat you, but only I can make sure that the other inmates don't eat you alive. You spent the morning in the kitchen, right?'

'Yes, with Chef Kristoff.'

'*Chef*, my arse! That guy's a schizophrenic who has no idea what he's cooking. He was an inmate in an insane asylum and ended up here because he tried to kill the real cook with a rolling pin. He has constant hallucinations and he's violent as hell. Would you like to have to work under the orders of a nutcase like that?'

'No, not at all.'

'So let's talk business.'

'I'm sorry, but as I said I don't get what you're saying.'

'It's very simple, Kirchner. They tell me your paintings are greatly esteemed in the capitalist market, and there are collectors willing to pay fortunes for them. Fine, so in return for my protection I'm going to want a few of your pictures. My men will drop by your place and pick up two or three paintings. Seems fair, doesn't it? Or do you want to carry on as a kitchen assistant?'

'All right. Take you want, as long as you don't hurt my family.'

'Kirchner, now you're offending me. For me, the family is sacred. It's the only thing you can't buy or sell.'

Koba took the lid off the saucepan and served Kirchner a rabbit stew with potatoes.

A WEEK later, around midnight, Kircher was dreaming in his bunk.

He was twelve years old again and was with his mother by a lake. It was a hot summer's day. The sun shone. The water shimmered. Butterflies and dragonflies fluttered about. His mother wore a white dress and sat on a towel; in his blue shorts, he was drawing in the sand with a stick. Lots of people surrounded them, but they were silent. Some were sunbathing and others swimming. A hairy dog wagged its tail by the water's edge. Presently he heard two voices above his head: 'You draw very well,' and 'You're very talented.' He looked up and saw the camp commandant and Koba looking at his drawings. The young Kirchner smiled at them, but a nude woman passed by and they followed her. Suddenly, like an apparition, Lia appeared at his side. 'Can I play with you?' She picked up another stick and began drawing in the sand. 'What are you drawing?' he asked her. 'A big yellow bird that will carry me far away from here,' said Lia.

Then he heard the sound his daughter was making, the whisper of her scratching the sand, of her spreading the grains. But Lia was immensely strong and at times the sound became a roar, only to soften again presently, and quickly increase in volume again. It was getting cooler by the lake. He moved his arm and began to draw again. At once he woke up. He searched for Lia in the dark, in vain. Scared, he called for his mother. The sound of the drawings had ceased.

Kirchner realized he had been dreaming and calmed down. Remembering his mother and his daughter brought a smile to his lips. He tried to cling to those fragments of the dream in the hope that his mind would return to them when he fell asleep again. He wished for another dream about them in which he hoped his wife would appear too. A dream that would free him from the camp, a dream from which he might not return. However, unexpectedly, Lia was drawing again. Kirchner raised himself in his bunk and looked in all four corners, but it was so dark he could not tell what was happening. All he could do was make out where the strange sounds were coming from – at the far end of the barrack, on the right side. He got up. Everyone seemed to be asleep. He put his boots on, and tiptoed in that direction. But he had not gone five meters before someone gripped his arm.

'Shhh. Go back to bed.'

Kirchner recognized Marius' voice and let himself be led back. When he reached his bunk he asked for an explanation. 'What's going on? Why did you grab me?'

'Keep your voice down. We'll talk tomorrow. Go back to sleep.'

It was not so hard to understand why Marius had pulled him away: They were drawing the great yellow bird on whose back all the prisoners would be carried away, far away from here. All but him. Because since they had found out that he was the protégé of the commandant and Koba, the other inmates had kept away, more from scorn than fear.

EXCUSED from felling trees and working in the kitchen, Kirchner was given the job of cleaning the barrack. He spent the morning sweeping and scrubbing the floor, but failed to find where the planks had been prised so that a tunnel could be dug. Nor had he understood how they could have got rid of the earth. At the end of the day, he meant to ask Marius. Meanwhile, the dust, the litter, the urine, the vomit and other body fluids spread over the floor took up all his attention.

When he had finished his task, he went out into the camp. The sky was still dark. The clouds looked like the armor of a tank that was crushing him under its tracks. The wind had blades that cut his flesh. Looking out through the barbed wire, seeing reality lacerated by steel, was the most upsetting experience of losing his freedom. He walked the length of the camp, kicking stones he found, and wound up by the fence. The closer he was to the barbed wire, the less was the distortion suffered by his field of vision.

A flock of wild geese crossed the sky. Their formation was an arrowhead shot into the blue.

Soon, two guards coming from the commandant's house stopped near him. They were the oldest in the camp and were nearly always together. One of them limped. They carried on chatting as if Kirchner were not there.

'You reckon there'll be a nuclear war?' asked the crippled one.

The question interested Kirchner, as he believed that humanity was fated to destroy itself in an atomic conflict. He turned his ears towards them to hear their conversation better.

'The Americans want to destroy us, but they have kids too,' said the other.

'Yes, the animals have the instinct to protect their young.'

'Sure, but they let them spend all day in front of the television eating popcorn, until they get obese. In the States, only the blacks do any sport. Boxing, athletics, basketball. The whites train them and watch the games. The Indians do fuck all, just live on reservations, where they give them whisky to anaesthetize them. I saw a documentary in the cinema where they showed all that.'

'If you saw it at the cinema, it must be true.'

'My son goes to the cinema all the time, he likes those black and white Soviet films. I don't like those movies, they're so slow, you can't understand what's going on, they're just for intellectuals.'

'I'd like my son to study so he won't end up like me. Become a doctor, an engineer.'

'I'd rather my son got a diplomatic post abroad.'

'Abroad?'

'Yeah.'

'And why the hell do you want your son to go and live in another country?'

'The world's huge, there's so much to get to know. So many beautiful cities. Only diplomats have access to stuff like that.'

'Yes, but that could be a problem…'

'What's the problem?'

'Those guys are exposed to temptation, the enemy makes them offers and sometimes they defect…'

'So what? No one ever wanted to come back, did they?'

'They don't come back because they aren't allowed to. There's no freedom in capitalist countries.'

'Look, I'm your friend. You don't have to talk to me like that.'

'What do you mean, like that?'

'Let's talk straight: this is where there's no freedom. What are we but guards in a concentration camp?'

'Mind what you're saying.'

'You aren't going to inform on me, are you?'

'I'm not one of them.'

'You know what? I'm sick and tired of this. I just want to go home.'

'What's stopping you?'

'Are you kidding? If I left here, the Party would never give me a job anywhere. They might even say I was an enemy of the people and bring me back here as a prisoner.'

'Come off it. If everyone worked wherever he felt like it, it would be chaos. Jobs are for life and that's the way it should be.

You've got to have rules and the Party knows what's best for us. I don't like being here either, but we've just got to accept that it's for the good of the people.'

The other guard was silent for a while and cleared his throat before he spoke. 'Before the revolution, my grand-dad had a farm. I still remember the cows and pigs. We had milk and fresh fruit. I used to play there with my cousins and we were really happy. Then they arrested him and he died in prison. Now the land is part of a farming co-operative and everything they produce ends up far away.'

'I'm sorry to hear about your grand-dad, but it was for the good of the people.'

'It might have been for the good of the people, but my grand-dad never exploited anyone. He and my grandmother worked their whole lives in the country. They couldn't read or write.'

'You know how it is: the innocent pay for the guilty. At times there's injustice, but the Party isn't to blame, it's the fault of bad officials.'

'Yeah… of bad officials.'

'And there's plenty of them, worse luck…'

'Our commandant, for instance.'

'Cut it out, let's change the subject, or this might end up badly for both of us.'

The guard who had just spoken started walking, the other hesitated a few seconds, but in the end followed, his body swaying owing to the effort of walking with his game leg.

At the end of the afternoon, when the prisoners came back to the camp, Kirchner went up to Marius as soon as he entered the barrack. Marius' shoulders sagged, he held his head low, and was pale, with hollow eyes and the wrinkles on his forehead deeper, and he coughed and struggled for breath. He was reaching the limits of his strength, since he had no protector who might relieve him of the hard labor. To Kirchner, the man seemed like a poorly-modelled wax figure, so he gave up the idea of questioning him. It was Marius who began the conversation.

'Come on, let's go to your bunk so we can chat.'

The other prisoners dropped into their cots, moaning and complaining. Marius sat down on Kirchner's without asking permission.

'Listen, you've found out what's going on, but you need to keep your lips sealed.'

Kirchner sat down next to him. 'Keeping your lips sealed is par for the course here, so that's not news. Don't you have anything else to tell me?'

'You ought to know that this is a more serious matter.'

'Yes, I know you're all going to escape and no one told me anything. Do you hate me that much?'

Marius wanted to laugh, but only managed to cough. 'You're wrong. It's Rufus and Zacko who want to escape. They started digging the tunnel and the other guys are helping them dump the earth outside so the guards don't find out. Anyone who wants to can escape too, but I don't think anyone will risk it. If they're caught, they'll be dead men.'

'And does Koba know about this?'

'Koba doesn't care.'

'But they're political prisoners. Hasn't Koba got a deal with the commandant to keep watch over those? Are they going to escape right under his nose? And will the commandant just accept that? I don't get it.'

Marius coughed again, then stroked his chin, locked his lips and stared at Kirchner.

'My dear painter, it's early days for you to understand everything that happens here. If you're surprised that women can come here, you'll be astounded by the rest. The rules outside just don't apply here. The truth is, there's only one thing you can be sure of in this camp, and that's that you can be killed at any moment. And the only defense you have against that is to keep mum and still. You may see an eighteen-year-old girl go into Koba's apartment, cases of whisky being delivered to the commandant, or two inmates digging a tunnel, and you don't open your mouth. You didn't see anything, you don't know anything, and you don't ask questions. If you're lucky, one day you may be able to reveal all this in your paintings.'

FOR the next two weeks, Kirchner continued to hear the digging soon after the lights went out, and he got used to sleeping in spite of the noise. Snores, noisome smells, and frozen feet were all worse nuisances. In the end he found out that the earth they had removed was taken outside in the boots of other prisoners, and he was offended that he was left out of the chore. He felt like talking to Rufus and Zacko and showing them his sympathy, demanding his share of earth to carry in his boots, doing anything that would prove he was not a spy or an informer, but he couldn't bring himself to do it. It was the same lack of nerve that prevented him from even considering the possibility of escaping too. Marius, who seemed more cadaverous each day, did not bring up the subject again, and Kirchner obeyed his rule about not asking questions. He kept to the camp routine as if nothing were happening.

One night, just after they had served the food made by Chef Kristoff, who had managed to make the potatoes taste of soap, and must have been in search of insects to throw them in the pan, Kirchner heard a roar.

'Enough's enough.'

Kirchner stood up and saw Rufus and Zacko on their feet.

'Yes, enough's enough,' Zacko went on. 'I don't know how you can eat this shit.'

'We have no rights. We're just animals,' Rufus said.

'You'd think it would be enough for us to be treated as slaves,' said Zacko.

'Because that's exactly what we are, slaves,' said Rufus. 'The Party says the revolution was carried out to free the people from exploitation, but the truth is, they became the new exploiters.'

'Has it occurred to you guys that we're cutting timber to heat the houses of the Party leaders?' Zacko said.

'Did you lot know that some of the timber we cut is exported to capitalist countries?' Rufus said.

'So they're our enemies, but we can still do business with them? And who makes a profit from that business? You reckon it's the people?' said Zacko.

'The Party, besides enslaving you, is fooling you. This is no re-education camp, it's a slave camp that feeds the vices of our leaders. They live like the bourgeoisie,' said Rufus.

'Wake up. Not one of you should be here, or forced to work anywhere. The time has come to start the real revolution,' said Zacko.

Kirchner was expecting Koba's men to step in and put a stop to the call for mutiny. However, the group of eight thugs who, according to gossip, usually thrashed any political dissidents who dared break the rule of silence, did not move a muscle. They should by rights have jumped on top of them the moment they uttered the first protest, but they simply ignored them. Just as people ignore someone in the street who talks to himself, none of the prisoners paid the dissidents any attention. Each one swallowed the nauseous paste they had been served as if those two men did not exist. Kirchner glanced at Marius in search of an explanation, but he averted his gaze. The rules concerning the running of the camp seemed comprehensible only to the man who had cooked the grub that had provoked the rebellion of Zacko and Rufus: only the deranged mind of a schizophrenic could follow the logic of a system based on so many contradictions. Kirchner, though, was at that moment forgetting what Marius had told him weeks earlier.

And, after several more minutes of seditious haranguing, emphasized by waving arms and blows on the bunks, the two political dissidents wound up quiet and eating their portion. A prisoner clapped his hands and another whistled.

That night Kirchner did not hear the usual noises from the digging of the tunnel. He heard the prisoners snoring, the moans of those who were ill, the words some uttered as they dreamt, and the scampering of the mice. Nothing else. Since he was listening for a non-existent sound, the other noises were a kind of hush, to his ears. Zacko and Rufus had terminated their project. The escape might be that very night.

Kirchner continued brooding.

Will those two escape on their own, or will others take the chance to join them? What will they do once they're out? Will anyone be waiting to help them? Will they try to get out of the country or go into hiding? And what if they're caught? Will they really be killed? For you it's too risky to join the fugitives, you're not in good enough shape to handle the flight, and if you run you've admitted your guilt and you'll never be able to go home again. Don't chance it. Your sentence will be commuted and soon you'll be back with your family once more.

The brushstrokes of his reasoning were precise, disciplined, without the slightest error, and yet the resulting picture did not comfort him. In the painting which had justified his decision not to run, all the lines pointed to the vanishing point of cowardice.

While he was moping over this, he fell asleep with his feet frozen.

Three hours later he woke to the yells of guards and the lights dazzling him. A tumult shook the barrack. The prisoners moaned and complained. The guards ran between the bunks, crowning anyone who was not on his feet. Some of the men fell out of their cots. Kirchner jumped on to the floor barefoot. The guards kept yelling orders, but the stamping of the boots on the planks and the punches produced more chaos than order. Presently Huss fired a shot at the ceiling and everyone shut up. For a moment, prisoners and guards were alike. Huss stood in the center of the barrack. He was wearing a new uniform and looked as if he had just had a shower. His gaze was serene and his lips wore a smile. He had no need to shout to be obeyed.

'Put your boots on, get in line, and get outside.'

The searchlights were on in the courtyard and the camp was bright. The dogs barked. All the guards were on duty. The commandant gave orders. The remaining prisoners formed a semicircle around the enclosure. In the middle, like actors in a play about to begin, were Rufus and Zacko. They lay on the ground, tied up and gagged. Blood ran down their faces. In spite of the ropes, they were shivering. All at once, the commandant moved towards them. The sound of his boots on the frozen ground echoed across the camp. The white brilliance of the searchlights wrapped him in a kind of aura. When he reached them he put his foot on Rufus' head and looked about, like a hunter showing off his prey before a photograph.

'You ought to know that it's impossible to escape from this camp!' he shouted. 'You see what happens to anyone who tries to run? These two prisoners have defied my authority and now they'll be punished. I hope this will serve you as a lesson. Guards.'

On his orders, four guards came over with buckets of water. Some of the prisoners whispered and a mist wafted about. The commandant stood back. Then the guards raised the buckets and emptied them over Rufus and Zacko. The sound of the water striking the bodies was like a pane of glass breaking. The two men whimpered and started threshing like colossal, crazed larvae. The guards kicked them and the commandant left.

Kirchner tried to intercede as he passed by him.

'Sir, please don't do this. It's inhuman.'

The commandant ignored him and a guard punched him in the guts so hard that Kirchner fell to his knees. Just then he heard a voice on the other side of the courtyard.

'Two less to feed. Anyone who dares criticize my potatoes can go in the freezer too.'

With his mouth agape and a demented stare, Chef Kristoff watched the torment.

For more than three hours Rufus and Zacko seemed to be connected to an electrical current: they shuddered, they writhed, rolled over, did everything they could to avoid freezing. Then their convulsions slowed down until in the end all that remained was the involuntary shaking of their bodies and constant coughing. Throughout this process, like chameleons, they had changed color: from beige to pink and finally white, only their eyes not undergoing the transformation. At last, first Zacko and minutes later Rufus, ceased moving. There were two snowmen in the camp.

It was too late for a yellow bird to appear and save them.

The prisoners went back to the barracks in silence. No one dared pass comment. Kirchner sat on his bunk and sobbed. When the lights went out, Marius came to him, put his hand on his shoulder, and sat beside him.

'Try and sleep, don't think...'

'This is a crime, a true barbarity. This commandant has got to be denounced and arrested. I can't believe the Party approves of such methods.'

'My poor painter, you see and still you don't believe. The Party won't arrest the commandant; on the contrary, they'll praise his efficiency. He had fallen into disgrace and now he'll be rehabilitated. Everyone knows he's an idiot and a weakling who acts tough at the expense of the prisoners.'

'I never thought he'd be capable of such a horrific...'

'Yes, what happens here is horrific. I've tried to tell you that. How do you think the regime stays in power, but through fear? Sure, there are people who support it, and you may have been one of them yourself, but most people just want to survive. They don't want to end up as snowmen. They don't want their kids to be frozen. And the Party knows that the day they abolish the camps and the brutality, the regime will melt like the snow in the sun.'

'I should have tried to stop them escaping. I'm to blame for this too...'

'No, it's not your fault at all. Calm down. I'll tell you how things worked out. They paid Koba to let them escape, Koba informed on them to the commandant, and the commandant let them escape so he could catch them and give a lesson to the rest of us. It was a good deal for the two of them. What's more, the Party has got rid of two dissidents, and had the justification for eliminating them.'

Kirchner shook his head and grabbed Marius by his uniform.

'So everyone knew that their escape was doomed and even so helped them? You too? You're all accomplices, you're...'

Marius freed himself. 'We're just men trying to survive. Don't judge us. If you want to get out of here alive, you might have to do the same one day.'

The next day, Kircher went back to felling trees with the other prisoners. He protected his hands and as far as he could, husbanded his strength, because he knew his privileged treatment was over.

When he got back from work he found out when he entered the barrack that another prisoner had arrived. He was middle-aged, short and dark, with signs of having been beaten up. Since the deaths of Zacko and Rufus, Kirchner had decided to keep away from the other inmates even more. For that reason he ignored the new arrival, even when he was given the bunk next to his own. However, when dinner was served, the new prisoner came over to him as if they had arranged to dine together.

'Are you the painter Ludwig Kirchner?'

Kirchner gave him a suspicious look and took his time answering. 'Yes, that's me.'

'My name's Jacob Levi. They warned me not to speak to you, but I'm not scared.'

'Why are you here?'

'It was Zdanhov who sent me here, because of a painting…'

'Me too. Are you an artist?'

'I was a collector.'

'You have a family?'

'My wife and my daughter have been sent to a concentration camp. I'm really worried.'

'Everything will be all right.'

'No, my friend, for us everything will go badly.'

'Maybe Zdanhov will be purged.'

'That bastard is really powerful and well protected. But even if it happened, another bastard would take his place and everything would stay the same.'

Kirchner scratched his head. 'Why are they so afraid of us when we don't even know how to use a gun?'

'In your case, because you use a kind of weapon they can't control. Nothing terrifies them more than a free mind that's capable of questioning the Party's truth.'

'But I never questioned anything...'

'Maybe not, but they knew you would, sooner or later. So they took pre-emptive action and sent you here. The Party doesn't like running risks. Prevention is better than cure.'

'You could be right. After what I've seen in this camp, anything is possible.'

'Don't be offended by what I'm going to tell you. My own taste leans towards classical art, and as I'm not an admirer of modernism, I've never been all that interested in your work. But I recognize that your paintings hold up a mirror to the suffering of the society we live in. Your work captures the reality, or as the Germans say, the zeitgeist, the spirit of the times. If the opponents of the regime could paint, they could do no better. Sooner or later Zdanhov was bound to put a stop to your daring.'

'That's strange: the camp commandant told me something of the sort.'

'I've been convicted for being rich, you've been convicted for being talented. It was easy for the Party to take possession of my wealth, but they know they'll never be able to take possession of your talent. You're in more danger than I am.'

Silvia

AT MIDDAY Silvia Lenka left the flat she shared with some of her fellow students at the university. As she opened the street door, brilliant light struck her face and forced her to close her eyes. Dazzled, she took from a pocket the Ray-Ban sunglasses that a French diplomat had given her and strode off. Her tall frame, voluptuous hips, delicate features and sensual lips, her black hair and sunglasses all attracted the attention of passers-by. Several men rubbernecked to admire her silhouette, while a number of women stared at her with scorn. Silvia was heading for the Faculty of Liberal Arts, where she was finishing a degree in History of Art, with a thesis on the painting of the sixteenth century, as well as working in the library.

Three years ago Silvia had landed this job, which allowed her for the first time to escape from the orphanages in which she had always lived. She had never known her mother, who had given her up for adoption, and had no idea who her father was. Her identity documents described her as a 'daughter of unknown parents'. She knew that somewhere there had to be a file recording the identity of her parents, and she had done everything in her power, including requesting the assistance of President Ionescu, to find them. In vain. In the institutions where she had lived, first they had told her that it was against the rules, then that a fire had destroyed all the files from that period, and finally that she should look to the future rather than trying to dig up the past. One night, when she was in bed with President Ionescu, he had promised to look into the matter, but even before he was snoring he had already forgotten it. Silvia tried to convince herself that her parents were dead and so it would be better not to know who they were, but the desire to discover her roots was like a tide that sometimes withdrew, leaving her floating in calm waters, only to return in colossal waves that swamped her with depressions.

In early adolescence she had had a recurring dream. She had a family: a father, a mother – who always had different faces – and sometimes even siblings, and they were all happy. Her parents doted on her. She played with them and hugged them. They took her to school and protected her from the rough kids. It was a marvelous family. But suddenly, the dream changed and the happiness evaporated. Her parents seemed furious with her, they told her she had behaved badly and would be punished. Silvia wept and asked what she had done wrong, but they gave no explanations. They went out and left her alone. It got dark and cold. Just then, she awoke in a panic, shouting for them not to abandon her. She still felt the kisses and hugs of her parents, and the warmth of their bodies; she could still hear their voices and she remembered their faces, so sharp and real. Afterwards she could never get back to sleep and for days afterwards she would be sad and withdrawn.

Her education had made her into a New Woman, utterly devoted to the socialist cause. The good cause, the sole cause that put human beings first. She found it hard to believe that sane people existed who failed to understand that it was the only alternative for humanity. Capitalism was a trap. The triumph of the workers' revolution in the rest of the world was inevitable, provided of course that the Americans did not destroy it in a nuclear war. Silvia wanted to build a better world. She felt grateful to the Party and wished to pay back to society the benefits she had received. Even so, she was aware that not everything was perfect. She knew people who had disappeared, she had seen men and women beaten in the streets, and losing their jobs, while others, mediocre ones, were promoted and prospered; she knew that Party leaders got mixed up in shady deals; she endured queuing for groceries and did not always get what she wanted; she resigned herself to showering with soap and presenting herself at Party functions without perfume or deodorant. Still, if all this happened it was because of sabotage by enemies of the people, it was because the system was evolving, because human beings had faults. The Party provided plenty of explanations and they all seemed logical and true to her.

However, the New Woman found herself facing an unexpected problem for which she was quite unprepared – something which should never even have happened, since it contradicted the principles of educational doctrine. In school and the Pioneers they had taught her to understand the Marxist dialectic, and identify the errors of capitalism, to defend the belief that the collective was superior to the individual, to show solidarity with oppressed groups, to handle arms and give First Aid, but no one had taught her how to control her heart.

In a while she was going to meet Leonidas Vall. Leonidas was the son of a doctor and primary school teacher and was finishing up a doctorate in Sociology. They had met through a mutual friend a couple of months ago and had begun dating. From the start they had clicked and she believed she had finally found a man who was like her – a man she could start a family with. Leonidas was cheerful, frank, and full of noble ideas; he helped his fellow students, did voluntary work and gave blood; he was kind to animals and she had never seen him angry or drunk. However, as she got to know him better, she had changed her mind. Little by little, she had begun to find him strange, even half-crazy, but recently a terrible suspicion had struck her: might she be involved with an enemy of the people? He refused to attend student meetings promoted by the Party, he changed the channel on TV when a Party leader came on, he laughed when in a group of friends someone had praised the cultural policies of Commissar Zdanhov, he spoke about freedom and democracy as if he were deprived of them, he asked her if she would like to live in another country, and sometimes he would disappear for days at a time without any explanation.

Silvia was scared. If it were anyone else, she would have acted as she had been taught, in the only correct way to act, as she would have with a criminal who had unmasked himself: she would have denounced him to the police. But she could not do that to Leonidas. She could not send the only person she had ever loved to a re-education camp. She would send her friends, professors, strangers, just about anyone except him. All the same, she had made up her mind to confront him today, force him to confess his guilt, even though she had no idea what she would do when he did.

The Faculty of Arts was a building from the previous century with a park-like garden. The trees and lawns exhaled a fresh scent and attracted birds. Leonidas was waiting for her by the iron gate. Tall and well-built, he had brown eyes, brown hair and a moustache. Dozens of students, staff and lecturers were entering and he did not notice Silvia's approach. She placed herself in front of him without offering her usual kiss. Leonidas tried to kiss her lips, but only encountered a cold cheek.

'We need to talk,' said Silvia.

'We are talking,' replied Leonidas, with a forced smile.

'It's a serious matter. Let's go over there,' she said, pointing to the garden.

They cut through the crowd in silence. The shade from the trees made the air cooler, and the other vegetation kept it humid. Their footsteps crunched on the gravel path. A few birds twittered. Leonidas knew what was coming and prepared himself for an interrogation. Ever since he had joined Solidarity, he had invented some plausible answers to the inevitable questions, whether Silvia or the police asked them, but now he could hardly remember them. Even so, he kept a cool front – that was the best way of showing his innocence. Silvia led him towards an empty bench beside the lake. They sat down, one on each end of it.

Silvia gazed at him in silence for a while, as if that might uncover his secrets.

'What's this about?' Leonidas asked. 'Do you think I've got another woman?'

'Don't treat me like an idiot. It's pointless carrying on with this farce. I want to know who you are and what you're up to.'

Leonidas bit his lips and scratched his moustache. 'Fair enough…'

'Your behavior isn't normal. You simply vanish as if people are on your tail, and give no explanations. You don't follow the rules, you don't co-operate. You speak in hints, you mystify. Sometimes you seem to be sounding me out, other times it feels like you're trying to pass on some kind of message, but it's obvious that you aren't happy with the Party. You actually seem to detest our comrades. You're…'

'I'm what?'

'Are you an enemy of the people?'

Leonidas laughed. 'I'm a friend of the people.'

Silvia pointed her forefinger and yelled: 'Don't mess around with me!'

'Are you threatening me?'

Silvia grabbed his arm. 'You fool, don't you see I love and want to save you?'

Leonidas shut his eyes, then hugged her. 'Silvia, don't ask any more questions, please. The less you know, the better…'

Tears fell from her eyes. 'No, Leo. Either you tell me or you'll never see me again.'

Leonidas took a deep breath, his head sinking. He was facing the worst situation he could imagine and he knew there was only one answer he could give. 'Then maybe it's better if we don't see one another anymore. I'm going.'

Silvia seized his hand. 'Don't do that. Trust me. I'll never betray you.'

Leonidas made no answer. 'Please,' she insisted. 'Have faith in me.'

Leonidas stroked his hair, then glanced in all directions to make sure they were alone. 'I did try to talk to you about it. Do you like living in your country?'

'Of course I like it. More than that, I'm grateful to my country. What would have become of me, an orphan, if the Party hadn't nurtured me and educated me?'

'In all civilized countries there are institutions to take in children. The difference is that when they become adults they can choose their destiny, emigrate for example, whereas we can't. We don't live in freedom. The popular democracy imposed by the Party is nothing but a dictatorship. Don't you realize there are political prisoners and concentration camps?'

'They're enemies of the people who want to destroy us. Criminals belong in jail.'

'No, Silvia, they aren't criminals. They're people who think differently from the Party. Wanting free elections is a basic human right.'

'Free elections? You call American elections free? The big capitalists finance the parties so they make laws that suit their interests. What choice do the workers have?'

'It may not be a perfect system, but at least there's more than one party and every four years the government changes. We're the ones who have no choice. Here it's always the same ones in power.

Ionescu will only give up power when he dies, unless he's toppled first.'

Silvia wrinkled her brow. 'Leo, are you taking money from them?'

'From whom?'

'The Americans – who else would it be from?'

Leonidas stood, bent to pick up a stone, and flung it with all his might into the lake. 'No, Silvia, I don't take money from anyone. I believe in freedom and fight for it. Look, you're a student of art history, haven't you noticed that five hundred years ago artists had more freedom than ours do now? If there had been a regime like ours, with a commissar like Zdanhov imposing rules and restrictions, do you think they could have had Leonardo's painting or Michelangelo's sculpture? Notwithstanding the Inquisition, they were freer than you and me. Art affirms freedom. Dictatorships asphyxiate the creative process. How can you spend your days in front of works of art, studying them with passion, and not understand that you live in prison?'

A muscle in Silvia's face twitched. 'Don't try to confuse me…'

'Quit fooling yourself. As soon as you're honest with yourself, you'll be ready to hear what I have to tell you.'

'But – does that mean you have nothing to tell me now?'

Leonidas sat down again. He pursed his lips until his tongue felt the hair of his moustache. 'What about you? Don't you have anything to tell me either?'

Silvia's eyes widened. 'Me? Like what?'

'Well, so it looks like you don't like giving up your secrets either.'

Silvia raised her voice. 'But what secrets? Just what are you insinuating?'

'The party receptions. I know only too well that they choose you because you're pretty and stylish…'

'Yeah, so what? In capitalist countries they call that being a model.'

'A model…'

'What's eating you?'

'There are rumors…'

'What rumors?'

Leonidas gazed at a treetop before he answered. 'Silvia, it's time you trusted me.'

'I don't know what you're talking about.'

Leonidas thumped the bench. 'Don't you? You just said you suspect me of being an enemy of the people – well, I suspect you of being a party whore.'

Silvia slapped his face, got up and ran out of the garden.

For hours she wandered about the city without purpose. Freedom had broken out in her mind, untrammeled, and upset all her ideas. In vain she struggled to impose order again and put back in their places all the foundations on which she usually rested. Having lost her self-control infuriated her so much that she had to use her legs to escape. The more she debated such thoughts as living in imprisonment, loving an enemy of the people, collaborating, informing, and prostituting herself, the swifter was her pace. People moved aside to avoid this woman with manic eyes who seemed capable of knocking down anyone who did not get out of her way. Men no longer turned their heads as she passed, and no woman felt scorn for her beauty.

Eventually, she found herself in the avenue where the museum of classical art was, and at last she knew where she was going. She climbed the stairway, passing two columns that held up the pediment of the entrance, greeting a guard she knew, walked along a corridor, encountering a group of students making a study visit with two teachers, and entered the main salon. To her relief, it was empty. Even someone breathing by her side could disturb her contemplation of works of art. This space full of treasures belonged to her alone. That was what she believed, without noticing that her desire to own the common heritage made her resemble a bourgeois collector more than a New Woman.

Silvia sat down before *The Trial of Christ by Pilate,* painted by Tito Nevet in the sixteenth century. The scene depicted was a salon in a Roman palace. There was a grey wall, an opening supported by two columns, through which light entered, and a floor of white marble flagstones decorated with black geometric designs. In the foreground was Jesus, wearing a white robe, chained. In front of him to the left was Pilate, wearing an iron breastplate and a red tunic, seated on a chair. Outside, seen through the aperture, the furious mob, their faces distorted as always when Jews were portrayed, were demanding the death of Christ. Pilate was interrogating him.

Was this the moment when he asked Jesus what truth was?

The contemplation of the painting was like a breeze that began to blow away the troubling thoughts, bringing with it no less worrying ones, all the same.

God doesn't exist, that's a scientifically proven fact, but that guy Jesus was an amazing person. He wasn't the first communist, as some ignoramuses claim. The classless society is also a society without religion, which divides people and creates a caste of priests. What's more, all these paintings show that the people rejected him, they didn't want him as their Savior, either on earth or in heaven. What he was, was a man crushed by the powers that be for not accepting the rules.

Silvia admired him for his solidarity with the unfortunate, and for the way he treated women – she remembered Mary Magdalene, the prostitute – but at the same time she rebuked him for his insubordination against the established order.

However imperfect it was, the Roman Empire was the best civilization possible at the time. The Roman heritage is apparent everywhere: in art, architecture, language and law. Everyone is proud of it. The world that came after its fall was barbaric. The destruction of order always leads to chaos. The Party is the order that Leonidas wants to demolish. If he had his way, chaos would succeed it, and then capitalist hegemony, which is nothing less than barbarism imposed on the workers. Leonidas is no savior. He's a madman, just as the Romans thought Jesus was.

The breeze blew from another direction and mixed everything up.

Yeah, but… why aren't there any paintings showing the trials of the enemies of the people? If art represents the spirit of an era, it should be shown in the museums. Isn't the subject just as important, and even educational? Why deprive students of the history of their country? Could it be that contemporary artists are afraid of portraying it? Might they even be banned from doing it? Is it possible that Leonidas was right and Tito Nevet was freer than I am? Have I been blind?

Simultaneously Silvia played the roles of Pilate asking complex questions and of Christ giving unexpected answers, but finally, instead of washing her hands, she ended up crucifying herself.

The group of students burst into the salon, running about and making a racket, boys and girls of thirteen or fourteen, tall and athletic. She glared at the intruders who had invaded her room, and swore at them. She felt like driving them out with a whip. A female teacher her own age in a daze tried to rein them in. No one took any notice. Silvia blamed her for the hubbub and hoped they would send her to a re-education camp. She was about to leave when she saw a boy touch Tito Nevet's picture, and ran up to him, grabbed him by the shoulders, and shook him.

'You imbecile. Hasn't anyone taught you not to touch works of art? If you lay a finger on it again…'

The students all fell silent and still. The teacher gaped at Silvia like an idiot. A guard appeared but did not speak either. The boy was paralyzed, expecting a slap as punishment. The figures in *The Trial of Christ* were livelier than this group. Silvia could hear her own breathing. She would never own Tito Nevet's painting, but right now she owned the museum. Suddenly she realized that she had taken the boy for Leonidas. She had released the rage the latter had stirred up on this kid. She let him go, straightened his jacket, and made for the exit.

When she got back outside, the sun had already set. The streets were full of people on their way home. Cars flashed past, this way and that, horns blowing and lights fencing. Silvia came into an avenue with bare trees and headed for the bus stop. She passed a shop that sold clothes she hated, and a group of six soldiers barely older than the kids in the museum. When she reached the stop she found eighteen people under the zinc roof. She joined the end of the queue and waited for the bus. A cold wind whipped her back. A drunk staggered by, insulting everyone. Presently the bus appeared at high speed, and braked abruptly; the squealing of the tires gave her goose bumps. Silvia squeezed into a cramped space and to start her journey home she had to lean against a man who smelled like vinegar. As she gazed out of the window she had the sensation that the world was slipping away from her.

No sooner had she opened the door of the flat than she smelled the food. She found her friends preparing dinner. Mucha, another art history student, wore an apron; Vania, a sociology student, was carrying plates; and Rita, a nurse, was opening the fridge. They were all bustling about restlessly.

'Where have you been?' Mucha asked.

'The way you look – has anything happened?' Vania said.

'Nothing happened, I've been in the library,' Silvia said.

'Put the glasses on the table and sit down. I'll serve,' said Rita.

All four of them sat at the round table, which was illuminated by a ceiling light. On top of a white tablecloth was a dish of roast meat, potatoes and vegetables; beside it stood a liter bottle of beer. The girls brandished their silverware like weapons, and the glasses rose and fell. To begin with, the talk was little more than praise of the food and complaints about their fatigue. Silvia ate in silence; the food struck her as tasteless. Little by little, the girls started gossiping about other girls and boys. Silvia did not hear them. On the tip of her tongue was the question that was burning her mouth. She looked at each one of them as they spoke and imagined how they would react. None of them had ever expressed any political opinion unendorsed by the Party. *Mucha's impulsive, she might answer with belligerence; Vania's always got her head in the clouds, so she might not pay any attention to the question; Rita's suspicious, so yes, she's the one who might guess something.* For the first time she understood that her friends – any one of them – could inform on her. Would they? Or would their friendship prove stronger than loyalty to the Party? She had to face it, before her meeting with

Leonidas, she herself would not have hesitated to inform on any of them if she had discovered that they were conspiring against the Party. All of a sudden her mouth was burning too much. Even the beer she gulped down was not enough to swallow the question.

'Do you like living in our country?'

The friends stared at each other in shock. Rita's fork froze just as she was about to put it in her mouth.

'What the hell are you talking about?" Mucha asked.

'Why shouldn't we like it?' Vania said.

Silvia flushed red. 'I suppose it was a stupid question.'

'Well, the truth is, we don't know anywhere else,' Rita said.

'I'd like to visit Australia,' Vania said.

'Australia? I heard the aborigines can't vote and they put them in concentration camps,' Mucha said.

Enemies of the people.

'Let's talk about the real issue,' said Rita. 'Where are all the hot guys in this city?'

'They must be in hiding,' said Vania.

'Talking of beauty, do you think the painters of the Renaissance were free to paint what they wanted?' said Silvia.

The three friends looked astonished again. Confusion and discomfort showed in their faces.

'That question doesn't sound like one you would ask,' said Mucha. 'Aren't you aware that they had an Inquisition, and an index of books banned by the Church?'

'Yes, but even so, painters had creative freedom. The interpretation of religious themes was very varied, and they could even paint pagan ones. Ever thought about that?' Silvia said.

'I don't know much about it, except that they were always painting nude women,' Rita said.

'They were private commissions, made by patrons,' said Mucha. 'At the time there were no museums, or public exhibitions. Those paintings were only seen by the owners of the house and their guests. That's the freedom you were talking about.'

'How about Adam and Eve? The Church let them be painted

nude,' said Vania.

'Adam always has a tiny prick and Eve is hairless. A subtle censorship,' Mucha said.

'A woman with no pubic hair looks horrible,' said Vania.

'There are people who are into that,' said Rita.

'Listen, if you do anything like that, we'll chuck you out of the flat,' Mucha said.

The three friends burst out laughing. Silvia drained her glass of beer at a single gulp. As usual she felt alone among them, unable to integrate, sick of their chatter and jokes, as if she did not belong to their group or any other. She said she had a headache and needed to lie down. She was wondering about the question Pilate asked Jesus:

What is the truth?

The next morning, just before she left home, she got a phone call. It was Ionescu's secretary, telling her that the president had scheduled a meeting at three-thirty. An important matter, she should not be late. This was how her dates with him were arranged, by a Party worker, as if it were an issue of importance for the country. That day, though, she asked herself:

Why do I sleep with him?

If she refused, she would lose the privileges and presents he gave her, she would stop eating roast beef, but surely they would not arrest her. Other women had done it, and apart from a few threats from the secretary who arranged the dates, nothing had happened. She did not love him, but nor was she indifferent to him. Not because of the gifts and benefits she enjoyed as the president's lover, but because she felt safe, protected by the older man. More than that: she felt good. She was no whore, since even if he had had no power, had given her nothing and had nothing to improve the quality of her life, in a moment of loneliness or maybe just out of curiosity about the age difference, for the pleasure of the flesh, or for no reason at all, she would have become Alfred Ionescu's lover anyway.

At three in the afternoon she decided her work at the faculty library was finished. That day she had verified a tendency she had noticed for some time in book searches: fewer students were interested in the works of Marx, Engels, Lenin, and other Communist theorists, while searches for the few foreign novels they had were increasing, as well as for history books on Europe and the United States. It was strange, and it made her ponder what Leonidas had told her. However, she had no desire to dwell on unpleasant subjects. She tidied her papers, said goodbye to her colleagues, put on a long coat and left the building. Outside, on the other side of the street, one of the president's black cars was waiting. The bodywork shone and the windows gleamed in the sunlight. Beside the car was the chauffer whose job it was to fetch the president's lovers.

Joseph was a bald man with a red moustache and a navy-blue uniform. The moment he caught sight of her, he straightened his jacket, raised his cap to her, and opened the door for her. For over a year he had been driving her here and there and had never addressed a word to her. At first, Silvia thought he was just a worker following instructions – keep quiet and don't ask questions – but, after several attempts to start a conversation, she discovered that he was deaf and mute. To speak of the president's lovers and his affairs could put the country's security at risk. Like a eunuch chosen to guard a harem, a deaf-mute had the perfect profile for someone who every day shared the cabin of his car with women who had seen the president naked.

Even so, the security chiefs failed to consider that Joseph had no need to hear confidences in order to know what was in the hearts of the beautiful girls he drove. Their secrets were written on their faces: some hated what they were doing and came out in a rage after their meetings; others enjoyed their duties no more but held back their tears when they returned; then there were those who went in and out as if they were doing a routine chore, neither pleasant nor unpleasant; and finally there was this odd girl he was taking now, the only one who seemed to really enjoy being the president's lover. If he could, Joseph would have taken them all somewhere else: to his own place. Every night he fantasized about possessing them, one at a time or in pairs or groups of three. In the solitude of his room, he spoke to them, gave them orders, yelled. Still, he made his choices: they all went to bed with him, furious, tearful, or indifferent – he would know how to treat them – except this girl with black hair and grey eyes. The reason was that Joseph had never known any women apart from prostitutes, and this was the only one who seemed not to be one.

Silvia scared him.

The president's residence was an eighteenth century palace surrounded by a wall with watchtowers. The building had a neoclassical façade, three storeys, and twenty rooms. The doors were armored and the windows bulletproof. The garden outside had flowerbeds, trees, shrubs, and two spouting fountains. Two guards at the entrance gates checked visitors' documents. A few people, like the People's Commissars and the president's lovers, were exempt from this inspection.

Without saying goodbye to Joseph, Silvia got out of the car, passed the saluting guards, and entered the palace gardens. The trees, the lawn, the flowers, the scents, the tinkling of the water, the buzzing of the insects and the birdsong always made her think that she had come to a paradise where, instead of being expelled, she was allowed in from time to time. At the end of the garden path, she climbed the five stone steps to a terrace with a balustrade and headed for the entrance to the palace. She greeted two more guards who stepped aside to let her pass, and entered a hall where one of the president's secretaries awaited her. The floor was pink marble, the walls were painted white, and beneath crystal chandeliers there were two rows of classical statues on pedestals: the Venus de Milo, the Discus Thrower, the Laocoon, Cupid, the Thinker, among others. The secretary led through the hall, then up a stairway of white marble with gilded banisters, and took her into a corridor hung with paintings of mythological scenes, and after passing six rooms, left her beside the last door on the right.

Next to the room, at the end of the corridor, illuminated by several spotlights, was the painting celebrating Ionescu's victories, painted by Kirchner, Lott, and other artists. The triumphant portrayal of Ionescu, with his rejuvenated face and muscular physique, attracted one's attention from a distance, and it was nearly impossible to go through the door without noticing it. That was its purpose. The president hoped that his lovers would lie down in his bed with the image of a handsome, virile man vivid in their memories. Then they would surrender themselves simply for the pleasures of the flesh, mad with desire, not out of duty. It never occurred to him that when he disrobed before them and revealed his flaccid, bent body, his skin yellowish and blotchy, that their shock and repugnance would be even worse. Silvia hated the picture for a different reason. She found the doll-like Ionescu ridiculous, preferring him exactly as he was. The composition itself and the treatment of color pleased her; the marching figures of the populace resonated with her, evoking for her the idea of a united family; and yet the image of the president was an element out of place, more suited to a fairy tale, and it turned the intended realism into a caricature, ruining the overall effect. Silvia was familiar with several paintings by Kirchner, whom she admired, and understood that there had been interference with his creative freedom. It struck her then that if Tito Nevet had received a similar commission from some prince of his time, or even a cardinal, he would certainly have been able to create a superior work without suffering pressure.

So she avoided looking at the picture.

Silvia knocked gently on the wood, turned the handle, and opened the door. As usual, the bedroom was at a temperature of twenty-four degrees Celsius, the double bed had silk sheets, and on top of a chest of drawers were two towels and two white dressing-gowns. Apart from a mirror in front of the bed, there was no decoration on the walls. The bedroom had one door leading to a bathroom, and another through which the president would enter, like a bull released from a pen. Silvia picked up a towel and went to take a shower. Minutes later, she was back in the room, and lay down in the bed.

The other door opened and Alfred Ionescu came in. He was sixty-five years old, a man of average height with grey hair and blue eyes. He wore a dressing-gown and slippers. He was wearing too much cologne. He smiled on seeing his lover. Silvia did what he expected: got out of bed, took two steps, and stood before him. She looked him straight in the eyes, as if she were challenging him. Ionescu loved having taller, stronger, younger women before him; instead of making him feel inferior, possessing them and dominating them made him feel powerful. He ran his hands over Silvia's body until they fell to her waist, then pulled her to him and began sucking her breasts.

Silvia woke first. Ionescu was snoring, his head on her chest. Silvia looked at his messy hair, his white skin, the ribs sticking out, the skinny buttocks and one foot with yellowish nails. The man who had ruled the country for so many years, feared by so many, was helpless now in her arms. If she smothered his nose and mouth he would cease to breathe and know nothing about it. Even so, or perhaps for that very reason, she felt a kind of tenderness for him.

As she stroked his hair, Ionescu woke up. He stretched, turned his head to look at Silvia and smiled. 'You're fantastic.'

'You were fantastic too.'

'I'm no spring chicken, but you give me so much energy.'

It was Silvia's turn to nestle against his chest – her way of showing affection without words. Ionescu kissed the nape of her neck. 'Ask me for anything you want.'

'I don't want anything.'

Ionescu smiled again. They all said the same thing in the beginning, with an insincere air of disinterest designed to increase the value of the gift. It was a game he enjoyed taking charge of, raising the stakes until they gave in.

'Would you like a dress?'

'No.'

'Do you need more food rations?'

'No thanks.'

'Would you like a weekend in the snow?'

'No again.'

'Opera tickets?'

'You offered me those last month.'

'Would you like someone to speak to your thesis supervisor?'

'Now you're hurting my feelings.'

Ionescu took a deep breath. 'My dear, I'm only trying to be kind, to thank you for these moments, for the life you give me. There must be something I can give you, something you'd like to be, perhaps. Come on, be frank, let's not waste more time with this silly game.'

Silvia raised her head from his chest, lay on her back and gazed at the ceiling.

'I'd like to be a Renaissance painter.'

Ionescu felt defeated. It was pointless trying to be nice to women, they were all the same. He shook his head, struggled to his feet, stepped into another pair of slippers and went for a bath.

Helena

AT EIGHT in the morning Helena Yava went into her office and sat at her desk. Her feet were cold and she had a headache. Through the window she saw grey skies and rain running down the pane. Thunder rumbled in the distance. She picked up a pencil, tapped it on the desk several times, and put it between her teeth, making it jiggle in her mouth. She opened a drawer. She took out a report on literacy campaigns carried out by her team, written by her assistant, Larissa Niek. Once again she read the parts she had underlined and for some minutes remained there thinking with her gaze lost in the storm.

Four years ago she had been appointed Commissar for Education by the Party when the previous commissar was purged. Helena had an excellent academic and revolutionary curriculum vitae: she had borne arms to defeat the last regime and her doctoral thesis in philosophy on Marx was considered a standard reference in the field. Helena had embraced the appointment with passion and the Party expected that she would be able to achieve what the preceding commissar had not been able to: the creation of the New Man.

The project of the New Man was reminiscent of the myth of the Flood, though without the initial destruction, as it proposed to improve humanity in a fresh start, with human beings who were immune to the ancient vices. The goal was to form citizens completely devoted to the cause who had never been tainted by bourgeois habits: men and women who considered the Party more important than their own families and never doubted their convictions; men and women ready for any sacrifice in order to build an egalitarian society, with no exploiters or exploited people. Of course that would only be possible if children were educated from the cradle in accordance with pedagogical principles approved by the Party. Unfortunately, though, there were obstacles to the success of her project. Certain Party leaders mistrusted some reforms she wished to carry out, such as replacing corporal punishment with service performed for the good of the school, or ending the separation of the sexes in all school activities. Besides, she was starting to doubt the competence and diligence of her subordinates, like Larissa Niek, with whom she had never had a good relationship, not since the days when they studied together. Would Larissa be capable of putting personal concerns above the interests of the nation?

Helena spat out her pencil, picked up her phone and ordered her secretary to call in her assistant.

Presently, Larissa knocked and came in. She had blonde hair which she always wore in a ponytail, and blue eyes. Without greeting her, she looked at her boss, expecting an order.

'I've been going over the report on the literacy campaign,' said Helena. 'We've managed to put all children in school, and have practically eliminated adult illiteracy, but it seems there are still problems with some peasants in the north.'

Larissa bit her lip. 'We can say that we have one of the best educational systems in the world. Our people have at last freed themselves from the darkness of ignorance, thanks to the ideals of the Party. As for those peasants, they're people who never accepted our agrarian reform and are constantly causing problems for the new agricultural co-operatives. The belief in ownership of the land was deeply rooted in their culture. For them, the profit motive is still more important than sharing resources with the community. That's why they don't co-operate with your literacy campaigns. In my view, it's a matter of sabotage…'

Helena interrupted her. 'What I've heard is that the peasants complain of being too tired to attend classes after a day at work, and that the teachers treat them like children. How do you answer that?'

"Our teachers are superb. I know lots of them personally and I can assure you that they are devoted professionals who take pride in their work of educating the people. As I just said, these peasants will never accept our revolution. They'll always be hostile to the Party. You shouldn't believe what they tell you. The peasant is a cunning creature.'

'My grandfather was a peasant.'

Larissa flushed. 'Of course most peasants are loyal to the party. What I meant was…'

Helena raised her right hand. 'There's a brigade of ten teachers working in that area, right?'

'Yes.'

'I want you to replace them with another in which the majority are women. I want to speak to them before they're sent to the countryside. Deal with this at once.'

Larissa gritted her teeth and closed her fists. 'Certainly, as you wish. Anything else?'

'Yesterday your secretary, Marina Ross, came to me complaining that she had been demoted, and her salary had been lowered.'

Larissa's eyes widened. 'I had no choice, she types so slowly and makes so many mistakes.'

Helena raised her voice. 'You think that's reason enough to lower the salary of a widow who has no one to support her? Where are your principles of solidarity? Don't you understand that the capitalist rules don't apply to communism? If the Party doesn't help her, what will become of her?'

'But...'

'You can demote her if you wish, but her salary stays the same. Got it?'

Helena picked up some papers by way of informing Larissa that the interview was over. The latter turned and left the office, chewing over insults to her boss.

Having settled these problems, Helena spent the rest of the day working on two important projects: the planning of the annual camp for all the Pioneers in the country – at the last one there had been inadequate water and provisions, a number of accidents during the war games, and several instructors had got drunk – and the introduction of sex education in the secondary schools – another reform that some Party leaders disapproved of, considering it an idea imported from capitalist countries that would corrupt the youth of the country. To ensure an effective plan for the annual Pioneers' camp she would have to replace some of the previous organizers, which would definitely make her more enemies, but would solve the problem. On the other hand, the introduction of sex education in the high schools required a more subtle strategy, maybe disguising the content in subjects linked to health or civics, so that she did not end up like her predecessor, accused of sabotaging the pedagogical efforts of the Party and sentenced to a re-education camp.

Nonetheless, despite the importance of these tasks and the risks they entailed, Helena found herself constantly distracted by another thought which brightened her grey day, like the sun that from time to time broke through a wall of cloud. The Pioneers' camp was abandoned, the educational reforms were postponed, and even the genesis of the New Man himself could wait, because she had something in her life far more important than the revolution – and something the Party could not give her: the warming up of her feet, the rest of her body, her heart, her soul, everything that made her a woman. In a few hours, in the safe haven of her flat, she was going to receive a visit from her lover, Ruth Meyer.

RUTH Meyer had met Helena Yava at a Party conference six months earlier, and since then they had kept up a clandestine relationship – which obliged them not to see one another for weeks. Ruth had married an army officer, because that was what her family, society, and the Party, expected of her. On her wedding day she believed herself happy, but two weeks later, she understood that she had made a mistake. Her husband just as quickly realized that his frigid wife had nothing to give him, and ended up with an extramarital family. They led separate lives, in a tacit agreement based on respect for the privacy of the other, thus avoiding a conjugal cold war, and even becoming good friends. But twelve years later, Ruth decided to put an end to the farce and divorced him.

She had made up her mind not to get involved with anyone else – male or female – but simply to devote herself to her work as a teacher of Educational Science when Helena came into her life.

Suddenly, everything changed.

Ruth's work fulfilled her, but Helena had more ambitious plans for her lover. On the one hand, she wanted to thank her and show her tenderness; on the other she was well aware that a People's Commissar should not be in a relationship with someone of inferior rank, even if the relationship was secret. This double necessity of proving her love for Ruth and satisfying her own vanity had led her to twitch the puppet strings of the Party. Ruth insisted she wanted no favors from Helena, as it was against both her own principles and the Party's to receive personal perks, and what was more, she did not feel up to playing any role except that of teacher. The firmness of her protests softened with Helena's first kiss, however, and after shedding a few tears to dissolve the dregs of her conscience, she felt an intoxicated acceptance of her lover's favors.

Thanks to Helena's influence, Ruth had been appointed Principal of the Boys' Orphanage at Tiers. In the eyes of the Party, anyone in her situation – the divorced daughter of a former businessman who had not taken part in the revolution – ought to have been distrusted and kept in inferior positions. But Helena knew very well how the Party functioned, and so, with a mixture of favors bestowed on some leaders, and slander against the previous Principal, she had managed to bring about a purge and appoint her lover in the post.

Ruth had found a scene of horror there. The old building that served as an orphanage was rundown: the walls splitting and stained, the ceilings cracked, the woodwork rotten, leaks everywhere, filthy bathrooms, and the playground invaded by weeds and brambles. The children and adolescents were malnourished, in rags, and in some cases, barefoot. There were two mentally retarded boys who had no extra educational help and could not even speak, and a blind boy who had also been excluded from the classes. Corporal punishments were constant, and included whippings and being put in chains. One boy who had anger issues was in a cage. Another had lost his hearing after a beating. Only cold water ran in the bathrooms, there was no heating in the dormitories, and the beds had bugs and were shared by two boys. The workers blamed the state of the orphanage on the lack of funds, but failed to understand that there were other ways of dealing with the boys' rowdiness. With Helena's help, Ruth had carried out restoration work, replaced workers, brought in new teachers, established new rules, and set up a carpentry workshop. She had promoted the adoption of boys by childless couples, through a policy of gradual development of intimacy that included weekends and holidays with the future adoptive parents. All the same, the first time she tried to caress a five-year-old, he shrank back, shaking like a frightened animal.

When Ruth left the orphanage the storm was over and stars already sparkled in the sky. Just like Helena, she had spent the day dreaming of her rendezvous with the lover she had not seen for a week. She had had to tell off a worker who was still beating unruly boys, discuss a roof repair with a builder, and return a delivery of spoiled chicken. Even so, all the while she was rebuking, calculating costs, and giving orders, her desire for Helena was interfering with her thoughts, softening words she meant to be harsh, complicating simple reasoning, and undermining firm decisions. Ruth smiled when she wanted to make her expression hard, could not remember what she was saying, and hesitated where she had been sure of herself. That day she had even managed to forget the problem that was driving her mad. Behind her back, two workers whispered that she must be ill, and a group of older boys put forward the theory that she was pregnant.

She got in her Lada and drove as if she were floating down the long avenues of the capital. The anticipation of the pleasures that awaited her transformed that noisy, uncomfortable machine into a silent ship, and the city into deepest space, where the lights of the streetlamps and cars were twinkling stars. So she did not hear the honking of angry drivers, or notice that she nearly crashed into a bus, or mind the wait at a crossing because of a broken down vehicle. Ruth was drifting towards a planet where only she and Helena existed, and the intervening distance was simply a vacuum.

Helena lived in a leafy area, on the top floor of a building with a view of the river. Ruth parked her car in the residents' private garage, greeted the porter and got in the lift. When she got out, she walked down the marble corridor, put her key in the lock and entered. The lights were on and she heard a Maria Callas opera. In the entrance hall was a vase of white roses – her favorite flowers. Ruth smelled them and kissed a petal. Then she went into the living-room. It had a wood floor and was furnished with a plum-colored three-piece suite, a mahogany table, a wall clock, a chandelier, a West German television set, four bookcases, three statuettes of African *Cokwe* art, and two paintings by Ludwig Kirchner on the walls. However, Helena was not there. Ruth threw a quick glance at the river view and turned towards the bedroom.

She opened the door without knocking.

Beneath the romantic light of a shaded lamp, wearing only a robe of red silk, lying on an Art Deco bed, Helena smiled at her. Ruth's eyes dilated and she began to undress. She had large, sagging breasts, a slightly swollen stomach, and legs so stout that her thighs touched. Thick tufts of hair sprouted from her armpits and pubis. Helena took off her dressing-gown too. Her figure was the opposite of her lover's, lacking flesh where the other had it in excess. She was thinner, taller, and had darker hair. On her abdomen a purplish scar from an appendectomy looked like a smile. Only in their hairiness did the two women resemble one another.

Ruth got into bed on her knees and Helena pulled her towards herself. They started kissing and caressing, slowly, each one selflessly prioritizing the pleasure of the other.

An hour later Ruth was the first to wake up. She tugged at the blanket to cover them and stroked Helena's hair. She woke up too and they embraced. For some time they stayed like that, without saying a word. Then, slowly, Ruth disengaged herself from Helena's arms and looked her in the eyes.

'I love you.'

'I love you too… Why are you looking at me like that?'

Ruth's face was grave. 'I wish I could live with you, go on holiday with you, and sleep in the same hotel room…'

'You know that's impossible.'

'Right, the party doesn't accept homosexuality. They claim to be progressive, but they're as backward as the bourgeois classes.'

Helena rose and sat on the bolster. 'For now they don't accept our relationship, but communism is a process in continual evolution, destined to reach complete perfection. One day, you can be sure, gay people will have the same rights as everyone else. Look at America, lesbians there are discriminated against even more, and black people are the target of racism. That will never change under the capitalist system, whereas there will be progress under socialism. One day a woman just like us could be the president. Now just try and imagine the Americans electing a black president. Can you imagine a black or Indian couple in the White House? It's simply unthinkable.'

Ruth sat on the bolster too. She raised her chin and touched her hair. 'I want to talk to you about something.'

'Go on.'

'It's a delicate subject…'

'Have we got secrets from one another now?'

'All right.'

'Fire away.'

'Last Friday, a party official came to the orphanage with a document stamped by the central committee and said that he had orders to take two boys of eight and nine years of age to spend the weekend in a mansion. He knew their names. I tried to argue that it was against the rules and he pulled out a pistol.'

'And who gave the order?'

'The signature was illegible, but I suspect Zdanhov. He had been there on a visit with other Party officials a couple of weeks earlier and he took an unusual interest in the kids.'

'So what's the problem?'

'It doesn't seem right to me, I can't see why an adult would take home children he doesn't know. If they were men or women, I could understand it. Is that how we're going to create the New Man?'

'Look here, Ruth, he's going to take them for a hike in the woods, a boat ride on the lake, he'll give them good food, presents, it'll be a blast for the kids when all's said and done. You should be happy that someone's taking an interest in orphans who've suffered so much. He's the father they never had.'

'Helena, I've got a bad feeling about it…'

'Don't be silly, Comrade Zdanhov is a great person.'

'He's sinister. He's got the eyes of a snake…'

'Careful what you say. If anyone heard you…'

Ruth grabbed her arm. 'Helena, you could help me, stop him taking those boys.'

'Are you mad? Don't you realize he's one of the most powerful men in the country?'

'You could talk to the president…'

'Don't meddle in this. Do you think the president gives a damn about two little orphans? If I bother him with a matter like this, the only thing I'll manage to do is get fired, and you, too. Have the kids made any kind of complaint to you, by any chance?'

'No, they haven't said a thing.'

'See? If they haven't said anything, it's because nothing has happened.'

'He gives them presents. He buys their silence with gifts and maybe threats too. You must know that these kids are very fragile, and easily manipulated.'

'You're speculating…'

'Helena, they came back terror-stricken. If you could have seen their faces. They started wetting their beds again, they had nightmares and woke up screaming in the night…'

Helena took a deep breath and scratched her chin. 'They've been traumatized by violence in the past. They'll have nightmares all their lives. They would need psychotherapy for years and years, and even then…'

Ruth shook her head. 'I know this was caused by their last weekend with Zdanhov. You know it too. You're just trying to fool yourself.'

'Listen, those kids have never had a chance in all their lives. This is the first time that someone powerful has reached out to them, and you know as well as I do that that's the only way you manage to do anything in this country. Look at us two. Wasn't it worth me helping you?'

Ruth got out of bed. 'How dare you compare our love to the abuse of those children? I'm leaving.' She started picking up her clothes from the floor where they lay scattered.

Helena got up too and seized her arm. 'I'm sorry, it was a poor analogy. Please don't go.' She kissed her neck. 'What I mean is that if Zdanhov has decided to become their daddy, there's nothing we can do about it. Neither you, nor I, or anyone. We're all orphans in this country.'

Ruth hugged her, tears falling from her eyes. 'I won't accept it, Helena. I can't accept that that monster…'

'My darling, it's possible that something happened, maybe, but it's more likely that nothing did. Come on, come back to bed.'

❧

Ruth

AT SEVEN o'clock the next morning, Ruth got back to the infants' school. The building was shrouded in fog. A watchman opened the gate, she crossed the playground, which was clean and tidy now, and went inside. The smell of fresh paint was still strong and the floor had not lost its gleam. The workers had new uniforms and greeted her as she walked down the corridors. She went into the kitchen to check that her instructions were being followed: the cooks wore hairnets, the floor and the benches were washed, and the bread, milk and fruit meant for breakfast were all ready to be taken to the tables in the cafeteria. In a few minutes, the boys would come down from their dormitories to have their first meal of the day.

While the children and adolescents were sitting down at the cafeteria tables, the noise of their conversation, their laughter, and shouts was rising, until it became a deafening racket. Two tables on either side, each with twenty places, divided the room; adolescents sat on the right side, children on the left. Until the food arrived, both sides seemed to be in a contest for a Pandemonium Trophy. Despite the best efforts of the workers, the new rules had brought about an increase in indiscipline, which at times verged on chaos. Ruth was trying to find a balance between the boys' rights on the one hand and the punishments that ensured order and healthy development on the other, but just then, a more pressing issue seized her attention. She was watching the behavior of Elias Roth and Tobias Munt.

Elias was eight, with curly black hair and grey hairs, while Tobias was nine, and had ginger hair and blue eyes. Elias was the son of a prostitute who had abandoned him at the door of the school, and Tobias was orphaned at the age of six when his parents had died in an accident at factory that made explosives. They were the two cutest boys in the primary school. Until they had started being taken to Zdanhov's mansion at the weekends, they had been playful, had got on well with their classmates, and behaved well in their classes. Elias enjoyed singing and Tobias loved drawing. But since then, everything had changed. Elias and Tobias had stopped playing, become silent, distracted in class, and sometimes aggressive with their schoolfellows and the staff. Elias no longer sang, and Tobias ceased drawing.

Ruth observed them with close attention. They sat at a corner of the table and ate in silence, slowly, with their heads lowered, while their fellows devoured the bread and butter and fruit, and spoke with their mouths full. Their eyes were red and swollen. Suddenly, from the other side, some of the older boys started throwing apple peel at them, to general laughter. A member of staff told them off and the two boys were left in peace.

As one of the teachers was absent that morning, the children's class had no lessons, and was sent to the playground. The sun was beginning to banish the fog but the cold remained. The shadows of two trees striped the cement of the playground. The children ran wildly this way and that, like animals suddenly freed. They chased each other, grabbed each other, and tumbled to the ground. Elias and Tobias, on the other hand, huddled in a corner. Their fellows mocked and insulted them when they passed by. Ruth heard ugly words and realized that there was no innocence in the orphanage – every secret of human perversity was known to the children. Elias and Tobias ignored them. They were as isolated as lepers and she had nothing to relieve their suffering, not so much as balm. Inside, pieces of their selves were breaking off and falling. How long could they bear it?

Presently a boy pulled Tobias' hair, and Tobias shoved him back. They started fighting with a ferocity that astonished Ruth. Their little bodies sustained brutal blows and kicks. In place of the New Man, the orphanage was creating rabid beasts. Blood ran down both faces. The other boys yelled in excitement. Elias fled behind a tree. Before any member of staff could separate them, Ruth ran towards them. By the time she pulled them apart, both boys had landed punches on her. Tobias had a split lip, but like the stillness that follows thunder, his fury had vanished. The other boy escaped the moment he could. Ruth was gazing at Tobias without knowing what to say when Elias turned up and clung to her legs. Amid the confusion caused by the arrival of several workers and the shouts of the boys, Ruth took the two back inside the building.

She led them to the classroom and treated Tobias' lip with oxygenated water and mercury. The cut was deep and the blood would not congeal, but Tobias gritted his teeth without a whimper. By his side, though, Elias shook as if he were the one who had had a thrashing. When she had finished taking care of Tobias, she realized the other boy needed more urgent care. She stroked his black curls, squatting down to make herself his size. Tears stood in his eyes and he sobbed. He opened his mouth and his lips twisted but he could not speak a word. A vein in his forehead throbbed.

Several times Ruth had tried to speak to them about the abuse, without success, and she was afraid that if she pressured them they would close up even more. But now Elias' tortured face overcame her prudence. She smiled at him and said in a gentle voice:

'Don't be scared. I'm your friend and I want to protect you, but you need to tell me what's happening to you at the weekends…'

Elias threw himself against Ruth, clung to her neck and burst into tears. Ruth hugged him back, pressing her face against his soft skin, and was unable to hold back her own tears. For several minutes the two sobbed and moaned together.

When at last Elias stopped crying, Ruth gently disengaged herself and looked him in the eyes. 'I will protect you. I promise you, no one will hurt you again.'

Only when she stood up did she realize that she had forgotten Tobias. As if nothing out of the ordinary had occurred, as if blood and tears were unimportant details in his daily life, he had sat at a desk and picked up a pencil and three sheets of paper. Ruth approached him cautiously.

Then she saw the drawings.

On one sheet, creatures with monstrous heads, humanlike bodies and booted feet were lying on top of little doll-like figures like those children draw. The disproportion in size was colossal. The dolls' mouths were twisted downward to show suffering, and lines near their eyes represented tears. The second sheet showed only the two little dolls, but while one continued to weep, the other snarled, with sharp, pointed teeth. And on the third sheet the same doll with snarling fangs was burying a spear in the chest of the creature who had attacked them. Ruth noticed that in the claws of all the portraits of the monstrous being was something that resembled a cigarette.

⚜

TWO days later, at around ten in the morning, Helena went to the Party headquarters to try and find out how her proposals for educational reform had been received. She was climbing the stone staircase of the five-storey building when she saw that Zdanhov was descending in her direction. Sunlight fell on his face. He seemed fatter and redder than usual. Zdanhov stopped to talk to her. Helena shivered.

'Morning, Comrade Helena. What brings you here?'

Ruth is right, he really does have a snake's stare, cold, venomous, as if he's hypnotizing us and preparing to attack.

'Good morning, Comrade Zdanhov. Work, lots of work…'

Zdanhov smiled. 'Our ministries of culture and education ought to have a closer relationship, since we both work for the same ends. Unfortunately, some excessively zealous comrades have created bureaucratic barriers which impede our co-operation. Don't you think?'

And why have you never married, nor had girlfriends?

'Yes, of course, we must unite our efforts…'

'For instance, I'd like to hear your opinion on the books we're approving for the libraries, and those we intend to remove. Once again, we have to strike a balance between the interests of the people and a blind censorship that would only damage our culture. I mean, we aren't the Inquisition, are we?'

No, no, you're out of your mind, Zdanhov may have certain faults, but he's not a child abuser, of course he can't be. The Party picks the best, the elite, the most perfect men and women who only desire the good of all.

'Comrade Helena, are you feeling well? You look a bit tired...'

'I'm sorry, comrade, I felt dizzy, but I'm fine now. Of course you're right...'

'Ah, I see we understand one another perfectly. I'll send you a list of books that I have my doubts about censoring. For instance, *Remembrance of Things Past* by Marcel Proust. It's a masterpiece, no doubt, but it's also a classicist work that defends the idleness of the bourgeoisie and the aristocracy. None of the characters work, they spend their lives at parties and dinners, humiliating the servants and abusing working girls, so the book may in fact end up corrupting our youth...'

Would you allow your nephew to spend time with him? You wouldn't, would you?

'Proust... He's a complex case...'

'I'll make you a confession: my favorite character is the Baron de Charlus. He's a vile guy, but his arrogance and snobbery are a delight. Really, the baron might be the best antidote to bourgeois tendencies. Who could possibly identify with that disgusting creature? What do you think?'

'The baron... yes, you're right. Look, I'll read the book again so I can give you a more informed opinion.'

'Yes, do that, I'll look forward to your comments. But read the original version, the translation in our language is a disaster. And now I must go, they're expecting me for lunch.'

Forget about it.

Zdanhov held out a sweaty hand, Helena shook his fingers and watched him amble down the stairs. Then Zdanhov put his hand in his jacket and took out a pack of cigarettes.

WHEN she got back to the office, she found a tall, well-built boy with curly brown hair and green eyes at the entrance to the building. He was wearing a white shirt, grey trousers that were too short for him, and old boots spattered with mud. The sun beating down on his face made his light skin gleam. The second he saw her, the boy came towards her.

'Comrade Commissar Helena Yava, I'm Hans Ross, Marina Ross's son. We came to thank you for what you did for my mother. I'll go and fetch her if you'll wait a moment.'

Helena told him to go inside and led him to the office where Marina worked. Helena opened the door and called her, to the astonishment of the other workers, and the chagrin of Larissa. Marina stood, straightened her dress, and tried to brush her hair with her fingers. Although she was smiling, her eyes were swimming.

'Comrade Commissar, my son and I would like to thank you for preventing my demotion. As you know, my salary and the pension I get are just enough to support Hans' studies. In theory education is free, but in practice there are plenty of expenses that the state doesn't cover. Hans has enrolled in the Police Academy, and is one of the best students there. I have the highest hopes that one day he will be an important man in our country. If you had reduced my salary, he would probably have stopped studying and started working. He's all I have in my life. Thank you, thank you so much.'

As she finished speaking, Marina seized Helena's hand and tried to kiss it. Helena slipped her hand out of the other's grasp. Marina lowered her head, sobbed, and said she was sorry. Helena held her shoulders and hugged her. Hans lightly touched the arm of the Commissar of Education, repeated his thanks, and moved away with silent steps.

Zdanhov

AT ELEVEN in the morning, Zdanhov arrived at his office and sat at his desk. As he always did before starting work, he cast an admiring glance at the works of art adorning his workplace. On the walls were a medieval illumination, a Byzantine icon, a baroque cross inlaid with precious gems, a map which showed a flat earth and two drawings of siege engines attributed to Leonardo da Vinci. The previous owners had been sent to re-education camps and Zdanhov had confiscated their possessions. In this way he had become one of the most important art collectors in Europe.

Presently he lit another cigarette and called his secretary to send in the playwright Albert Remus, who had been waiting to see him for two hours. Zdanhov had just read his play, *Hope,* which told the story of a revolutionary – Lazlo Tiers, who had risked his life to topple the last regime – and he intended to explain the alterations he considered necessary.

Albert Remus was a Party member and one of the few dramatists allowed to stage his works. Before the revolution he had written novels and plays about relationships between the sexes in which he dissected love, treachery, and revenge. He had been translated into a number of languages and praised in the international press. After the revolution, following the imprisonment of some of his colleagues, he had changed tack in his writing, glorifying the regime and separating the characters into good ones and evil ones. He had lost the respect of his colleagues and his wife, and was no longer translated abroad. But his freedom was assured.

He entered Zdanhov's office with his hat in his hands and his shoulders slumped. He had very short, white hair, and wore glasses with lenses so thick that they magnified the size of his greenish eyes. He waited until Zdanhov gave him permission to sit down.

'Remus, I've already read your play, *Hope.* We'll have to make some changes to your main character, Lazlo.'

'Isn't it good, Comrade?'

'It's too good.'

Remus fidgeted in his chair. 'I don't get it.'

'Remus, this isn't a children's play. The characters can't be too perfect, saints without a blemish. Who's going to believe that? You've created a character who was the best student in his school, a superb sportsman, devoted to his parents, with several women falling in love with him, who develops a political consciousness and leads a resistance group without committing a single mistake, never failing to risk his life to save his comrades. It's not plausible. The adult audience is not retarded, they want people of flesh and blood, with virtues and vices. Complex beings they can identify with. We aren't in North Korea, are we?'

'Comrade, I just thought that…'

Zdanhov thumped the table. 'Don't interrupt. The Party doesn't want propaganda, it wants literary works of enduring value. In a hundred years my plays, our plays, should still be read and staged. You used to write plays in which the characters had doubts, hesitated, they had to make choices and didn't always make the right decisions. That's what made you a great author. You need to transfer that complexity to Lazlo and the other characters. Take Superman's cape away from him and show his vulnerability. Find inspiration in Shakespeare, Chekhov and Brecht. I mean, you know them better than I do.'

Remus took out a handkerchief and wiped the sweat from his brow. 'Can I speak?'

'Who's stopping you?'

'Comrade, what you're asking me to do is really risky and might not be interpreted well by the Party. As you know, I can create complex characters who are capable of noble acts or petty ones, the very creatures of flesh and blood you want. But I'm afraid that that may not be what the Party wants to see in the theatre. Some of my fellow writers are being re-educated for daring to deviate from the rules…'

'Are you insinuating that I don't know the rules?'

'No, not at all.'

'What then?'

'I just wanted to…'

'What?'

'Nothing. I'll work on the play. It's the greatest challenge of my life. I'd like to ask you to give me some time.'

'Remus, you see those works of art on the walls?'

'Yes…'

'Every one of them was created at time when one false step by an artist could lead to his death, and yet their creators had the boldness to create something unique, to transcend the limits and reach the sublime. You know why?'

'No…'

'Because they were not just geniuses, but brave too. You see what I mean?'

'Yes…I suppose so.'

'Take advantage of what you think is a threat to transcend yourself too. This truly is the greatest challenge of your life. Don't weaken at this point which is so important for our country. Don't disappoint the people.'

'No, comrade…'

'I'll give you a month to improve the play. You can leave.'

Remus lowered his head and moved towards the exit of the office. He was pale and he trembled. None of the characters he had created had felt so much terror.

After getting rid of Remus, Zdanhov called for his chauffeur, who took him to Jacob Levi's historic mansion. Even though he had not received the telephone call he had been hoping for, he could not resist going to see the excavation work.

The sky was clear and the day windless when he got into the car. He sank into the leather seats and stopped seeing the light pouring in through the windows, or hearing the engine, because he was starting another journey which took him far, far from there. He saw classical architecture, electric colors, blue, green, red, and yellow bodies stretched and twisted, dramatic faces, violent movements and whiplashes, oh what beautiful whiplashes. Everything was perfect in that world created five hundred years ago.

Built by an aristocratic family on a country estate, the mansion had been purchased by Levi ten years before the revolution. During the German occupation, it had been the quarters of a general who was so confident of victory that he intended to seize his spoils after the war – which meant that it had remained in the country. It was a Baroque building of the eighteenth century, two storeys, with twelve bedchambers, two dining rooms, a library with over a thousand volumes and rare manuscripts, and an art collection that included Ming vases, ivory Ottoman chests, Indian statuettes, African masks, Greek and Roman sculptures, Gothic relics, medieval armor, and paintings from a number of periods and styles: Renaissance, Mannerist, Baroque, Neoclassical and Impressionist. The outstanding picture in this priceless collection was El Greco's *Jesus Driving the Money-Changers out of the Temple,* for which various European and American museums had offered a million dollars.

As soon as he had sent Levi to a concentration camp, Zdanhov seized his collection, but he had never been able to find the Greco painting. He had installed a squad of five museum technicians to turn the mansion upside down. They had knocked down walls, used sniffer dogs, and tortured Levi personally, but even so they had been unable to find the hiding place where he kept it. Zdanhov's fascination for the painting was not purely aesthetic. He believed that that picture was one of the best proofs that Jesus was the first communist to fight the bourgeoisie of his time that way. Aside from the religious issue, he identified with the figure of Jesus struggling against the exploiters of the people to create a fairer world. The only way to deal with capitalists, in the past or the present, was with the whip. That was the only way to drive them out of their financial temples.

In desperation, he had ordered excavations on the estate, in locations chosen by himself. Since he could not bring himself to destroy the French garden in front of the façade of the mansion, he commandeered a team of laborers from a public project and had them dig behind the building. He himself knew that it was no more than a hunch doomed to fail, but even if the chances of finding a chest containing the canvas buried were infinitely small, he had to try, at least.

When he arrived, he found himself at a scene of battle. There was a crater in the earth, mounds of soil everywhere, dirty walls, and dead moles. Zdanhov was so horrified that his cigarette fell from his lips.

'Stop at once, you barbarians.'

The workers gaped at him, stupefied, sweat pouring down their faces. They were used to hearing the most idiotic orders from Party leaders, but this Commissar did not even know what he wanted. They would have purged him then and there, if they could have.

Zdanhov turned his back on them, went around the mansion, passed through the garden, climbed the staircase and entered the building without wiping the dirt from his shoes. He called Pietr Schwartz on the telephone and asked him to bring Levi back from the re-education camp for another round of interrogation.

The next morning he went to the Lubianka Prison. It was a concrete building surrounded by walls, in a lonely spot. It had been designed for two dozen prisoners, but housed three times that many detainees. On arrival, the prisoners underwent a full body search, had their fingerprints taken, and were photographed full face and in profile. Then the prisoners were interrogated before they were sent to re-education camps or shot. Some died under torture; others went mad. It was a rare one who did not confess something, whether true or false. There were group cells where dozens of men had to sleep on the floor, and individual cells three meters long and two high. None of them had windows or sanitation. In the summer, temperatures could exceed thirty degrees Celsius, and in the winter they could drop to minus ten. The prisoners had the right to daily exercise in a yard; the duration depended on the guards' mood. Apart from a monthly visit from a nurse, the only medical care they received was during the interrogations.

Thanks to this care and to Zdanhov's hope that after a spell in a re-education camp he would eventually give in, Jacob Levi had survived Lubianka. Because of sleep deprivation he had seen monsters climbing the walls, and he had been revived with buckets of water after electric shocks, and he had lost three fingernails ripped out with pliers, but he had not broken. However, it had never occurred to him that Zdanhov might send his wife and daughter to a re-education camp too.

The jailer thrust a key into the lock and the cell door opened with a noise of grating metal. Jacob Levi got up from his cot. He was wearing a brown uniform with no buttons, and broken sandals. He had lost ten kilos. His face was cadaverous, his eyes goggled, the veins in his neck were dilated, his front teeth were rotten and broken, his mouth was twisted because his jaw was fractured, and part of one ear was missing. His body gave off an acrid smell. Zdanhov did not suppress an expression of disgust on seeing him.

'What do you want?'

'You know very well what I want.'

'I've already told you everything. The painting was sold to a foreign collector. At this moment it must be in a villa in California…'

'A lie like that isn't worthy of an intelligent man like you, Levi.'

'It's worthy of you.'

Zdanhov wrinkled his brow and closed his right fist. 'Why are you so stubborn about hiding the painting, if you know very well that the rest of the collection belongs to me?'

'For that very reason. At least there's one work of art that hasn't fallen in your hands.'

Zdanhov took a pack of cigarettes out of his pocket. 'Want one?'

Levi raised his hand. 'No. Concentration camps are very effective at eradicating vices.'

Zdanhov lit a cigarette. The smoke calmed him. 'Listen, Levi, I understand that you hate me. Our relationship didn't start the best way. We're living in difficult times and men like me have to take hard decisions. But I'm a collector, just like you. Whether you like it or not, we have something in common that the majority of men will never understand. In other circumstances we might even have been friends.'

'We have nothing in common and I will never be your friend.'

'All right, maybe I went too far with that about being friends. But you've got to admit that we're among the few people in this country who recognize that art can redeem Man from his animal state. As you know better than anyone, our regime is brutal, I don't deny it, but if we deprive it of art we make it inhuman.'

Levi shook his head. 'Do you really think you can get round me with idiocies like that? In other circumstances I'd be laughing at you and spitting in your face.'

Zdanhov shut his eyes for several seconds. 'Levi, be reasonable. Don't you understand that I'm the sole Party leader who loves art and culture? I'm making a colossal effort to preserve the artistic plunder of our country. Every single work of value has been catalogued and stored safely. I'm going to leave a very important heritage for future generations. One day we could have one of the best museums in the world. Doesn't that have any value for you? Do you know what would happen if other Party leaders were in charge of this artistic heritage? The most likely outcome is that they'd sell it to foreigners and put the profits in their bank accounts. If the El Greco ends up in the hands of another leader, then most likely it will wind up in America.'

Levi twitched his lips into a smile, showing what was left of his teeth. 'Let it wind up in America, then, or on Mars, just as long as it stays far away from you. And as for museums, the only one this country ought to have is one devoted to terror.'

Zdanhov took a deep breath to control himself. 'Listen, I'll offer you freedom and the chance to leave the country, if you tell me where you hid the painting.'

'Freedom? You killed my family. You can't offer me anything now.'

'I never killed anyone. There was a flu outbreak in the camp and a number of women died. I'm sorry for your loss.'

Levi took a step forward and raised his voice. His eyes blazed. 'You're not sorry about anything. They died because they had no medical assistance. You could have saved them, but you're a monster and you let them die.'

'Calm down, Levi. Discussing the past won't bring your family back to you. And you're wrong if you think I can't offer you anything. I can rehabilitate the name of your family, leaving you and honorable legacy for the future.'

Jacob Levi spat to one side. 'Posterity will see justice done to the Levis, but drag the Zdanhovs in the mud.'

Zdanhov threw his cigarette down and punched Levi, flinging him against the wall.

'You Jews are always causing trouble. Why hasn't anyone liked your race since the time of Nebuchadnezzar? Why? Because your race has always considered itself superior to all the others, because you've always been thieves, because you've always conspired against authority. Hitler was right, there's no possible remedy for you. Guard!'

Just as he had been instructed to, the guard appeared with a whip. If Levi failed to deliver the painting, then they would both recreate part of its main scene. For several minutes, Zdanhov became a furious Jesus lashing the Jewish moneychanger. There was no classical architecture, no electric colors or elongated bodies, but there was far more violence than El Greco had tried to show. Even so, Zdanhov was mistaken: not everyone could be freed from bestiality by art.

The sky was starting to cloud over when Zdanhov came out of Lubianka Prison. He was sweaty and his heart beat wildly. He had finished his cigarettes. He needed a little boy, any boy, not necessarily the dark one or that redhead, what were their names? That's right, Elias and Tobias, those were their names, he needed to give them love, all the love he felt inside himself and could not share with women or men, it was like a ring of diamonds that could only be entered through the fingers of children, those beautiful, delicate angels for whom he had kept his most priceless treasure. Why didn't they understand that? Why couldn't they see that he was the only person in the world who loved them and cared about their future? Why? Why did they have to force him to use the whip?

Still, it was too risky to take them out of the orphanage during the week. His reputation as People's Commissar for Art and Culture could not be tarnished. When the chauffeur left him at the door of his house, he found Ruth Meyer awaiting him.

Olin

INSIDE the home of the People's Commissar for the Economy, the clock struck two in the morning. Igor Olin closed and squeezed his fist as if he were recharging a battery inside himself. Suddenly, he would start to pace this way and that; then he would stop and gaze out of the window of his flat. Sometimes he spoke to himself. He sweated. That night his son Aliocha had not stopped coughing and had vomited four times already. Should he take him to the hospital, or trust in the nurse who was in his bedroom?

Aliocha's birth had been a double tragedy. His mother had died during the delivery and he had sustained serious brain injuries. The Party had provided three nurses to take care of him twenty-four hours a day, but there were times when even they were unable to lessen the suffering of the poor child. Aliocha was four and he was bedridden. He was not strong enough to stand, he could only move one arm, and his neck kept toppling him over on his right side. He could not speak, beyond a few moans, he used nappies, and had to be washed and fed.

Igor Olin had expected a strong, healthy son like himself, for whom he dreamed of a radiant future: as a great athlete, a remarkable student, with lots of girlfriends, and one day, he would be president of the country. Aliocha's birth had been the worst blow he could bear. He felt horror, repugnance and hatred for that freak, and he would have handed him over to an orphanage if his own reputation would not have been damaged by it. In the early days, when Aliocha was always accompanied by a nurse, he avoided being with him, in an attempt to forget the problem. But unfortunately the problem did not disappear. One night when the nurse had to go out for a few minutes, he went into his son's room, and seeing his halfwit expression, his vacant gaze and the drool running from his mouth, he had the urge to pick up a pillow and smother him. Everything would be over in a minute and maybe it would be better for the unfortunate boy. The nurse might suspect something, but she would never dare to accuse the powerful People's Commissar of killing his own son. Olin got as far as picking up a pillow and staring at Aliocha as if he were an enemy he had to eliminate, but in the end he dropped it and burst into such a wail that he had to hide so that the nurse would not see him in that state. From that night onwards, his attitude to his son began to change. At first he started to feel sorry for Aliocha, but after a while that sense of pity changed too. Aliocha could not help being like that, Aliocha was a human being, Aliocha was his own flesh and blood. Before long Igor Olin loved his handicapped son as he would have loved the normal son he would have liked to have. Moreover, the People's Commissar for the Economy redoubled his support for hospitals and centers that looked after handicapped children. He had also managed to persuade President Ionescu to create a rehabilitation center for the handicapped, which, out of solidarity, the president had named The Olin Center.

After a while he could not stand it any longer, and he went into Aliocha's room. It was dimly lit and smelled like a hospital. The nurse had put him on her lap and managed to get him to sleep. Seeing him in the arms of the woman, with a serene expression, relieved of his suffering, Olin smiled and tears ran down his face. Without a word, he left the room and went to bed.

In bed, with the light off, he did something he had not done for over ten years: he thanked God and said a prayer. Religion had been banned at the time of the revolution and Olin had been one of the most ardent supporters of the eradication of the 'opium of the people.' The churches had been bulldozed and the priests arrested and sent to re-education camps. All the same, Olin understood that night that, faced with Aliocha's suffering, he had no other remedy but to appeal for divine aid. The Party was able to offer him three nurses, the best specialists in cerebral palsy, and the best machines imported from capitalist countries, but what Aliocha needed was a guardian angel. More than that, he needed a miracle. Olin had been brought up in the Christian faith, and for many years had been a devout believer, until he had given up his religion for Marxism. It was the same faith that seized him now, with the desperation that turns the believer into a fanatic.

Then he remembered Father Ivo, his old confessor. Along with other priests, Ivo had been sent to a re-education camp, and Olin had not lifted a finger to prevent it. That man had been his friend, and he had turned his back on him. Ivo had educated him, protected him, and been at his side whenever he was ill, but Olin had forgotten him. He had not had the courage, nor wanted to commit himself, or know anything about his fate. And yet a single telephone call could have saved him. What unpardonable treachery and cowardice! Might God have punished him for this with Aliocha's affliction? Olin tossed and turned in bed. It was high time to correct the mistake, expiate his sin. How could God help him when he had allowed a priest to perish in a re-education camp? As long as Ivo were not free, Olin was unworthy of divine mercy, and should not even dare to talk to God. It would not be possible to free all the priests, but at least he could liberate Father Ivo.

And what could he offer Pietr Schwartz, the chief of the secret police, in return for freeing Father Ivo? He fell asleep pondering the matter.

When he got up, he went to see how Aliocha was doing. He approached the bedroom on tiptoe and pressed his ear to the door. He heard nothing, which meant that Aliocha was asleep. He opened the door slowly and peeped in. The nurse switched on a lamp and the halo that surrounded her made her look like an angel. The angel made a sign with her head that Aliocha was fine. His suffering was over. For Olin it was the confirmation that God had heard his plea – and at that moment his faith became invincible. He closed the door and blessed himself. Now he had to free the priest.

Olin knew that Schwartz always ate in the same restaurant – known simply as Number 12 – and he would try to arrange to have lunch with him. When he reached his office he told his secretary to contact Schwartz. An hour later, the Chief of the Secret Police was on the telephone with the Commissar for the Economy.

'Olin, your secretary tells me you want to have lunch with

me.'

'Yes, could I meet you at Number 12 at noon?'

'Of course, but I suppose you have something to tell me?'

'Certainly, but it's not a subject I can discuss on the phone.'

'Are you afraid it's tapped?' Schwartz let out a laugh. 'You're right to think so, even my phone is under surveillance.'

'Is it arranged, then?'

'Sure, come at half-past twelve.'

Before the revolution, Number 12 had specialized in French cuisine and had been called Noelle, the name of the owner. Then the restaurant had become the property of the state and Madame Noelle had been sent to a re-education camp, where she had committed suicide. However, apart from the change of name and owner, the business kept the same staff and carried on serving French food. It was decorated with a black and white mosaic, had a ceiling and walls of wood, and three chandeliers. It had eight tables, each covered with a white cloth, and chairs upholstered in red velvet. The waiters wore uniforms and gloves. The cellar was still well-stocked with wines from France, Italy, Spain and Portugal. The restaurant's clients were Party leaders, diplomats, and their guests.

Olin arrived ten minutes before the appointed time, and found Schwartz seated in a corner. Olin declined a waiter's assistance, greeted the Yugoslav ambassador, who was with his wife, and joined Schwartz. The police chief was drinking Sauvignon Blanc from a bottle in an ice bucket. He gave Olin a suspicious look.

'Sit down.'

'I'm grateful for your time, Schwartz. I appreciate French food too.'

'Olin, you didn't come here to discuss cuisine, did you?'

'No.'

'So what is it?'

'All right, let's not waste time.'

'It must be something important.'

Just then a waiter appeared, notebook in hand, to receive their orders. He cleared his throat to attract their attention. Schwartz raised his head slightly and said, 'The usual, two portions.' Then he picked up the bottle and filled Olin's glass. Olin tasted the wine and showed his appreciation.

'Where were we?' said Schwartz.

'Do you remember the first measures the Party took, with regard to religion?'

'Course I do, great times. It was a great decision to destroy the churches and put the priests to work in the camps. Our people were completely subjugated by religious superstition, and the priests would have done everything in their power to sabotage our work. We never could have changed the mentality of the people as long as there were charlatans promising them a paradise in heaven. That's what makes the church so dangerous for us. The priests lead the masses to direct their energies to the hereafter, while we want them to work to build a society in this world. To tell the truth, speaking of those people makes me sick.'

Olin scratched his neck and bit his lower lip. 'Sure, I totally agree, but there's a special case…'

Schwartz raised his eyebrows. 'A special case?'

'Yes, a priest who helped my parents a lot, and who my mother always asked me to look out for.'

Schwartz drank his wine at a gulp. 'Why now? Didn't your mum die five years ago?'

'That's true, but since then I've felt that I've betrayed her memory. I need to put a full stop to the subject. Put yourself in my place, wouldn't you do the same? Your mum was probably brought up in the Christian faith too…'

Schwartz began drumming with his fingers on the table. 'Olin, this is an odd way to go about things. You don't expect a People's Commissar to approach another and ask him to free an enemy of the people.'

Olin took a deep breath. 'Fine, Schwartz, let's make things crystal clear.'

'Isn't that what we've been doing?'

Olin repressed a laugh. 'Tell me your price for freeing the

priest.'

Schwartz put on a shocked look and took his time answering. 'It's also dangerous to try to bribe the Chief of the Secret Police.'

Olin looked him in the eye. 'Your wife is an engineer in a phosphate fertilizer factory near Witten…'

The point of Schwartz' tongue flicked his lips. He only replied two seconds later. 'The bureaucratic procedure for freeing an enemy of the people is complex…'

Olin tapped a glass with his fingernail, making it ring like crystal. 'It might be possible to promote her to director of the factory, with her salary doubled, in spite of the bureaucratic procedures…'

'Director? Double the salary?'

'Yes.'

'It would only be fair that her talents were recognized. What about the present director? What are you going to do to him?'

'Leave that problem to me. The priest's name is Ivo Karlovic. He's in Systa Re-education Camp.'

'Tomorrow that priest will be making a lovely train journey. After that he's your responsibility. If he gets into trouble again, he's going back to the camp.'

Olin held out his hand. 'Agreed. But if your wife does anything daft, she'll be fired too. An eye for an eye, a tooth for a tooth.'

The waiter brought two steaming plates of Coq au Vin just as Olin rose and left the restaurant. He was famished, but he could not bear to eat with that man.

TWO days later, at two in the afternoon, his driver took him to a suburb where Father Ivo's only surviving relative lived. His informers had confirmed what he had foreseen: since his church had been demolished, the only shelter the priest could find was in his sister's house. It was a concrete block of flats in an area with no green spaces. In the past Olin had praised this kind of collective housing, but now this form of urbanization struck him as horrible. The overcast sky made the scene even more depressing. Rubbish littered the pavements, streetlamps were broken, and there were stray dogs. A group of boys played football. Noisome smells assaulted him as he got out of the car, and he soiled a shoe on a viscous mass. Tenants' faces appeared in windows, intrigued by a visitor who had the use of an official Party car. The People's Commissar for the Economy was recognized at once.

Olin approached the entrance to the building where Father Ivo's sister lived. The intercom system for the flats was cracked, and electrical wires were visible. Olin carefully put a finger on the bell. He heard a woman's voice and asked to speak to Father Ivo Karlovic, saying he was a friend. The woman was silent for several seconds, and then finally told him to wait. Ten minutes later the door to the building opened.

The man who appeared was unrecognizable as Father Ivo, who had always been cheerful and smiling, clean-shaven, with black hair and grey eyes. Before him was an old man with white hair, and a face disfigured by scars, who glared at him. The kind expression of the priest who had always forgiven the children had given way to an air of ferocity. A much-mended grey suit that was too big, and shoes with no laces, made him look like a tramp.

'Father Ivo, I'm Olin, do you remember me?' He held out his hand to him, but the other did not take it.

'Don't call me father.'

'What? I don't understand.'

'You understood all right, I don't want anyone to call me father.'

'But you were ordained, you confessed me so many times...'

'Yes, I was once a priest, but now I'm nothing. You accomplished what you wanted to. You destroyed my faith.'

Olin started sweating and shook his head. 'Please, explain yourself.'

'You communists put me in places where I found out that God can't exist. I was in the concentration camps for ten years. Sure, in the early days I tried to hold on to my faith, but in the end

I had to make a pact with the devil to survive. The Christian God of goodness and mercy isn't much good in your camps. Animals don't pray, they eat each other.'

Olin was disconcerted and tried to gain time. 'Look, wouldn't you like to get in my car so we can discuss this better...'

'No.'

'I ask your forgiveness. They must have treated you very badly...'

'Don't ask for my forgiveness because you won't get it. That they beat me, and made me endure cold and hunger wasn't the worst. The worst was that they turned me into an animal. Besides not being a priest any longer, I'm not a human being either.'

'Don't say such things. You're traumatized, but in time that will pass...'

Ivo raised a hand to interrupt him. 'Shut up. You have no idea what I did to survive. I killed a man so I could keep his rations. I strangled him with these hands,' he said, showing them to Olin, 'and it was like killing an insect. I felt nothing at the time, and I feel no remorse now. I informed on other prisoners to get revenge on them, knowing they would be shot. I enslaved a boy who ended up in my cell. You want to hear more? Or do understand that you can't count on me for anything?'

'Father... sir, my son is handicapped and needs your blessing. I only ask that you come to my house and see him. You are bound to feel pity for the poor creature. He's innocent, he has no consciousness of evil. He doesn't even know that he exists.'

Ivo closed his lips. For a few moments, Olin thought he recognized the priest of old: the ferocious look seemed to soften, his neck distended and his head leaned towards his right shoulder, his hands searched for one another and his fingers entwined, and he sighed. Olin ventured to touch his arm. Ivo pushed him away.

'I'm sorry about your son's problem, but I can't do anything for him. I'm a murderer, understand?'

Olin stared at him, unable to speak. More than the words, it was Ivo's dead eyes that silenced him. For a moment, he thought he might rescue the old priest from hell, but at last he understood that that man no longer existed. Meanwhile Ivo turned his back on him, went back into the building and slammed the door behind him.

Inside a car parked nearby, one of the agents appointed by Schwartz to watch Ivo had photographed the meeting and would write a report for his boss.

On the journey back, images swam together in his mind, of grey buildings, the tormented face of the old priest, and of Aliocha drooling. That was the world, and those the creatures, that he had created. The car proceeded down the long traffic-free avenues, but Olin was trapped in his labyrinth. He was beginning to realize that he had become someone far worse than that man who had been a priest.

♛

Leonidas

AT EIGHT in the evening, Leonidas Vall opened the front door of his flat. Two young men came in, one of them with black hair and a beard, the other with brown hair and a fair moustache. They were Cornelius Hass, a secondary school teacher, and Rado Kholl, a swimming coach. They had been invited for dinner, it was just a dinner for friends – that was what they would say if any neighbor informed the authorities about the meeting. Cornelius and Rado were part of the faction of Solidarity that supported the use of violence to defeat the regime. Disappointed by Jacek's leadership and unable to persuade the other members of the need to alter their means of resistance, they had decided that the time had come to act alone. As a precautionary measure, Leonidas never met more than two conspirators together; decisions taken were later relayed to other members during casual meetings or at work. In this way up until now they had foiled the vigilance of the secret police and their informers, but none of them had any illusions about that; sooner or later it would cease to work. Being captured was only a matter of time. It was all the more reason for them to act swiftly.

Leonidas led them to the kitchen, seated them at a table with a white Formica top, and served them bread, pickles, and smoked fish from a can. He opened a liter bottle of stout for them to drink. For some minutes they ate and drank without talking, as if storing up their energy for the test to come. Cornelius devoured pieces of smoked fish with bread, Rado drank half the bottle of beer, and Leonidas finished off the jar of pickles. A belch from Rado was the signal that it was time to discuss the subject that had brought them together.

The three looked at each other.

Leonidas spoke first. 'As I've told you before, our target should be the phosphate fertilizer factory at Witten. We've got several friends working there, and thanks to the nature of the raw materials it will be easy to bring about an explosion and a fire.'

Cornelius scratched his beard. 'Yes, without question it's one of the best targets to weaken the regime. But how can we be sure we won't kill workers, too?'

Rado nodded. 'Unfortunately you can't guarantee that, can you, Leonidas?'

Leonidas took a deep breath. 'We've gone over this before. The truth is that I can't guarantee there won't be any innocent victims, but that's the price we have to pay to defeat the dictatorship. Is there another way? Has our colleagues' strategy of peaceful resistance had any effect whatever, apart from them being sent to re-education camps? We face a violent enemy who only understands the language of violence. The only way we can defeat him is through terror and sabotaging the economy. I'd like to eliminate Ionescu and all the other People's Commissars with a bullet in the back of the neck, but that's impossible. We don't have the means to carry out assassinations like that, and even if we did manage to kill them, they'd be replaced by bastards just like them. What they can't replace so easily is a ruined factory. It will be through the paralysis of the economy, which is already so weak, that the regime collapses. Our men in the factory will take every possible precaution so that there are no victims.'

Cornelius and Rado exchanged looks, the muscles of their faces tensing.

'We're talking about ammonium nitrate,' Cornelius said.

'A highly explosive and inflammable compound,' Rado added.

'Our guys will only trigger the sabotage of the warehouses once the factory has closed and the workers have gone home. There's a security guard who will be taken to the other side. Done like that, it's unlikely there will be any victims.'

'All right, but something unforeseeable can always come up,' Cornelius said.

'They might decide to work overtime or something,' said Rado.

Leonidas grabbed the bottle and filled their glasses. 'My friends, nothing unforeseeable will happen. The manager of the Witten factory is the most foreseeable person in the world, and all he wants to do is go home as soon as possible. We're going to blow it up because that's our duty. If we can't agree on that, we may as well give up altogether.'

Cornelius and Rado gulped their beer but said nothing. Both pictured huge flames, burnt bodies, and ambulances.

Leonidas understood that before he could set the factory on fire, he would have to play the part of a fireman. 'I take full responsibility for what happens. Are we agreed?'

Cornelius and Rado nodded, but one of them was staring at the pickle jar while the other's gaze was as dead as the smoked fish's.

Leonidas got up to fetch another beer bottle. When the fridge door slammed, his colleagues started with fright.

Schwartz

PIETR Schwartz was the second most powerful man in the country. Ionescu controlled the army, but he was the lord of the secret police – the so-called *National Security* – as well as the regular police, the informers and all the mechanisms necessary for the functioning of the regime's repressive apparatus. People said he was the only man who could not be arrested – even Ionescu himself might end up in jail, but not Schwartz. His men controlled the media, the schools, the hospitals, the arts centers, sports clubs, and officers' messes, in fact any place which had meetings of more than two people.

Nothing happened in the country that he did not know about.

At eight o'clock on a Monday morning, Schwartz entered the *NS* building. It was a concrete structure with four floors and a basement, situated in a square in the city center which had a bronze statue of Ionescu. The severe façade was no different from those of other minimalist buildings built after the revolution, its only distinction being that two uniformed guards watched the entrance. Every crime committed in Slavia was reported to the *NS* headquarters, which then had the task of filtering them: murders, rapes, assaults, and other violent felonies were left to the regular police, as long as they did not involve any opponent of the regime; crimes against the state such as sabotage, conspiracy, civil disobedience, slander or libel against the regime, reading banned books, or attempts to escape from the country were investigated by *NS* itself. The time of the offence, the source who had revealed the crime, the details and conduct of the agents sent to the place where it was committed were the starting point for their investigations.

Schwartz passed the guards without greeting them, entered the atrium of the building and at once encountered secretaries and other workers milling about. They all stepped aside for him, with a nod of their heads. Schwartz strode along a corridor of grey granite with white walls and neon lights in the ceiling. The clicking of the secretaries' heels matched the tapping of typewriter keys in the offices. Just as in a factory the noise of the machines indicates that goods are being produced, at *NS* this sound of women in movement and of typing meant that the surveillance of the enemies of the Party was working. The bustle of the secretaries – even if its objective were to relay useless information – and the constant production of reports – even if they served no purpose – formed some of the cogwheels that moved *NS*. If the noise of the heels and the typewriters ever slackened, Slavia would be at the mercy of its enemies – which might not even exist. The archives in the basement would continue to be swamped with new documents, which, like waves sweeping the sea clean of debris, were tossed with the old ones into a never-extinguished furnace.

Schwartz got into a lift, pulled the security grate to, and ascended to the top floor, where his office was.

He took from his pocket a long key, inserted it in the lock, turned it twice, and opened the armored door. Only he had access to this space; the cleaning staff had to perform their work in his presence. The office was eighty square meters, with a blue carpet, white walls, a vast window overlooking the square, and a private bathroom. It had four bookcases full of law books, books on criminal psychology, history and geography, as well as reports and other information considered important. Side by side on one of the walls were maps of Slavia and Tiersk. On his desk were a globe the size of a beach ball, and two telephones. In a safe beside it, he kept a collection of documents that he regarded as his greatest triumph: the biographies and confidential data on all the Party leaders, including the president and the People's Commissars. His power resided in his ability to use this information, like holding a knife to the throat of a particular person; nearly all the leaders had done something in the past that made the knife sharp enough to cut them; some, however, would suffer only a surface cut, from which they would swiftly recover, while others, unfortunately few in number, ran the risk of being beheaded.

Threats from opponents of the regime did not worry him currently. He knew of the existence of a group of dissidents, but according to reports made by his men, the group was divided and disorganized and its activities were inoffensive. They were a band of idiots who so far had not even been able to start a strike. Besides, if he arrested every intellectual who protested, and eradicated all resistance to the regime, the Party might be tempted to curtail his powers, to regard him as an official who was not much use, as it had with so many others. So it was important that these guys from

Solidarity, and other rebels, carried out some subversive activity from time to time, continued to represent some kind of threat that they yelled and made a ruckus of, so that the *NS* could justify its existence and its funding.

Its real enemies were inside the Party.

Schwartz opened a chest and took out some folders full of typed pages. Although he knew practically all the information by heart already, exploring the past of the Party leaders had become an obsession with him.

He opened the dossier on Alfred Ionescu and reread the parts he had underlined.

Grandson of a Romanian immigrant, he was born in 1914. His father was a cobbler and his mother a fruit seller. He attended primary school and then, at the age of ten, began working as an assistant to his father. At fifteen he was sentenced to two years in a reformatory for young offenders, for stealing the purse of an old woman. When he was freed, his father refused to accept him back in the home, and he was forced to enlist in the army. At twenty-three he reached the rank of sergeant. A year later, while at a camp in Rhur agricultural district, he was accused by peasants of raping several women. The army filed away the complaints, but Ionescu received a reprimand.

Schwartz picked up a copy of this document.

In 1940, during the German invasion, he joined the secret resistance movement. In 1941 he organized a series of attacks on Nazi targets. That year, he became the commander of the Resistance. There are rumors that he killed the previous commander. After the expulsion of the Germans, he participated in the revolution that brought in the new regime. In 1946 he was promoted to colonel. That year he accused four officers of superior rank of counter-revolutionary activities, leading to their execution by firing squad, and took charge of a factory that made army uniforms. A subordinate wrote a report accusing Ionescu of embezzling factory funds; nothing happened to Ionescu, but the author of the report was sent to a re-education camp. In 1947, during military exercises in the country, he was suspected of raping two girls. This time there were no charges, and the army did not carry out an investigation. In 1959, following the death of the previous president, he was able to forge an alliance of military officers and politicians that enabled him to take power. He maintains a Swiss bank account with a balance of ten million dollars.

'With a thief, a rapist and murderer as president, it's no wonder the country is in the state it's in,' Schwartz said to himself. 'How is it possible that this guy always managed to get off scot-free, and go so far? Would it be possible in a capitalist country?' On top of the table, Schwartz spread out the photographs attached to the dossier: pictures of a young Ionescu in the army, saluting, and later of the colonel receiving medals, and finally, in civilian clothes, pictures of the president on official occasions, drinking with friends, and in the company of young girls. Schwartz pulled a face in disgust.

He put it all back in the file and picked up the dossier on Zut Zdanhov.

Zut Zdanhov was born in 1925 to parents who were both primary school teachers. He completed his education at university, where he graduated in Archaeology at the age of twenty-three. He became a high school teacher and in his first year of service was suspended after having been accused of sexual harassment of his pupils. The father of a pupil cudgeled him and he was hospitalized for a month. At the time of the Nazi invasion he recovered his post as a teacher, and was suspected of informing the invaders of the whereabouts of hidden Jews. During the occupation he lived comfortably and moved to a larger apartment. On the expulsion of the Nazis he underwent a volte-face and became a fervent communist. He began as a ground-level militant, but soon gained leadership status thanks to his speeches at party meetings. He escaped accusations of collaboration made by other teachers because someone protected him (who probably had information that could have compromised the new party leaders.) Eventually he managed to have his accusers sent to re-education camps. In 1950 he was appointed secretary to the People's Commissar for Culture and Propaganda. He began to get involved in the confiscation of works of art, and to visit orphanages in order to seduce minors. In 1955 Ionescu purged the former Commissar and offered Zdanhov the position. Since then, he has appropriated over a hundred works of art that belonged to museums and private collections. With the help of Ivan Fiorov, a gangster who goes by the nickname Koba, he has sold some of these works abroad. He has a bank account worth two million dollars in Switzerland, and has abused more than forty boys.

'A pedophile thief in charge of Culture and Propaganda. This country really needs a massive purge.' Schwartz flipped through a pile of photographs of Zdanhov at various times in his life – the young teacher, thin and with a taciturn air; the teacher rehabilitated by the Nazis, heavier and smiling, the assistant to the Commissar for Culture, seated at his desk; the rapist of children leading two of his victims to his car – and there were fifteen similar photographs; and the art thief contemplating a painting in a museum.

Schwartz put back the information in the file and picked up Igor Olin's dossier.

Igor Olin was born in 1918, the son of a tax clerk and a domestic servant. He completed his university career at university, where he graduated with a degree in Economics, with the highest marks that year. He became an Assistant Professor of Statistics at the age of twenty-three. With the German invasion he was expelled from the university and joined the resistance. Nothing worthy of note is known about him during that period, except that he met his future wife, Raisa. After the revolution he joined the party and was given back his post at the university. He wrote various articles on problems in capitalist economies. He was admired by his colleagues and respected by his students. In 1950 Ionescu invited him to become Commissar for the Economy. He suffered a deep depression when his wife died in childbirth. He was left with a handicapped child and has lent his support to people with similar problems. He requested the liberty of a priest from a re-education camp, without expressing any motive. No foreign bank accounts in his name have been discovered.

'Hasn't this guy ever made a false step in his life? The request to free the priest was weird, but apart from that, there seems to be nothing you could point at. It's not normal. How did he manage to reach the position he's in without support or alliances? I'll have to investigate his past more.' Schwartz flicked through the photos of Olin – smiling with a group of graduating Economics students, looking more serious with another professor, then a wedding photograph and a picture of him when he was appointed People's Commissar.

Next Schwartz picked up Helena Yava's dossier, but he put it back on the desk. It gave him no pleasure to reread the biography of that woman. Just like Olin, she had a clean profile, too perfect for a People's Commissar. She seemed to genuinely believe in her mission. She had never stolen, or killed anyone. There was nothing that could compromise her, apart from some intrigues and the fact that she liked women, which was general knowledge, and which the Party tolerated.

Then Schwartz began to consider his other obsession: trying to figure out how it was that the enemy was beating them. Before the Party and in public he had to affirm that capitalism was decaying and doomed, but he knew that the truth was different. The pop culture created by the Americans had not only spread across Europe but propagated itself around the whole world, a wave that never stopped growing, sweeping the entire planet, even penetrating communist countries. A bloodless revolution. The young, and also people old enough to have more sense, had lost their minds. They were addicted as if to narcotics. How was it possible? What was the secret? At the end of the day, what was so fascinating and irresistible about the music, the films, and the fashions of the capitalist system? Schwartz opened a drawer and took out a cassette from a box that Slavia's ambassador to France had sent him. The ambassador's job was to collect information on the political, economic, and cultural activities current in Paris. However, lately it seemed that he too had become fascinated by pop culture. He had started going to discotheques. The ambassador had told him that it was all the rage, that that song by a French singer, sung in English, was playing on radios and was heard everywhere in the world. Thus it was important material to analyze. Schwartz inserted the cassette into a player beside him and started to listen:

'We were born to be alive…' Patrick Hernandez sang "Born to be Alive".

Schwartz listened to the song with some apprehension. Much as it was hard to admit it, that thing, that idiotic ditty, sounded pretty good, it had rhythm, it hit him deep inside.

What can classical culture do against this damned music that casts a spell on people? Between visiting a museum or a discotheque, it's obvious which young people will choose. They don't need missiles to beat us. They've created a pied piper of Hamelin who leads our youth wherever he likes. We tell them to defend the fatherland, they tell them to enjoy life. What can we do about it?

The telephone rang. Annoyed, he picked it up and heard one of his secretaries:

'Comrade Commissar, I'm sorry to disturb you, but it's your wife…'

'Put her through,' he said in a brusque tone.

Right away he heard Luda's voice:

'Pietr, Roman's had an accident at school…'

'What?'

'Yes, he split his head open during playtime.'

'Is it critical?'

'No, but he's had five stitches.'

'Have you brought him home?'

'Of course. He's resting in his bedroom.'

'I'll be right there.'

Schwartz quickly put the papers back in the chest and left his office at a run.

The Schwartz family lived in a flat with five rooms in a residential area reserved for party officials and diplomats. The decoration was austere, with a wooden floor, sparse furniture, and empty walls. A television set made in West Germany was the only luxury they allowed themselves. The couple understood that their son's character could not be formed into the image of a New Man if he benefited from privileges. Capitalist luxury corrupted. Books, puzzles, maps and educational games were the toys the twelve-year-old Roman had the right to have.

Panting, Pietr Schwartz opened the front door of his home. His wife and child were waiting for him in the entrance hall. Luda was short, with brown hair and brown eyes, and she wore a black skirt and a blue blouse; Roman was nearly as tall as his mother, with curly fair hair and blue eyes; he wore grey trousers and a white shirt. They were leaning against one another with the worried expression of people expecting to be told off. But Schwartz hugged his son as if he had escaped from an airplane crash.

'Roman, are you all right? What happened?'

Suffocated by the hug, Roman could hardly speak.

'Let him go,' Luda said. 'Let him answer.'

Schwartz released him, but stared at the stitches on his scalp.

It could have been serious.

Roman had split his head open through disobeying the school guards, climbing a tree and falling from it, but in his version he became the victim. With the gravest air he could muster, he told his lie.

'Dad, we were playing football, and a kid tripped me and I hit my head on the cement.'

Luda's eyes widened, but she did not contradict him.

'Who was it? What's his name?'

'Pietr, these things happen. Leave the boy in peace.'

Roman realized he had created a problem and added another invention.

'It was Johann, but I tripped him up earlier. We're friends...'

Schwartz grumbled and turned to Luda.

'Yes, Pietr, they're friends, and Roman doesn't want you to do anything to punish Johann.'

'No, dad, everything's fine.'

'All right. But at least you gave him a couple of punches?'

Two hours later, at seven-fifteen, the Schwartz family sat down to dinner. The father sat at the head of the table, with his wife on his right side, and his son on his left. The cook had prepared roast chicken with potatoes, and boiled vegetables. Schwartz was abstemious, and the only drink he allowed at mealtimes was water. Luda sliced the chicken leg with a huge knife, and as was the custom, first served her husband, then her son, and finally herself. Without taking her eyes off the chicken, she turned towards Schwartz:

'Look, because of Roman's accident I forgot to tell you that I've got to go back to the factory.'

Schwartz looked at her in amazement. He detested being surprised by any deviations from routine, and this was the second time it had happened today.

'Go back to the factory? But aren't the premises closed by now?'

Luda placed her knife on the plate. The crease between her eyebrows became a curved furrow.

'Yes, but I've got some important matters to deal with.'

Likewise, wrinkles around his eyes, nose and mouth disfigured Schwartz's face.

'What matters?'

'Thanks to your influence I was promoted, but no one is helping me understand how to manage the factory. I've been treated with mistrust and hostility. I've heard quips and jokes. It seems they liked the previous manager. I've got to make a massive effort. There are technical details I don't understand, and I don't want to appear incompetent to the other engineers and workers. What's more, I left work unfinished because of Roman's accident. I really have to go back, you understand?'

Roman butted into the conversation. 'It's thanks to the fertilizers from the factory that we're eating these carrots and cabbages.'

'Be quiet,' his father said.

'Pietr, let him speak. He's learning important things.'

Schwartz felt sorry and stroked his son's cheek. The lines on his face were no longer a caricature of anger, but of resignation.

'All right. If it's so important, you can go back to the factory.'

Luda kissed his face and served him chicken.

'I want to prove to everyone that I wasn't promoted to manager because I'm your wife. I want to show them that I'm competent and can raise the factory's production. I have heaps of ideas for improving methods of manufacture, reducing energy consumption and stimulating the workers' productivity.'

Schwartz attempted a sad smile while he cut a piece of meat. 'And you'll succeed because you're a true professional.'

Luda looked him in the eye and bit her lip.

'There's another subject I need to talk to you about…'

'What?'

'I suspect that the previous manager cooked the books and reports, and that the factory is in a much worse state than we thought. I'm afraid there have been huge losses and the factory is bankrupt.'

The information was not news to Schwartz. It was all in his dossiers.

'Unfortunately, that may have happened.'

Once more, Luda's eyes widened. 'You knew that? So why didn't you accuse him at party meetings, or tell the president? He's been hiding losses of millions. And if he's done that, other factory managers might be doing the same thing.'

Schwartz shut his eyes for a moment. His face wrinkled again.

'These are very complex, confidential matters. We can't discuss them in front of our son.'

'May I speak?' Roman asked.

'No,' said Schwartz and Luda simultaneously.

'And go and wash your hands,' Luda added.

'But I've already washed them.'

'Wash them again,' Luda said.

'Right now,' Schwartz said.

Roman pushed his chair back and got up abruptly. He realized the conversation was taking a turn that contradicted everything he had been taught so far, in school and at home, and he could not bear to be excluded.

Luda lowered her voice. 'If you were running the country, none of this would happen. This isn't the course we hoped to take to build socialism. You know better than I do how many dissatisfied people there are in the party, don't you? To your face, all they do is give praise, but in private all they talk about is corruption and robbery. The president and the People's Commissars aren't respected any more. It's going to end badly.'

Schwartz stroked her left hand.

'Luda, one day things will change. I'll take care of that. But for now, for the sake of the family, it would be better if we didn't mention the subject again.'

Luda sighed. 'All right, I'm just an engineer, aren't I?'

Schwartz kissed her, his eyes brimming with tenderness.

'You're my wife and the mother of my son...'

'Right, right...'

'What time are you coming back from the factory?'

'Fine, I won't say anything else about confidential matters. I'll be at least two hours. I don't know when I'll get back home.'

'Are you going already?'

'Yes, I've lost my appetite.'

Luda got up, kissed his cheek, and left.

As soon as she had closed the door, Schwartz's expression turned somber. He had said too much. The conversation should never have taken place. For now he had managed to persuade her not to ask more questions, but sooner or later, Luda would return to the charge. She would be able to pick up the thread in which the banned subject was tangled. So it might be better to tell her the truth. But which truth? The truth about the People's Commissars? About the state of the country? About himself? Schwartz felt that his head might explode, and shut his eyes. He tried to think of something pleasant, of life's pleasures. It was in this moment of weakness that the enemy assaulted him with one of his most effective weapons. Without any warning, the damned song sprang up again:

'Born to be alive...'

♛

Luda

WITH her cap on, and a long coat and thick gloves, Luda got in her Lada and set off on the twenty kilometer trip to the fertilizer factory at Witten. The sky was full of stars and the road seemed to lead to them. In daytime, because the surface was so poor, it took fifty minutes to get there; but as there was no traffic at night she expected to arrive in half an hour. The yellow light from her headlights dissolved in the darkness, and she could hardly see two meters ahead. But Luda accelerated without noticing the poor visibility, since her thoughts were taken up with even darker matters.

She tried to concentrate on the problems at the factory, but these were tangled up with the problems of the Party, the discontent of the people and the future of the country, which in its turn led to the biggest problem of all: at the end of the day, who was her husband and what was he doing? Until she had been appointed manager of the factory, she had seldom asked him anything about his work. From the start, the young engineer had known that being involved with a member of the secret police meant not asking certain questions. Some words, like freedom and dictatorship, resembled certain chemical elements that when mixed, produced explosions. Pietr told her that he looked after the nation's security and that was all she needed to know. The stability of her marriage rested on her respect for this rule, which became stricter still when he was made director of *NS*. Her friends who were married to party leaders all acted the same way: they could speak to their husbands about anything, except politics. Conjugal intimacy excluded it, in the bedroom there was no place for the Party. But the rule had been broken and Pietr himself had spoken to her about forbidden subjects. Even though it had only been for a few seconds, it had opened a breach. The questions, doubts and protests that had accumulated over the years could no longer be contained.

How many men might he have arrested? How many might he have sent to concentration camps, or to face firing squads? How many have died because of his decisions? And why has he protected some but sentenced others? Is the person who scrawls a protest on a wall a greater enemy of the people than someone who conceals a factory's losses, or someone who gets rich at the Party's expense? It's pretty obvious that selfishness and greed are not qualities that only apply to capitalists. How do I explain all this to Roman?

The light her mind shone on these matters was even weaker than her headlights. The road of her life had suddenly become as black as a moonless night. And since she could neither brake nor turn back, all she could do was keep going sightlessly, until one day lightning struck her blind.

A lorry appeared on a straight road, with its headlights undipped. Incandescent with rage, Luda undipped hers too. The lorry driver began blowing his horn but did not dip his lights. At the moment she passed the lorry, Luda had to close her eyes and nearly lost control of the car. Squeezing the wheel hard, she shouted: 'Damn you, watch out or my husband will send you to a re-education camp.'

As soon as she made the threat, she felt ashamed of herself. Did she think she had the right to send people to prison too? What kind of human being had she become? Was it the revolution, or marriage, or the Party that had turned her into an uncaring creature?

For a few moments, she wanted to disappear in the darkness.

At the end of a bend she saw a set of points of light at the end of the road: a glittering geometric figure. It was as if a few stars had fallen to the earth to form a little firmament.

She was arriving at the factory.

It was an industrial complex two hundred meters long by a hundred wide, composed of five units. A barbed wire fence surrounded it and twenty spotlights illuminated it. The factory employed ninety-six workers. There should have been a guard at the entrance to open the gate for her, but she saw nobody. Luda looked at her watch: it was five to nine at night. She decided not to blow her horn, half in fear of disturbing anyone, and got out of her car with her keys in her hand. Her breath condensed in the cold air. She put the key in the lock, struggled to turn it, opened the gate, entered, and closed it again. In front of her were the units that produced ammonium nitrate, with their four gigantic chimneys. The offices were in an area on the left hand side of the factory, and she had about forty meters to walk before she got there. On the way she would pass a warehouse where they stored the raw materials, such as sulphur, phosphorus, potassium and ammonia. Luda strode head, taking in at a glance the huge structure of steel and concrete where the production cycle began. In her head marched the numbers of the reports that she knew had been doctored.

She was just arriving at her destination when the explosion took place.

Leonidas Vall's men had enlisted the guard, and an hour earlier, he had opened the door for two operatives who placed a bomb in the raw materials warehouse, which was set to go off at nine o'clock. The explosion would start a fire of such proportions and intensity that when the firemen arrived, they would be able to do little more than watch the hellish spectacle of the factory being devoured by flames. The guard had been instructed to leave the site, await the explosion nearby, and telephone the police at once to inform them of the accident. He would explain that when the explosion took place, he had been behind the factory, and thus had escaped unhurt. During the investigation that would follow, the experts might or might not discover that it had been an act of sabotage, but Leonidas had given instructions that they should convince the guard – a semiliterate man – that the fire would destroy all the evidence and it would be impossible to come to any definite conclusion; he would only have to blacken his face and clothes with the soot from the explosion to make his explanations credible. 'We are at war and at times there are innocent victims,' was how he justified himself in the face of the embarrassed looks of his comrades.

When the firemen arrived they had to use masks to cross the cloud of black smoke so they could fight the bluish blaze. Temperatures of close to a thousand degrees Celsius kept them at a distance, so the jets of water from their hoses hardly reached the flames. They were knights armed with buckets, battling a dragon who spat fire from his mouth. When some of the men started vomiting because of the toxic gases, the fire chief ordered them back to a distance from which it was impossible to put out the flames. In the end the dragon would devour itself. At eleven o'clock the next morning, the fire was declared extinguished, but nothing was left of the Witten fertilizer factory but a smoking carcass of steel and concrete. In the aftermath in the cinders, beneath a heap of twisted steel, the firemen found some of the calcified bones of Luda Schwartz.

♚

Karlovic

THE ECONOMIC effect of the sabotage planned by Leonidas Vall's group was achieved, as the losses caused by the destruction of the factory plunged the nation even deeper into the red. All the same, the terrorist attack and the death of Luda Schwartz produced the opposite reaction to the one Leonidas had hoped for: the citizens united in defense of the government and in condemnation of the enemies of the people who had committed such a barbarous act. The next day, the newspapers and the television showed shocking images of Luda's burnt bones among the rubble. Zdanhov, the Commissar for Culture and Propaganda, took charge of the news and instructed the directors of the media on how the event should be presented: as a crime against the nation that killed an exemplary worker, perpetrated by criminals in the pay of capitalist powers.

On television, at dinnertime, President Ionescu made an unexpected appearance to condemn the attack. Assuring the nation that it had been planned by the American secret services, he appealed for the denunciation of the saboteurs, and promised that they would be severely punished. Then, contrite, he announced two days of national mourning. While the news was being read, the female newsreader began weeping when she referred to the death of the engineer Luda Schwartz.

Demonstrations took place, some spontaneous, some organized, in which thousands of citizens took to the streets to demand justice – the death penalty – for such a heinous act. In the street, in bars, and at work, everyone discussed the terrorist act and the feeling of revulsion was unanimous. Luda's image began to appear on murals, posters, and banners, transformed into a martyr for the revolution. Her death shocked even those who were dissatisfied with the regime, and doubt set in: the regime was bad, for sure, but the guys who wanted to replace it were just as capable of committing atrocities. So why change?

Schwartz was in his office when he heard about his wife's death. A shaking, stammering secretary told him she had something very serious to say, and as soon as she had given him the news, fled. For several minutes Schwartz paced up and down, shaking his head, with his mouth agape and a vacant look; then he hurled everything he had in the office at the walls, yelling until his vocal chords gave out; finally he fell to the floor and wept until he could weep no more, with his face buried in the carpet.

When at last he pulled himself together, with his eyes bloodshot, his nose red and his lips pale, he began the counter-attack. He gave instructions to his men to arrest and torture anyone they suspected; they would have to make at least two hundred arrests. Among them he marked the name of Ivo Karlovic. That damned priest, and Igor Olin too, were responsible for Luda's death. He could not do much against the People's Commissar for Culture, but the priest would not be spared.

Half an hour later, the guard was arrested on the factory premises. He was wandering without aim, shaking his head, and mumbling mindless phrases. He would pick up handfuls of ash and gaze at them with a half-witted air until the wind blew the ash away. Ten minutes of interrogation in Lubianka brought him back to his senses. He made a full confession: he had been recruited by a group of enemies of the people, had opened the gate to terrorists who had placed the bomb there, and then had fled the factory at once. The electric shocks also set the mechanism of betrayal working: he supplied the names of the dissidents who had recruited him. These were arrested the next day, and although they withstood half an hour of torture, they too ended up confessing that they were enemies of the people, and squealing on their comrades. Cornelius and Rado were taken in hours later, but Leonidas managed to escape. The following day, Adam Jacek and another twenty members of Solidarity were arrested too.

At two in the afternoon, Ivo Karlovic was caught in the street when he left home to buy cigarettes. Led by a brigade commander called Markus Richter, three *NS* agents surrounded him and ordered him to get into their car. Karlovic looked at them as if they had just asked him for the time. He offered no resistance, as if he were expecting such a fate. As this was the response the agents hoped for, the correct procedure for any person detained, they did not beat him up when he got in the car. On these missions, agents only spoke with Richter's authorization, and he, as he sat beside the driver, kept a grave expression on his face. He did not enjoy carrying out the task he had been given. His uncle Adam, who had taught him to read and ride a horse, had been a priest. It was painful for him to even think about it, but luckily, he had died before the revolution. Although he was grateful to the Party for the post they had entrusted him with, he did not agree with religious persecution. Having faith was no crime, and it was not right to harm priests. However, when the Party gave him orders, he had to obey.

At last, they reached a wood, and the agents told Karlovic to get out of the car. He obeyed without a protest. On his face was not a trace of fear or surprise. One of the younger agents opened the boot of the car and took out a spade. Then they lined up behind Karlovic and Richter told him to go ahead. They walked for several minutes, penetrating deep among the trees and scrub. The light and temperature were falling. They could hear whistling and buzzing. At times, a twig cracked beneath a boot. Once again it was as if Karlovic were back at the concentration camp, on his way to work; except that this time he was not going to chop down trees, but dig his own grave.

At a certain point, Richter told him to stop, turned around, and stared at him. The condensation coming out of their noses mingled. Richter wanted to express something – friendliness, compassion, forgiveness – but Karlovic's face was a mask devoid of any feeling. Richter lowered his head and began to move away. He would carry out his mission, but was not obliged to see the outcome. The other agents found this behavior odd in a chief who usually took it upon himself to press the pistol to the back of the neck of the victims, but they asked no questions. They gave the spade to Karlovic and told him to dig. Meanwhile, as the chief was not nearby, they started to have fun with their victim. 'As you're a priest, you can say a prayer,' one of the agents joked. 'Don't worry, you're sure to go to heaven,' said another. They all laughed at the gags. Karlovic's face altered. His jaws tightened and his eyes narrowed. He no longer believed in God, or considered himself a priest, and yet those morons had offended him. At the moment of his death, his feeling for the sacred was again as strong as it had been when he entered the seminary. A blasphemy had caused a malfunction in the clockwork mechanism of his obedience. Karlovic turned and spat in their faces. The agents' fingers pressed the triggers, the pistols roared and Karlovic's body dropped to the ground. Birds fluttered off, scattering, and animals hid in their holes. It was half-past three. They discharged the rest of their fury on the corpse with kicks, not so much for him spitting, as because now they had to dig the grave themselves in which they would throw the old priest. Far away, invisible to his subordinates, Markus Richter whispered a prayer in which he asked forgiveness of his uncle for taking part in the murder of a priest.

Helena and Schwartz

A WEEK later, the body of Ruth Meyer was found by a hunter in a wood about twelve kilometers from Tiers. She was half-naked and showed signs of having been subjected to violence. The investigators concluded that her death had taken place a week earlier and the cause was strangulation. Ruth was taken to a morgue and her body was identified by a niece. The workers at the orphanage had informed the police of her disappearance, but no one had said anything to Helena Yava. Helena had called her twice and found it odd that Ruth did not answer. She was worried, but since at times Ruth went missing without warning her, and since they had a clandestine relationship, she tried to persuade herself that it was a normal occurrence.

Her secretary informed her of Ruth's death just as she would have informed her of the death of any minor official of the regime. Helena was signing documents and became paralyzed, with her pen suspended millimeters from the paper. The secretary, supposing that she was telling her an exciting story, got closer to the desk and revealed all the details of her death. On discovering that Ruth had been murdered and left in a wood, Helena released a bellow that sent the secretary flying out. Instantly she pictured Zdanhov strangling her. It was obvious what had happened: Ruth had gone to confront him with the abuse of the children and Zdanhov had killed her.

She began to rack her brains for a plan to incriminate him. She could not rely on the police to carry out an independent investigation that would lead to jail for a man like Zdanhov. Tears and mourning would come later; all she wanted now was vengeance.

With her elbows on the desk and her hands supporting her chin, Helena tried to find any proof she could bring up against him. Her eyes glazed. She chewed a pencil. She breathed slowly. After a while digesting it all she realized she had no proof. The only thing she could do was make up evidence, and run the risk of being found guilty of perjury. However, if she involved Ruth herself in the accusation, no one would be able to contradict her. She would simply be the vehicle that brought the thoughts of the victim to the knowledge of the police; and these, though invented, would tell the truth as they would be legitimized by her murder. It would be as if Ruth had sent a message seconds before she was killed. In the end, it was the Party itself that had taught her that the truth was something fabricated in one's own interests. The investigators would believe her because of her position and because she had no motive to wish to harm Zdanhov. Then it would be her word against his. It might not be enough for a court to find him guilty, or perhaps even to try him, but it would damage his career severely. At the very least it would keep him away from children for a while.

ARRESTING everyone involved in the terrorist attack on the Witten fertilizer factory – except Leonidas Vall, who was believed to have fled the country – and having had them executed, along with the priest, had somewhat placated Schwartz's rage. Luda had been avenged. Even so, his mourning was surrounded by clouds as black as the ones that had followed the explosion at the factory. Whichever way he turned, all he found was a darkness that burned his lungs.

He was in his office analyzing the progress the investigation was making when his secretary brought in a dossier on the death of an orphanage director named Ruth Meyer. Although he did not recognize the face in the photographs, her name was not unfamiliar. Schwartz scratched his chin and closed the report on the investigation. He looked up Helena Yava's file and confirmed that she had been her lover. It was very odd indeed for the girlfriend of a People's Commissar to appear strangled in a wood. That made Helena Yava the main suspect. Jealousy? Revenge? However, a woman did not use her hands to kill; knives, revolvers, or poison, certainly, but not brute force. Intrigued, Schwartz continued to read the report. Apart from the fracture of the larynx, the victim's face was covered in hematomas and her jaw, nose and several teeth were broken; under her nails, blood and traces of skin were found, which indicated that she had fought with her assailant; she was semi-nude, but had not been raped. The woman had been beaten and killed by someone stronger than herself, almost certainly a man. The crime had been committed somewhere else, which meant that the murderer had the resources to transport the concealed corpse to the wood. Undressing the victim without carrying out a sexual attack might have been an attempt to leave a false trail. Schwartz began to sketch a profile of the killer, although he could not understand what motive the man might have had for killing a lesbian. Then he found an unexpected clue. A witness had seen a woman resembling Ruth Meyer near the home of Zut Zdanhov at seven in the evening, and that was the last time she had been seen alive. The house was in a sparsely-populated area and was enclosed by walls. It would not have been difficult to kill someone inside the home, put her in the boot of a car, and take the corpse far away.

Zdanhov? Why the hell would that maniac want to kill a lesbian?

Schwartz did not have to ponder long to find the answer. The question he still could not answer was what he was going to do next. Zdanhov or Yava? He could frame either of them. Which sacrifice would serve his interests better? Which of the two People's Commissars would be more valuable? He smacked the globe and set it spinning. The world accelerated right before his nose.

An hour later, at five in the afternoon, he received a telephone call from Helena Yava, asking for an appointment. He told her he would see her at once. And a thought germinated in his mind that had not occurred to him: if justice were done, then he should be rewarded. The Commissar for Education could not get her lover back, and so she had come to demand the head of the murderer. He was in a similar situation and for that reason would make a demand too. Luda had been given the honor of a state funeral, and her name had been given to a square, but that was not enough. Nor was shooting her assassins. His vengeance had run out with their death. The time had come to prepare for his future and Roman's, in fact to behave as the other Party leaders had behaved before they took power.

The black cloud that had wrapped him since Luda's death did not dissipate, but now he was beginning to learn how to breathe toxic gases.

Helena Yava arrived at the *NS* headquarters twenty minutes later. An official awaited her: he led her to Schwartz's office and opened the door for her. Helena felt uncomfortable the moment she trod on the fluffy carpet. Schwartz was waiting for her on his feet, and went to meet her and shake her hand.

'Comrade Helena, welcome.'

The closed expression on the Commissar's face did not change as she greeted him. Schwartz invited her to sit down and she did so but kept her trunk stiff, with her hands close to her chest and her knees together.

'The subject that brings me here is serious. I have important information on the murder of Ruth Meyer, the director of the orphanage.'

Schwartz faked a look of amazement and rested his chin on a fist.

'Information? What information?'

Helena took a deep breath. 'I'm Ruth's friend and two weeks ago she told me she had received death threats.'

Schwartz raised his eyebrows. 'Death threats? And who threatened your friend?'

Helena leaned towards the desk. 'Zdanhov.'

'Zdanhov? Are you accusing the Commissar for Culture and Propaganda? That is a very serious allegation, comrade.'

Helena raised her chin. 'I give you my word that Ruth told me several times that Zdanhov had threatened her with death because she had found out he was a child molester. He sent people to fetch children from the orphanage then bring them back to his mansions, where he raped them.'

'That's another very serious allegation.'

'Don't be cynical, Schwartz. I'm sure you already knew of Zdanhov's perversion.'

Schwartz drummed on the table. 'Then I'm sure you are equally aware that I know that Ruth Meyer was your lover. And that will be public knowledge if you become a witness in the prosecution.'

Helena pursed her lips. 'I have nothing to hide.'

'Continue.'

'Two days before she disappeared, Ruth told me that she was going to confront him with the abuse and tell him that if he did not stop picking up children from the orphanage, she would accuse him before the Central Committee of the Party. And that's what happened. She must have gone to his house or else they met somewhere that he killed her. Then he took her corpse to that wood so that everyone would think it was a crime committed by a delinquent.'

Schwartz almost smiled and set the globe spinning. 'So your friend carried out a kind of blackmail on Zdanhov.'

Helena raised her voice. 'Preventing children from being molested is not blackmail at all. It's a civic duty. She asked him for nothing in return.'

'How do you know that?'

'I knew her very well and I know that her only goal was to protect the children. They were like her own children.'

'And what was your position when she told you that she was going to confront him with the abuse?'

'I tried to dissuade her from talking to Zdanhov. I told her it was very risky, and he might even kill her.'

'By the looks of it, your friend didn't listen to you.'

Helena let her hands fall from her chest and opened them.

'She was desperate and felt guilty because she had been unable to prevent what was happening. She did what her conscience dictated and showed incredible courage. Aren't those the moral principles the Party transmits to the citizens?'

Schwartz stroked his cheek and looked at her askance. 'There's something I find hard to believe. Your lover was getting death threats and yet she decides to meet the guy making the threats...'

'Yes.'

'And all you did was try to dissuade her? A woman in your position could have done much more. For example, you could have come to talk to me before such a tragedy took place. Where are the astuteness and perspicacity that enabled you to reach your office?'

Helena reddened and an eyebrow twitched. 'Yes... you're right. I admit that I should have acted differently. I feel guilty that I didn't foresee what happened, and the only way I can make up for my mistake is by telling the truth.'

'Are you prepared to sign a deposition accusing Zdanhov?'

'That's why I came here.'

'You're aware that it will be matter of your word against his, and that obviously he will deny everything. And that if you can't prove what you allege, you will end up in dire straits. You may be sent to a re-education camp.'

Helena raised her voice once more. 'I am ready to accept all the consequences. And I'm counting on your investigation to corroborate my testimony. Given what I've told you, and bearing in mind what you already knew about Zdanhov, it won't be hard for your men to find the evidence that will incriminate him. They can begin by questioning the workers at the orphanage.'

Schwartz closed his fists and frowned. 'Comrade, you're playing a dangerous game. I don't like to be told how to do my job.'

'Don't take offence. I don't mean to lecture you. There's been a crime and I have come to give my testimony so that the murderer can be sentenced. It's only in capitalist countries that the powerful escape justice, isn't that so?'

Lia and Roman

MARIA Kirchner was unable to hide from Lia for very long the fact that her father, Ludwig Kirchner, was in a re-education camp. At Lia's school her classmates pulled apart the story that her father was working away from home. 'Enemy of the people,' two boys shouted at her one morning, 'your dad was arrested for being an enemy of the people.' Then other classmates joined them, and in less than a minute, Lia was surrounded by dozens of boys and girls insulting and threatening her, because the daughter of an enemy of the people also inherited the guilt. In the grounds of the high school, in a grassy area which had two-hundred-year-old lime trees, subject to their shouts and shoving, Lia underwent a kind of purge. Finally, with her body bruised, her hair disheveled, and her dress torn, she was saved by two staff members who intervened when they felt her punishment was enough. The violence of her classmates was not what hurt most, but the brutal discovery of the truth. If her own mother lied to her, who in the world, from now on, could she rely on?

From that day forward, Lia became an outcast at school, as most of her schoolmates kept away from her, with the exception of a few other unfortunates whose parents had also been labelled enemies of the people. Even the teachers grew harsh with her, and started to demand more of her than of the other pupils. The transformation of the daughter of an enemy of the people into a New Woman required sacrifices and redoubled efforts.

It was Roman Schwartz who had informed on Lia, since he had heard his father referring to Ludwig Kirchner's sentence, and he took part in her punishment. He had stopped speaking to her months ago, and had even gone as far as pushing her in the corridor. For some days, though, Lia had noticed that his aggressive attitude had changed. Shyly, and only when none of his classmates were with him, Roman began to greet her again, and show her little courtesies, like letting her pass through a door ahead of him, or picking up something that had fallen from her satchel. The hatred that had inflamed the blueness of his eyes had died down to a dull, sad color. The death of his mother had changed his perspective; something hidden had revealed itself. Roman began to understand that Lia must feel as lonely and lost as he did. The grief of being an orphan raised an enemy of the people into a friend of the people.

One Saturday, Lia rose at six because she had to be at the headquarters of the Pioneers Movement within an hour. The entire youth of Slavia from the age of ten to fifteen were members of the Pioneers, and the instructors used to say that they were their second family. They camped in the mountains, played sports, entered contests, and learned to serve the nation. The Pioneers were going to take a group aged between thirteen and fifteen into the country so they could see how agricultural co-operatives worked, and so they could help the farmers. From time to time the idea of collaborating with the regime that had sentenced her father rose up in Lia; to subdue it, she told herself she was just going to spend a day with Roman, nothing else.

She put on her blue skirt and white blouse, and tied the red scarf round her neck. As she left home, she found an orange sky, and the first rays of sunlight piercing a cloud. The day was windless and the air was hot.

When she got to the headquarters and saw Roman she felt her heart beating. The instructors made them line up, then counted them, and only then did they get into the buses. Lia managed to find a seat parallel to his on the other side of the aisle. The seats were all broken, with exposed springs, the engine made a snoring noise, and the luggage racks shook. Suddenly the bus set off and everyone clapped. The trip lasted an hour, and during all that time the instructors were explaining that Slavia was building a better world, while the United States only wanted a nuclear war; luckily, the Soviet Union had more advanced missiles and satellites that would protect them, and capitalism was on its last legs. After saluting President Ionescu, the Pioneers promised to give their lives for the country, and to denounce enemies of the people. Finally, they roared out patriotic songs.

While they sang, Lia and Roman were glancing at one another, and at times, Roman dared to smile at her. The other Pioneers were having fun, the instructors were drinking vodka, and no one noticed. Except for Micha, Zdanhov's nephew. Before Lia was denounced as the daughter of an enemy of the people, he had declared his love for her. Lia gave him a compassionate smile, and told him it would be better if they were just friends. Humiliated, Micha was brooding over revenge.

When they reached the agricultural co-operative they found three houses, painted white, with thatched roofs, a wooden barn, and further off, two brick buildings which, they were told, housed pigs and cows. On the left side were wheat fields, and on the right, vegetable crops. The stench of manure hovered over everything. The buses passed through the farm gates and parked by the main house. Some thirty men and women awaited them. The instructors got out first. A bearded man met them and greeted them with embraces. Then he led them to the peasants, where they seemed to inspect some of them: they squeezed their arms and made them open their mouths. Only then did they let the Pioneers out of the buses and have them line up again. Lia had expected country people to be young and strong, but these peasants seemed old and tired to her. The women wore headscarves and the men wore caps. Lia had never seen such sad-looking people.

Could any of them be enemies of the people too, and be here for their re-education?

The bearded man turned round, made a fist, gave a patriotic speech, and finally, told them to go and pick tomatoes. The sun was already burning her head, the light was blinding, and she was thirsty, but Lia knew that a Pioneer never complained. Soon, they were given baskets and sent to follow a group of peasants. The instructors and the bearded man went towards the house, telling jokes and laughing.

Roman took the opportunity to walk by Lia's side as they proceeded to the tomato fields. She had noticed that the peasants were not as old as they looked, in spite of their wrinkled skin and slumped shoulders. Out of pity, perhaps, she tried to talk to them, but they turned their faces away and did not answer. After a while, it began to seem as though the farm was endless. Earth got inside her shoes. She was sweaty and she still had not picked a single tomato.

The tomato plantation covered an area bigger than a football pitch. The green leaves and red fruit contrasted vividly with one another. The aroma was similar to that of grass. Black birds flew overhead, and brilliant insects crawled about. Crickets and cicadas chirped. Then a woman clapped twice – her hands looked like an animal's paws – and started giving instructions.

'Pay attention. First of all you are not allowed to eat a single tomato. Your job is to fill the basket and empty it over there,' she said, pointing to a group of carts. 'But make sure you don't crush them. Form a straight line and all move forward at the same time. Let no one fall behind or waste time talking. Watch out for snakes and scorpions because there's no nursing station here. Anyone's who's thirsty, come and see me. Time to start work.'

The Pioneers spread out and the tomato field turned into a green stain with white and red spots on it. Plucking the fruit and shaking the foliage created a rustling that drowned out the birdsong and insects' chirping. They all threw themselves into the work so they would be praised for their productivity. A wasp stung Lia at one point, but she put up with the pain and carried on working with her swollen hand. After an hour her back ached and she had blisters on her fingers, but she wanted to prove that the daughter of an enemy of the people could produce as much or more than the others.

Even so, exhaustion defeated her in the end. As she tripped on a stone she dropped the basket and a few tomatoes rolled on the ground. For a few moments she was disoriented, and just stared at the red balls without moving. Roman stopped working and came to her aid. His caress on her arm awoke her from her torpor.

'You OK?'

'Yes.'

The pair knelt and filled the basket again; then, each of them holding a handle, they took it to a cart to empty it. Two peasant women whispered as they passed, but when Lia stared back they dropped their eyes as if they were scared.

Later, Lia had the urge to urinate and went to a bushy area set aside for the girls. It was a quiet area some hundred meters from the tomato plantation. Since there was no one there, she squatted and relieved herself without constraint. When she was finished and preparing to go back, Micha appeared. He had taken his shirt off and was bare-chested. He stood in front of her, raised his arms and flexed his muscles. In the sun his sweaty body shone.

'Feel my muscles.'

'I don't want to, leave me alone.'

'Why not? You think you're better than all the rest?'

'Don't be daft.'

Lia turned her back on him. Micha grabbed her by the neck and started kissing her by force. Lia tried to get free, but he was stronger. She yelled. Micha covered her mouth and dragged her into the bushes. Lia's lip was bleeding. Micha called her names as he tried to rip her clothes off. Lia could hardly breathe and felt herself fainting. All of a sudden, Roman was there and he punched Micha and knocked him down.

The pair stared at one another, Roman panting and Lia shaking, unable to say a word.

Micha got to his feet and ran away.

Then they took a step forward and fell into one another's arms.

Schwartz and Zdanhov

AFTER two weeks of collecting more evidence to corroborate that accusation that Zdanhov had killed Ruth Meyer, Schwartz realized that he would be unable to make any more progress. The witnesses he had got only proved that on the day of her death, the director of an orphanage had visited the home of a man who had been abusing children at that same orphanage; and just days earlier, the abuser had threatened the director with death. It was enough to condemn an ordinary citizen, but not a People's Commissar. A person like Zdanhov could never be convicted unless he were caught in the act. And as for sex with children, the Party would not waste time on a detail of the private life of one of its leaders. Those orphans and foundlings would just have to be grateful that the regime had taken care of them. All the same, facing the scandal that the revelation of the case would cause if it reached the ears of some diplomat or foreign journalist, the Party would not hesitate to deprive him of his post.

Zdanhov knew that, and it was the trump card Schwartz would play against him. By telephone, he requested that Zdanhov should appear at *NS* headquarters the next morning.

Eleven o'clock sunlight was shining in Ionescu Square when Zdanhov arrived at *NS* headquarters, driven by his chauffeur. He wore a grey suit with a white shirt and black tie. As he got out of the car a flock of pigeons took off; the sound of their wings beating filled the square. Zdanhov raised his head and gazed at a blue feather blowing past on the wind. Then he spat to one side and headed for the building. As if he were the head of the secret police, he entered without showing any ID to the agents guarding the door, got rid of the secretary who was supposed to accompany him by swatting at her with his hand, strode along the corridor, forcing officials carrying reports to swerve out of his way, went up in the lift, and headed straight to Schwartz' office on his own. He went in without knocking and wiped his feet furiously on the carpet. As the blinds were half-shut and the dim light was in his eyes, all he could make out was a shape seated at the desk.

'Comrade Zdanhov, how have you been?' said Schwartz without rising, pointing at a chair for Zdanhov to sit down.

As if the seat were covered in dust, he blew on it. 'Comrade Schwartz, I've been fine, but you didn't call me here to discuss my health...'

'You're right, it's to discuss the health of someone else.'

'What?'

'Do you know a woman named Ruth Meyer?'

'No.'

'She was found dead. She was the director of an orphanage.'

'Never heard of her.'

'She was strangled somewhere we haven't determined yet, and left in a wood. Doesn't that seem strange to you?'

'Nothing surprises me anymore.'

'She was a lesbian.'

'Women like that don't interest me.'

'In my opinion, it's a sexual perversion. In our society perversions should be eradicated. Don't you think so, Zdanhov?'

Zdanhov fidgeted in his chair. 'Listen, Schwartz, what are you driving at with this daft game?'

'In our society, there shouldn't be any men who abuse children, don't you agree? That's something the degenerate bourgeoisie does, isn't it?'

Zdanhov blanched. His eyes were practically popping out.

Schwartz took a photograph out of his draw and threw it on the desk. It was of Zdanhov leading a child to his car.

'What is this?' Zdanhov shouted. 'What are you insinuating?'

'I'm not insinuating anything, I'm showing you that I have proof that you're a pedophile. My men have been watching you for a long time.'

Zdanhov stood up with his fists clenched.

'Sit down. Don't make the situation worse.'

For a moment Zdanhov froze, but in the end he obeyed. His mouth was twisted and he had a downcast look. 'Tell me what you want and get it over with.'

'Pay attention. I know you killed Ruth Meyer. You killed her because she knew about the abuse of the children and she was about to report you to the Party's Central Committee.'

'That's absurd, I didn't murder anyone.'

Schwartz raised a finger to stop him speaking. 'It's useless to deny it. I have witnesses who saw her go into your house, and a signed declaration by a friend of the victim accusing you of making death threats several times to her, because she had said she would report you.'

Zdanhov thumped the desk. 'That's a lie. I never threatened the woman.'

'Listen, whether you threatened her or not is irrelevant now. She's dead and I have sufficient evidence to bring you to trial. You may even be absolved of the crime, but your career as a People's Commissar will be over. As you know, the Party dislikes scandals.'

Zdanhov grasped his forehead, unable to say anything. Schwartz went on: 'And that's not your only problem. You're also guilty of appropriating works of art that belong to the people, and of selling some of them to foreign collectors, which has made you millions of dollars that you keep in a Swiss bank account. And that, as you know very well, is far more serious in the eyes of the Party than abusing children.'

Zdanhov raised his eyes. 'It's money that you're after…'

Schwartz set the globe spinning. 'Your account in Switzerland will be transferred to my name in exchange for me closing the investigation on the lesbian's death. Or better yet, we'll find some unlucky bastard we can pin the blame on. And you can keep the paintings, of course. I'll never be able to understand how a painting could be worth more than a house. At the end of the day, capitalism really is an aberration.'

Zdanhov wiped his forehead with a handkerchief. 'How can I be sure that you'll keep your word after you get the money?'

'From the moment the account is transferred to my name, you'll have proof against me. Our agreement requires a pact of mutual silence. You can carry on playing with the boys, you can sell a few paintings, you can do what you like. I won't bother you again, comrade.'

♚

Ionescu and Olin

IT WAS ten o'clock at night and Alfred Ionescu was looking at the sky through the window of the office in his palace. Venus stood out from the blackness of the firmament. The few visible stars were just a scattered dust that highlighted the planet's brilliance. That night Venus was the ruler of the universe, but its dominions did not extend beyond the cosmic darkness. The contemplation of that lost heavenly body, with its equally intense and useless brilliance, began to cause Ionescu discomfort.

He sat at his desk and went back to reading the economic report they had given him that afternoon. The five-year plans were producing excellent results: agricultural production had grown 15%, industrial production had grown 10%, the GDP had grown 14%, the rate of inflation was at zero, and so was the unemployment rate. Just like the first time he had seen it, Ionescu was unable to finish reading it: none of it was true. Despite the efforts of his assistants, rumors about the lack of food in the stores had reached his ears. On one of his rare excursions from the palace, he himself had seen the queues in front of food shops, and hunger was stamped on their faces. A squalid woman with sunken eyes and a crying child on her lap had made a strong impression on him. Those two unfortunates were not included in the reports; that mother and her child were part of the cosmic darkness that he reigned over. He could no longer fool himself with fantasies of continual economic growth and prodigious development. There was not even the faint glimmer of stardust in the gloom of his realm.

The People's Commissar for the Economy would have to come up with an explanation. He picked up the telephone and dialed Igor Olin's number.

Olin was watching the nurse change Aliocha's nappy when he heard his phone ring. He decided to ignore it and continue to follow the careful attentions given to his son. Aliocha's inexpressive face seemed to be animated by a smile when the nurse spoke sweet words to him; he responded to them with sounds that resembled the purring of a cat; in this way a dialogue took place between the two, as simple as it was intense. Olin wanted to take part too in this magical moment with his son, but he did not know how to; when he was alone with him, Aliocha's gaze seemed vacant, and his caresses, instead of awakening him from his torpor, ignited something like rage. And it was even harder for him to do anything now because the telephone would not stop ringing. The nurse and Aliocha did not hear it and their intimacy only grew, but for Olin the spell was broken. Annoyed, he left the room and went to answer the call. He was getting ready to reprimand the person making the disturbing call when he heard the voice of President Ionescu.

'Comrade Olin, I hope I'm not disturbing you at this hour.'

Olin gritted his teeth and gripped the receiver with all his might. 'Comrade President, you never disturb me. To what do I owe the pleasure of this call?'

'I need to speak with you urgently.'

'Of course, I'll be in your chambers first thing in the morning.'

'I need you now.'

Olin made a furious grimace and gripped the phone again. 'Now?'

'Yes, be here in half an hour,' he said, hanging up.

Twenty minutes later, Olin arrived at the presidential palace and was taken by a bodyguard to Ionescu's office. He entered a salon with a chandelier, landscape paintings on the walls, a portrait of the president himself, and bookcases; the wooden floor was covered with a red Turkish carpet decorated with blue and yellow geometric designs. Ionescu was seated at his desk, and he stood up to greet Olin.

'Comrade Olin, thank you for coming. Please sit down.'

Olin shook the cold hand and forced a smile.

'Comrade Ionescu, what is bothering you?'

Ionescu returned to his desk and looked at him gravely. 'I want to know the real situation of our economy.'

'I think we have already sent you the reports for this year. You should find all the information you need in them.'

Ionescu sighed. 'Olin, let's not prolong this farce. I want to know what's really going on in our country. What state is our economy in? What are we producing? How much foreign debt is there? How many people are unemployed?'

Olin stroked his hair. 'No reports with that information exist.'

'What?'

'We don't have any kind of true study of our economic situation. All we have is what you've read.'

Ionescu got out of his chair. 'But that's absurd. Are you all insane?'

'Comrade, no one had dared write such reports because they've been afraid of being considered traitors or saboteurs or something that might get them sentenced to a re-education camp. As you must remember, some of your policies have encouraged that kind of behavior. The importance of "good news", of "raising the morale of the people," of "avoiding pessimism", and opposing "defeatism." I myself have taken part in what you called a farce. What choice did I have?'

Ionescu sat down again. A lock of grey hair hung down over his forehead.

'So we have no idea how we're doing?'

'Well, we have some idea.'

Ionescu gestured with his right hand as if he were begging from Olin. 'Speak.'

'You won't like what I'm going to tell you.'

'I command you to tell me the truth.'

Olin stared at him without fear. This would be his revenge for forcing him to leave home at that hour and abandon Aliocha.

'Very well. Our economy is near collapse. We owe billions in foreign debt. If we didn't have fixed prices, inflation would be out of control. There are thousands unemployed. We don't even produce a sixth of the goods we need. In terms of food, our agricultural production is diminishing and of poor quality. If it weren't for the support of the Soviet Union, we would have people dying of hunger.'

Ionescu shook his head. 'But explain to me how that could happen.'

Olin felt a perverse pleasure in tormenting Ionescu. 'Our investments only generate losses. Our factories are obsolete, badly managed, and our workers are not motivated. There's a lot of waste and theft too. In agriculture it's the same. The methods of production are outdated, the agricultural co-operatives don't work, there are ruined crops because no one harvests them, and cereals that rot in the silos, and the peasants don't work hard and steal the food. And when there are droughts or heavy rains at the same time, we have a catastrophe.'

Ionescu listened to him with his eyes shut. 'We've got to replace the managers of the factories and co-operatives at once. We also need to educate better meteorologists…'

Olin interrupted him. 'Comrade, unfortunately that won't solve a thing. That's not the issue. The issue is our system of production.'

Ionescu raised his voice. 'Are you questioning the wisdom of a planned economy?'

Olin shrugged his shoulders. 'You asked me for the truth, didn't you?'

Ionescu got up and started pacing the room. He took deep breaths to calm himself down. Olin had to keep turning his head to follow him.

'The effectiveness of the planned economy has been scientifically proven. It's beyond discussion. What was this country before the revolution? The people lived in misery, exploited by half a dozen bourgeois families. We brought equality and justice, dignity and hope. We put an end to child labor, and illiteracy, we vaccinated and offered healthcare to children, we got the young to practice sport and sent them to universities, we created dignified jobs for the adults and gave them social security, we built housing for the homeless, and sports pavilions and cultural centers, roads and bridges, we provided plumbing and sewage, banned prostitution and gambling, and set the tramps and the priests to work. What other country in the world, apart from our allies, can boast of such progress? The problem is sabotage. We're infested with saboteurs and you should know that better than anyone.'

'Certainly, sabotage is a problem all right...'

'In that case, why didn't you declare that at once as a cause of our economic results? Don't you understand that everything you mentioned is a kind of sabotage? Poor management, theft, waste, low productivity, these are all methods designed to ruin our economy. And isn't it true that the Americans have even invented ways to alter the climate so as to ruin the agricultural production in socialist countries? Those satellites they're always sending into space... NASA...'

Olin scratched his chin and bit his lower lip. 'Comrade, you know as well as I do that those rumors about the Americans disturbing the climate were made up by the Soviets. No educated person believes in such rubbish.'

Ionescu wrinkled his brow. 'Maybe not, but you never know what they're up to. They've got nuclear missiles aimed at our country, haven't they?'

'Comrade, please listen to me: we're facing a serious problem and we need to take drastic measures. If we don't, there will be a mass uprising.'

'Yes, we need to shoot the saboteurs.'

'Shooting the saboteurs won't improve the situation. Nor will printing more money, as it will only increase inflation even more, and lead to a bigger black market.'

'All right, so what do you propose we do?'

'We need to make economic reforms with the greatest urgency.'

'Economic reforms? What are talking about?'

'Comrade, as you know, Lenin himself made reforms to save the Soviet economy.'

'Are you referring to the New Economic Policy?'

'Yes. One step back, then two steps forward.'

Ionescu went to the window and gazed for a few moments at Venus. Abruptly, he turned. He was pale and his shoulders slumped. 'So you want us to give up the five year plans and allow capitalist initiative in our country? Permit the existence once again of small firms in industry and commerce? Let the peasants own their own lands again and sell their own produce? Salaries set by the market and foreign investment?'

'As a temporary measure, naturally, until the economy improves.'

Ionescu shook his head. 'Our Soviet allies would never allow anything like it. Didn't you see what happened to Hungary and Czechoslovakia? They don't tolerate dissidence. Do you want to see their tanks in our country?'

'We don't want to go as far as the Hungarians or the Czechs. It's a question of diplomacy. We need to persuade them that it's absolutely vital we make some reforms to save communism.'

'Don't be ingenuous. In the end they themselves rejected the reforms of the new economic policy. They'll just tell us that it was a mistake we shouldn't imitate, and that the only way is the planned economy. They'll also tell us to shoot more people. As you know, they think we're too mild in that respect. Do you think I have the power to contradict them?'

Olin smiled. 'In that case, we simply won't tell them. It's high time we took decisions without asking their permission. The Russians can't tell us what to do. Don't tell me you aren't sick to death of them?'

For a time Ionescu was silent. 'It's a risky game. I might be deposed and convicted of treason.'

'If there's a popular uprising, or worse, a military coup, the same thing will happen. As you remember, in Portugal there was a coup d'état.'

'Yes, but that was a fascist dictatorship.'

'A dictatorship…'

'I need to think...'

'Comrade, all we have to do is let the peasants go back to farming their own lands and selling a few products and there will be an increase in the food supply. Even that will solve a lot of problems. If there's food in the shops again, the danger of an uprising disappears.'

Ionescu squeezed his face with both hands and took a deep breath. 'All right. Arrange that, discreetly, but make it clear that it's a temporary measure. Don't let the peasants start having bourgeois aspirations. I'll speak to Schwartz so he doesn't interfere in the process.'

'Yes, it's vital that his men don't start arresting the peasants. Besides, I'd like to not have any problems with the other People's Commissars. Every last one of them just seems to look out for their own interests. We haven't played on the same team for ages.'

'Don't worry. None of them will contradict me, for fear of losing their privileges. They...all of us, Olin, we all work hard to deserve our standard of living, isn't that so?'

'Sure, we work hard...'

'You're right, if the peasants sell a few potatoes and carrots, it won't bother anyone. As for the Russians, I agree with you, it's none of their business how we govern ourselves.'

'It will be a small step backward so that we can take a giant leap forward.' Olin felt ridiculous as he uttered these words.

'We're agreed then. Guarantee the food supply to the people and you will be well rewarded.'

'I'll do everything in my power, but don't expect quick results. We're starting from zero. There's a very rigid infrastructure that we have to dismantle. It'll be a slow process and there will be resistance.'

'Go ahead.'

Ionescu turned back to the sky lit up by Venus and discovered that new stars had come out. He smiled. Olin watched him for a few seconds until he realized, with relief, that he could leave. He knew that the measures he had proposed would have a modest effect, and only a radical change of economic and political policy could prevent the ruin of the country, but that did not worry him much.

When he got back home, Aliocha had fallen asleep and the nurse was seated by his bedroom door. She was a woman of forty or so, short and stout, with grey hair that was always tied back and black eyes magnified by the thick lenses of her glasses. She was wearing her usual white coat and flat shoes, which were enormous because of her swollen feet. Olin realized that he did not know her name – she was simply called 'nurse', just like the others. After she had told him that Aliocha was fine, he wanted to prolong the conversation, ask her how she managed to communicate with the child, ask her to teach him the mysterious language that only the two of them knew; in other words, he wanted her to give him the key to his son's heart. But he only stared at her, unable to say a thing, as he lacked the courage to admit his love for Aliocha.

On the other hand, the nurse was just as capable of decoding Olin's facial expressions, and of understanding that this was the best way to communicate with the important People's Commissar. Communication with the father was not so different from communication with his son; in fact, she even used more words with Aliocha than with Olin. She smiled at him and nodded her head, as if she could absolve him that way of any remorse he had, and at the same time, the gesture gave him permission to go to bed. One day, if he continued to try to get closer to his son, he would finally manage to win his affection, without her help or anyone else's.

Olin went into his bedroom, and before he said his prayers, he wondered what the country would be like if this woman were the president. A sick country needed someone who knew how to take care of it, and who understood the language of the people, a task Ionescu was not qualified for. If she were in charge, there would not be any privileged people, or hungry people, or innocent people sent to concentration camps; if she were in charge, maybe not even he, or any People's Commissar, would keep his position; if she were in charge, they would not need to take steps backward before they could take steps forward. Once he was under the blankets with his head lying on the cotton pillow, he pressed his hands together and began a prayer in which Aliocha and the economic reforms both figured. The reforms were not intended to save the country, but to assure the future of his son. For that to happen, however, another miracle was necessary.

♔

Kirchner, Levi and Steiner

FOR some days now Kirchner had been feeling ill: he had a cough and a fever. But it was after a day of exhausting work, when his sweating body had been exposed to glacial winds, that he began to shake, feel bodily pain and find it hard to breathe. That night he hardly slept, tormented as he was by a temperature of 39 degrees Celsius, a constant cough, and congestion of his nasal passageways. His thirst was unbearable, but he had no water to drink. In the morning, when the guards came to fetch them for work, he did not want to show weakness and joined the other convicts for the usual tree felling.

Levi was the first to notice that he was not well. 'Kirchner, you're ill. You shouldn't go to work. Talk to the guards and ask them if you can stay and rest.'

'I appreciate your concern, but this is nothing. I've just got a cold. The fresh air will do me good.'

'Sorry to insist, but if you get a respiratory infection here, you've had it. You won't get the right treatment. Look what happened to Marius. Don't you think that...'

Kirchner coughed, doubling over. When he recovered, he pulled his friend by the arm to put an end to the conversation. 'Levi, let's go to work.'

Once more the day was cold and windy. From time to time the sun peeped out of the clouds, only to vanish again. Marching slowly, with his head bursting and cold sweat on his skin, Kirchner survived the walk to the tree felling area, breathing with ever greater difficulty. It was as if a barrier that impeded the inflow of air had been raised in his lungs. The alveoli were imprisoned in a concentration camp overrun by a virus. His immunological system had been defeated by pneumonia. This was the penalty for inadequate food, poor sanitary conditions, overwork and exposure to the cold. Each coughing fit was followed by an expectoration of yellow mucus and blood. At such times, Kircher grabbed whatever was in reach – the carts, the trees, or other prisoners – so that he would not fall. Used as they were to these spectacles, which preceded the collapse of many, the guards tolerated his slowness. Huss even offered him water, and when they arrived at the forest, signaled to the other guards to leave him in peace.

However, Kirchner had decided to prove that he was as strong as the rest, and needed no one's protection. He did not need the commandant's favors, or Koba's. There was a picture he wanted to paint for them, in which there was nothing to see but the letters, in broad brushstrokes, of the word 'respect.' To make himself respected in the concentration camp had become essential for the painter. By now he hardly cared if anyone considered him guilty or innocent, but he could not allow them to consider him a spy, or worse still, a privileged guy. This would be the hardest work he had ever carried out in his life, shaped and molded in his own flesh, but he would put up with any torment to complete it.

When he tried to pick up an axe to chop down a spruce tree, he felt that he was going to faint, and allowed himself to fall to his knees. A pile of dry leaves crackled beneath him. Kircher let go of the axe and leaned against the tree that he could no longer cut down. The trunk of the spruce seemed as comfortable to him as a pillow. All at once, he saw the world spinning: images got mixed up, voices and sounds were confused, and the smells nauseated him. As he coughed, he released a jet of blood. He wiped his mouth with his hand and stared at that reddish mass that had come out of his lungs. Then he remembered what Levi had told him. Marius had died for lack of proper medical attention and the same thing could happen to him. There was something even more important than making himself respected: survival. He hugged his uniform to his body, brought his arms up to his chest, bent his knees, and stayed like that, quivering with fever and coughing.

He seemed to hear Levi's voice when he felt some arms picking him up and putting him in the cart. By then he already had a temperature of forty-one. On the way back to the camp he became delirious, seeing Lia and Maria hovering over him like two angels coming to take him to heaven. They smiled at him and told him not to be afraid; he tried to stretch his right hand towards them so that they would take it. He wanted nothing else but to die peacefully, and, in the company of his wife and daughter, leave forever this world that had treated him so badly.

He had been lying in his bunk for half an hour before the camp nurse came to see him, accompanied by Levi. He was a boy of twenty-three they called the Messiah. He wore a white coat and thick glasses, and had his head shaved. His knowledge of nursing had come to him through being a veterinarian's assistant. He was carrying a bottle of vodka and two enormous pills wrapped in newspaper. He saw that Kirchner was struggling to breathe, coughing and bringing up blood, and was as pale as a corpse. He scratched his head and finally questioned the patient. 'How do you feel?'

Levi interrupted. 'Can't you see he's so ill that he can't speak?'

The Messiah looked at him with indignation. 'Are you trying to teach me my job? Are you a doctor by any chance?'

'No…'

'Then shut up, because you're not helping the patient.'

Levi took a deep breath and restrained the urge to punch him.

'All right then,' said the Messiah, 'I'll examine him. Get back, get back.'

He placed his hand on Kirchner's burning forehead and let

out a whistle.

'He has a fever. A high one. No need to use a thermometer.'

Next he took his pulse and stared at his watch. For some seconds he did that, until suddenly he flung Kirchner's arm aside as if he were throwing something in the rubbish.

'No, he really isn't well.'

Levi gritted his teeth, but said nothing. The Messiah carried on speaking as if neither he, nor Kirchner, were present. He was angry. 'I know the work is hard here, and conditions could be better. But if the sick would just come to me earlier they wouldn't reach this state. Only when they're at their last gasp do they remember to call me, and then they expect me to work miracles. At the end of the day, it's their fault. On the other hand, the one who suffers is me. Sure, if they die it's my professional reputation that's put in question. How am I going to explain to the commandant that he's lost another worker? I could be fired. These people are so ungrateful.'

Levi could not keep silent any longer. 'Excuse me, but what are you going to do to save him?'

The Messiah sighed with annoyance and adjusted his glasses. 'What am I going to do? Well, I'm going to do what's in my power, and that's all you can expect. Two aspirins and half a glass of vodka. And don't start whining, because this is no hospital. Maybe he'll get better, who knows? Unfortunately this guy isn't very strong, I've seen tougher-looking women and suckling pigs. Even if he'd never come here, he wouldn't have made his century. Pray, pray if you're his mate. Tomorrow I'll come and see him at the same time.'

Then the Messiah opened Kirchner's mouth, slipped the two pills inside, and made him take a few sips of vodka. Kirchner had an even more violent coughing fit, and spat out the tablets, along with blood. The Messiah wiped his hands on Kirchner's uniform and shrugged his shoulders. He turned to Levi.

'As you can see, the patient rejects the treatment. In such a case even the best doctor in the world couldn't treat him. He's a psychiatric case. Anyway, that's enough for today.'

The Messiah turned and left.

The other convicts had been watching the scene and making commentaries, but none of them appeared to care what the painter's fate would be. They quickly forgot the dying man and took up their usual conversations.

When dinner time came around, Levi went to ask for the guards' help. Beside a steaming pot of potato soup, he tried to persuade them to set the case before the commandant. The guards resisted the idea, arguing that it would not help him, and they might be punished. Levi shouted that a man was dying and they were responsible for whatever happened. The steam from the soup seemed to thicken his words. One of the guards slapped him and told him to shut up. Some of the prisoners told him to shut up too, as he was holding up their dinner. At that moment, Huss came into the hut. His face was tired and his tone was not threatening.

'What's going on here?'

No one opened his mouth. Levi moved towards him and the guards let him pass. He halted close to Huss and grabbed him by the sleeve. 'Kirchner's dying. Help him.'

Huss jerked his arm to get Levi's hand off it. 'They told me the nurse has treated him. I can't do anything else for him.'

'You could set his case before the commandant…'

Huss shook his head. 'That would only make it worse. This guy isn't in the commandant's good books any more. If I were to disturb him at this hour, he might order me to hose him down with leave him to freeze during the small hours.'

'But…'

Huss gave him a shove. 'Don't keep on. He's an enemy of the people and he came here to be re-educated. Suffering and pain are part of the sentence. This here is like when they used to dunk witches in the old days, except there are no innocent ones. If he survives it's because fate decreed that he should become a better citizen.'

Huss turned his back on him and left, accompanied by the guards. The only sound in the dormitory was their footsteps on the wood floor. The steam from the pots of soup was dying down. As soon as the door closed, Levi went back to Kirchner. Once again the painter was delirious, and murmuring meaningless phrases. His breath sounded like the moaning of a kitten. Levi wiped the sweat off his brow with the sleeve of his own uniform. Just then, someone approached.

'Koba could help this poor bastard. He's a rich painter, isn't he?'

Levi stared at the man before him. He was plump and had scars on his face and forehead. He recognized him as a murderer sentenced to life imprisonment for killing a family with two children.

'Yes, he could pay with his paintings. You work for Koba? Then go and ask him for help before it's too late.'

The man gave a signal to another prisoner, who went to a window and called a guard. The two spoke. The prisoner appeared to be giving orders to the guard. A moment later, the guard set off running.

Within fifteen minutes the dormitory door opened again. It was Fiorov, accompanied by a guard. He was wearing a black suit, a white shirt, and polished shoes, and his face was freshly shaven. The prisoners stepped back to allow him to pass with more fear than they had shown Huss. Some greeted him and he raised his hand like a politician making a victorious wave to a crowd. A fragrance of lavender snaked through the smell of sweat.

'Where is he?' asked Fiorov. All the prisoners pointed at Levi.

Fiorov approached Kirchner's cot and stood there looking at him. The painter was still struggling to breathe, shivering with fever, and coughing. Fiorov shut his eyes for a moment.

'Poor devil, it's worse than I expected.'

Levi, who had stepped back a step, moved closer to him. 'Please help him, you're his last hope.'

Fiorov scrutinized him from head to foot. 'You're the Jew, the art collector?'

'Yes, but I have nothing left. No property. If I had, I'd give you whatever you asked for to save him.'

Fiorov twitched the corners of his lips. 'I see you're the painter's friend.'

'I'm the only friend he has in the camp and I know he'd do the same for me if I were ill.'

'All right, as he may not be able to hear me I'll deal with the matter with you. Bringing a doctor here will cost me a lot of money. This guy succeeded in pissing off the commandant and that's why the price of a bribe will be high. I'm going to have to pay for breaking the camp rules and I'm going to have to pay for the commandant's pride. Get it?'

Levi nodded his head. Fiorov went on:

'A few weeks ago, I made an agreement with this guy that I'd protect him in exchange for a few of his paintings. Now the price for bringing a doctor here is the whole of his work. Everything in his house will be confiscated by my men. Fair enough?'

Levi scratched his head. 'I don't know. I can't promise anything. I don't have the right.'

Fiorov raised his voice. 'Have we got a deal or not?'

'Yes, yes, call the doctor.'

'I can't do a thing today. Right now the commandant is probably getting drunk on the whisky I gave him, along with a few chicks, and he wouldn't like to be disturbed. What's more, he ended up hating the painter after he questioned him in public. The commandant loves the money and luxuries I provide him with, but even an idiot like him has his pride. I've got to bring it up gently. Tomorrow, the moment he wakes up, I'll talk to him.'

Fiorov turned his back and made for the exit. All at once, he turned back:

'Listen, Levi, what you did has made an impression on me. The camp hasn't turned you into an uncaring creature who only wants to save his own skin. That's rare. You're an unusual guy. Trustworthy. One day, when the regime changes and you get your art collection back, I'll do business with you.'

The following morning, at eleven o'clock, Fiorov, wearing the same suit from the night before, but with a blue tie, entered the commandant's office. The latter, in civvies and with scruffy hair, greeted him with a handshake. The sunlight coming through the window lit up both men.

'Come in, Ivan.'

'Stanislau, thanks for seeing me so early.'

'Well, that's what friends are for.'

'Have you still got a few bottles of whisky?'

'Actually, I've only got one case left…'

'Ah, then I'll try to get you some more. This one comes directly from Scotland.'

'Thanks, it's one of the best I've ever drunk. Will you have a glass?'

The commandant went to fetch the bottle to serve Fiorov. The pair clinked glasses. The sunlight turned the whisky golden.

'Tell me how I can help you. Have you had a problem with one of the guards?'

Fiorov cleared his throat. 'Stanislau, it's a delicate subject.'

The commandant's face tensed. 'Mmm, here come problems. Ivan, you know very well I can't let you out of the camp.'

'That's not what I want.'

'What then?'

'I'd like you to let a doctor come to the camp.'

The commandant's face broke into a smile. 'Why didn't you say so? Of course you can bring a doctor in. Do you feel ill?'

'It's not for me.'

The commandant frowned. 'Who is it for then?'

Koba put his glass on the commandant's desk and looked him straight in the eye. 'It's for the painter, Kirchner.'

The commandant winced. 'That guy's insubordinate. He had the gall to give me orders in front of the guards and the prisoners. Let him die and you won't lose a thing.'

'He's a great artist.'

The commandant made a gesture of disdain with his hand. 'A great artist? He's just a bit better than me. He was lucky…'

'Stanislau, his paintings sell for millions of dollars in capitalist countries.'

'Capitalists have very weird tastes. Their art is getting worse and worse. Look at abstract art, all those squiggles all over the place, anyone could paint a picture like that.'

'Look, Stanislau, I'll never be able to understand why one work of art is considered valuable while another that's nearly identical isn't. Religious paintings, for instance, they're always the same thing: Christ on the cross, the Virgin and a bunch of angels. Anyway, what matters is how we can make a load of money at Kirchner's expense if we keep him alive. All we have to do is stop him dying, then make him paint new pictures. I'll take charge of getting them out of the country and then we split the profits fifty-fifty. How does that sound to you?'

The commandant went to the window and stayed for some time with his back to Koba. 'What if he refuses to paint, since he's a prisoner? As you must know, it's not easy to make someone create works of art against his will.'

'If I say I'll send someone to kill his daughter, he'll start painting right away.'

The commandant turned round and combed his hair with his fingers. 'I want seventy per cent of the profits.'

Koba pretended to haggle. 'Sixty.'

'Sixty-five.'

'Deal.'

The commandant clapped once, convinced that he'd driven a hard bargain. 'You can call the doctor, then get that moron to paint a picture a week. And now I think of it, show my drawings to the foreign collectors who buy Kirchner's work. Who knows if they won't buy them too?'

'Of course I'll show them. You're very talented too, Stanislau.'

The pair shook hands and Fiorov left, his smile turning into loud laughter as soon as he was well away from the commandant's office.

Six hours later, the doctor arrived at the concentration camp.

Doctor Max Steiner was forty and a specialist in respiratory illnesses. He worked in the state hospital in Tiers, and had been consulted by the leading figures in the regime. He had saved the lives of many patients, who deluged him with presents on his birthday – woolen sweaters, scarves, eggs, fruit. He pretended embarrassment at receiving the gifts, but deep down he thought he deserved such rewards. Koba's men had offered him a hundred dollars – the currency used on the black market – for him to accompany them on a car journey to a concentration camp where he would treat a patient with pneumonia. Dr. Steiner knew he had no choice, quite apart from the fact that the hundred dollars was triple what he earned at the hospital. So he picked up his case and put in it the medical instruments and medicines he would need to treat the sick man.

The moment the gates of the camp opened, Dr. Steiner shuddered as he once had twenty years ago when he first witnessed the autopsy of a corpse. The dusty ground, the miserable huts, and the fence of barbed wire which enclosed everything with its lacerating spikes all evoked the end of life, just as the disemboweled body of the dead man had. When he was a medical student he had been surprised by something he had imagined but never seen; now that he had dissected so many corpses himself, he was again surprised to find that the imagination falls short of the horror of reality, whether that be human flesh or a concentration camp. But Dr. Steiner screwed up his courage as he had during that class when they had made him remove a liver with cirrhosis, and he walked into the camp prepared to be autopsied by the violence of the regime.

Dr. Steiner was a true communist who was grateful to the Party for allowing him to study and become a doctor, in contrast to his parents who had never had such an opportunity. He could not understand how there could be people who were discontented and even capable of wanting to destroy the regime, when it guaranteed work, housing, healthcare and education to all citizens. Just what did they have to complain about, really, if in capitalist countries the people were enslaved and lived in misery? Obviously such ingratitude deserved to be punished. Thus it was that re-education through work seemed to him an irreproachable form of justice. However, what he was seeing now was not consistent with the humane treatment the regime proclaimed that it provided to dissidents.

The commandant was warned that he had arrived and came to meet him. He had put on his uniform, polished his shoes, and combed his hair. The sun was disappearing, and a damp wind was blowing when the two shook hands.

'Welcome, Doctor...?'

'Steiner.'

'My name's Stanislau Yovic and I'm the camp commandant.'

'I believe you have a sick man in a serious condition?'

The commandant shrugged his shoulders. 'Maybe, I don't know much about medicine.'

The doctor was suspicious. 'Could you take me to him?'

'Yes, but first I'd like you to take my blood pressure and listen to my heart. I might as well take advantage of your visit. This camp is ruining my health. As you must understand, a commandant can't allow the prisoners to take priority over him. Discipline has to be very strict here, or we have problems. We're re-educating enemies of the people, dangerous guys.'

Before the doctor could utter a word of protest, the commandant took his arm and led him to his office. Far away, at the entrance to his own dormitory, Koba watched the scene, shook his head, and went back inside where roast pork and a bottle of Bordeaux were waiting for him on his dining table. Before he ate he went to basin with warm water and washed his hands.

It was almost an hour later before Dr. Steiner was able to get away from the commandant in his office. Besides the medical exams, he had been forced to drink toasts with whisky, look at the commandant's drawings and listen to a dissertation on the degeneracy of modern art and the injustices inflicted on certain artists. When he got out he no longer knew for sure what the terms friend or enemy of the people meant, or which side he was on.

Accompanied by a guard, Dr. Steiner entered Kirchner's dormitory as fearfully as he had when he had done his first examination at the Faculty of Medicine. No sooner had he stepped on the floorboards and started to walk between the prisoners, than the terrible questions his teachers had asked him came back to him:

'Is a pancreatic abscess synonymous with an infected necrosis? How would you define a pulmonary embolism? What are the symptoms of a malignant neoplasia?' And he realized that at that moment, not only had he been incapable of responding, but he had been unable to remember any of his medical knowledge at all.

For a few moments, he wondered if he really was a doctor.

The guard pointed to the cot in which Kirchner was lying. Dr. Steiner began shivering as if he himself were a patient with a fever, and dropped his case on the floor. Levi guessed who he was and came over to him.

'You're too late, doctor, the man died half an hour ago.'

Dr. Steiner stood staring at Ludwig Kirchner: the thin body, the white hands with blue veins, the curly hair, the wax-colored face, the sunken eyes, the hairs growing out of his nose, the open mouth from which a trickle of blood ran. This man would not offer him woolen sweaters, or eggs, or fruit.

Two greenish flies flew over the corpse. Their buzzing was the only sound in the hut.

Dr. Steiner felt as if he had failed an examination.

'If you had come earlier, maybe you could have saved him,' said Levi.

Dr. Steiner could not say a thing, or even understand if he was hearing a question or an accusation.

'Maybe a penicillin injection, or some other antibiotics,' Levi said.

Dr. Steiner felt like injecting himself with a load of medicine. The flies grazed his lips and he did not feel them.

'But it's not your fault, doctor.'

If it was not his fault, then whose fault was it?

For the first time in his career, he was not capable of touching a corpse.

Leonidas

LEONIDAS Vall was walking through Vienna's Judenplatz. Summer had begun, but a cold wind was blowing and grey clouds filled the sky. Leonidas had managed to cross the frontier to Austria, where he had been given the status of political refugee.

For months before the attack on the factory he had prepared his escape, without telling his companions. He knew that there were some border checkpoints in the mountains that separated Austria and Slavia, but the distance between them was ten kilometers, and what was more, the guards spent the nights drunk or asleep. On a night with a new moon, the barbed wire fence could be cut without anyone noticing. Hundreds of people trying to leave the country without authorization had been caught, and even killed, but many others had managed to escape. Because he had camped nearby in his time in the Pioneers, Leonidas had some knowledge of the lie of the land, which he supplemented with a study of the geography, local maps, and navigating by the stars. He needed water and food for one day, warm clothes, boots, a woolly hat, gloves, a torch, a compass, and wire cutters. A day before he made the attempt, at midnight, he would travel the hundred kilometers from Tiersk to Rudden, the city on the Austrian frontier. It would take about two hours to get there, as long as he was not stopped by any police checks – and if he were, no explanation would convince the agents and he would be detained. Then, before he reached the city, he would make a detour towards the mountains, and when he could go no further, try to hide the car as well as he could, covering it with vegetation. He would go on towards the border on foot. He estimated that he would have to walk for over three hours. Aside from the frontier guards or some night reveler who might inform on him, he could have dangerous meetings with wolves, boars, or even bears.

Since the cuts in public spending imposed by Olin had necessitated saving on fuel, Leonidas did not come across any brigade or police car. The trip went by without incident apart from him having to deal with the risk of his Lada's engine not starting when he set off. Later, he decided not to waste time hiding the car, and headed for the mountain. It was two degrees below freezing, and foggy, and the ground was wet and slippery. The climb was harder and slower than he had expected. The light from his torch was swallowed up by the darkness, and Leonidas kept getting lost in the gloom. He met with a barrier of trees and bushes, along with rocks and uneven ground, which forced him into a ferocious struggle with nature. He tripped and fell several times, ran into branches and thorns, and nearly broke a foot in a hole. After half an hour, he had skinned knees, a torn ear, and his face crisscrossed by cuts. He was panting. About then, he started hearing the howling of wolves, which, blending with the hooting of the owls, made him lose track of where he was heading. However, the desire for freedom invigorated him and sharpened his senses. Leonidas climbed the mountain like an animal pursued by hunters. He was leaving a trail of blood, but he did not pause. It was better to die than be caught.

Three hours later, staggering, he reached an area of the mountain that had been cleared of trees and realized that he was at the border between Slavia and Austria. In spite of the darkness, the barbed wire fence glimmered. Leonidas dropped to his knees and stared at the phenomenon like a believer before an idol. Could it be a will o' the wisp? Or an effect of the fog? Might it be the reflection of starlight? Where could that impossible light come from?

The barking of a dog awoke him from his trance. A patrol was approaching and he would have to cut the wire quickly. He took the wire cutters from his pocket and attacked the wire in a frenzy of clips; in a trice, he made a gap in the fence as if he were cutting a sheet of paper. Then he hurled himself through it, and, torn and bloody, let himself roll down the mountain on the other side.

At eleven o'clock in the morning he reached the town of Laa an der Thaya.

Everything he saw was unfamiliar and strange. The town was clean, the buildings in good repair, the cars modern, and of unknown brands; the shop windows were full of food, clothes, toys, books, medicine, sporting goods and many other things that did not exist in his country; the people were wearing fine clothes in a variety of styles, and excellent shoes, they smelled nice, smiled, and the most surprising thing of all was that some of them were fat.

Presently, the smell of hot bread assailed his nostrils, and, as if he were caught by a hook, pulled him in that direction. Leonidas went into the baker's and stood staring at an abundance of food such as he had never seen. The passers-by crossed to another pavement, frightened of that ragamuffin who pressed his forehead to the shop window. The loaves, cakes and croissants were snakes that hypnotized him. Finally, he went inside. The thirty people there fell silent. Leonidas raised his arms as if surrendering himself, said he was a political refugee, and asked if they would give him a roll of bread. Behind the counter, the owner hesitated a few seconds, his hand tempted to pick up the phone and call the police, but he ended up serving him breakfast. In the meantime, two police officers who had been following him for several minutes entered the baker's too. They were wearing blue uniforms with white stripes, black boots, and holsters with pistols at their waists. Politely, but with their hands near their guns, they approached him. Leonidas shook; even so, he did not stop eating while he talked to them. The officers signaled him to calm down, waited until he had finished his meal, then took him to the station.

After an hour's interrogation, he was taken to Vienna, where he would be given authorization to reside in the country, and the status of a political refugee.

In the welcome center where they took him next, he had a hot shower and a meal, and a medical examination, and then he went to bed at once and did not wake up until the next day. When he got up, he went to the bathroom to shave off his moustache. Then he put on the new clothes they gave him, had breakfast, and talked to a worker at the center who gave him some money. Because he was afraid of spies who had infiltrated the country, he avoided contact with the other refugees. Even after they had told him that he was a free citizen, the only duty he needed to fulfil being the center's curfew of nine o'clock at night, he asked permission to get to know the city, and only then did he leave.

The splendors of Vienna were beyond his dreams: the city had architectural styles as varied as the Gothic, Renaissance, Baroque, Neoclassical, Art Nouveau, Art Deco, Beaux-Arts and Modernist, instantiated in buildings like churches, museums, opera houses, public institutions and private houses; it had enormous avenues and squares, parks with trees and lakes, modern public transports, and most fascinating of all for him, shops full of every kind of product imaginable, and cafes and restaurants serving delicious-looking drinks and meals. And everyone had the means to take advantage of this horn of plenty. It looked as though in Austria, and doubtless other capitalist countries too, any citizen could enjoy the luxuries available only to a People's Commissar in Slavia. It seemed to him now as if capitalism put into practice the egalitarian principle of communism, while communism worked like capitalism but only for the ruling class.

So it was that two hours later he found himself in the Judenplatz, stunned and confused. It was eleven in the morning. The sun had broken through a grey sky, but the wind was still cold. The sensation of freedom, of being able to go where he liked, knowing that no one was following him or would stop him, was intoxicating. Presently, without thinking what he was doing, he raised his arms and shouted: 'Down with the dictatorship, death to Ionescu, freedom for Slavia!' Right away he stopped himself, embarrassed, and looked around himself on all sides, fearing they would arrest him. But no policeman appeared, and apart from a couple who took him to be a lunatic, the other onlookers ignored him. Leonidas took a deep breath, shook his head, and smiled. Freedom was a new toy he still did not know how to use.

After making several circuits of the square, he sat at a café terrace and asked for a coffee. Ever since he had crossed the frontier, he had not stopped thinking about the consequences of his attitude, but the stress of the escape, the questioning he had been subjected to, the astonishment at the novelty, and the exhaustion that it had all caused, had prevented him from reflecting on what he had done. Now was the time to do so.

No, you had no choice. If you'd been caught you would have been shot, and that would have been the end of the only resistance they feared. What would the others do without you? Nothing. They talk, they conspire, they hope for the defeat of the dictatorship, but they don't act. Only by sabotage and guerrilla warfare can we beat Ionescu. No people has ever won its freedom by entering into dialogue with its oppressor. Force is the only language they understand. Gandhi's passive resistance only worked because he did not face fascists or communists. In Slavia, he would not have lasted two days. And I shouldn't blame myself for Cornelius and Rado not wanting to escape too. It was their choice. You couldn't tell them you were planning to flee. Probably they would have abandoned the terrorist attack, called you a coward or even a traitor. Neither of them would have informed on you, but you didn't know if they would tell their wives. They would never have spoken of the bomb, as they were involved, but they could have said that a friend was going to run away from the country. It wouldn't have been the first time that happened. If they believed the bonds of loyalty had been broken, very likely they would have felt no obligation to keep a secret. Then the ladies would tell a friend and a few hours later you would be in Lubianka. I did what I had to do and I'm free to continue the struggle against the regime. I shouldn't feel remorse. What I should feel is proud of myself. Maybe others will even follow my example, it might encourage more dissidents to plan attacks and escapes from the country. The bomb will explode in a few hours' time and that's all that matters. If the watchman has any brains, there will be no victims.

Right then, the waiter brought him his coffee. The man entered his field of vision, but it was only the chinking of the cup that woke him from his reverie. Turning his head, Leonidas looked with astonishment at the cup that held the steaming drink. It was white porcelain, painted with a pink-fleshed cherub who had blue wings. The handle formed a perfect circle that harmonized with the pottery. Together, it seemed the ideal place for a fluttering angel. Used to earthenware crockery, or cups of aluminum or thick glass, with no design whatever, and no decoration but the national flag or the hammer and sickle, he was again surprised by the sophistication of the simplest everyday objects.

Does beauty require freedom?

While he was enjoying his coffee, two girls who looked like twins to him sat at a nearby table. They were brunettes, with mirrored sunglasses, red lipstick, white leather jackets, short denim skirts, green tights, and boots with colossal heels. They spoke loudly. As one of them said something, the other responded with laughter. *Being free means laughing.* Leonidas captured their smell of sweet perfume, and ran his eyes over their legs. Desire obliterated politics. Leonidas shut his eyes and tried to imagine them naked, but it was Silvia, dressed, who appeared to him.

Then he remembered their farewell.

On the morning of his flight he had followed her from her home to the museum. He had waited until she sat down in front of a picture, and then, as if he were a visitor who did not know her, he sat down on a bench facing the other way. No one else was in the salon. The silence was total. Silvia picked up a sheet of paper and a pen and started to take notes. Just then, without turning his head, pretending that he too were contemplating a painting, Leonidas addressed her in a whisper:

'Don't move. I've come to say I'm sorry.'

Silvia shivered, a chill freezing her back. She did not answer.

'Silvia, I'm going to leave the country.'

Silvia raised her voice. 'What?'

'Speak softly. I'm going to be forced to leave.'

'You mean you're running away, right?'

'Yes.'

'If you came here to tell me that, this time you've got to tell me everything. And don't be afraid of compromising me: I'm not stupid. I know you belong to the resistance. And if you're running away it's because you're planning an attack on the regime. Are you going to kill the president?'

'Shhh!'

'Nobody's listening to us.'

'No, I'm not going to kill anyone.'

'Then what are you going to do that's obliging you to run away?'

'There's going to be an act of sabotage…'

'Where?'

Leonidas was silent.

'Where?'

'A chemical fertilizer factory.'

'A fertilizer factory… Witten?'

Leonidas nodded.

'But that's really dangerous. There could be explosions, and fires.'

'That's just what we hope for. To put an end to the factory's production and make the regime weaker and more dependent on foreign aid.'

'What about the people who work there? What will happen to them? And what about the consequences for the rest of the population? A fall in agricultural production will cause even more hunger. Have you even thought about that?'

Leonidas smoothed his moustache. 'We're fighting a war. At times there are innocent victims.'

'Innocent victims? And you think you have the right to choose who those victims are, as if you were God. You haven't asked them what they think of your terrorist attack, or whether they are willing to be sacrificed for the sake of your cause, have you?'

'*The cause belongs to the whole people. You have to pay a price to win freedom.*'

'*So why don't you pay that price?*'

'*I risk my life, I'm going to have to leave my country and may never be able to come back. Is that so little, do you think?*'

Silvia did not answer.

Leonidas tried to stroke her hair, but she pushed him off.

'*Go away, Leonidas. Go and be the people's liberator. Blow up the factory and make our lives even more miserable. Go, but don't come back. I never want to see you again.*'

Silvia stood up and left without looking back.

Leonidas left the price of the coffee on the table, stood up and left, looking ahead.

II

PERESTROIKA

✤ 1989 ✤

STALIN must be spinning in his grave, and Lenin, if he were not a mummy, would be too. The communist system is on the verge of collapse. Three years ago Gorbachev initiated *Perestroika* and *Glasnost* in the Soviet Union. The high costs of the arms industry and the war in Afghanistan, technological backwardness, low productivity in industry and agriculture, corruption and the falling standard of living had all led Gorbachev to start a radical transformation of the economy and politics of the Soviet Union. The economy had been opened to private initiative and foreign investment, imports were allowed, prices were no longer regulated, the currency was introduced into the international financial system, subsidies and limits on production were abolished, and the bureaucracy was eliminated. To sum up, the market was allowed to function. At the same time, the government began to democratize the Soviet Union, allowing freedom of expression. It also sought an understanding with the United States to put an end to the Cold War. Finally, Gorbachev addressed the countries that made up the Eastern Bloc and told them that from now on they were free and each of them would choose its own path. The Soviet Union would no longer tyrannize them. In other words, they could maintain their dictatorships or have free elections and accept the will of the people – which would certainly mean taking another direction.

At the same time that East Germany began to demolish the Berlin Wall, in Slavia, with the same fury and hopefulness, Ionescu's regime was being toppled. The strength of the cement that held the stones together was being tested. The cracks ran from the base to the top.

To begin with, on a sunny morning in November, it was just a few dozen people who took to the streets to demand changes, but others joined them until there were hundreds of demonstrators, and by the end of the afternoon, thousands of citizens concentrated in the main squares of Slavia, demanding an end to the regime. The people shouted Freedom and Democracy and the police and soldiers, astonished, let them march, let them yell, let them wave placards, flags, and torches, let them offer flowers without knowing what to do. Orators climbed on to statues of Ionescu, spat on him and called him dictator and murderer, then began to insult the other party leaders, saying disgusting things about the regime and demanding free elections, and the police and soldiers, with flowers in the barrels of their guns, had no idea whether to arrest them or applaud them. Photographs of Ionescu were set on fire, as were flags of the Soviet Union, and ration books, and the police and soldiers wondered if they should lend their lighters or matches. All this was painted and written on the walls of public buildings, while the police and soldiers simply watched the subversive artists appreciatively, and quietly, so as not to disturb the creative process.

And the next day they patrolled the empty squares, which were full of rubbish, broken glass, missing shoes, torn posters, pools of vomit, and smelled unbearably of beer and urine, and they just stared at the walls of the filthy buildings, the plants uprooted from their flowerbeds, and the toppled statues of Ionescu. They stared and could not tell if all this was bad or good. If they were facing the end of the world, or its beginning.

These men who had been trained to suppress demonstrations and protests without questioning their orders, who loved laying into people with their truncheons, and loved punching, and kicking, using water cannon and stirring their dogs to a fury, these men who were so excited by blood, shouts, and people fleeing in panic, and after the clean-up operation, loved torturing those taken to Lubianka and other jails, did not know what to do. Their helmets and body armor protected them from sticks, stones, and knives, but were ineffective against the people's happiness. Why did the people not want to fight against them, why, on the contrary, did they give them flowers, food and beer, call them brothers, and invite them to join them? They had been taught that whoever protested against the regime was in the pay of capitalists, and must be the enemy of the people, and yet, if it was the people itself that had taken to the streets to protest, at the end of the day, who was the enemy?

In fact, none of the leaders, from Ionescu to Schwartz, knew what to do. They could not order in the tanks, or order the troops to open fire on the crowds, because they no longer had Gorbachev's support, nor could they arrest everyone and send them all to re-education camps because they would need a camp the size of Slavia, nor could they even try to explain to them that the Americans were manipulating them because no one was listening, and they could not wait until they got tired and went home because the people had gone berserk. They could do nothing. The worst of it all, however, was the feeling that they had been stabbed in the back. It was treason. Nor was it just their backs that were stabbed; other sharp blades menaced their heads.

It was like a French Revolution upside down, in which the people considered the Party as a sort of monarchy that deserved decapitation. Maybe they would not reach the point of cutting off their heads and holding them by their hair to show them to the crowds, but whatever happened after the fall of their Bastille would not be pleasant either. Terror was the word that best defined the mood of Slavia's leaders during Perestroika.

Terror.

Helena

ALL the same, there was one leader who knew immediately what to do. Helena Yava wrote a letter of resignation, and even before she received a reply from Ionescu, joined the protestors. Unlike her comrades, she was not afraid of taking to the streets and mixing with the people. She knew she might be insulted and attacked, but it was worth running the risk.

Since Ruth's death she had devoted herself even more to the work of educating children and molding adolescents. Nothing interested her any longer except creating the New Man – the dedicated, hardworking, honest men and women who would channel all their energies into the fight against capitalism and the struggle to build a better world. With the unexpected support of the Commissar for the Economy, Igor Olin, Helena managed to get some of her reforms approved, such as doing away with single-sex classes, and introducing sex education, and in the beginning, she was proud of her efforts. However, in the past few years, what she saw did not correspond to the goal she had set. The youngsters were garbed in odd clothes, the boys wearing jeans and flowery shirts, and the girls wearing clinging mini-skirts and high heels; the boys let their hair and beards grow and the girls painted their faces and nails; they listened to rock music, spoke rowdily, went to parties instead of taking part in cultural and sporting activities organized by the Party, and they kissed in public without embarrassment, and some even took drugs.

Could you only build a new humanity after the destruction of the Flood?

At six in the evening, Helena tied a white scarf over her hair and went into the street.

At the window of her flat she had been watching the demonstrators marching up the streets towards the central square of Tiers. Most of them were boys and girls. They were dressed in the style of the West, in brightly-colored clothes, they sang, shouted 'Freedom!', waved placards and flags, drank beer, and hugged and kissed. This was the New Man she had created. Certainly, they were dedicated, good students and workers, and they had moral values, but instead of fighting against capitalism they wanted to defeat communism. It was then that Helena's world turned upside down. She could either carry on that way, with her attitude that it was the crowd that was standing on its head, like flies walking on the ceiling, or she could change her viewpoint, which would mean moving to the other side of the world, like a driver who realizes he has taken the wrong road and does a U-turn. On coming down from her flat into the street Helena decided that from now on she would always keep her head up, even if she saw everything upside down.

It was already dark and the street lights were on. On the pavements, groups of demonstrators shouted slogans against Ionescu. On the roads, the cars blew their horns and the drivers stuck their arms out of the windows, making the victory sign. Altogether, they were making a tremendous racket, as if that could bring down the regime's walls of Jericho.

A group of some thirty boys and girls was just passing when she left home. They were children of the middle and upper classes that the regime had brought up and their parents watched their revolt with incredulity. Threats of cuts to their pocket money, expulsion from home, and even a beating did not deter them. They knew they were taking part in a historical transformation that went far beyond their country and their own lives. They knew they were writing the future. *Perestroika* had elevated them to the position of minor gods in a titanic struggle; later, come what may, they would become human again. Most of them were completing university degrees; some were already working. A blonde girl wearing jeans and a green polo-neck sweater called out to her.

'Join us, granny. Don't worry, no one's going to take away your pension. I'm Sonia.'

Helena hesitated, but when she realized that no one recognized her, she ended up going with them. What did she have to be afraid of? She herself had molded them in the schools and universities. And now that they were not restricted in any way, she could truly evaluate her work. Would these New Men and Women behave in a civilized way in their protests, or like barbarians sacking Rome? One of the lads carried a torch in his hand... Helena's fears grew smaller the further she walked with them, and the more she allowed herself to catch their high spirits. They told jokes, chatted to policemen they met, and did not break shop windows, or spit on the ground, and they continued to put their beer bottles in the rubbish bins.

No, it was not hate that motivated them, but hope.

The girl who had called her began to speak to her again:

'Granny, do you know what we're doing? We're choosing our destiny. Up till now they decided what was best for us, as if we were children. From now on we want it to be us, the people, who make the decisions. And for that we need freedom and democracy. Do you know what that is, democracy? Not the direct democracy they imposed on us – that of the People's Commissars – but true democracy, one citizen, one vote. You've never heard of this, have you? It doesn't matter, they kept you in ignorance for a long time. A granny like you is a victim of the regime too. They don't have to kill us or beat us for us to be victims, you see? But things are going to change and everything is going to be all right. The main thing is that you're having fun.'

Helena smiled and stroked her cheek. Shortly after, a boy with long hair and a beard and a chain round his neck joined them, hugged the girl, and kissed her on the lips. Despite the shouting and the tooting of the horns, Helena managed to hear the sound of that kiss, which stayed in her memory, forever afterward associated with what happened that night.

Some hundred meters further on, coming from a perpendicular street, there appeared a group of a dozen men armed with truncheons and iron bars, who started to taunt the protestors. Besides insulting them with obscenities, they called them traitors. They were young and middle-aged men. All were tall and well-built. They wore a mixture of civilian clothes and military camouflage. Their black boots shone as if they had been polished for a party. The way they were arrayed in two ranks showed that they had combat training.

Helena recognized one of the men: Joseph, Ionescu's driver. His usual sullen expression had changed into a mask of rage. The quiet, polite chauffeur, who had driven her on a number of occasions, had not merely exchanged his blue uniform for a grey camouflage. His hands would not have the task of opening doors, turning the steering wheel or changing gears, nor would his feet depress the accelerator, the clutch, or the brakes. None of these girls awoke sexual desire in him, the impulse to kidnap them and rape them in his room. Right now he was a street fighter, just like any other troublemaker thirsting for violence. Was he there on Ionescu's orders, like a dog faithful to his owner? Or was he just defending his job? Whichever it was, Helena did not have the slightest doubt that Joseph, whatever smiles and tips she might have given him, would be capable of splitting her head open with his iron bar.

Led by a man with a shaved head who gave commands in gestures, Joseph's militia began to chase Helena's group. Like a pack of hyenas they kept a safe distance, but tried to surround them, starting from behind. However, it was not an isolated prey, but thirty, that these hyenas chased. In spite of the predator's instinct and the iron bars, their inferiority in numbers did not allow them to begin an attack from which they would emerge victorious without losses. They snarled that they were going to kill them, they mimicked beating them with the bars, they spat on them, but they did not dare do more. Joseph tried to be as aggressive as his comrades, brandishing his weapon and roaring, but while they showed the confidence of professionals trained to fight, he was awkward and clumsy as he waved his truncheon, as if they had told him to pilot a plane without giving him the necessary instruction.

Helena's group responded to the insults and threats with shouts of 'Freedom!' and 'Democracy!' as well as spitting back. They still formed a cohesive phalanx, not one of them showing fear or the desire to flee, and it struck Helena that this spirit of unity and fearlessness had been forged in the groups of Pioneers which they had all belonged to.

Meawhile the girl put her hand on Helena's shoulder. 'Don't worry, granny, I'll protect you.'

Her boyfriend, who was always close by, also tried to reassure her. 'If we don't show any fear, they won't attack us. This is just a maneuver to intimidate us. Hold your head high and look at them with scorn. In no time at all they'll be gone.'

Just then, Helena heard shouts behind her, and then the sound of running feet. It was a group of fifty miners who were also on their way to the main square. Formerly one of the pillars of the regime, since *Perestroika* the miner's union had changed its position. The awakening of their political awareness made them understand that they got miserable wages and worked in dangerous conditions, which led them to support the demand for democracy. They had seen that a militia was menacing a group of protestors, and had come to their aid. Unlike Helena's group, they were armed with sticks, iron bars, chains and knives. Just like Joseph's militia, they believed that force was the best way to solve their problems.

Suddenly the leader of the militia gave the signal for retreat and the hyenas fled before the herd of elephants that was about to crush them.

The march continued, with the miners escorting Helena's group now. They wore their work overalls and some wore their helmets too. A smell of sweat and coal clung to them. Now the militia had run away, they tried to hide their weapons as if they were embarrassed by their show of strength. The two groups exchanged friendly words, as well as beer, cigarettes and food, but quickly enough the communication between them slackened, just as if two strangers had met in the street, and after asking directions of one another, had found there was nothing else to say. Each group began to ignore the other. They walked in the same direction, but with their backs turned to each other. The only exception were the pickup lines some of the miners, who were more interested in seduction than politics, directed at the girls. Other miners belched after drinking beer and broke the bottles on the pavements and still others urinated wherever they felt like it.

The girl shook her head and confided to Helena: 'Don't take offence, granny. These roughnecks are victims of the regime too. They're sons of dirt-poor people, who Ionescu used for cheap labor. He pretended to educated them and give them social rights, but what he really wanted was to domesticate them. I'm a medical student and I can assure you that most of them will have respiratory problems before long and some of them will die prematurely. We have to be tolerant with these people. Maybe their kids will be more civilized.'

Her boyfriend turned to them again and gave his opinion, too. 'This is yet another proof that a classless society can never exist. The communist regime wanted to impose it by force and this is the result. They don't want to mix with us. Their idea of democracy is not the same as ours. They're here because they think that with capitalism they'll earn more money. If Ionescu had the money to double their wages, they wouldn't be on our side. In fact, they'd be against us. In a fair society, we who are going to be the doctors, teachers, and engineers, have the right to earn more than they do and have a better standard of living.'

Helena felt like telling him that the miners were not as crude or stupid as they seemed to think, and might even be able to teach them things they were unaware of, but she knew that would cause an argument. So she let them carry on thinking that they were talking to a simpleton like the miners, because only thus would they reveal themselves as they really were. Already she had discovered that these New Men and Women, however loyal and brave they might be, had class prejudices which she thought had been eradicated. They were almost bourgeois.

In the meantime, the noise of a crowd yelling, ever more loudly, shook her out of her reflections. The roar came and went, doubling in strength, like waves succeeding each other as the tide rises. They were approaching the central square.

Thousands of people filled the square, squeezed between the buildings and the raised beds for the trees. The entrance at which Helena had arrived was like a full bottleneck. The crowd shouted 'Freedom!' and 'Democracy!' and the ground practically shook. They started launching rockets and the air was soon saturated with the smell of gunpowder.

Seeing the happiness of the people, and their lack of fear, with so many emotions released in her, Helena remembered Ruth. She had dreamed of this moment of freedom, and maybe before anyone else, had foreseen it. How Helena wished she could have been there. Among these thousands of people they would not have had to repress her feelings, pretending they were just friends, holding hands in secret and murmuring in one another's ears so that no one could hear. If Ruth were alive, right now she would hug her and kiss her without caring what other people might think. Even if the New Men and New Women showed they had sexual prejudices – and nothing would surprise her any more – she would not be intimidated.

Democracy can mean love, too.

A ladder allowed someone to climb up onto the bronze statue of Ionescu, and a megaphone was passed to a speaker. However, Helena was unable to understand what criteria the brigade who controlled access to the statue used to decide who had the right to speak. The democratic process sometimes struck her as complex and confused.

At this demonstration shouldn't everyone have the right to say what they want?

The orator was a young man with red hair and a beard, wearing jeans and a black jacket. His voice was hoarse from having made so many speeches in the past week. He held the megaphone with his right hand, while with his left he pointed his index finger to emphasize his rhetoric. When he began to thrash the regime, Helena felt that he was speaking to her personally, and mentally, she responded to him.

'A regime with political prisoners and concentration camps is a criminal regime...'

Yes, you're right and I myself was part of a criminal gang. I was never responsible for anyone going to prison, but I was complicit. What can I do to redeem myself?

'They should all be tried and sentenced...'

Go ahead and try me, I have no fear. Just don't forget that murderer, Zdanhov.

'In the new society we want to create, there will be no place for anyone from the old regime.'

That's going too far. The country can't dispense with technicians and others with expertise simply because they worked with the regime. How much choice did those thousands of people have? I want to help build a better society. I'd go further: it's my right to do so.

'We want to live in freedom and democracy...'

Yes, but what does freedom mean? Each person doing exactly as he likes? And how do you prevent the people being manipulated by the demagogues who are going to appear? Those questions need to be clarified.

'We've had an appalling education, they brainwashed us and prevented us knowing what was going on in the world...'

No, that's untrue, your education from primary school onwards has been rigorous, and the curricula included all the important disciplines in both the sciences and the humanities. You can accuse the regime of everything, except giving you a bad education.

'The Europeans and the Americans are our friends, and they want to help us...'

If you knew a little history, you'd know that there is no friendship between nations, only mutual interests.

Presently, in the middle of the crowd, she saw her old secretary, Larissa Niek, shouting and holding up her fist. She was calling for an end to the regime too. Helena had demoted her and she had become a typist. Helena watched her for some time: she had scruffy hair, popping eyes and a gaping mouth. She looked like a crazy woman. Her idea of democracy must have been different from Helena's too. For the first time since leaving home, she wondered what would happen if certain people took power after the regime changed.

Just then, another orator climbed up onto the statue. He was middle-aged, and wearing a brown suit with a white shirt and a blue tie. He had brown hair and a moustache. He had his own megaphone, which was superior to the previous one. As if the regime had already been deposed and this was an electoral campaign, he announced the creation of a new political party, the Freedom Party, and started making promises. His party would bring about spectacular economic development, so that in ten years Slavia's wealth would come close to Switzerland's. Jobs would be created for everyone and salaries would equal those in the capitalist countries of Europe. Taxes would be reduced. Education and healthcare would remain free. Workers would retire at sixty. Pregnant women would stop working at six months, and maternity leave would be two years. Hospitals, universities, museums, theatres, football stadiums and swimming-pools would be built. Crime would be eradicated and begging prohibited by law.

Not once did he mention freedom and democracy.

Even so, the crowd applauded him with enthusiasm.

Helena listened, intrigued. The ambition to bring Slavia in line with the capitalist countries, along with social security and support for the arts and sports, were all praiseworthy, but these promises all seemed too easy to her. He said that he would do a great deal, but did not explain how he would do it. As someone who knew that any reforms met with resistance, even in a dictatorship, Helena suspected that the Freedom Party's plan would prove unviable in a democratic regime.

The girl spoke in her ear: 'Don't believe this guy. He belongs to a mafia controlled by a guy called Koba, whom the regime protects. These guys are dangerous and they want to trick the people. If they take power we'll have another dictatorship. The old People's Commissars will become entrepreneurs and seize the principal sources of wealth in the country.'

Helena could not contain herself any longer, and dropped the disguise of the half-witted old lady. She gestured that they should move away so she could make herself heard. They stood beneath a tree.

'I'm afraid you're right, Sonia. Changing the regime is risky because the democracy is a complex, contradictory system, and it's unfamiliar to our people. People can be easily manipulated, as we are witnessing. Whoever has the financial means to organize propaganda campaigns may be able to persuade the people to vote for a program that will only bring them suffering. The human mind is always receptive to accepting information that gives it pleasure and comfort, at the same time disconnecting the sensors that identify that information as false. Nobody wants to hear the truth, if it's unpalatable. Using democratic means, a party can install a dictatorship. The future of our country doesn't seem radiant to me. We're entering a labyrinth and we don't have the slightest idea how to find our way. We're not going to have any thread of Ariadne to help us, but we are certainly going to meet many minotaurs. This man may be one of them.'

The girl could not have been more stupefied if Helena had beaten her arms and begun to fly. Because in fact that was what she had just done, ascending from the ground of illiteracy to the heights of knowledge. And the flight had been so sudden and unexpected that the girl could only gape, stunned, at the strange woman who hovered a couple of meters above her. She realized that she too, just like the crowd who had been listening to Koba's man, had been manipulated from the start.

Seeing that she was disoriented, Helena smiled at her and stroked her cheek once more. Sonia turned her face away and took a step back. Her muscles had tensed as if she had just been threatened.

'Who are you? Why did you infiltrate our group?'

Helena admired her attitude, but could not resist treating her the way she had been treated. 'I'm the one who has molded you since the day you started school. You are the New Woman that I idealized. So I'm your second mother. But don't worry, the main thing is that you're having fun.'

Sonia's gaze oscillated between fury and fear. She had no idea whether she was facing a crazy woman, or was being mocked, or if this woman was speaking seriously. She had left home to demand the end of the regime and had been prepared to be threatened and attacked. She was not afraid of the miners or the other militias. She accepted the risk of a beating or even death. However, she had not been prepared for what was happening. The behavior of this woman gave her the creeps. The old woman was insinuating that she, Sonia, had been a mere puppet in her hands? In search of support, she shouted for her boyfriend. But when he came up beside her, she realized that she did not know what complaint she could make. In the end, what could she accuse the old woman of?

'What's going on?' the boy asked her.

Sonia felt ridiculous. 'Nothing, I'm just tired.'

Helena interrupted her: 'We're all finding that democracy demands a lot from us.'

The boyfriend nodded his head. 'Maybe you should be at home in bed by now.'

'I've slept my whole life. I'm just waking up.'

'Let's go,' Sonia said, taking her boyfriend's hand and joining the group again.

Helena understood that she was not welcome and remained alone. The memory of Ruth was enough for her to feel that she had company.

Meanwhile, the orator had climbed down from the statue to make way for someone else. Helena saw a girl a few years older than Sonia climb the ladder and position herself on the pedestal of the statue with the agility of a cat. Her brown hair was tied in a ponytail and she wore a white dress. The light of the streetlamps seemed to be directed at her. The crowd clapped for her and Sonia's group cheered for her as if she represented them. The girl raised her arms to thank them with the self-assurance of someone used to speaking in public. A gust of wind blew out her dress as if it were the sail of a ship. The girl held herself firmly, offering her face to the cold. Quickly she made a signal with her right hand and the crowd fell silent.

Lia Kirchner was about to speak.

Zdanhov

ZUT Zdanhov was one of the members of the regime who was most taken by surprise, and puzzled, by the protests that began with *Perestroika*. If the people were discontented and protesting, it meant that his work of propaganda and the promotion of culture had failed. Naturally that traitor Gorbachev was the main culprit of this mess, but he, Zdanhov, could not absolve himself of all blame. What could he do now to upend the situation? Constantly in the newspapers, on the television and the radio, one heard that capitalist forces were behind the demonstrations, that the people were being manipulated, that the end of communism would be an unprecedented tragedy. President Ionescu himself had given a speech live on the evening news, warning of the dangers of *Perestroika*, appealing for popular resistance to it, and guaranteeing that as long as he was alive, there would be no change. Next, the television showed a montage of images of President Reagan, Prime Minister Thatcher and Pope John Paul II, of the American army with tanks and missiles, of the Vietnam war, of the police charging black demonstrators and films about slavery, of the Wall Street Stock Exchange and sacks full of dollars, while a journalist with a cavernous voice explained the capitalist and Catholic conspiracy which had given birth to *Perestroika*. They had also had murals painted, and had created patriotic posters, resorting to the best artists, which tried to show that the nation was under attack by foreign forces and resistance was imperative. Finally, they organized a football match between the national team and Romania which, in spite of a sympathetic referee and linesmen, ended in a no-goal draw.

Nothing worked.

Zdanhov realized that the end of the regime was inevitable. The question was what would happen afterwards. He would lose his privileges, they would confiscate his works of art, and might even arrest him. Nor was it only his political responsibility that concerned him; the possibility of being accused of the abuse of minors was even greater. What could he do? Since Schwartz had forced him to hand over the money in his Swiss account, he had managed, by making use of Fiorov, to sell more works of art abroad, and once again he had a million dollars in Switzerland. It was enough for him to be able to escape to another country and devote himself to his pleasures in peace. On the other hand, if he were tried after the fall of the regime, he ran the risk of extradition, at any rate in the civilized countries which were worth escaping to.

President Ionescu had called a meeting – the third since the beginning of the protests – for the following day, and Zdanhov, like the other People's Commissars, had no solutions to present.

Zdanhov was thinking in his office when his secretary knocked on the door. The People's Commissar for Culture and Propaganda twitched at the noise of the knuckles on the wood. It was as if a pair of tongs had ripped out his thoughts. He shouted furiously:

'Who is it?'

'Comrade, it's me. May I?'

'Come in. What was it?'

The secretary stayed some three meters from Zdanhov's desk.

'I have important news to give you.'

'Important? Everything that's happening these days is important, you idiot.'

'This is different.'

'Come out with it, then.'

'The French Consul, Foucault, is making clandestine pornographic movies to sell abroad.'

'Foucault is making pornographic movies?'

'Yes.'

'Tell me more.'

'He's taking advantage of the confusion brought by *Perestroika* to persuade young guys and girls to earn a few dollars by acting in sex films. He tells them it's a form of protest against the regime, a form of liberation, that in the United States it's normal for young people to do such things in the universities, that these films are a kind of avant-garde art and one day they'll be famous.'

'And they believe that?'

'I don't know whether they believe it or it's only for the money, but Foucault has already made at least three porno films and it seems they're being sold in France.'

'What a bastard, but what else could you expect from a capitalist?'

'He's written books against capitalism.'

'That must have been a propaganda tool, to trick them. As you can see, this Foucault is a double agent. He's trying to make our country a laughing-stock.'

'Maybe, but now is not the perfect time to expel him. We may need French aid. There are plenty of people in that country who still support the regime.'

'Yes, you're right.'

'We've got to be realistic.'

'Are the films any good, at least?'

'They're excellent, the French have a knack for the cinema.'

'Have you got one for me to watch?'

'Here you are.' The secretary handed him a Sony video cassette. It was called *The Revolt of the Working-Class Women* and it was the story of three female workers who decide to become the lovers of foreigners to free themselves from sexual repression.

Foucault

MATIEUX Foucault, the French Consul in Slavia, had been appointed to the post two years before. He was a professor of sociology at the Sorbonne who had written an essay that showed how capitalist society organized education so as to perpetuate the dominance of the ruling classes – the bourgeoisie and the clergy – over the lower classes. Beneath a cloak of seeming democracy, capitalist society reproduced the authoritarian, classicist models of the past, which for that reason was against the interests of the majority of the people. Among its many forms of repression, bourgeois morality consolidated the submission of Woman to the patriarchy, reducing her to the position of wife and mother, with the support of the Church. Thus, with the aim of restoring to the people its freedom and rights, and to promote the emancipation of women, he urged that socialism should replace capitalism. Although the book was ignored by the public, it was praised in French academic circles, which had brought a certain prestige to Foucault.

Since they had no one better available, the French government decided to send him to Slavia as its consul. Foucault accepted, because they offered him a salary superior to the one he earned at the Sorbonne, which would help him pay the mortgage on a house in Paris. His duties consisted mainly of promoting French culture in the country. At first, Foucault threw himself into the work with enthusiasm, holding weekly cinema sessions, art exhibitions and conferences in the consulate, which seldom attracted more than five people. Soon, he began serving French wine at these events and the audience tripled. In the end, he reduced the promotion of French culture to wine-tasting and cheese-tasting, and it turned out that the consulate was too small for the hundreds of people who appeared.

Foucault's admiration for a regime which put his theories into practice altered quickly too. His euphoria turned, in less than a month, into depression. He had believed he was going to a place where the sun rose equally for everyone, but all he found was gloom. Slavia was the poorest and least developed of the Eastern bloc countries, and made Romania seem enviable. Its leaders had created a repressive system based on the army, the secret police and the concentration camps, which made capitalist oppression look like a children's game. The people lived in fear, hunger, and humiliation. The leaders did what they liked and lived in bourgeois comfort. Even so, Foucault believed that communism was a process that developed by stages, the ascent of a mountain with a range of levels. And for now, Slavia was still at base level. Well, at times, it was actually below base level.

To fight his disenchantment, at first he tried to write a new essay on the evils of consumerist society, but far as he was from the shops and supermarkets of Paris, he was unable to direct his gaze at the object of his criticism. Then he began to drink too much, but he was promptly reminded that France could not present herself drunk before Slavia. Until finally he found the thing that gave him most pleasure and made him feel fulfilled (as well as helping him forget the miserable country in which he had landed up): women, who were prettier and looser than French ones.

Foucault had found that Slavia's women, even on an inadequate diet, and subject to terrible working conditions and abuse from parents, boyfriends, and husbands, were most attractive, and what was even more interesting news, they loved foreigners. So it was that the French Consul, succumbing to the temptations of the flesh, started to collect mistresses, and then, succumbing to the temptation of greed, realized that he could earn money using them – and thus pay off the loan on his house. The porn industry was growing thanks to the invention of video, and the appetite for exotic women never stopped rising. Now Slavia, like Thailand, offered all this for half a dozen dollars. And instead of feeling like an exploiter of women and poverty, Foucault convinced himself that his films contributed to the undermining of the conservative values of capitalist society and the hypocritical morality of the Church. Although they seemed to parody communism, in fact their goal was the destruction of capitalism. Bourgeois morality could be annihilated by sociological analysis or by a four-way orgy – those women were the antithesis of submissive wives and mothers. The people had never understood academic language, but they would understand the language of the body. If the masses had ignored his book, they would not resist his films. Both appealed to a revolt against the system. The consumption of pornography had become an act of rebellion.

With the winds of freedom brought by *Perestroika*, it became easy for Foucault to recruit actresses and actors – two men per movie were enough, but he needed at least four women – for his pornographic films. Besides his own mistresses, he approached potential candidates near the universities, sports clubs, and factories. He was looking for girls of between eighteen and thirty years of age, tall, curvaceous and pretty, and he offered them a hundred dollars (and fifty dollars to the men.) He soon discovered that there were plenty of girls willing to be filmed in sex scenes for that amount, and because they knew that the films could not be shown in their country (or at least not to the majority of the population.) Faced with such a plentiful supply at the workplace, with the women coming close to attacking each other when approached in a group, Foucault did not defy the capitalist laws of supply and demand: the salary dropped from a hundred to eighty dollars, and to thirty for the men. Then he undertook a kind of casting in his flat, where he judged the gifts and talents of the girls. The choices were hard to make, as they all put out in order to get the role, which caused him considerable physical exhaustion. Once the actresses were selected, he took them and the actors to a house he had rented and started shooting. The technical equipment consisted of a single Sony video camera, and the screenplay, of his own authorship, was nearly always the same: with no preamble a group of women appeared in a room which had a double bed, exchanged a few words about communism, capitalism and women's liberation with an intense expression, and suddenly began to caress each other, kiss, and undress, giving themselves up to a lesbian orgy on the bed. Minutes later, one or two naked boys appeared in the room, who also said something in favor of women's rights, then joined the orgy. From then on, Foucault gave complete freedom to the actresses and actors, as long as they carried out every kind of sexual practice, and that the women yelled like crazy.

He never ceased to be surprised by the conviction with which they played their roles, the daring and imagination of these women – in Paris, even with professional actresses you would never achieve such convincing acting. One day, in wonderment, he asked them if their violent orgasms were real, to which they responded with surprised stares, as if to ask if that were not the natural outcome of an orgy. In this way, Foucault strengthened his belief that it would be through the wild sexuality of young women educated by the communist regimes that capitalism would begin to be demolished.

In any case, the distribution of his films in France, through a Parisian production company that bought the rights from him and paid him royalties, gave him an annual income a hundred times higher than his investment. Foucault paid off his mortgage and started to consider buying a place in the country. The French public never discerned any political message in the films, let alone a defense of feminism or an incitement to revolution, but on the contrary scenes of real sex with beautiful women from an exotic country. This was rare in the market and gave it a high value.

The demonstrations against the regime in recent days had awoken in Foucault's imagination the desire to make a new porno film outdoors that would capture the historic events in progress. Something along the lines of Eisenstein's *Battleship Potemkin*. To him *Perestroika* seemed like an anti-communist conspiracy devised by the Americans, but even so, the cinema ought to make use of the boundless energy being released. And in all likelihood he was the only foreign film director in the country – that was how he thought of himself – who had the desire to explore the people's revolt. His idea was that the actresses and actors would join the demonstrations, shout slogans, make the peace sign and provoke the police, while he filmed the protests and movements of the masses; if there were confrontations and spontaneous violence, one of his girls with her head split open, or one of his boys kicking a policeman on the ground, that would be perfect, because it would make the film look more real. He would film the demonstration from start to finish and then choose the best scenes. The next day, the sex scenes would be filmed in the rented house or even, daring to prolong the initial realism, in a public place in the open air, such as the wood not far from the city. Then he would edit all the material he had shot, combining the real protests with the orgies, until he had a pornographic film an hour and a half long. He would call it *Perestroika in Bed*. Of course it would be hard to associate the film with anti-capitalist protests, in fact it would seem like a defense of capitalism, but in Foucault's mind nowadays profit weighed more heavily than ideology. The house in Paris and the place in the country were well worth a hiatus in the political struggle. Anyway, one way or another, for good or ill, capitalism always triumphed, everywhere. Besides, the film would be condemned by conservatives and the Church, and that in itself would be a victory.

ZDANHOV had phoned the French Consulate and had spoken to Foucault. The Consul had arranged to meet him there in two hours. Zdanhov had decided that, given the delicacy of the issue, it would be better to hold the meeting in the consulate. In his Ministry, surrounded by armed guards and grey walls, Foucault would feel threatened, which would not help the negotiations. You could not be too careful when it came to dealing with the French.

The French Consulate was situated on a tree-lined avenue full of mansions built by the upper bourgeoisie of Tiers, which the state had confiscated after the revolution. The embassies of Yugoslavia, Bulgaria, Poland, China, Egypt, Angola and Cuba also occupied these buildings.

It was a neoclassical design of two storeys with a terrace and a small garden. The façade had two columns supporting a curved pediment and was painted white. The door at the entry was of glass and iron with decorative details imitating Art Nouveau. On the ground floor was a kitchen and two salons, one for the cultural wine and cheese events, and the other used as a dining room. On the first floor there were two bedrooms and an office which dealt with bureaucratic business, such as obtaining a visa for entry into France, a scholarship financed by the French government, or ordering magazines or books approved by the regime. Access was open to all citizens, but the people knew that entering a western consulate without first notifying the police of one's motives might be considered an attempt to defect, which would be punished by a concentration camp sentence. Thus, except for the events promoted by the consulate – and even those were frequented by other diplomats and the families of Party leaders – very few people dared show themselves there. Five months earlier a student had gone in to request political asylum and Foucault himself had called the police to come and pick him up. He had done it because he thought the regime's image would be weakened even further by yet another defection to the West, and above all, because he did not want any hassles with Paris. Since then, the doors of the consulate had remained shut.

Zdanhov's chauffeur parked at the entrance to the consulate and the People's Commissar for Culture and Propaganda got out of the car and went into the building. The sky was clear and the sun was at its zenith. A strong breeze blew. Zdanhov walked through a garden full of wilting flowers and weeds, climbed the two steps that led to the entrance patio and rang the bell. Foucault opened the door a little later.

'Good morning, Commissar Zdanhov, please come in. May I offer you a glass of champagne?'

'No, thank you.'

'Then come with me, please.'

Foucault led Zdanhov into the salon for cultural events and pointed to a blue sofa with yellow stripes on which both men could sit. Sunlight entered through a window and formed a rectangle that extended over a brown carpet. On the walls were reproductions of paintings by Matisse, Léger, and Picasso. Zdanhov considered the absence of works of art by 'real artists' as a slight to his country by the French. All the same, he decided to pay a compliment to start the conversation: 'The consulate is really well decorated.'

Foucault smiled. 'You think so? It's my own work. Anyway, with the money I have at my disposal I couldn't do much better. But tell me, Commissar, what subject did you wish to speak about?'

Zdanhov cleared his throat. He looked at one of the Picasso prints – *Portrait of Dora Maar* – and that deformed, weeping face, with the handkerchief in her teeth, horrified him.

'I came here to discuss your films.'

'My films?'

'Yes, your films... how should I describe them? Erotic, no, artistic...'

'Ah, those films.'

'Yes, those.'

'Are they illegal?'

'Well, to tell the truth, we don't have any particular law that regulates such activities. If you'd filmed the girls near a military base it might be considered espionage, but that's not the case. However, the government could take the view that you're using the country's human resources without asking for authorization. A few years back the National Geographic had to pay thousands of dollars to be able to film some beetles that live in our forests. What's more, some comrades who are less sensitive to culture might consider that you're producing pornography. And then there's the question of avoiding taxes. In fact, this could become complicated for you, and cause a serious diplomatic crisis.'

'I see. And you've come here to help me solve these problems?'

'Yes. I can not only grant you permission to film wherever you like, but also put at your disposal high quality equipment, and more picturesque scenarios where you'll be able to use the talent of your actresses to the full.'

Foucault's smile returned. 'An interesting offer. And what do you want in exchange?'

'I imagine you've already guessed, haven't you? We're in the middle of a time of historic change and the future of the country's leaders doesn't look too rosy…'

Foucault's smile vanished. 'Political asylum.'

'Yes, in Paris if possible.'

'It's a very delicate matter and the response doesn't depend solely on me.'

'I know that your academic work is based on a denunciation of the capitalist system.'

'That's correct.'

'Well, what's happening with *Perestroika* is a conspiracy of the Americans and the Vatican against communism. So if you help me you'll be guaranteeing that in France my voice will be heard, condemning what's happening.'

Foucault shook his head. 'Commissar, unfortunately I think the opposite. It's true that my work exposes the dark side of the free market, but if I help a communist leader escape to the West I'll be contradicting myself, and contributing to public opinion being swayed into believing that capitalism is the best of systems.

Neither of us wants that, do we?'

Zdanhov gritted his teeth. 'Monsieur Foucault, let's be frank. Your films are simply pornography, disgusting pornography that exploits poverty-stricken women who are hungry.'

'It's your fault that they're hungry.'

'Don't interrupt. You're in total contradiction with what you claimed in the past. You've sold your soul to the devil for a few francs. All that interests you now is getting rich.'

'Don't get on your high horse with me. Your regime is a dictatorship that arrests, tortures and kills people. And you, the People's Commissars, only care about money.'

Zdanhov took a deep breath. 'In that case, why did you agree to come here? We've all taken decisions determined by our personal interests. They offered me a position and I accepted it because it gave me power and I believed I was serving my country. You did the same and perhaps you never even considered the interests of France. Maybe that's why communism hasn't worked. Human beings think first of themselves, then of others. Or else they don't think of anyone else at all. Existence is a sinking ship, and each of us tries to save himself. The world has never worked any other way. But right now we have the chance to be real communists, and help one another, instead of both of us drowning.'

'I don't follow your meaning.'

'In this country it's traditional to express ourselves with metaphors, but it seems you don't appreciate them.'

'I prefer the objective discourse of scientific analysis to the subjectivity of poetry.'

'As you wish, in that case. Either you help me or I'll have you expelled, today.'

Foucault got up and started to walk to and fro. His back was slumped and his grey hair fell across his face. He took his time to answer. 'As I told you, the granting of political asylum doesn't depend on me. France has never sheltered any foreign leader who fled his country.'

'Except for the African dictators who deposited millions in

French banks.'

'And have you got millions to deposit?'

'I have a million…'

'I'm sorry, but in France that's small change. Go to the shops of the couturiers or the jewelers in the Champs Elysees, buy a painting or an antique, and it's all gone in a morning.'

Zdanhov flushed. 'I have valuable works of art that could be donated to the Louvre.'

'Yes, but reporters would discover where they'd come from and it would be a scandal.'

'Only in capitalist countries do such things occur. In the end, shouldn't journalists be the greatest defenders of culture? And aren't there plenty of works of art in the Louvre that were pillaged by Napoleon and other French conquerors? They stole half the treasures of Egypt. They sacked Portugal. What harm would it do to have my paintings in a corner there? Would tourists ask where they'd come from? Do you think it's better for them to be sold on the black market to some collector who'll keep them in a safe?'

'I agree with you. The vital thing is to show the art to the public, come what may, but France is a nation full of contradictions. As de Gaulle used to say, it's impossible to govern a country that has more than two hundred cheeses. Are you sure you really want to live in exile there? England or Italy would be better choices.'

'Unfortunately, the diplomats from those countries are not making porno films.'

Foucault looked at his suede shoes. 'Give me a while. I must speak to Paris.'

'One week.'

'If the response is negative, you should consider not expelling me. I could be useful to you anyway.'

'How?'

'If the regime falls by any chance and you end up on trial, you're going to need the help of France. If you expel a French diplomat, you certainly won't have it. But if I'm here at such a time, you'll have an important ally by your side. I can influence western opinion. I have influential friends in the universities and the newspapers. Imagine the French intellectuals declaring to the media that the former Commissar for Culture, Zut Zdanhov, had nothing to do with the repression of the regime, that he is the victim of a witch hunt, and so on. Imagine an international petition demanding your freedom, and other forms of pressure. The new authorities in Slavia would not be able to resist them.'

Zdanhov looked at him with mistrust. He was being told the story of a film he did not believe in, but right then any illusion was preferable to reality. He got up, glanced at the lacerated face of Dora Maar again, and left without shaking Foucault's hand.

Schwartz

SCHWARTZ considered himself even more to blame for what was happening than Zdanhov did. The implausibility of the event, its absurdity and the imminence of the tragedy had left him incredulous and paralyzed, like someone who has seen an extra-terrestrial spaceship land on his property. He could not call the firemen or the ambulances because they were already there, incorporated in his own person; but fireman Schwartz had no idea how to turn on the hoses to extinguish the fire, and paramedic Schwartz was incapable of using his instruments to save the victims. These last, however, instead of yelling for help and moaning, were jumping for joy and celebrating the disaster. So it had to be an off-course extra-terrestrial spaceship, because the inhabitants of Slavia he knew would never behave that way. Or else, as in those American science fiction films he secretly enjoyed, they had undergone a collective brainwashing by those very extra-terrestrials who were, in fact, the Americans and the Vatican.

His informers had warned him that there would be street protests – which was common knowledge – but he had never imagined there would be millions of protesters or that they would demand the end of the regime. From the information retrieved from his millions of files, nothing had indicated that such a catastrophe might occur. The submissive populace who feared the tortures of Lubianka and the re-education camps would never dare to defy the government. And why should they if the government gave them everything they needed? That was the question for which no answer could be found, except for an extra-terrestrial conspiracy. That answer, however, led to another question that even the most daring conspiracy theory had no response for: how had it been possible for the Americans and the Vatican to bring about such a brainwashing of the people of Slavia without him and the other commissars having noticed a thing? The Americans may have invented a secret technology for espionage in space, and sophisticated weaponry for long-distance destruction, but they had not invented any invisible and impalpable method for altering people's minds. The censorship had blocked the films, the plays, the books, the newspapers and the music of the capitalist countries – their dreaded secret weapons – the few citizens of those countries who lived in Slavia were watched and had scant contact with the people – the French consul had been taking advantage of the women, but right now that was irrelevant – and the Americans had not even tried to broadcast their subversive radio to the country. Slavia was an isolated island. So how was it that they had managed to rub out all the years of communist education and propaganda, and replace them with the capitalist dream? Where were the New Men and Women that the incompetent Helena Yava was supposed to have molded? What had become of the discipline and loyalty inculcated in the youth who belonged to the Pioneers? And was there no one among the older generation who remembered how they had lived before the revolution?

At the start, Schwartz believed there would be a few hundred protesters, badly organized and lukewarm in their convictions, whom he would be able to disperse and arrest, as long as he used all his strength. When the creature that threatened the regime was overcome by a violent blow, it would retire to its burrow and even dare to peep out. And here instead was a gigantic monster in the streets, a Leviathan that *Perestroika* had given birth to, roaring and spitting fire, against which he was all but powerless. Worse still, sooner or later the monster would come for him and the hunter would turn into the prey. When that happened, he would find no burrow in which to take refuge.

President Ionescu was old and had shown his weakness when he rejected the advice to crush the revolt by hurling the army against the people, using tanks, planes, and the rest of the military forces. Schwartz could not rely on him, nor on his colleagues who were equally scared and seemed more intent on saving themselves than the regime. The vessel was sinking, the captain lacked the strength to turn the wheel and the rats were looking out for a chance to abandon ship. All he could do was face the storm of Perestroika alone.

Without letting anyone know, Schwartz had created militias to deal with the protesters. The personnel had been recruited from among the secret police, the regular police, the military, professional athletes and other men for whom the fall of the regime might cause problems or danger. He had managed to bring together a thousand men, who were divided into squads of twenty. The training was carried out by military instructors in the forest, and they were given carte blanche to use any means necessary, including shooting to kill, to intimidate and disperse the protesters. Some of the militias had succeeded in scaring off protesters and delaying demonstrations in the squares, others had suffered merciless counter-attacks, and many of their members had been wounded and many more, like Joseph's militia, dared do little more than insult the protesters. A week after the start of the demonstrations, the militias had killed twelve people, lost four themselves, and eighty had deserted. Another mission of the militias was to beat up journalists and public figures who took advantage of the relaxing of the censorship to write articles praising democracy. In this task they had had more success.

One Saturday morning, Schwartz travelled to a rendezvous in the forest to watch a militia training session. Because of the political instability, and because he was travelling to an isolated spot, he took along two bodyguards. The sky was grey and there was fog. The car exited the main road and continued on a dirt track full of holes for another half a kilometer. Then it stopped. The driver stayed in the car while Schwartz and his men went into the wood. As they walked through the trees the fog grew denser, wrapping them in a vaporous mass that prevented them from seeing their hands in front of them. Trees, rocks, and the earth all began to vanish. The path they had followed so far was erased and what was left before them seemed not to exist. Schwartz had to feel his way forward to protect himself and allow one of the bodyguards who knew the place to precede him. Presently the bodyguard whistled, and at once from the left, as if the forest itself were responding, they heard a similar sound. Their ears were the only compass they had to find their way. Whistles on one side and the other followed and Schwartz and his men changed course. It was as if two birds who wanted to begin a mating ritual were trying to find one another; in this case, not to create new life, but if necessary, to put an end to it. A turn to the left forced them to descend a hill. Putting his boot on a mossy area, Schwartz skidded, fell and rolled out of control for a few meters. The bodyguards did not restrain their laughter before helping him to his feet; and in that mockery, that absence of fear of their superior, Schwartz heard an echo of *Perestroika*. With his trousers smudged by moss, his jacket covered with dry leaves, his hands scratched and his face bleeding, the Chief of the Secret Police looked more like a prisoner who was about to be executed deep within the forest.

Suddenly a louder whistle broke through the fog and struck them like an arrow.

The three men had reached a clearing where a stream ran. Out of the mist the militia men started to appear. One here, one there, beside the trees; armed with sticks and iron bars, they looked like warriors from long ago ambushed in the forest. Markus Richter was the instructor. He knew that *Perestroika* would bring an end to the persecution of priests, but he was equally aware that with the fall of the regime he would lose his position and be judged for his crimes. With so many sins on his conscience, joining the revolution would not save him from hell. In camouflage, he approached Schwartz, saluted him, and shook his hand.

'Comrade, we've already warmed up and we're ready to start the training session.'

'Show me what you can do,' said Schwartz.

Just then the sky started to clear and sunlight penetrated the glade.

On a command from Richter the twenty men formed a line. They were about a meter apart from each other and had their sticks and iron bars resting on their shoulders. They stared at an imaginary spot as if the anti-regime protesters were there. Richter made a signal with his hand and they began the attack. Yelling, they took a step forward and made three blows in quick succession: two meant for the head and a horizontal one aimed at the ribs or kidneys. They repeated the attack again and again until they had taken ten steps. Then they turned around and carried on beating the imaginary enemy three times until they were back at the starting point. Richter followed them at close quarters, correcting some and encouraging others. He called for greater speed, greater power and better balance. He shouted at them and at times walloped them. 'Kill them. Have no mercy!' he growled. These words were like a shot of adrenalin in the militiamen, making them strike even more furiously; rage contorted their faces and their mouths foamed. In spite of the shouting, the hiss of the weapons slicing the air was audible. The ancestors who had killed and died in these forests could not have been more ferocious and cruel to their enemies than these warriors.

The exercise lasted ten minutes and at the end of it they were exhausted.

Markus Richter let them drink water and rest for two minutes, but without allowing them to sit down. The men were sweaty and their faces were red from the effort and their fury. They panted.

Not one of them spoke, as if the brutishness of the state they were in had annulled language. On the edge of the clearing, leaning against a pine tree, Schwartz nodded to signal his approval. Even more than the way they handled their arms and their physical strength, it was the ferocity of these warriors that pleased him. Richter understood how to control them, understood how to flick the switch that unleashed violence: the switch was hatred. It was through hatred that a fighter got a shot of energy that made him invincible. Schwartz imagined them let loose in the streets of Tiers hunting down protesters like famished wolves chasing after sheep. He imagined them breaking up demonstrations simply with their yells and their deranged glares, chasing protesters in flight, catching some and smashing them to pieces. Cracked skulls and broken bones, burst organs, and blood, lots of blood. He smiled. Yes, even he would feel terrified if that militia appeared in front of him.

Richter clapped his hands to end the break. The men quickly lined up and the instructor told them that now they were going to train for situations of unarmed personal defense, in which they would be attacked in the same way as in the previous exercise. To show them, he called on a militiaman with an iron bar and told him to give him a blow to his skull. The two men were in the middle of the clearing, just two meters from one another. Everyone was watching them. The sunlight lit up their right side and cast two long shadows. The only sound was the far off tweeting of a bird. Suddenly the militiaman lifted his iron bar and took a step forward to attack, but the instructor beat him to it and intercepted his arm with his left hand while he pushed back the man's chin at the same time with his right hand, and tripped him. The militiaman fell on his back and the instructor raised his boot and struck a blow with his heel just centimeters from the man's face. All this took no more than two seconds.

'You can break his nose, burst his liver or crush his balls,' said Richter, turning towards the other militiamen. 'The main thing is not to give him time to react. Then raise your head to watch out for other possible attacks.'

Schwartz applauded and even his bodyguards, who were scornful of such training methods with amateurs, were impressed by the ease with which the instructor had foiled the attack.

The militiamen formed two lines, one facing the other, to practice this exercise. Richter ordered the line to his left to attack the line to his right so that the latter could repeat the sequence of defense and counter-attack he had just taught them. His command started the exercise. However, this time the majority of the men being attacked did not succeed in following the sequence of grabbing the arm, pushing the chin, and tripping the assailant over. Scared of the possibility of a club or iron bar crushing their skulls, they were incapable of responding in the right way. Some got in each other's way, others froze. They suffered blows on their hands, their arms, and heads, and only those who fell back managed to avoid being hurt. There were bruises and bloody wounds. If this had been a real situation, they would have been beaten or even killed. They began to argue, blaming each other for the mess.

Furious, Markus Richter halted the exercise with a shout and went to fetch a first-aid case. No prayer could help him.

Schwartz's two bodyguards laughed.

He scratched his neck and bit his lips. He felt tired, his body aching and his feet pinched by his boots. The humidity of the forest made him sneeze. The tweeting of the birds perforated his eardrums. He glanced at the sky and it seemed to him that clouds were covering the sun again. Suddenly, he thought of Luda. *What would she think about what is happening? Was it because of Roman that I created these militias? Am I defending the regime or simply defending my family?* Nothing seemed to make any sense. He took a few aimless paces this way and that, as if he did not know where he was going. He heard the instructor directing the militiamen, but he was no longer watching what they were doing so as to correct their mistakes.

Schwartz realized then that it was all over.

There was no point trying to convince himself. Even if he had a hundred thousand militiamen at his disposal, all experts in martial arts, he would not be able to stop the protests. *Perestroika* would tear them apart with its claws, crush them with its feet, and swallow them in its monstrous maw. Nor was it worth clinging to the theory that the Americans and the Vatican had been the authors of *Perestroika*. The monster had been created by communism itself: *Perestroika* was the poisonous waste produced by the Soviet Union, thousands of Chernobyl nuclear power stations exploding one after the other, due to design defects. And these men who were training to face the protesters would find themselves as defenseless against the radiation as the unprotected men sent by the Soviets to put out the nuclear fires. Many would die or be gravely injured for a lost cause. The difference was that there had been anti-radioactive equipment which could have been used at Chernobyl, while there was no protection in existence against the radiation that *Perestroika* was releasing in Slavia. He would not be accused of negligence, but that did not lessen his responsibility.

He made a signal to his bodyguards and left.

On the way back, a bolt of lightning split the grey sky, then the thunder exploded, and finally it started raining. Inside the car it was dark. The four men travelled in silence. The sound of the rain drumming the car roof and the effect of the water pouring down the windows made Schwartz feel as if he were drowning in the sea. He glanced at the driver and the bodyguards and asked himself if they were still loyal. *They are not stupid and they are planning their future. They no longer believe – if they ever believed – that the Party is their family. How long will it take them to abandon me and join the uprising? And what then? Will they say anything in my favor at my trial, or will they volunteer to execute me?*

He was pondering all this when, in the center of Tiers by now, the driver slowed down and said there must have been some kind of problem. Schwartz opened his window, and with his face in the rain, saw there were policemen in the road, signaling to cars to slow down. They were two small, thin officers, their hair dripping and their uniforms and boots soaked, for want of protection against the rain. The fury of their signals to the cars seemed more for the purpose of keeping themselves warm than to carry out orders. *Those wretches are sinking too. Only those who have been adherents to* Perestroika *will find a place in the lifeboats. For the rest, instead of lifebuoys, there will be axes to chop off the fingers of anyone who tries to hold on to the vessels.*

A bolt of lightning struck the roof of a building near the police officers and the immediate crash of thunder made them cringe. The sopping grey uniforms, the boots dragged through puddles of water, the shadowed faces and the hair plastered to their foreheads made them look like a species of insect caught in the rain.

When the car came to a stop, Schwartz thought he was about to face a demonstration against the regime. The very fury of nature could not hold back *Perestroika*. His bodyguards guessed the same and took out their guns; the driver locked his door. However, there were no crowds in the road. It was just an accident in which a bus had collided with a lorry, had been hurled against a barrier and then flipped over. The four men were so relieved that they did not have to face protesters that they got out of the car and stood in the rain to gape at the accident. The rain was not something that froze their bodies, but a caress of nature; the water that ran down their faces removed any remnant of pity for the victims.

The red bus lay smoking on the asphalt. One of the wheels was still turning. The windows were broken and the panels dented. The front door had disappeared. Blood and oil glinted in the water. There was a stench of petrol. Inside people were calling for help, outside there were corpses and injured people lying on the pavement. However, no ambulance came to their aid and the only care the injured received was given to them by ordinary people. There was insufficient fuel, insufficient parts, and insufficient goodwill on the part of the drivers of the ambulances and paramedics to help at accidents. Schwartz walked towards the crash, followed by his men. A shower beat against his face and his chest.

Suddenly the engine of the bus caught fire and the people trapped inside broke out in desperate shouts. Those who could move threw themselves out of the broken windows, risking cuts on their hands and faces. The rain, instead of dousing the flames, seemed to fan them. Schwartz started running. He did not see a burning bus with passengers imprisoned inside, but the Witten fertilizer factory where his wife had died. Luda was still alive and he was going to save her. He should never have let her leave her home at that hour, nor have made that proposal to Olin to free the priest in return for her promotion, nor should he have hidden the fact that he arrested, tortured, and killed men, nor should he have considered her less important than the Party. Never. But now he would make up for the mistakes he had made. He would pull her out of the flames, hug her, beg her forgiveness and then take her home to show to Roman so he would stop crying and have his mother once again. Schwartz ran up and down the bus from one side to the other searching for Luda, seeing the faces of the people who were frantic to escape the flames. He banged on the windows, cut a hand, freed himself from the arms stretched out begging for rescue, ignored the shouts for help, until he saw a woman lying on a seat, with a bloodstain on her back and her neck drooping like a wilted flower, and thought he had discovered Luda. It was her! Even though he had not seen her face, he was sure he had found his wife. Luda was this woman with the brown hair and she had only fainted. All he had to do was fetch her, give her a little water, and everything would be all right. To find a way in, he punched a one-eyed man whose head hung out of a window and began to climb into the bus to save his wife. Just then, as he was crawling inside the vehicle, his bodyguards put an end to his delirium by grabbing his arms and legs and dragging him out.

When at last they released him, one of the bodyguards tried to bring him back to his senses. 'Comrade, you can't do anything for those people. It's too dangerous to go into the bus. It's all going to burn.'

Schwartz was soaked and one hand was bleeding. Instead of having pulled him out of a bus, he felt they had rescued him from the seabed. That bottomless ocean, dark and cold, was where he had sunk since Luda died. A bolt of lightning and a burst of thunder shook him. Schwartz looked at the bus, at his bodyguards, at the two stunted policemen, and at the buildings around him, and lowered his head like a child caught doing mischief. He could not explain to himself what had happened and he felt ashamed. *Perestroika* had driven him crazy.

Meanwhile, a number of people on the pavements and in the stopped cars had recognized the Chief of the Secret Police. If it was unusual to see him on foot in the street, it was stranger still to see him looking like a beggar, trying to get into a burning bus and being pulled out by his bodyguards. With *Perestroika* everything seemed possible, but this scene was unimaginable. Everyone was talking about him, some laughing, others insulting him. Someone threw a beer bottle that shattered at his feet. Schwartz no longer frightened anyone and the people would not miss this chance to settle scores. Realizing that their boss could be lynched at any moment, the bodyguards took out their weapons again. However, Schwartz signaled them to put the guns away. He could not show that he was afraid of the people, or give them more reasons to hate him. He heard the insults, saw people pointing their fingers at him, felt the fury in the air, but continued calmly. They might accuse him of many crimes, but they could not accuse him of being a coward. The cowards were these protesters who only found the courage to take to the streets after that traitor Gorbachev had betrayed the regime and encouraged the riots.

Meanwhile, it stopped raining.

He was just reaching the car when a woman dressed in black, her hair grey and her face sagging, came running up to him. Supposing her harmless, the bodyguards let her pass. The woman tripped and almost fell in front of Schwartz. She was out of breath and had to recover before she was able to speak. The corner of her mouth twitched and her voice came out shrill and piercing: 'My husband? Where's my husband?'

Schwartz knew he was being accused of the disappearance of some man, one of the thousands he had silenced to protect the regime. He had no idea who it might be. A saboteur? An intellectual? A spy? Not so long ago he would have slapped her without a second thought and turned his back on her, but today he was unable to ignore her. The suffering she showed was not alien to him. The loss of a family member had created a point of contact between the pair of them.

'If you tell me his name...'

'Kirchner, Ludwig Kirchner,' said Maria. 'He was sent to a concentration camp and I've never heard from him since. Is he alive? Tell me.'

Schwartz searched the threads of his memory, and tangled up in one of them, the face of the painter appeared. Yes, he recalled a modern painter, a creator of strange images with deformed human figures and violent colors; he had been caught in some purge or other and accused of denigrating Ionescu's image. An absurd accusation, like so many that had condemned innocent people, simply to keep the populace in fear, or for personal revenge. Zdanhov had been responsible for his prison sentence and deportation, he remembered. That thief and child molester had managed to ruin a harmless painter and his family, since, more than likely, the man must have died by now. Schwartz himself had had nothing to do with that purge, but he felt obliged to give the woman an explanation. There would be no news on the television lamenting the death of the painter, nor official speeches praising him, nor streets named after him. The only consolation for the death of her husband this woman might have would be the words he addressed to her.

'Madam, on behalf of the government of Slavia, I regret what happened to your husband, the painter Ludwig Kirchner. It was a huge mistake that can never be rectified...'

Maria seized the sleeve of his jacket and interrupted him. 'What are you saying? What have you done to my husband? Is he dead?'

Schwartz did not attempt to free himself. 'Honestly, I don't know. But you had better prepare yourself for bad news. Few survive more than two years in the re-education camps. I will investigate and I promise I will be in contact...'

Maria beat Schwartz's chest with her fists and yelled:

'Murderers! Murderers!'

By then a crowd had gathered around them, hurling thunderbolts and lightning. The two traffic policemen were inadequate lightning rods. The people too began calling them murderers and spitting on them. They were getting closer and closer. This time the bodyguards did not hesitate: they took their guns and fired into the air. The crowd dispersed. Maria fell in a puddle and lay there, prostrated. Schwartz fled to the car and they tore away. He realized now that the catastrophe of *Perestroika* was even worse than he had thought, and that there was nothing he could do but escape from the burning bus his country had become.

Olin and Fiorov

FOR Igor Olin, the menace brought by Perestroika extended far beyond the end of the regime, and touched Aliocha's fate. It was a tentacle that after crushing the government would strangle his son. Olin accepted the loss of power, the blame for the failure of the economy and even for the violence perpetrated against the population. He had collaborated, made pacts, benefitted. What he could not accept was that his son would lose the care given him by the nurses, and in the event that he, Olin, died first, that his son might end up in a place where he was maltreated. Aliocha would be one of the first victims to be swallowed by the monster Gorbachev had created. To save him, he needed money. Far more than he had earned up till then in his post as People's Commissar for the Economy. For the first time since he had come to power, he regretted that he had not followed the example of the other commissars and members of the Central Committee of the Party. They had taken advantage of their positions to get rich. They had done illicit business deals, embezzled, and robbed state enterprises. No one had accused them because that would have meant being instantly accused themselves. There had been a pact of silence similar to the one in the Mafia. Without question his comrades had secret accounts in capitalist countries and could retire like princes. While he, the man who directed the economy, had not managed to save a cent, nor to take measures against the inevitable fall of the regime, nor to assure his son's future.

The time had come to do something. But was there still time?

Olin knew the whereabouts of a man who could help him earn money. After lunch, his driver took him to the outskirts of the city where there was an isolated villa by the forest. The property was on a hill surrounded by walls topped with barbed wire. At the entrance was an iron gate and a sentry box in which there was a guard armed with a machine gun. The building was a modern design in concrete, composed of three modules, with glass doors. Olin's driver got out of the car to announce the identity of the visitor. At once two furious Rottweilers appeared and hurled themselves against the bars of the gate. At a whistle from the guard, the dogs kept still, although they continued to growl. There was a short conversation between the two men, the driver showing ID and the guard returning to the sentry box to open the gate. The driver came back to the car and they entered the property. There was a lawn, fruit trees, and a pink marble fountain sprinkling water. The car followed a fifty-meter drive that led to the main building and parked in a patio in which there were four cars, two motorbikes and two bicycles. When Olin got out of the car he found another two security guards awaiting him. They wore suits and black ties. One of them, a short, stocky man, addressed him: 'Comrade Olin, don't take this badly, but I have to pat you down.'

Olin raised his arms like a delinquent caught by the police.

'You can go ahead, but the driver can't go in,' said the guard.

The other guard pointed the way with the palm of his hand and led him towards the house. The door was open and Olin went in. A middle-aged woman with an apron and a scarf over her hair appeared and barred his way. 'Don't you know how to knock before entering?'

Olin looked back for the guard who had brought him here, but he had vanished.

'I'm sorry…'

'You think you're high and mighty, don't you?'

'I thought that…'

The woman raised her hand to cut him off. 'That's enough. Come with me and don't touch anything.'

Olin crossed an atrium with a floor of exotic wood and followed her along a corridor with white walls to a glassed-in salon. The décor combined modern and antique furniture, oriental vases, African carpets, leopard skins, silver dishes, with maps and paintings by Ludwig Kirchner on the walls. While he was gaping in astonishment at the miscellany, Olin smelled cologne. Only then did he notice that someone was seated in a leather armchair in the corner of the salon.

'Commissar Olin, you are the last person I expected to come and visit me. I see that you've met Irina, my housekeeper. When I'm obliged to travel, she's in charge here.'

Olin turned his head and saw Fiorov. He was wearing a grey suit with a white shirt and a red tie. In his hand was a glass of brandy.

'Ivan Fiorov, forgive the intrusion…'

'Don't worry about it, I'm used to the government intruding on my life. You can't break old habits. Sit down,' he said, indicating a wooden chair in the middle of the salon.

'I've come to speak to you on my own behalf.'

'That means you have problems. Serious problems, if the party can't help you.'

Olin faked a smile. 'Most importantly, how have you been getting along?'

'Much better than when they put me in a concentration camp.'

'I'm sorry about that…'

'No, you aren't. You were one of the members of the regime who clamored for me to be arrested. You never accepted me doing business beyond the reach of the state, and you always despised my activities. I was a prisoner for a year because of you. The sentence was ten years and I had to pay nearly a million dollars to get free...'

'The one who gave the order for your deportation to the camp was Schwartz.'

'Another bastard who secretly bought the merchandise I sell. You were the ones who should have been arrested. All of you. You're the criminals, the ones who steal from the people and kill. Worse still, you destroyed the dreams and hopes of a nation. If it were up to me, you'd all rot in a concentration camp.'

'Your wishes may well come true.'

Koba put his glass on the floor, got up from his chair, and began pacing up and down.

'That's enough, let's come to the point. What do you want from me?'

'I need to make some money.'

Koba laughed. 'Make some money? But aren't you the Commissar for the Economy? All you have to do is divert funds into an account in Switzerland. Do you want me to show you how to do it?'

'I know how to do it. But right now at this point in the crisis, it's no longer possible to siphon off funds without arousing suspicion. The country is bankrupt...'

'It always has been. If there's one thing you people don't know how to do, it's managing public funds.'

Olin pretended to ignore the dig. 'Fair enough. But now the situation is critical. Any movement of monies would have to be justified far more rigorously.'

'So what's your plan?'

'I persuade the president that there's a chance for the country to make a good foreign investment that will bring in quick profits and enable us to face our financial problems. I make him believe that with a certain amount of economic recovery and redistribution of wealth we might be able to hold out against *Perestroika* and the regime will survive.'

'And you think he's going to believe that? He's old, but he isn't losing his mind yet.'

'Since we lost the support of the Soviet Union we've been completely isolated. A desperate man will cling to any lifebuoy, won't he?'

'Yes, you're a perfect example of that truth.'

Olin looked at the floor, dumbstruck for several seconds. 'Right… to start with, I might be able to get hold of two million dollars. As I assume that you have a profit margin of over a hundred per cent in your business dealings, I propose a fifty-fifty split on whatever we make. The other half, along with the initial investment, will have to be returned to the state. In other words, I want half a million dollars.'

Koba shook his head. 'Even as you're planning a sting on the nation's finances you want to carry on being an honest man. Can you square this with your conscience? You're an odd fish, Olin.'

'Are you in or not?'

'Sixty per cent for me and forty for you. Take it or leave it.'

'All right.'

'Great. You will transfer the money to this account,' and handed him a document that looked as if it had been prepared beforehand for this purpose. 'In a few months, you'll get your share. And you aren't going to ask me if you can trust me, are you?'

'If I didn't trust you, I wouldn't have come. Just one question. How are you going to invest the cash?'

Koba gave him a shifty look. 'What do you care? What matters is the profit.'

'If you don't mind, I'd like to know what you're investing in right now.'

'All right, since you insist, I'll tell you. Drugs.'

A chill crept up Olin's spine. 'Drugs?'

'Yes, cocaine, heroin, hashish, all kinds of pills. It's the business of the future. *Perestroika*'s opening the gates to drugs. People have been imprisoned so long that now they don't know what to do with the freedom approaching. They think it's modern, or want to copy the Hollywood stars, or just escape from the reality of all this garbage. I mean, who am I to blame them?'

Olin turned white. 'I don't like it. Couldn't you invest in some other business? Alcohol, food, clothes?'

'None of those can compare with the profits you make from drugs. Pornography makes money too, but in our country people don't have video equipment.'

'I know, but...'

Fiorov stepped right up to him with his fists clenched at his waist. 'But what? You come here and now you want to teach me my business? What do you know about capitalism? Nothing.'

Olin fidgeted in his chair. 'Capitalist countries don't traffic drugs.'

'That's what you think. What's more, profits from drugs are invested in the stock markets and legitimate businesses. Do you think the Americans, the English, the Swiss and the French turn down this kind of money? Do you think anyone asks if the notes are dirty or clean? The richest countries in the world arrest the little dealers, but carry on doing business with the big ones. The money's all the same, and if they started investigating the provenance of all the fortunes that keep the capitalist system working, you'd have a global economic collapse. So we're just going to follow the rules already in place.'

Olin lowered his head. 'All right, but could we at least ensure that they don't sell drugs next to schools or to minors?'

'Unfortunately details like that are beyond my reach. I can't control the behavior of the dealers. This is one of the difference between the communist system and the capitalist system that you still don't understand. The state, which in this case is me, doesn't control, or interfere in the economic lives of its citizens, which in this case are the dealers. They're free, they can take risks, get rich, or wind up in prison. But don't worry, kids don't have the money for drugs, and they aren't interested in them either. They only start wanting to experiment when they're sixteen, and at that age they're already practically adults.'

'Adults?'

'Sure. At sixteen I was already selling homemade vodka.'

'I beg you to be careful…'

'Look, Olin, a lot more people die from alcoholism than because of drugs, and yet no one wants to ban vodka, do they? And what about tobacco? Did you know that tobacco causes cancer and a load of other diseases? Have you considered how many millions would lose their jobs if we did away with alcohol and tobacco? These vices make people happy, and in the end, they're going to die anyway. If there weren't so much hypocrisy, they'd legalise the consumption of drugs too, and sell them in chemists. But if they did that they'd end up losing money.'

'These are different matters…'

'Listen, do you like modern art?'

Olin threw him a suspicious look. 'What's modern art got to do with this subject?'

Fiorov approached one of Kirchner's paintings, and standing on one of the leopard skins, contemplated it with the air of a connoisseur. 'Did you know that a lot of modern art, literature and music was composed under the influence of drugs?'

'Maybe that's why I don't understand modern art.'

'Right, that's the usual mistake. Modern painting wasn't made to be understood, but felt. Just like music. And sensibility is like class: not everyone has it.'

Olin realized that Koba was trying to humiliate him, but he kept up his side of the conversation. 'Maybe it can be cultivated, but it certainly can't be bought.'

Koba ignored the dig. 'You see those people?' He pointed at one of Kirchner's paintings. 'They seem anguished, frightened, suffering, but do you think there's any message? Of course not. Just feel the images, as if they were a perfume.'

'I suppose your dogs must have sniffed out drugs in these canvases.'

Fiorov slammed the wall so hard that one of the paintings nearly fell down. 'You're an ignorant fool. I was thinking of showing you an El Greco I acquired recently, which you could easily have learned how to appreciate, but I've changed my mind. It'll stay in the safe.'

Olin did not answer. Fiorov went on. 'Listen, soon your regime will collapse and you're going to need a lot of money to survive. Lawyers, bribes, a deposit account in some country willing to take you in. If you had no qualms of conscience during the years you were crushing the people, surely you aren't going to worry now about some white powders that a few nutcases like to snort and shoot. I'll tell you something else: drugs are going to turn a lot of women into whores so they can keep up their habit, and as I control that business too, it will make me even richer. And I'm even thinking, when your regime is finished, of opening a rehab clinic for addicts. In the capitalist system they call that controlling the process from start to finish.'

Olin's mouth twisted and his eyes widened. 'You're the devil in the flesh.'

Pacing slowly, with his hands behind his back, Fiorov came close to him again. He wanted to put an end to their talk. 'I'm the devil, sure, but it was you people who created this hell. I adapted myself to it, just as you're adapting yourself now. Only the fittest survive in the law of the jungle, don't forget.'

The thought of Aliocha made Olin shut his eyes for a moment. He stood up and was about to shake Fiorov's hand when the latter addressed him again. 'Wait.' Fiorov picked up a sheet of paper, wrote some names on it and handed it to Olin.

'What's this?'

'I need you to do something for me. Make out some documents with an official stamp declaring that these men received payments from the State.'

Olin examined the names on the list, intrigued. 'Payments?'

'To put it another way, make out some documents proving they were regime informers.'

'And were they?'

'Probably not.'

'So why do you want to frame them?'

Koba shook his head. 'I don't want to frame anyone. This is just for my security, in case any of these gentlemen decides to make problems for me. A man like me always has enemies, in any regime. It's better like this than shooting them in the back of the neck, don't you think?'

Olin took a deep breath. 'All right, I'll do it. You'll have the documents in the next few days.'

'Terrific. Our partnership is starting on the right foot.'

The two men shook hands and Olin left. Just as he was getting into the car, Irina and the Rottweilers appeared. She muttered something against Olin and the dogs would have bitten him if he had not shut the door.

All the way back home, Olin chewed over that implacable judgment of Fiorov's: *Only the fittest survive in the law of the jungle.* How could Aliocha, the weakest of the weak, survive then? Even if he managed to earn millions of dollars, could he guarantee that after his death Aliocha would not be robbed and cast into a care home? As he was finding out, stealing, even from the strong, was dead easy. And trust and loyalty, in ideas and people, had a price, just like any other merchandise; and that price, in these turbulent times, was very low. Even if he were to become the richest boy in the world, Aliocha would always be a weakling at the mercy of predators, condemned to suffering and extinction. Would not Fiorov himself be the first to sniff out his blood and avail himself of his wealth? He, or other even worse vampires, would pursue Aliocha, surround him, and in the end drain his blood. And no one would rise up in his defense, not the friends he had never had, nor the distant relatives, nor even the nurses who had taken care of him. For a few moments, as his horror overwhelmed his pity, the idea struck him again of putting an end to the suffering, sparing him the law of the jungle declared by *Perestroika*. Then he shook his head and shouted, 'No! No!' to the astonishment of the driver who peered at him in the mirror.

Olin's car proceeded along an avenue of grey buildings, quite treeless. The sun was hiding behind the clouds. A hole in the tarmac caused a jolt that put an end to his reflections. Looking through the window he saw people hurrying along the pavements. Men, women, adolescents and a few children, all trying to survive the death rattle of the regime. *Are these the ones who will consume the drugs I'll be financing? What effects will heroin, cocaine, and synthetic drugs have on the lives of these people? They certainly won't be creating works of art, music or literature. How many will become thieves or prostitutes? How many will die of an overdose? Or will they know how to benefit from freedom without ruining their lives? Will they discover that they can beat their wings and ascend all the way to heaven?*

This was the thought he tried to hold on to, a sort of Garden of Eden in place of the jungle, where human beings would know how to co-operate instead of competing and destroying each other. Aliocha would have a chance of surviving with dignity in this new reality. Olin was elaborating on this idea, steeling himself against the jolts caused by the holes in the road and the sight of addicts shooting up, when he noticed that they were going past his old secondary school. The syringes pierced the tenuous calm he had achieved. A terrifying drug had entered his bloodstream and was starting to make him suffer.

'Stop here,' he told the driver.

Once the car was parked outside the school, Olin got out. It was a two-storey building in the architecture of the early twentieth century. It had cracked walls, flaking paint, and broken windows. The garden had not been tended for months and the gate was rusty. Dozens of pupils of both sexes were going in and out just then. They spoke in loud voices, shouted, and laughed. Some pairs of sweethearts kissed one another. Two boys fought playfully. The adolescents were living out the euphoria of a permanent *Perestroika*.

Olin watched them, a cigarette in his hand, and amazement on his face. He had not paid any attention to the behavior of young people for ages. He had forgotten the authenticity of their emotions. With them, everything was intense and sincere. They lived as if the world were about to end at any moment. Death, on the other hand, was something that did not exist, as false as a white hair or a wrinkle.

Nor did the future or the past exist. Only the present, the moment, this instant, interested them. Olin imagined Aliocha developing strength in his muscles and energy in his brain, and waking up and springing out of bed like a Lazarus revived. He would run towards these adolescents, join in their games and pranks, yell, utter the same kind of nonsense they did, test his strength against another boy, embrace a girl. Then, out of nowhere, he would appear as a man, or maybe an older boy, and tell them that he had something for them to try. Something they did not yet know, which was the best thing in the whole world. Something that would make them fly, rise to the stars, and see wonders never before seen by anyone. And it was free, they didn't have to pay a penny, the first time they tried it, it would be a gift to them from a friend. There was nothing to be afraid of, it was good stuff and would not do them any harm. It awakened the mind and made people more intelligent. It aroused desire and made sex more thrilling. There were scientific studies that proved it. All the film stars, footballers, and cool people had already tried it. It was in fashion. People took it at all the parties. It was only pussies and uncool people who didn't try it. Only those who had no idea how to enjoy life would refuse the powders and pills he had in his pockets.

Olin had his eyes closed and a hand pressed to his forehead. Some of the pupils passing by him guessed that he was ill. They avoided him as if the pain he was showing were contagious. He was the kind of man they feared, and not the dealer. He represented everything that their short experience of life had taught them to despise: pain, despair, and defeat. The dealer, on the other hand, sold them the euphoria, the pleasure, and the craziness that in their innocence they could not recognize as the beginning of a suffering that would make that man almost happy by comparison.

Olin, however, felt worse than a heroin addict going through withdrawal. The Rottweilers of his guilt were tearing him apart. He was about to destroy the lives of these adolescents in order to save the life of his own son. And what before had seemed a necessity to him, now struck him as a crime. He ran back to the car and ordered the driver to pull away. He was unable to look through the car windows at the adolescents who no longer even remembered he had been there. It was the executioner who needed a hood to hide from his victims.

'Where to, Commissar?' asked the driver.

Olin did not know. He did not want to go the ministry and work, nor go home and face Aliocha, nor go anywhere else at all.

'Just drive and don't ask questions,' he said.

The driver took the car on circuits through the streets of Tiers for several minutes. *Perestroika is driving him mad*, he told himself as he took the opportunity to drive through the parts of the city he liked best, and watch the girls on the pavements.

If he could have, Olin would have gone into a church to confess his guilt and beg God not to discharge his rage on Aliocha, but they had all been shut or demolished, and the priests imprisoned or killed. There were no sanctuaries where he could take refuge, no priests to whom he could confess, and there was not a single sacred image or icon before which he could surrender and accept his penance. He was thinking all this when an idea struck him.

'To the Museum of Ancient Art, as fast as you can,' he told the driver.

Minutes later, Olin was at his destination. He got out of the car, climbed the stairway, passed the two columns that supported the pediment at the entrance, greeted a guard, walked down a hallway, passing a group of noisy pupils accompanied by two teachers who had just finished their study visit, and entered the main salon. Here was the painting he was seeking: Tito Nevet's *The Trial of Christ by Pilate*. Olin had not set eyes on the picture for over thirty years. Even so, the scene of Jesus Christ's interrogation in a Roman palace by Pontius Pilate, while a furious mob demanded his death outside, fascinated him just as it had the first time. Olin sat down and forgot what he had come here for. The trial and sentencing of a man who only wanted equality for human beings was for him the supreme symbol of the injustices of the world.

Yes, Christ was the first revolutionary to give his life for the noblest of causes. The Party had not been capable of understanding his message. The Party should never have banned the Christian religion or persecuted its faithful. It should have found a point of contact with Christianity, and learned how to absorb its strength. The new theories of Marxism should have been able to encounter a dialectical synthesis that reconciled the poles that had never been in opposition. Heaven on earth. The Soviets had made a pact with Hitler, but they had not wanted to make a pact with the Church. They had visited the United States, but they had not been to the Vatican. How absurd. How different everything might have been if the communist regimes had had the Christians on their side, the power of their faith to face suffering with, and the ability to forgive which would enable them to accept injustices. After all, the Church itself rested on an authoritarian power, and condemned profiteering. They were not that different. Christianity could have supplied more and better arguments against capitalism. The sin of greed, the sin of usury, the rich unable to enter the kingdom of heaven, so much powerful rhetoric to set against it. As well as Jesus himself, the saints could have been presented as examples of revolutionaries who gave their lives for a cause similar to socialism. Saint Guevara. Perestroika itself would never have been more than a passing fad, if the Party had known how to treat Christians differently. But the Party had continued to insist that religion was the opium of the people... and it was then that Olin awoke from his daydream.

The opium of the people was himself. He was the one who was ready to supply the people with drugs which would alienate and destroy them. What was he doing there? How could it have occurred to him that he might find redemption for his crime in a museum, before a five hundred year old painting? Such nonsense would not even occur to the most tripped-out drug addict. There was no forgiveness for someone who became a drug dealer. He deserved a mob even more violent than the one in the painting to drag him through the streets and crucify him, without a trial.

Olin got up and left.

Ionescu and Olin

ALFRED Ionescu no longer read the reports on the economy or read the dossiers on the plans for the country's development. If he had not banned the arts of divination and arrested all the psychics and astrologers, he would have consulted them. But he could not even do that. However, he had received information which, while it did not fit into soothsaying, seemed like something out of science fiction, and to which he clung as his last hope of solving the problem of *Perestroika*.

That was why he had called Igor Olin to his office, to explain his plan. It was five in the afternoon when the Commissar for the Economy arrived. Ionescu was on his feet waiting for him and went to greet him. Olin had not seen him for a month and found him frail. However, that weak old man, with his jacket buttons badly done up and a urine stain on his trousers, seemed cheerful.

'Have you ever heard of Ciclosporina?' asked Ionescu.

'No, is it a new weapon?'

'Yes, you could consider it a powerful weapon…'

'I'm afraid we don't have the money for military expenses…'

'Olin, I'm talking about immunosuppressants.'

'I know little about that subject. Are you suffering from a serious illness, Comrade?'

'My illness is truly serious: it's called *Perestroika*.'

Old man, you finally flipped. Olin felt like leaving and never coming back. He pulled himself together, though, and tried to focus the talk on the only subject that interested him.

'I imagine you've summoned me to analyze the situation in the country, is that right?'

Ionescu's eyes shone. 'Right. That's why I spoke to you about Ciclosporina.'

'Comrade, maybe it would be better for you to rest now; we could meet again tomorrow. The reforms we agreed to make take time to bear fruit, and I still don't have good news for you.'

'Do you too think I'm not capable of governing the country?'

'No, I would never think such a thing.'

'Of course you do. All the Commissars think I'm finished. But while you lot have not been able to find any solution to taking on *Perestroika*, I've found out something important.'

He's out of his mind.

'Please explain to me.'

'Let's sit down. I'll explain everything: during my last appointment with my personal physician, Dr Max Steiner, by chance he spoke to me about immunosuppressants. For the sake of conversation, I asked him a few questions and ended up learning that thanks to these medicines it's become possible to transplant organs, which until now has been practically impossible. They prevent the patient's immune system from rejecting the donor's organ. Get it now?'

Olin looked at him, intrigued. 'Yes…'

'And that could be the solution to all our problems.'

'What are you talking about, Comrade?'

'You still don't get it, Olin? There are millions of people in the world desperately waiting for an organ that will save their lives. They can't wait months or years. Among these millions, there are thousands in Europe, Africa, Asia and the Americas who have the money to buy them. The traffic of organs has become a big business. For some time the Chinese have been doing it with prisoners sentenced to death. The time has come for us to do the same.'

'How?'

'We'll export the organs of our deceased. Every day dozens of healthy people die in accidents. We can execute some prisoners too. Can you imagine how many millions of dollars we can make? And there's no need to worry about ethical questions, since a dead man doesn't need his organs for anything. Do you think it's preferable for them to be eaten by worms, or incinerated? Isn't it much more ethical to use those organs to save a life? Think of the child who's dying because he has a diseased liver, and ask yourself if there's anything nobler than giving him the chance to carry on living.'

Olin was going to reply, but he kept quiet. How could he criticize dealing in organs, when he had already begun dealing drugs? Ionescu was right. The traffic of organs saved lives, whereas the traffic of drugs destroyed them.

'And how are we going to export our product?'

'To do that, we need the help of that gangster, Koba. Do you know him?'

Olin blushed. 'Yes, I've heard of him.'

'He's the worst kind of scum, a man who would sell his own mother to make a buck. Still, at times we need him. The sabotage of our economy by the capitalist countries forces us to resort to guys like him. He's a necessary evil. In this business of organ traffic, he's the right man to find us customers. He's got the international contacts in the networks of organized crime, which people who need transplants resort to. He'll be our middleman. All we have to do is instruct our doctors to start harvesting organs from the corpses of healthy people.'

'He's going to want a hefty commission…'

'Yes, very likely. That's why I'd like you to take care of the matter in person. Negotiate with him. Right now, you're the person I trust most.'

'I'm grateful for your trust in me, but aren't you afraid that the capitalist press could take advantage of this to blacken the name of our country?'

'You're still worried about our image? Ever since the revolution the capitalist press has never stopped criticizing us. We're beneath Ceausescu's Romania and Hoxha's Albania. We don't have children chained in the orphanages, do we? Even so, Slavia is considered the most miserable country in the Eastern bloc. The damage is done. They can't blacken us any further.'

'Well, if you look at it that way…'

'We've got to act like the Chinese. They use all the means at their disposal to get benefits and they don't give a damn about the condemnation of the western world. The Pope, the Queen of England, the American President, can all criticize them harshly, but it makes no difference. The Chinese have even worked out how to use foreign criticism to increase the patriotism of the people. They know how to rule a country with a billion inhabitants. There will never be any *Perestroika* there, believe me.'

'The Chinese are making impressive economic reforms. One country, two systems.'

'As you know, I was never keen on those reforms. Let's get some profit from our dead people, since we can't rely on the living ones any longer.'

Olin shook Ionescu's hand and left. As he was going down the stairs of the presidential palace he started wondering if they could use any of the organs of someone who died of a heroin overdose for a transplant. Not the liver, but maybe the lungs… Then another, even weirder thought struck him. *Apart from the flesh, could anything else from a human being be transferred to another when he had an organ transplant?*

⚜

Ionescu and Silvia

AN HOUR after Olin had left, Joseph parked the car in front of the Presidential Palace and Silvia Lenka got out. She was wearing a black jacket, a white blouse, a red miniskirt and boots with high heels. She had had her hair cut and dyed blonde. She was wearing a perfume with an aroma of tangerines. At first the guards did not recognize her, and almost forced her to show her ID.

Silvia had received the usual call from Ionescu's secretary, but this time she had been ready to refuse the invitation. *Perestroika* had aggravated her concerns about the nature of the regime. On the one hand, it was proving that people could demonstrate freely, without being suppressed by the police – in spite of the violent militias who attacked them – but on the other, the fact that there

were so many people – nearly everyone, even her own friends –
who wanted change was a sign that something was going badly. As
if this anxiety were not enough, Ionescu insisted on knowing what
she thought about the events, forcing her to probe the wound. So
she had to lie, pretending ignorance of politics; she did not know
exactly what was happening, but sure, it had to be a conspiracy
organized by the Americans, and naturally she had full confidence
in the government. With slight variations, she always ended up
giving these replies, to mistrustful looks from Ionescu. Today,
however, she felt she could not keep up the farce.

For some time there had been no sex in Silvia's meetings with
Ionescu. Little by little he had become incapable of performing,
and the last time he had tried, he had had chest pains that he feared
might be a heart attack. Scared, Silvia had begun to caress him,
but ended up telling him off as if he were a naughty child. Even
so, they lay down naked together in bed as if they were incapable
of relating to one another any other way. Then he told her stories
of his childhood, recalling moments from the past, transported
himself to a time she had never known and introducing her to
people who had since died. At such times Ionescu became a happy
child again, who played and was loved, with no threats to his
happiness. His voice altered, acquiring childish tones and picking
up grammatical mistakes, his gaze lost itself beyond the walls, and
his hands fluttered as if he were conducting an orchestra. Silvia
listened in silence, stroking his hair and his face. Sometimes, he
fell asleep and started to snore; she would cover him with more
blankets, kiss his forehead and go away.

Silvia entered the bedroom, looked at herself in the mirror,
and shook her head. She was already regretting her hair cut, and
regretted dyeing it that color even more. Whatever had she been
thinking, wanting to copy an American actress she had seen
in a film? How could she have let herself be influenced like an
adolescent? Or had she really felt the need to change her image?
Was she sick of herself and wanting to be someone else? Might she
have a *Perestroika* inside herself?

She was pondering this, and trying in vain to find a flattering angle, when Ionescu came in. He was wearing a white dressing-gown and slippers. He was coughing. He did not seem surprised by the change in her, as if he had expected it, not that he showed any pleasure.

'A new fashion. I preferred the old one,' he muttered.

Silvia made an effort to smile and went to kiss his cheek. Then she sat on the bed and got undressed. Ionescu appreciated her curves with the same desire as ever, but he no longer touched her. Licking his lips and making a kind of roar were all the signs of lust he had left. Once Silvia was naked and lying on the bed, he took a little box out of the pocket of his dressing-gown, undressed, and lay down facing her. His coughing had stopped.

'I brought you a present,' he said, handing her the little box.

Silvia's eyes shone. 'Thank you.'

'Open it.'

Silvia untied a pink ribbon and opened the gift. It was a pair of triangular earrings, in gold filigree. 'They're beautiful.'

'Put them on. I think they'll go well with your eyes.'

Silvia sat up in bed and inserted the earrings in her ears.

'Only use them on special occasions.'

'Like this one.'

Ionescu showed his yellow teeth. 'I'm glad and I have good news to tell you. I'm going to solve our economic problems and put an end to *Perestroika*.'

Silvia bit her lip and drew up her knees. Problems were coming. 'Oh yes?'

Ionescu lowered his voice. 'It's a state secret but I'm going to tell you. We're going to export our blood.'

What crazy scheme had he come up with now?

'Blood?'

'Yes, I've given orders for a national harvest and the blood we get will bring in a profit of many millions of dollars when it's sold to countries that need it. We'll have new harvests each month and so we'll have an inexhaustible supply. If you hear any rumor about a state business involving the hospitals, you know, it will be the sale of the blood. Don't believe the gossip. I'm the only one who knows the truth.'

Silvia attempted another smile, but her mouth took on a sad expression. 'I see, blood.'

Ionescu leaned on an elbow in bed, supporting his head with his hand. His face wrinkled up like a plastic bag. 'There will be money to increase salaries and pensions, and to guarantee social security and the distribution of food. People will stop protesting and before long no one will remember *Perestroika*. The solution to our problems is in the people, in its energy and vitality. If we unite and learn how to take advantage of our resources and our human potential we can take a great leap forward. Then we'll no longer depend on the Soviet Union and we'll become one of the most advanced countries in Europe…'

Poor devil, he's finally flipped completely. What will happen to him when the regime falls? Will he end up begging in the streets?

'It's all going to go well, yes it is… Why are you looking at me like that, Silvia?'

Silvia gulped. 'No reason. I was just listening…'

Ionescu's cheerfulness vanished. His eyes turned dull. His wrinkles, the rings under his eyes and the pallor of his skin all became more marked. His mouth opened and a thread of drool slid out of it. He coughed again. He turned to the other side of the bed and stared at the ceiling. Silvia laid her head on his thin, cold chest.

'What's the matter? Have I done anything to hurt your feelings?'

Ionescu neither answered nor moved. Silvia shook him to make sure he was alive. Ionescu slowly turned his face towards her. His voice was a moan.

'No my dear, you haven't done anything.'

'I don't understand a thing about politics.'

Ionescu stroked her neck and touched one of her earrings. 'Yes, you do. It's because you understand that you don't believe it will work, isn't it?'

'I...'

'Listen, it's pointless carrying on pretending to be a bimbo. I know you better than you think. I'd like to think there's another reason for you being here with me, but the main one is that I'm the president. You're young and pretty and I'm old and finished. Each of us plays our role...'

Ionescu paused and took a deep breath. Silvia shut her eyes, embarrassed.

'You don't believe it and you may be right, as even I am starting to think that all is lost and nothing can save us. Not even the blood we're going to export...But the best thing for you is to know nothing about it.'

Silvia opened her eyes. Her face was tense and a crease appeared between her eyebrows. 'It's true, I no longer believe that any measure you take can prevent the collapse of the regime. I used to believe that the Party wanted the best for us and knew what was best for us. They taught me that capitalism was evil and our model was superior. I've never known any other reality or any other way of living. The regime is the only family I've ever had, and that's why it's molded me from head to toe. My way of thinking, my way of being, my way of dressing. Everything. I am your creature. All the same, I'm not here just to serve the creator. I like being with you. But the people are angry and I'm part of the people too. Part of me is with you and part of me is against you. I don't know what's right or wrong any more, I don't know who I am, nor even where to go. I had to dye my hair to try to be myself, to try and escape, to... oh, I don't know. I feel I'm coming apart. It was all just an illusion.'

Ionescu embraced Silvia and laid his head on her bosom. 'I only wanted the best for my people, I did what I thought best, I had to take hard decisions. I made mistakes too, sure, but who doesn't? I'm not a saint, but a man. Governing a miserable country that's subjugated by the Soviets and threatened by the Americans hasn't been an easy task. You can't even imagine. I put up with everything while the Commissars robbed the people. I sacrificed myself for the country. What for? These people who are protesting forget that they studied in the schools I created, and make use of the hospitals I built. Do they know what it was like to live before the revolution? Without me, they'd all be serfs in the country, or exploited factory workers. Many women would have to become prostitutes or abandon their children. Many would have died for lack of medical care. They should be grateful, but instead of that they want to topple me. At the end of my life everyone hates me, I don't have a single friend, a single person I can confide in. Only you. And now I don't know what to do, everything is truly lost. I'm scared, Silvia. What are they going to do to me? Do you think they'll kill me? Help me.' Ionescu started weeping on Silvia's chest.

THAT night, Ionescu had a nightmare.

He was running barefoot through a thick, dark forest. Without knowing why, he was being chased by a band of men who had dogs for tracking him. He tripped on stones, scratched his face on branches, dunked his feet in puddles, but he managed to prevent them catching him. His pursuers, who were carrying torches, howled like wolves as they chased him. Ionescu was terrified. Suddenly he entered a clearing through which ran a stream. In its bed, Silvia was bathing, naked – with her hair cut and dyed blonde. Ionescu ran towards her and asked for her help. Silvia smiled, emerged from the water on top of a scallop shell, and held out her hand to him. But when Ionescu gave his to her, she pulled him and made him fall into the stream. Right away his pursuers arrived, seized him, dragged him into the middle of the clearing, tied him to a tree trunk and started dancing around him like deranged savages.

'Now we've got you we're going to remove your organs and sell them to the Chinese,' one of the men said. 'Please don't, I'm old and my organs are no use any more,' said Ionescu. 'Capitalism,' said another man, 'in the capitalist world there's a market for everything. Even an old carcass like yours can bring in a few dollars.' 'Yes,' said Silvia, 'your eyes and kidneys will feed a family for a month. That's fair, isn't it?' Ionescu looked at her. 'Silvia, you know I'm a good person. Don't let them do this to me.' Silvia burst into sarcastic laughter. 'A good person? But wasn't it your idea to make use of the organs of the dead without consulting their families? That's what a bastard would do. You deal in human flesh and now you're going to taste your own poison.'

The moment she said this, she threw the gold earrings in his face. Then one of the men put on a white apron, took out two huge knives, and sharpened them against one another. The blades glittered and the metallic noise made Ionescu tremble. He noticed that the man who was about to disembowel him had the face of Igor Olin. '*Perestroika* is starting,' said Olin, smiling. Silvia took a step forward, with her hand raised. 'Wait, let's call his victims, come on, come on.' From nowhere there appeared dozens of women, young and old, thin and fat, plain and pretty, all with their fingers pointing at Ionescu. Some carried children. 'It was him,' they said. Silvia shouted, 'Cut his balls off so he learns what happens to rapists.' Olin dropped Ionescu's trousers and brought the knives close to his testicles.

At that moment Ionescu woke up shouting, soaked in sweat.

From that day onward, Ionescu started isolating himself, giving orders that no one should disturb him when he was locked inside his office. He ate little at meals but drank too much. In bed he faced nights of insomnia. When he dreamed, Silvia appeared in the arms of other men, beside herself with pleasure. Little by little, he grew thinner, paler, and developed rings beneath his eyes. He wandered around the palace like a ghost and spent hours on the balcony gazing at the horizon. If anyone asked him if he needed anything, he did not respond; on the other hand, he sometimes spoke to himself. Finally he lost interest in governing the country, and in the protests caused by *Perestroika*, and left the decisions to the Commissars.

A week later, before sunrise, the door of his room opened with a crash and in surged a group of soldiers, pointing machine-guns at him.

'You've been deposed,' the commander said. 'Get dressed. You're under arrest.'

Ionescu shrugged his shoulders and obeyed without a protest, as if his arrest relieved him of a burden. He did not ask who the leader of the coup was, nor what they wanted, nor what would happen to him. Nothing. He put on a new suit, pulled on his shoes, without socks, and allowed himself to be handcuffed. The soldiers dragged him along as if he were any old prisoner. He traversed the corridors with his eyes on the floor. He passed servants, officials, and bodyguards, and not one of them said a word. Some of them even looked happy. Only Joseph, when Ionescu was getting in the car that would take him to Lubianka, raised his hands to his face, not hiding his shock. Not long after, a group of servants took down from the wall the painting of Ionescu's triumphs painted by Kirchner, Lott and other artists, kicking it until it split, drinking toasts with champagne pillaged from the cellar, and burned it at the entrance to the palace.

♔

Schwartz

THE SAME day, Schwartz appeared on television, announcing Ionescu's imprisonment, the end of the regime, and the call for free elections. 'The dictatorship is over. From now on, we will live democratically,' were his first words. He was wearing a blue suit, a white shirt, and a grey tie. His face was made-up with cosmetics and he smiled constantly. Next he said that until the elections were held the country would be governed by a provisional cabinet of honest, competent men who would ensure the continued functioning of state institutions – but without mentioning the names of any of them. He promised that all the crimes and violations committed by the regime would be tried by an independent court – it had not occurred to him that in democracies all courts were independent. He appealed to the people to remain calm, and asked the citizens to go about their lives normally – hoping that if they did so they would not engage in reprisals or witch-hunts. Finally, in the kindest voice he could manage, he announced that a new era of hope and prosperity was beginning and Slavia's future was radiant. The moment the broadcast was over, Schwartz stopped smiling, stood up and left the studio, escorted by five armed men.

As the head of the armed forces was Ionescu, Schwartz had no difficulty persuading the military that the regime was doomed and their only hope of salvation lay in supporting him in a coup d'état. The people had lost their fear, he told them, *Perestroika* was unstoppable and the change was irreversible. However, if they themselves led the new revolution then they could control the process that followed on from the installation of democracy. If they failed to, they would face tragic consequences. In other words, they risked being arrested, tried, and convicted for crimes ordered by Ionescu. At the end of the day, they had only obeyed orders. The duty of an honorable soldier was to respect the hierarchy. All the same, people were thirsting for revenge and Ionescu's blood would not satisfy them. Someone else would have to be hurled on to the funeral pyre that was supposed to purify Slavia. Now if they controlled the settling of scores, they could secure not only their own survival but also their honor. It was not enough to escape conviction, it was important also to keep their families' good names. There were plenty of people who could be sacrificed to placate popular anger – really guilty ones who had got rich at the people's expense, and who were preparing to flee the country. He, Schwartz, would take care of the matter.

Schwartz's plan was to accuse the other People's Commissars – whom he had not informed of the coup d'état – making them scapegoats for the regime's crimes. Just as in many revolutions of the past, in which members of a toppled regime had led a coup, and thus washed off their own guilt and escaped punishment for their crimes, Schwartz hoped to bring about the same happy ending for himself. During the period of revolutionary turbulence, the people acclaimed any leader who had the courage to free them and give them some culprits to satiate their desire for revenge. While the euphoria lasted, the leader of the coup was considered a hero, whose history was not questioned. Later, certainly, someone would point an accusatory finger, but by then he would already have assured Roman's future, by leaving the country and living in exile in a safe place.

Seconds after Schwartz's broadcast, the people flooded the streets, not to celebrate the fall of the regime, but to demand his imprisonment too. There would be no democracy as long as the evil Chief of the Secret Police remained in power. They demanded a complete change of all leaders and the punishment of all the guilty. They threatened to take justice into their own hands. Instead of placating their rage, Schwartz had reinforced it.

Several hundred protesters, at the instigation of Fiorov and his men, turned up at the station and stormed it, taking it without resistance. Wearing a black suit and a white shirt, Fiorov appeared live and called for a revolt against Schwartz, whom he considered the true culprit for the crimes of the regime. He described himself as a victim of the regime and a simple man who spoke for those who had no voice. He praised the people and exalted their courage. He begged them not to let themselves be fooled, and to stay united. He told them to fight without mercy and promised that victory was nigh.

Two attacks followed, on the headquarters of National Security and on Schwartz's fortified residence, both guarded by soldiers and policemen. The forces of public order fired rubber bullets and real bullets, while the protesters threw stones and Molotov cocktails. During the disturbances twelve people were killed, and dozens injured. The image of a fallen girl, fainting in a pool of her own blood, shocked the world. The United States, Canada, Japan and various European countries called for the will of the people to be respected, and threatened a trading boycott. The Pope said he was praying for Slavia. Gorbachev warned of the possibility of civil war. Fiorov appeared on television again and blamed Schwartz for the violence. The number of demonstrators rose. There were desertions in the police and the army. At last the military arrested Schwartz and took him to Lubianka.

A PROVISIONAL government made up of civilians and military officers took power until elections could be held. The government was faced with the problem of trying those responsible for the crimes of the former regime, without resorting to dictatorial methods, and avoiding the settling of personal scores. At the same time, so as not to paralyze the country, it was necessary to preserve the armed forces, the civil service, and Ionescu's specialized officials, even if they had taken part in repressive acts. The decision caused protests, and people said that many criminals would escape scot-free, but only Ionescu, and some People's Commissars and Commandants of concentration camps, were tried.

The trials of members of the regime accused of crimes were carried out by judges who had in the past sent people to the re-education camps, and who had benefitted from the support of the regime. The Ministry of Justice made an unsubstantiated accusation, and nominated several witnesses who were deceased. The defense lawyers argued that the accused were heroes who had served the nation and defended it from its enemies. They reminded the judges and juries of the threat of nuclear war that had hung over the country, and the circumstances of the Cold War in which they had governed. They remembered the public and social works that had been offered to the nation. They mentioned progress in the areas of literacy, culture and sport. They conjectured that the establishment of democracy could lead to regression and only posterity could judge the accused. Ionescu and Schwartz remained in silence during their trials. A bomb threat meant that the court had to be cleared. Stones were thrown at the windows. In the end, both men were sentenced to twenty years in prison, but weeks later the Supreme Court decreed that all the political crimes committed in the time of the last regime, either by the government or the opposition, were given amnesty for the sake of national reconciliation.

ONE measure taken by the provisional government was the expulsion of the French Consul, Matieux Foucault. The series of pornographic films entitled *Perestroika in Bed* was considered an insult to the country, an exploitation of the misery caused by the communist regime, and an affront to the dignity of the women of Slavia. It was useless for Foucault to argue that the films were an act of resistance to the dictatorship, and that in France they were esteemed as avant-garde works that transcended the limits of the cinema to explore the links between sexuality and repression. Pasolini, he claimed, had done something similar with his *120 Days of Sodom* to expose the fascist violence of Mussolini, and at the time no one had understood him either. The great work of art was always ahead of its time. How could a country that proclaimed itself free and democratic censor culture and persecute a film director? Was that how they intended to get into the European Economic Community? The civilized world would not forgive such an affront.

They gave him twenty-four hours to leave the country.

Fiorov

FOLLOWING the process of the transformation of a nationalized economy into a free market economy, the public industries were privatized. The transitional government chosen by the military created a commission of experts to pick the best proposals made by economists and entrepreneurs. The process was quick and caused criticism: that it had been poorly organized, lacked transparency, and even corrupt. The evaluative criteria and the values of the bids were not revealed. Two journalists who attempted to investigate the process received death threats and one was run over. Groups of citizens who tried to protest in the streets were beaten by militias who appeared to enjoy police protection. An entrepreneur promised he would reveal a scheme of personal favoritism and corruption, but on the day when he was scheduled to give a press conference he sent notes to the newspapers declaring that he had been mistaken and he had not had any proof. Finally, the public companies who distributed gas, water, and electricity, as well as the main public bank and the television station, all ended up in Fiorov's hands. The media wrote that the privatization of the public companies had taken place according to the rules of free competition, and that the country would benefit from the fact that they had not been bought by any foreign groups. With his face improved by plastic surgery, Fiorov appeared on television and announced that the exploitation of human beings by the state was at an end, and from now on the workers would be better paid and enjoy more rights. Profit, he said, would come later. The next week, his new companies changed their names, and half the employees were made redundant, with no compensation.

⚜

Silvia

AS SOON as she found out that the directorial board had been changed of the orphanage which took her in, Silvia once again went in search of the documents that would allow her to discover the identity of her parents. Since the last time she had tried to get information, the building had deteriorated. The three-storey mansion built at the start of the century had a dirty white, cracked façade, windows with rotten wooden frames, and an entrance door whose paint was flaking off. It could not have contrasted more strongly with the beginnings of life that it sheltered inside. Silvia arrived at ten and the sunlight striking the building was like a finger pointing out its decay.

She was received by a young girl to whom she explained the reason for her visit: she had been brought up in the institution, and now they lived in freedom, she had the right to know who her parents were. For that reason she wished to speak to someone in a senior position. The girl looked confused and asked her to wait, indicating a wooden bench. Silvia sat down to wait. After five minutes a tall, elegant, woman appeared, with brown hair and eyes, wearing a blue skirt and jacket, and white shoes. She was smiling. Silvia smelled her scent and thought she must be one of the hundreds of pretty women whom the new authorities, in their eagerness for renovation, had chosen to replace the old officials who had been loyal to the regime. She was the director of the orphanage but could just as easily have been the director of a gymnastics school, in charge of gastronomy fair, or on the jury of a beauty contest. In other words, her only qualification for the post was the ability to read and write. It struck Silvia then that in the past she too might have been the lover of one of the members of the regime, perhaps even Ionescu himself.

'Good morning. My name's Irina and I'm in charge of this home. How can I help you?'

Silvia shook the hand with red-painted fingernails. 'Good morning, my name is Silvia Lenka. I was brought to this home for adoption by an unknown mother. I'm here to try to find out her identity and also to find out who my father was. I need you to let me consult the records.'

Irina stopped smiling. 'Well, that's not a regular request. The old regulations prohibited the consultation of the records, and the new ones haven't been finalized yet. There are ethical questions involved. As you must understand, it's not the same thing as finding the owner of a lost cat. I suggest you put your request in writing...'

Silvia stepped so close to her that she was within a palm's

breadth of her face.

'Listen, I'm no cat, but I have got sharp nails and I can scratch. I've been trying for twenty years to find out who I am. The last regime denied me the right to find out who brought me into this world. It denied me the right to have a beginning, an identity, to be a person like other people. Yes, I was treated like an animal that's found in the street and brought home. It's true I was well treated. I can't complain that they took care of me nor of the education they gave me, because if I hadn't been looked after I probably would have died. But that's not enough. The most important thing is missing. Something you have: a family, even if they're dead. A mother and a father. You understand? The time has come for me to know the truth and neither you nor anyone else is going to prevent me from finding out.'

Irina recoiled two paces and tottered on her high heels. A corner of her mouth trembled. Her voice came out feeble: 'I'll see what I can do…'

'You can take me to the records. It's the only thing I care about. Now.'

Irina scratched an ear, her bracelets jangling together. Silvia did not take her eyes off her, forcing her to drop her gaze. Although the former directors had defended the secrets of the house as if they were guardians of a temple, practically kicking out difficult intruders, Irina simply wanted to get rid of this unexpected problem. In seconds she concluded that if they really lived in a democracy now, nothing could happen to her if she provided the information this aggressive woman demanded. Freedom was just that: being able to consult documents. Was it? Or was it not? There were classified documents, state secrets, but no, wanting to know who your mother was could not possibly harm the nation. Even if they reprimanded her or fired her, she was sick of this depressing, smelly house already, with its runny-nosed little orphans. Her boyfriend – an entrepreneur of imported products – could probably get her a better job. A woman like her ought to be directing a museum or an art gallery. Pretty things. She nodded and made a sign to Silvia to follow her.

The two women walked along a poorly-lit corridor, climbed stairs that squeaked at every step, turned to the left and followed another shadowy corridor until they reached its end. There was a wooden door reinforced with sheets of metal. Irina took out a key ring and opened it. Silvia could smell the mildew. The room was dark and Irina groped around on the wall in search of a switch. She turned on a neon light and went to open two windows. Silvia found herself in a large room of some ninety square meters, with cabinets pushed up against the walls that rose to the ceiling, and other smaller cabinets in the middle of the room. The larger ones had shelves and were stuffed with papers. The smaller ones had drawers but were equally crammed with records. There were cobwebs and dust everywhere.

'This is the memory of the house,' said Irina. 'The archives are organized in chronological order and each shelf or drawer has the corresponding year marked on it. From what I've heard, recently no one bothered about keeping documents. You can look for your file. When you've finished, knock the door. Good luck.'

Irina turned and left. She would not expose herself to the risk of being scratched by some lost animal again.

Silvia stood and stared at the cabinets, paralyzed. She was just steps away from finding out who she was, but instead of feeling euphoria, she was afraid. She had supposed that the moment she entered the archives room of the orphanage that had adopted her, she would hurl herself at the documents like a madwoman, and yet she was incapable of moving. The door to the past might destroy her future. The very handle was a white-hot iron. Suddenly, everything was up in the air. In the end, what was the truth?

Do you really want to know who your mother and father are? If they're dead, how will it help you? And what if you discover that you're the daughter of a prostitute? And what if you discover that you're the daughter of a woman linked to the regime who rejected you out of selfishness? Will you find any peace? Or will you feel even more disgusted and insecure? If bitches don't abandon their puppies, what kind of woman was she who carried out such a barbaric act? Why didn't the woman who gave birth to you solve the problem right away by having an abortion? Because that's exactly what you are: an abortion created by the regime.

Tears ran down her face as she chewed over these thoughts. She leaned against one of the cabinets and slid down until she was sitting on the floor. She propped up her chin on her fists. Her hair had already grown out enough for the drops from her eyes and nose to dampen it. Her head hurt and her back was cold. She started coughing. She felt wet and realized she had emptied her bladder. She gritted her teeth, clenched her fists, and let out the loudest shout she had ever uttered. Then she got up and approached the cabinets.

1957 was the date she was looking for.

She found a shelf at the top of a cabinet with an enamel tag indicating that year. She found a ladder, climbed it, and took down the first folder on the left. It had over six hundred pages. Silvia climbed down and placed it on top of one of the smaller cabinets. Contact with the records was unpleasant. The texture of the paper was rough and the smell repulsive. The pages were yellow and handwritten. It was hard to understand them. Little by little she began to decipher the texts, and realized that most of the documents did not even refer to the adoption of children. They were accounts, staff orders, house rules, bills and receipts, personal messages and even doodles.

She was not expecting it to be easy and she continued her research. She got used to the handwriting. After a while, in a few seconds she could tell if a document interested her.

After two hours she had completed her task. She fetched the next folder and began to analyze its pages once more. She was exhausted, hungry, and her eyes smarted, but she could not stop. This folder took her half the time of the first, but she found nothing. She repeated the process with no luck with two more folders. Finally in the middle of the afternoon, Silvia feared that her heart might burst. She had found a stamped page that mentioned her name:

A child of the feminine sex, baptized with the name of Silvia Lenka, was handed in for adoption on 2 March 1957 by Iva Masa, inhabitant of the village of Rhur, born in 1942...

Silvia read the document several times. Her hands did not stop shaking. She kept repeating her mother's name as if she were under a spell. 'Iva Masa, Iva Masa.' She takes the sheet, puts it in a pocket and leaves the archive room. She had a glassy gaze and her neck was stiff. She passed a number of workers at the home who regarded her in astonishment, but none dared question the woman who was talking to herself. When she found herself in the street, the sun had already set.

'Iva Masa, Iva Masa.'

The next day, early in the morning, Silvia caught a train that would take her to the city nearest the village of Rhur, and finished the journey by bus. In all, the trip took five hours.

Throughout the journey the thoughts that had occupied her mind all night continued.

My mother was a peasant when she had me. She wasn't a whore, or an important person. What now, is she alive or dead? What will I say to her, if I find her? How will she react? Will she embrace the prodigal daughter or reject her like a leper? And what will she look like if she's alive? Will she be well-preserved, or aged by work? And what would she have been like when she got pregnant? Tall, dark, and pretty, just like me? A cheerful, kind peasant whom everyone adored? I wonder if she was happy in her little rural world, if she was loved by her parents and siblings. And how did they treat her after they found out that she was pregnant? They can't have been happy about it. Would she have been driven away like an animal, or forgiven? Did she give me up for adoption of her own free will or was she forced to? What must our separation have been like? Has she thought of me every single day? Or might she have wanted to forget me? And who will my father turn out to have been? Some neighbor boy she used to play with? An older peasant who seduced her? A stranger who was passing through? Will I find any relatives?

The questions buzzed inside her head. On the train, on the way to the bus station and right up to her final destination, Silvia went through a whirlwind of emotions: she was serious, she smiled, she wept, she fed her hopes, she prepared for disappointment, and ended up exhausted, empty of feelings. When the bus arrived at the village, she felt strangely calm. She would definitely find the family she had never had, even if everyone had died. She was about to heal the wound and become a person like everybody else. She would no longer have the nightmares in which her parents abandoned her.

It was a settlement on a mountain slope, inhabited by three hundred people. The houses were of granite, with thatched roofs, all clustered together, which meant that the lanes were narrow and winding, making a knitted web that linked them all. In the middle of the labyrinth was an open square with a whitewashed church that was over a hundred years old. Beside the village were cultivated fields, stables for animals and massive trees. The climate was cold, wet and windy, even in summer. The mountain air had a fresh scent that only disappeared during the growing season. Attacks on the henhouses by foxes were frequent. At times, wolves came down the mountain and killed sheep. The villagers also feared snakes, scorpions, and wasps.

Dressed in her best clothes, wearing her gold earrings and carrying a handbag, Silvia got off the bus and gazed about. A mist was creeping down the mountain, streaming along the village streets, and seemed to be coming to meet her. The grey cotton skirt-suit she wore was not much use against the moist cold. Her stockingless shoes sank in the wet grass. Silvia began to shiver. She had prepared phrases for every situation she might encounter – introducing herself, explaining why she had only come now, and asking for forgiveness – but she could not remember any of them. Once again she started repeating the name of her mother as she moved towards the houses: 'Iva Masa, Iva Masa.' Like a cabalist intoning some magic formula in order to bring about a revelation, Silvia offered up those two words. Just like the Jewish magus, she was standing before a Tree of Life, where the mystery of her origins would be explained.

As she walked through the lanes of the village she passed an old lady at her window, and a man leading a goat tied by its horns, and she saw two children playing football. She was incapable of questioning any of them, so she decided to walk around the whole village. She smelled the aroma of freshly-baked bread and walked towards it. She came to an alleyway with irregular cobblestones, tripped, and nearly fell flat on her face. Laughter broke out behind her, but when she turned around she could not see anyone. At the same time she heard someone knocking a window shutter in the other direction. She began to suspect that someone was watching her. She was an intruder whom the villagers would keep an eye on. Did they fear that she had come to rob them or commit some other vile act? They certainly would not view her as a friend. If she made a false step, she would be thrown out before she could learn anything. Before she asked any questions, she would have to show that she didn't constitute a threat to the village. Instead of continuing to climb, which made her seem to be trying to hide in the fog, she decided the most sensible course would be to return to the entrance to the village and wait until someone came to her. It was as if she were asking permission to be allowed to enter.

Minutes later, there appeared a white-bearded man carrying a stick in his right hand. He was wearing a beret, a coat, a white shirt, grey trousers, and clogs. His blue eyes kept blinking. His mouth was half-open, revealing the absence of an incisor.

Silvia supposed he was the village headman or mayor.

The man planted his stick in front of her to establish a distance between them.

'What are you doing here?'

Silvia forced a smile. 'My name's Silvia Lenka. I'm a professor of art history and I've come to ask for some information.'

The man twisted his nose. 'Information? There's no information here for anyone.'

'Iva Masa, I'm looking for a lady called Iva Masa.'

The man's face contracted, multiplying his lines and wrinkles. He gripped his stick hard, making the thick tendons in his hand stand out. He scrutinized Silvia's face, suspicious on principle of her identity. Then he walked right round her observing her in minute detail. Finally, with his face practically stuck to hers, he whispered:

'Iva Masa died many years ago. It'll be better for everyone if you go away.'

Silvia felt a knot in her throat. 'She died…'

'She died!' he shouted.

'How?'

'A fever. Get lost.'

'Please will you tell me if any relative of hers is alive?'

The man moved away from her and took a deep breath. His eyes were lost in the void. He scratched his head. He spoke to himself in low tones. 'I knew this was going to happen, but she'd never forgive me if I…'

Cautiously Silvia stepped towards him. 'Pardon?'

The man awoke from his trance. A new, less hostile, expression appeared on his face.

'Do you believe in God, girl?'

Silvia stared at him, stunned. She intuited that he wanted her to say she believed.

'Yes…yes.'

'Do you believe God punishes us in this life?'

Silvia nodded her head. Tears ran down her cheeks.

'Then you know what you did, don't you?'

'Yes, I do…'

'God sent you here to punish you.'

Silvia wept and sighed. She could no longer say anything.

'Instead of crying, you should pray. You're not to blame for being born, but you're here for a reason. Wait while I go and call someone.'

In no time there appeared a woman of forty dressed in black who also wore clogs. Silvia looked at her features: her cheeks, nose, lips, grey eyes and black hair were all similar to her own. She had no doubt: she was from her family. Would she be an aunt, a sister, a cousin? She felt an urge to hug her, but restrained herself. This woman might be of her own blood, but she was not happy to see her. The way she looked at her even suggested pure disgust. As the woman did not speak, Silvia risked a question.

'Who are you?'

The woman bared her teeth as if snarling. 'I'm Iva's cousin and there's no one else left alive.'

Silvia's eyes bulged. 'Cousin…'

'Now you can go away. You already know everything there is to know.'

'Wait, I'm the daughter of Iva's who was given up for adoption. We're from the same family.'

The woman spat to one side. 'You're not from my family, you're the devil's daughter. Get out of here and never come back.'

They're all mad.

'I'm sorry, but I don't understand. I'd like to talk to you about my mother and also find out who my father is. I'm only asking you for a few minutes of your time. Then I'll go away and never return. I haven't come searching for money or any inheritance, if that's what you're thinking.'

The woman clenched her fist in threat and shouted: 'I told you, you're the devil's daughter. Begone, creature.'

At that moment, the church bell began to toll. From out of the mist there appeared men and women, some of them armed with sickles and hoes, and they lined up behind Silvia's cousin like a Praetorian Guard. Silvia could hear their breathing: a sort of thick snore that the ringing of the bells could not drown. These people seemed capable of lynching her, her mother was dead and her cousin rejected her, and yet she would not leave. There was still so much to find out. What secrets was the village hiding? Silvia did not budge. She had faced more terrifying threats than these peasants. Meanwhile the light strained through the fog began to disappear and it got colder. An old, fat woman came towards her then and shoved her, making her fall. Lying on her back, Silvia saw the peasants coming closer. They were nearly on top of her, but they neither touched her nor said anything. The acrid smell of their bodies was sufficient warning. She stood up slowly, avoiding sudden gestures, and began to withdraw as if she were facing wild beasts. Once she had put some distance between herself and them, she turned her back on them and started running. Just then a band of children appeared, chasing her and throwing stones at her.

Scared and confused, Silvia went to look for somewhere to sleep in the nearest town. During the two hour walk she never ceased wondering what the reason was for her having been expelled from the village like that. Why had they called her *daughter of the devil?* Peasants were superstitious and believed in demons, ghosts, and witchcraft, but this was something else. Her birth had been associated with some flesh and blood disaster. Had the family of her mother killed her father to avenge the honor of the daughter? Could she be the daughter of a priest? Or could Iva Masa have prostituted herself? She set herself to conjuring up suppositions involving tragedies and catastrophes that only puzzled and drained her.

She reached a place called Hara and in the main street found a two-storey house with a sign reading *Pension*. She went in. The receptionist, a blonde boy with a spotty face, was asleep with his head on the counter. Silvia knocked on the wood and woke him up. He looked at her with astonishment. Silvia asked for a room and something to eat. The boy found her attractive and tried to flirt, but her expression shut him up. The boy lowered his head and went to the kitchen to fetch a bowl of milk and a slice of bread. Silvia took the food without looking at him and climbed up to the first floor.

She was sitting on her bed eating, with her feet in a bowl of hot water, when she heard someone knock the door. She thought it was the receptionist and muttered a swear-word. She dried her feet, put on slippers and went to open it. There was a middle-aged woman, tall and thin, with a red face and a headscarf. Her voice was as gruff as a man's.

'Are you Iva Masa's daughter?'

Silvia regarded her with distrust. 'Yes, and I've brought documents to prove it.'

The woman made a gesture to indicate that she had no interest in seeing them, and entered the room. A lit lamp with a shade projected an elongated shadow of her on the wall.

'And do you want to know who your father is?'

'Of course, it's very important for me to find out my origins. But who are you? And why did they throw me out of the village?'

'I'm Rhana, the midwife. I was a friend of your mother's and it was I who helped bring you into the world. You took three hours. It seemed like you didn't want to be born.'

Silvia trembled. 'So you know who my father is?'

'I do.'

'Tell me, please. I'm not leaving here until I know the truth.'

'Sit down, I'll tell you everything. They arrived at dawn, put up tents and started their exercises...'

'Who were they?'

'Soldiers.'

'My father is a soldier?'

'Don't interrupt, let me finish.'

'Sorry.'

'When they finished the exercises, at noon, they started hunting the girls.'

'What?'

'Shhh. Your mother had taken the sheep out to the graze and she was alone on the hill. She was a girl of fifteen and she'd never even kissed a man. She hardly knew how babies were made. She used to believe everything they told her like a child. The commander of the soldiers approached her smiling, saying he needed some information, then he threw her on the ground and molested her.'

Silvia went pale. 'It can't be, there must be some mistake.'

'There's no mistake, your mother was raped, she got pregnant and she was forced to give you up for adoption. You can't imagine how she suffered. Her father wanted to throw her out of the house, people stopped speaking to her, and once they caught her and shaved her head and soiled her face with sheep dung. The called her the soldiers' little whore. If she hadn't been so religious, she would have aborted you.'

Tears slid down Silvia's face and her voice came out in a moan: 'And who was…this…this commander?'

'Your mother didn't know his name, but she never forgot his face. One day, she saw him on television. He was older, but she didn't have the slightest doubt that it was him. She started yelling and I think it was then that she lost her mind for good.'

Silvia grabbed her by the arm and shouted, 'But who? Once and for all tell me who my father is.'

The midwife gazed at her and sighed. She put her hands on her hips and her shadow on the wall resembled an amphora.

'Your father is the president.'

'What? What are you saying? Which president?'

'Ionescu: you're the daughter of the devil.'

Silvia's face distorted into a grimace of horror. She stood up, shaking her head and pacing up and down.

'No, it's not true. My mother must have been mistaken. She was traumatized and…'

The midwife gripped her by the shoulders and held her still. Her smile was malevolent. 'No one was mistaken, my pretty one. She identified him whenever he appeared on television, in the newspapers or on posters. There could be a hundred people around him and she never hesitated. She always recognized the devil wherever he was. In fact, you only have to look at your face, at those eyes of yours, and you can't have the slightest doubt who your father is. Now do you understand why they ran you out of the village?'

The violence of Silvia's shove was directed at the midwife's revelation, but it was she who struck the wall. The amphora broke and Silvia ran barefoot out of the room. She flew down the wooden stairs, passed the receptionist at a run, opened the door and went into the dark.

For half an hour Silvia ran without any idea where she was going. The cold that froze her feet and the stones that lacerated them did not stop her. She had fallen twice, but rebounded and rose. Her hair was disheveled and her gaze crazed; her clothes were torn and filthy. She breathed greedily. Her heart was an atomic bomb. At times she shouted like a lunatic. The few people she passed feared she would attack them. She was getting further from the town and entering a plain. On the ground was wet grass and animal burrows. The moon filled the sky with a halo around it. Half a dozen stars strayed about, lost. Silvia ran more slowly, then began to walk, and finally limped. She was about to be catch by herself. In the mountains a wolf howled, but she heard nothing. Nor did she see a flock of birds migrating to the south. When she tripped over a hole, she fell and hit her face on a rock. She no longer had the strength to get up. She began to drag herself along like a slug, tearing her elbows and knees with each centimeter she progressed. She managed to go on a few more meters but in the end she exhausted herself. For a few minutes she stayed in that position, with her head laid to one side on the grass. Then she turned over and gazed at the sky.

It was to the darkness that stretched beyond the stars that she started to speak.

She cursed Ionescu for having raped her mother, she cursed her mother for not aborting her, she cursed the dictatorship for allowing the powerful to abuse the weak, she cursed *Perestroika* for having brought freedom, she cursed democracy for allowing her to find out the truth, she cursed Irina for letting her consult the files, she cursed Leonidas for abandoning her, she cursed the God she did not believe in, she cursed Jesus for having created the illusion that men were good, she cursed the village that had expelled her, she cursed the world, she cursed life and she cursed herself for being the devil's daughter.

She no longer had any tears left to weep, nor felt pain, nor revulsion, she no longer felt anything. Nor did the wounds on her body hurt her. It was as if she had been sedated. Her mind emptied but a single thought remained. A lost wave that could as easily fade away as grow. However, some electromagnetic process stimulated it and the wave began to tremble and propagate itself throughout her mind. The void called it. The wave responded by growing faster. Like water flooding a house, it inundated every compartment. Finally, it took its place and dominated the being that had given it birth. Then, Silvia was just a single idea.

She gathered the strength to sit up then, took out her earrings and put them between her teeth. She brought her left wrist up to the pointed gold posts and started tearing at her veins. Then she raised her right wrist and repeated the motion until she had opened those veins too. She fell on her back, shut her eyes, and let the blood run out.

Leonidas and Lia

WHEN he found out that the attack on the factory in Witten which had killed Luda Schwartz was included in the amnesty for blood crimes perpetrated during the previous regime, Leonidas returned to Slavia. While he was in exile in Austria he had tried in vain to contact Silvia and his comrades in the resistance. The letters were intercepted and the phone calls interrupted. So he had ended up losing contact with both. If it had not been hard to find his old comrades again, Silvia seemed to have vanished. He had gone to look for her in the house she had lived in with her friends and not even they lived there anymore. He had been to the Liberal Arts Faculty and only managed to learn that she had finished her degree. He had found friends they had in common, but none had been able to give him an address or any contact information. One of them told him she must have emigrated. So he gave up trying to contact her. In his life there was something more important: recuperating the political power he had lost, which meant taking up the leadership of the party his comrades were forming.

Leonidas found a very different country from the one he had left a few years before. However, it was not in its economic or urban development, which ran up against decades of backwardness, that he noticed the difference. In fact, new problems had appeared. With the end of state monopolies and the opening of private enterprise had come the appearance of shops and supermarkets offering goods that had not existed – especially foods – but the prices were so high that the majority of the population could not afford them, despite the increase of salaries. They called this inflation and said it was caused by the low productivity of the workers. Another grave problem was the end of lifelong jobs guaranteed by the government. The number of unemployed people continued to rise in spite of their professional qualifications, which forced thousands of people to immigrate to the richer countries of Europe. Those who stayed were attracted towards crime and prostitution.

All the same, there was an atmosphere of euphoria, of hope and dreams, to which people surrendered with an almost religious fervor. The older ones wanted to recover the time they had lost, and the younger ones believed in the happiness they were promised. People supposed that it was enough to participate in the building of democracy and make use of their civic rights for anything to be possible. Everyone was convinced they had the solutions for the country's problems. Everyone became an expert in politics, economics, finances, and even a range of cultural subjects. The people now had millions of omniscient commissars who with a magic wand could transform Slavia into a rich, developed, just country. Some went even further, proposing a kind of universal panacea to benefit humanity. In these early days of democracy, the sense of the ridiculous was a forgotten quality. Nor were a sense of humor or tolerance much in evidence. Political discussion had become an uncontrolled passion that often led to conflict, and sometimes to violence.

The Solidarity movement was in the process of becoming the Democracy Party. They had opened a headquarters in a building in the city center and there was a meeting scheduled for three o'clock on Saturday to vote on the statutes and the mission of the party. Two days in advance, Leonidas found out about this by chance, because no one had invited him. He began to realize then that it would be much harder than he had supposed to achieve political power after the fall of the regime. The *Perestroika* train had not waited for him. It had left at high speed, leaving him standing on the platform. Now he had to chase it and jump on to the engine in motion.

At ten in the morning on Saturday, wearing jeans and a white shirt, Leonidas left the pension where he was staying. He wanted to wander for a few hours before attending the meeting that would transform Solidarity into the Democracy Party. Ever since his arrival he had sought contact with people in the streets; he wanted to see how they behaved, what they said to each other, and what they might tell him. Only thus could he understand what was happening and in which direction society was going.

As he passed along an avenue for the first time he saw a series of posters of the Freedom Party pasted on the walls of buildings. The sunlight made them gleam. Some posters showed the name of the party in black letters, a blue dove as a logo, and the slogan *We Shall Overcome* in red. Others had nothing but the face of the leader of the party: a bald man with dark eyes and thin, smiling lips. Leonidas got closer and recognized him: it was Ivan Fiorov, also known as Koba. For some time he stood staring at the image to make sure he was not mistaken. He felt a chill along his spine, and a bitterness in his mouth. He clenched his fists and his teeth, and finally spat at the posters. Had he risked his life fighting against the dictatorship just so the biggest criminal in the country could create a party and stand for prime minister? What democracy could allow such a thing? And what kind of citizen could vote for him?

He was pondering this when he heard shouts. He looked around but only saw passers-by and cars. The rumpus did not come from the avenue he was in, but from a perpendicular street. He moved that way at a quick pace, nearly knocking into the stick of a blind man who was coming from the opposite direction, and turned at the first crossing on the left. It was a pedestrian street with granite paving-stones, full of clothes shops and bars. Sunlight fell obliquely on the facades on the right-hand side. Some twenty meters ahead, Leonidas found a group of people arguing. Men and women of various ages were shouting and waving their arms to emphasize their arguments. Shopkeepers were peeping from their doors, afraid the disturbance might damage business. Passers-by paused and sometimes joined in the dispute. Leonidas swiftly realized the reason: one group was pasting up posters of Koba and another group was trying to prevent them. His first impulse was to join the group who opposed the gangster's propaganda, but he held himself in check. He would be a neutral observer.

A man in a blue suit and a black tie managed to shout louder than the others and make himself heard. 'So we've got rid of the dictatorship and yet now we aren't free to defend our political ideas? In a democracy everyone's free to express his opinions and stand for office. If you don't like our party, you've got a good solution: don't vote for it. But you don't have the right to ban it. If you prevent us from putting up posters you're behaving like the police of the old regime.'

Although he hated to admit it, Leonidas could not refute the argument of Koba's supporter. Yes, even an utter bastard had the right to make his voice heard and have it subjected to the people's scrutiny. In Vienna, he had seen the election of corrupt politicians and former supporters of Hitler. Besides, the behavior of the others was not so different from the police who in the old days had confiscated the propaganda that he and his comrades had tried to circulate.

From the other group, a woman of thirty in blue corduroy trousers and a yellow sweater answered. 'That's demagogy. In all democratic countries there are political groups who aren't allowed to advertise. Nazi and racist parties are banned. We don't accept that a gangster who was in league with the previous regime and made a fortune at the people's expense can stand in the elections as if he were an exemplary democrat. You can't whitewash history.'

Fiorov should have been tried too for the crimes committed by the dictatorship. As he wasn't, it's our civic duty to stop him taking over the country again.'

Leonidas agreed with this argument too. If the Ku Klux Klan could not stand for elections in the United States, and neither could the neo-Nazis form a party in Germany, why on earth should Slavia not impose the same constraints on antidemocratic movements and collaborators of the old regime? It was not a matter of subverting the rules of democracy, but of strengthening them. However, Fiorov was neither a Nazi nor a racist, nor had he sent anyone to the concentrations camps; he himself had been a victim of that punishment. Seen like that, who in the end was right?

Meanwhile the dispute was continuing.

The man in the blue suit said, 'The simple truth is that Ivan Fiorov played a vital role under the dictatorship for managing to import goods that were scarce in the shops, and for giving work to lots of citizens. You should be grateful to him.'

'Those goods were contraband and they ended up in the hands of party leaders who used public funds to buy them. And the only people he gave jobs to were thieves and murderers. We owe him nothing,' said the woman in the yellow sweater.

From that point on, everyone started talking at once although no one managed to make himself heard. The words were rats, biting each other. Koba was the rabies that was driving them mad.

'He's a hero…'

'A gangster…'

'If it weren't for him…'

'He's got millions in Switzerland…'

'Ingrates…'

'Murderer…'

Leonidas was pondering the complexity and contradictions of democracy when violence erupted. Without warning, a boy with a shaven head kicked the belly of the woman in the yellow sweater, bringing her to her knees. At once, the members of the two groups fell on each other and twenty-two people were fighting. They punched, kicked, elbowed and head-butted. Some grabbed each other and rolled on the ground, others slammed into the walls or shop windows. The shouting got louder. Blood ran down faces. The man in the blue suit had a broken finger. Suddenly a blade shines in the sunlight. Leonidas sees it searching its way through the fighters until it finds the back of a tall, strong man who has already knocked down three opponents with punches. The man let out a scream, froze, and finally fell on his face. A bloodstain soaked his shirt. 'He's dead,' someone shouted. There was silence. The group who had been pasting up posters of Koba started to flee, supporting their wounded as best they could. The other group vanished too, each one running in a different direction. The murderer's knife remained on the ground, blood dimming the gleam of its blade.

Before long, the siren of a police car sounded. The shopkeepers shut their doors. The bystanders broke away running. The dead man lay alone. Leonidas approached him and squatted down. He had turned his head to the right, his eyes were open and his tongue stuck out between his teeth. Leonidas guessed he was no more than thirty. Leonidas felt even more hatred for Fiorov than pity for the victim.

For several hours Leonidas wandered around the city without ever going far from the headquarters of the future Democracy Party. In the sky a blanket of thin clouds had appeared, which the sun was unravelling. Leonidas imagined various ways of removing Fiorov from politics, but the only one that seemed to work was physical elimination. A bomb. As if it were a matter of crushing an insect, the victim of the fracas already forgotten, Leonidas evaluated the chances of blowing up his car or some place where he was giving a speech. The problem, he realized, was that he no longer had the means with which he had fought against the dictatorship. And even if he regained some political influence, would he be able to persuade anyone to plan a terrorist attack under the democracy?

Presently, as he passed beside a park with trees and wooden benches, he heard a hawker. He had a strong voice that carried over the noise of a nearby lawnmower.

'MacDonald's hamburgers, original recipe.'

Overlaying the smell of cut grass, Leonidas caught a combination of aromas in which grilled meat predominated. His stomach dilated and contracted like a pair of bellows. Looking about, he saw a short, stocky man with red hair and blue eyes, dressed in white. Beside him was a cart with a parasol where he cooked the food, and on top of it was a rolling pin. Ever since *Perestroika* fast food stands had multiplied. The quality of their products, however, was far from great. Whether hamburgers, pizzas, or sandwiches, there was always some adulterated ingredient: the flesh of dogs, cats, and mice were all used. As they did not need licenses, and there were not even any inspections, each of them did as they liked. Leonidas forgot the bombs and went over to him.

'Good morning, what's in your hamburgers?'

The vendor raised his eyebrows, as if the question were offensive. 'What's in my hamburgers? Didn't you hear what I said? It's an original recipe, what a question.'

Leonidas took a deep breath. 'And may I know what's in your original recipe?'

The vendor's eyes seemed to catch fire. He raised the rolling-pin and squeezed it.

'As everyone knows, MacDonald's original recipe consists of bread, minced beef, bacon and potatoes.'

'French fries? As a side for the hamburger?'

'Of course not. Roast potatoes, inside the bread.'

'Sorry, but I've lived abroad and I've never eaten a hamburger like that.'

'Have you ever been to America?'

'No…'

'Keep quiet, then. You know nothing about it. Take one, try it,' he said, handing him a roll of bread with the ingredients he had described, 'and if you don't like it, you don't pay.'

Leonidas regarded the hamburger with suspicion: the bread was dark, the minced beef reddish, the bacon yellow; only the roast potatoes looked good. However, hunger triumphed over mistrust and Leonidas wound up bringing it to his mouth. It tasted better than he had guessed. It had some secret ingredient, surely a spice, that he was unable to identify.

'Isn't it delicious?' asked the vendor, picking up the rolling-pin again.

'Yes, it's good.'

The vendor flashed a triumphant smile and put down the rolling-pin.

'How much is it?'

'It's on the house. Chef Kristoff is in a good mood.'

It was savoring the strange hamburger that made Leonidas remember the man who was stabbed to death an hour earlier. Only then did he pity the man's fate. The poor soul would nevermore enjoy the pleasures of life. If the death of a human being owing to a political dispute seemed to him part of the rules of the game, the deprivation of a delight as simple as a meat sandwich struck him now as a crime. Leonidas chewed the last bite more slowly, trying to extract every flavor of the hamburger and exploring its textures, as if he owed that much to the dead man. The fat running between his fingers did not bother him; he licked it off as if it were something precious that could not be wasted. At that moment he experienced the closest thing to a spiritual enlightenment he had ever had. When he finished eating, it struck him that instead of a bomb, Koba deserved to be poisoned.

Twenty minutes before the start of the meeting of the Democracy Party, Leonidas entered the headquarters. At the entrance were dozens of people he did not know, and who did not recognize him either, conversing. Young and middle-aged men and women, wearing fine clothes, and perfumed as if they were at a party. They had glasses of wine in their hands and they smoked. A tall, pretty girl was dancing, shaking her head and hips. A group of boys with long hair were shoving each other and laughing. A man with sunglasses and gel in his hair was speaking English, showing off. Leonidas watched from a distance, as if he were afraid of mixing with them. *Who are these people? Do they represent the people who are going to elect the rulers of the country? They look more like the children of the old leaders and the new entrepreneurs who have benefitted from the transition to democracy.*

Instead of what one might have expected, no one was talking about politics. Leonidas began to eavesdrop on their conversations, picking up phrases here and there.

'I heard they're going to open a Benetton store soon…'

'I bought Boris Becker's tennis racket…'

'My husband's going to take me to Mauritius…'

'You just can't find a decent pair of shoes in our country…'

'Is your son going to study in a Swiss school?'

For a few moments, Leonidas felt like planting a bomb for them, right there, to shut them up for good. In his contact that day with life in the streets, he had picked up enough information about what was happening: a gangster was preparing to take over the country, some people were protesting and ran the risk of being killed, while others seemed to be interested in everything but politics. Democracy might become a dangerous game. The ones who knew best how to play it were criminals, opportunists, and madmen.

He passed through the people, pushing some and treading on the toes of others, and went through a narrow door into the building. The light of the outdoors gave way to shadows; a muggy smell took the place of the fresh air; the temperature rose. Leonidas found himself in a windowless courtyard and from there he moved into a corridor until he could no longer hear the hubbub of the street. He passed people, but nobody spoke to him or asked him any questions. He found people drinking and talking, leaning against the walls, one guy who seemed to be snorting cocaine and pair of lovers kissing greedily. He realized the party meeting would not be in that part of the building and turned back. Then he followed another corridor, wider and better-lit; there too there were a lot of people, but no one was drinking. At last, Leonidas reached a kind of auditorium whose doors were open. It was a space with room for three hundred people and a stage with brown leather chairs; the ceiling had spotlights, the walls were white and the floor was covered with a blue carpet. The smell of paint and leather indicated recent renovation to welcome the party conference. Leonidas was observing the room when a tall, pretty woman, with a notebook in her hand, addressed him.

'Would you like to become a member of the Democracy Party? It's two dollars to enroll and a dollar a month.'

'Dollars?'

The girl flashed an embarrassed smile. 'As you know, since the liberalization of the market, our currency has devalued a great deal and the dollar has become the de facto currency. But when our party is in power there will be significant economic growth and our currency will be strong again. First, we have to win the elections.'

Leonidas hesitated, but ended up putting his hand in his pocket and giving her two-dollars. The girl's eyes gleamed.

'Thanks a lot. Would you like to put down your name to speak too?'

Leonidas gave her his name and left. Meanwhile, the auditorium was filling up. As if they were in a holy place, the people whispered and showed a different kind of composure. But the aroma of the perfumes was still intense, and mixed with the smells of leather and paint, they infested the air. It nauseated Leonidas. Suddenly, silence fell. Adam Jacek and six of his old comrades had arrived. They carried briefcases and documents under their arms. As they passed him they turned their heads away. One of them murmured a curse which Leonidas realized was meant for him. Some of the group sat in the first row of the auditorium while the rest occupied the tables and chairs on the stage. The other people began to sit down too and Leonidas himself looked for a seat.

The first Democracy Party Conference was about to start.

In the first half hour the statutes of the party were read and approved by a unanimous vote. In essence, a political organization based on Social Democracy was created, and there was a vote by arms in the air on the principle of a leadership mandated for four years, which would enjoy full powers to choose the electoral platform. Next, two candidates for the leadership of the party presented themselves, one composed of Adam Jacek and his comrades, and the other by an unknown person called Tadeusz Khun. Both advocated a model combining capitalism with state intervention based on the regulation of the economy for the distribution of food, the maintenance of social security, education and public health, culture and sports, close ties with Europe and the United States, and entry into NATO. During this time, apart from the representatives of each candidate, thirty people who had enrolled to speak were given the floor. Leonidas listened to the candidates' presentations – which all seemed the same to him – the proposals, the solutions and the digressions of twenty members of the party, and after two hours, finally he had the chance to speak.

On hearing his name, he stood up and moved towards the stage where there was a microphone for speakers. He was climbing the steps when he started to hear whistles and insults. He halted and turned. It was Adam Jacek's group heckling him.

One of his old comrades stood up and pointed his finger at him. 'We don't want murderers or traitors here. You're guilty of the deaths of Cornelius and Rado. Get out.'

From another corner of the auditorium, a man Leonidas did not recognize shouted too.

'Our party must not have people like him. He will ruin our reputation. We've got to expel him at once.'

Close by him a woman got up. 'For once in your life, do the decent thing. Disappear.'

Leonidas looked around, haplessly. Other people began to insult him, and some threw paper balls, plastic cups, and lighters at him. The auditorium was an ogre. He was about to leave when a woman stood up and managed to shout above everyone else:

'That's enough! You're the ones who should be ashamed. This man risked his life so we could be here. We owe him our freedom. Thank him, instead of insulting him.'

The protests ceased. People looked at each other. Adam Jacek made a sign to his comrades so that they would not react. No one dared speak. Leonidas looked at the woman who had defended him, still more dazed than he had been.

Then Lia Kircher left her seat and moved towards the stage. She was wearing a white dress with a green scarf around her neck; she wore high heels and her hair was tied up with an elastic band. As she reached Leonidas she took his hand and led him like a child. The people supervising the debate on the stage made no protest. Lia stamped on the floor, thumping the wood like a drum; she marched like a general who has conquered territory; Leonidas took insecure, silent steps. When she reached the microphone, she stared at the stupefied audience for a while. She was punishing them with her silence. Then, she started to speak:

'Congratulations. Right at the formation of a party that calls itself democratic, you try to prevent a citizen from speaking. And what's more, a hero who took on the dictatorship when the majority of you were obeying without protest. So do you think you're better than him? Do you think you have the right to judge him? Well, let me tell you, you are cowards and ingrates. If it were up to you, we'd still be ruled by Ionescu. A country with no memory that doesn't recognize who gave its freedom back to it is condemned to return to totalitarianism. This man, Leonidas Vall, did what was necessary to weaken the dictatorship. In a time of violence when human life was worth nothing, he paid them back in the same coin. There was a victim, it's true, and I'm truly sorry about it. But we can't say she was innocent. She was a pawn of the regime. The fact is that there would continue to be hundreds of victims, and who knows if you or your children wouldn't be among them, if the regime had not been worn down by acts of propaganda and sabotage. Do you know of any revolution in which blood wasn't spilled? Do you think the historical figures who fought for freedom in France and the United States were pacifists? Are you forgetting the bombing of civilian populations in Nazi Germany? Does anyone mention that when they celebrate VE Day? And what would you call the movements for freedom in the African colonies?'

Lia paused and glanced around the audience to see if anyone would object. No one said a word. Adam Jacek was a pressure cooker about to explode, but the steam was escaping from some other side than his mouth. Lia dominated the auditorium as if she had cast a spell over it. Even Leonidas was more stunned than embarrassed.

'My father was one of the victims of the regime, as you well know. That doesn't give me any special status to give you lessons in democracy, but it taught me something that a lot of you still haven't learned. A dictatorship is composed of murderers, and eliminating them is a legitimate act of self-defense. But we've spoken enough of the past: it's the present and the future that interest us. There's a figure linked to the old regime who wants to take power. If he wins the elections, our country will be turned into a paradise for gangsters and the corrupt even worse than the dictatorship. Democracy will give way to the law of the jungle. Repression and fear will return. Social inequality will increase. Europe will drive us away and no civilized country will want to have diplomatic relations with us. He's our true enemy. We have to be united to defeat him by democratic means. Do you understand?'

Lia paused once more, and again no one questioned her. She was beginning to feel weary and she had a headache. She understood that she had achieved her aim and if she carried on speaking she would end up breaking the spell. 'So I'll pass the microphone to our comrade Leonidas Vall, as he has a lot to teach us about how to face this threat.'

Leonidas was pale, his left eyelid was trembling, and his mouth was dry. He did not want to speak now, he no longer had anything to say. He felt more of a stranger there than when he was in exile. In a few minutes he had gone from murderer to hero, from devil to angel, from undesirable to saviour of the nation. He only wanted to get out as quickly as possible, but the hundreds of eyes riveted on him in the audience were like iron balls chained to his feet. Maybe they would have forgiven him the death of Luda, but they would not let him go without speaking. They would demand some sort of contribution so the party would win the elections, and he could not even remember what he wanted to say. Did he want to influence the party? Take over the leadership? Stop Koba taking over? Bombs? None of that mattered to him now. He only wanted to never again see these people against whom he had no weapons. The murmuring that rose from the audience pierced his eardrums. The ceiling lights dazzled him. The smell of paint burned his windpipe. Lia understood what was occurring and decided to cut the current. She raised her arms and returned to the microphone.

'He prefers not to speak while the conditions for having a calm debate are absent. It's a humble attitude that we should applaud. We'll give the floor to the next speaker. Thanks.'

Once again she took him by the hand and led him off the stage. As they crossed the auditorium everyone rose to their feet. Some clapped their hands, others looked disappointed, and again the word 'murderer' was heard. Lia raised her head while Leonidas looked at the floor. She saw eyes following them, he saw stationary shoes. In the corridor which led to the exit door, they find the man who sniffed cocaine lying on the floor. They stepped over him. When they reached the street, they stopped and gazed at one another. The setting sun was disappearing behind pink clouds. The air was cold and humid. Neither was able to speak.

Jan and Stefan

THE GROUP of twenty-six neo-Nazis met every evening at eight o'clock in the center of Tiersk to start hunting those they considered the enemies of Slavia, the parasites, the inferior races, and the degenerates. It was made up of young men between the ages of eighteen and thirty. There were students, building workers, electricians, male nurses, taxi drivers, shopkeepers, security guards and unemployed people. They practiced martial arts, boxing, and bodybuilding in the gymnasiums. They practiced fighting techniques in the street. They had shaved heads, and tattoos of swastikas and skulls, and wore black clothes and army boots. They went about armed with truncheons, knuckledusters, chains, and knives. As there were few blacks in the country, and most of the Jews were rich and well-protected, their victims were immigrants from Albania and Romania, gypsies, tramps, homosexuals, alcoholics and drug addicts. However, in the event that they did not find any of those, any citizen they happened to meet could become the target of their beatings. They had started patrolling the streets two months ago, and already had attacked over seventy people, two of whom had ended up dying. As well as interrogations, anyone who wanted to join the group had to undergo a test that consisted of beating up a designated victim, alone. The violence and mercilessness of the attack were vital for being accepted. Hesitation meant rejection and a thrashing. The police knew them, but did not mind them, as they thought they helped clean up the streets and intimidate gangsters. So they were allies, in a way.

That night one of the neo-Nazis named Jan had brought along a candidate for joining the group, and he was going to be put to the test. Jan was the only member of the group who had read Hitler's *Mein Kampf* and knew anything about European History, the Second World War, and the western democracies. Jan worked in a butcher's, had finished high school, used a library, and bought books about politics and history at the stands of second-hand booksellers in the streets. The other neo-Nazis had vague ideas about these subjects, which bored them, to tell the truth, as violence fascinated them more than ideology. As there was thus a sort of hierarchy in which punches and kicks ranked higher than knowledge, Jan, in spite of being a reasonable fighter, had never managed to achieve influence over his comrades. They called him 'the intellectual,' pejoratively. All the same, no one doubted that he was the best person to recruit the new neo-Nazis because he prepped them in minute detail before they were put to the final test. In the last six months he had introduced three new candidates, and only one had been rejected, because in a street fight he had been unable to beat a Romanian immigrant who had stabbed him in the arm.

The new candidate was a boy of twenty called Stefan, fair-haired and blue-eyed, and muscular thanks to boxing and full contact. Jan attended the same fighting school and had been impressed by the power of Stefan's punches and the ferocity of his attacks on his opponents – the trainer had several times had to restrain him from causing serious cuts. One day he had invited him to train with himself, and after a bout in which both ended up bleeding, had taken him out to drink a few beers. That was how the recruitment process began. Jan asked questions and learned what he wanted to know: that Stefan lived with his mother and had never known his father; Stefan had given up studying and made a living by expedients like working as a bouncer in bars or entering illegal fights; Stefan had no girlfriend nor any real friends; Stefan knew little about politics, history, or culture in general.

Jan understood then that underneath the armor of the hardened warrior, an insecure child was hiding, who could easily be manipulated. First, he praised his strength, his courage, his fighting skills, and even the shape of his biceps – and Stefan smiled, avid for recognition. Then he told him that he believed Stefan would become a professional fighter capable of competing abroad – and Stefan started punching the air. Only after half an hour of conversation and four beers did the political indoctrination begin. Did Stefan know that the country was being robbed by Jews, by immigrants, and by scum who did not work but received social security payments? Of course Stefan had never thought about any of that. Did Stefan know that the inhabitants of Slavia were a superior race who were being corrupted by mixing with inferior races? Stefan did not know that either. Did Stefan know that within a few generations the country might be overrun by foreigners? Stefan shook his head again. So, something had to be done. Stefan agreed. Since the politicians were corrupt, it had to be the citizens who would fight for their country. Stefan agreed again. Slavia had to be purified and that struggle was starting in the streets. Stefan smiled; this was something he understood. Would he like to join a group of brave lads who were defending their country? Did he have the courage to take on the Jewish scoundrels, the immigrants, the queers and drug-addicts? Did he have the urge to break teeth and skulls? Yes, yes, they could count on him, said Stefan, they could count on him to start beating the hell out of those sons of bitches.

Jan had no need to peer further into the abyss that had opened in Stefan: on the surface there was sufficient hatred, revulsion and ignorance to make of him an attack dog.

The night was warm and the sky was full of stars. A group of neo-Nazis had met in an old district of the city where restaurants, bars, clubs and brothels were beginning to appear. It was a pedestrian street, wide and well-lit; the walls of the buildings were covered with graffiti and there were rubbish bags on the ground; some corners smelled of urine. The place attracted many people, but a clearing formed around the neo-Nazi group. No one dared approach them and some went away as soon as they saw them. The bar owners greeted them with their heads lowered and offered them beers. The restaurant owners asked them if they would like to eat anything. No club bouncer barred entry to them. The neo-Nazis loved such gestures; the fear they inspired made them feel powerful and invulnerable, lords of the streets. They were loud, they pushed each other, showed their knives and simulated fight scenes, letting out tremendous yells. At such times everyone stared at the spectacle of them showing their strength, and straight away many people left.

When Jan arrived with Stefan he saluted his comrades by raising his right arm and went up to the leader to present the candidate. Stefan looked at the tall, well-built, red-haired man with blue eyes, who wore a ring with a steel skull, and his expectations were met – he was before a warrior. He let the other examine him from head to toe with a cold regard as if he were a doctor looking for a disease. He knew he would pass the scrutiny.

'My name's Tobias and the first thing you've got to learn is that I'm the boss here.'

Stefan nodded.

'I've heard you can fight.'

'I can.'

'Are you ready to fight for your country?'

'I am.'

'Has Jan explained to you what you have to do to be accepted?'

'Yes.'

'In that case that's enough questions for now. Let's see what you can do.'

Tobias whistled and all the neo-Nazis turned in his direction. His athletic physique and furious face made an impact even on the ones who had known him for some time. Despite his dark clothes, all the lights seemed to be trained on him. 'Let's go,' he said, and started walking. The group followed him, with Jan and Stefan at his side. The neo-Nazis' boots made the cobblestones shake. Some of them thumped doors as they passed them, others smashed their glasses on the ground, and yet others whipped out their knives. Everyone made way for them, the men more scared than the women.

The hunt was on, and Stefan, the beginner taken by his friends for his baptism by fire, was beside himself with excitement. He was electrified: his heart beat hard and his eyes shone. He held his head high, smiling, and at times made little leaps. Next to Jan and Tobias, he felt as if he were in the presence of two older brothers who would test his bravery. He was already picturing himself beating up an immigrant, a druggy, a homosexual or a gypsy. They were going to love his punches and kicks, they were going to see that he was as strong as the others, maybe even stronger, more violent, more of a man. He would pass the test with flying colors. And then, along with these new friends of his, he would fight for the salvation of his country.

By now they had got further from the district of bars, and were walking along narrower streets, which were deserted and ill-lit, when they encountered a middle-aged man coming from the opposite direction. He was a secondary school teacher who had had dinner with some relatives and was on his way home now. Faced with the neo-Nazis, whom he had detected by the racket they made long before he reached them, the man reacted as if a herd of bulls were charging down the street: he hugged the walls and slid along in the hope of passing them unnoticed. He actually scraped his nape of his neck against the walls, so intense was his desire to disappear from the sight of the menacing band. He sweated, his teeth chattered, and his heart raced.

Stefan was the first to see him and he scented blood. As the man was coming from the direction opposite his own – from the left – he took a few paces to the right to be able to catch him. Stefan began clenching and unclenching his fists, and wiggling his neck and shoulders as if he were preparing for a boxing match. He was five meters from the man, and he had already lowered his head in an attitude of submission. When he came near, Stefan grabbed him by the throat and immobilized him.

'Who are you? What are you doing here?'

The neo-Nazi group stopped and they all watched Stefan and his victim. The man tried to speak, but the chokehold on his throat prevented him. He stammered some hoarse noises and groans. The neo-Nazis laughed. Suddenly, Stefan head-butted him in the face, which broke his nose and knocked him to the ground. Then he kicked him several times. The neo-Nazis applauded. Finally, a kick to his head made him lose consciousness. The neo-Nazis spat on him. One of them opened his fly and urinated on his face. Panting, Stefan turned in triumph towards Tobias. He only needed the final approval of the leader to be admitted to the group.

However, Tobias did not wear the expression Stefan had expected. His gaze was still cold and his face muscles were contracting. He took a step towards Stefan.

'You think you're tough, don't you? Who told you to beat this guy up?'

'I...'

Tobias raised his hand and flicked Stefan's forehead. 'Shut up. You only open your mouth when I tell you to. Understand?'

Stefan reddened, but nodded his head.

'What you just did was an act of disobedience which is enough to get you expelled. But as I'm in a good mood today and you've already shown that you're a bit dopey, I'm going to give you another chance. I'll tell you who to attack and only then will you act. Understood?'

Stefan nodded again. Tobias turned his back on him and set off walking once more. The rest of the neo-Nazis went on their way in silence now. Jan moved away from his guest and joined the tail of the group. No one wanted his company. Now it was Stefan who wished he could find a crack in the walls where he could disappear. The blood he had on his hands and clothes shamed him. The reprimand had been a gust that had scattered like dust his political indoctrination: the fatherland, the immigrants, the Jews and drug-addicts – what did he care about any of those? He just wanted to be a professional fighter and earn tons of money. Were these the guys who would take care of his mother when she was ill? Was that Jan really his friend? What was he doing there, in the end? He walked through the city center for a quarter of an hour and his legs felt leaden and his feet hurt. He wanted to leave and he actually considered running for it, but he was afraid of being caught. He had already grasped the fact that, owing to his previous haste, Tobias would give him a tougher test than he had planned; for sure he would have to fight one or more opponents who were strong and capable of hurting him too. So he decided to muster his strength again, transform his humiliation into hatred, and even if he had to beat up someone who had done him no harm, give the group of neo-Nazis and their leader a lesson. Then, when they bowed before his bravery, he would show his indifference; and when they finally let him go, he would never see them again.

Stefan raised his head once more, straightened his spine and gritted his teeth. He placed himself beside Tobias in an attitude of challenge and kept giving him sidelong glances. Jan understood, came closer and tried to pull him away by his arm – but Stefan pushed him away. If he had to, he would fight this guy who was a hand's width taller and weighed at least ten kilos more. Tobias, on the other hand, ignored the provocation and concentrated on finding a victim or executioner he could deliver to Stefan. They passed by a number of men, some of whom appeared to be from abroad, others who were effeminate, some drug addicts, and others who were burly, more than enough to set against Stefan, but Tobias let them go unmolested. He was looking for something else. Jan and the other neo-Nazis were just as puzzled as Stefan. They had themselves been subjected to the trial by fire in order to join the group and other men similar to the ones they met had served just fine for a beating. Would he be forced to fight with a policeman? None of them, however, dared question Tobias. More than once the leader had demonstrated that he did not tolerate questions, suggestions or doubts. The cancer of Democracy that was corroding the country, he had said once, would not grow in his group: blind obedience to the leader was the only way to keep the group united and capable of defeating its enemies. This brief speech, accompanied by a slap administered to a boy who had contradicted him, were sufficient to clear up any of the neo-Nazis' questions about the rules and moods of the leader.

By now they had reached a square in the city center. It was one of the places where a statue of Ionescu had been pulled down during *Perestroika*, and then the figure of the first king of Slavia had replaced him on the pedestal. Around the monument were flagstones, wooden benches and trees. There was a vandalized telephone box and a litter bin with no bottom. A few people were walking and a policeman leaned against a lamp and smoked. Tobias led the group to the doorways of the shops and blocks of flats. Jan was the first one to guess what was reserved for Stefan. He pulled a face and shook his head. At that moment he too wished he could get away and forget that night.

The mother and her two-year-old child were lying on a piece of cardboard box and had covered themselves with a plastic sheet.

They were wearing dirty, torn clothes, and were barefoot. An acrid stench rose from their bodies. They were Albanian immigrants forced to beg by a gang who confiscated the money they got. The Albanian mafia had released sixty women with their children in Tiersk, which brought in a daily income of a thousand dollars. The beggars worked all day from dawn until ten at night and received two dollars a day. If they tried to escape, rob their bosses, or even failed to meet the minimum targets, the mothers were punished with beatings, and the children with cigarette burns. The police did not harass these women because they constituted an extra source of income for each officer, who was free to extort whatever sum he thought right or demand sexual favors. As for Fiorov, he charged the Albanian mafia twenty per cent to allow them to operate in his country.

Tobias came closer to the woman and her child and stared at them for a while. She had her legs apart and her arms crossed. She was breathing deeply. Jan, Stefan and the other neo-Nazis kept several paces away from them, as if those two wretches were a threat. Suddenly, Tobias shoved the woman with his boot so that her forehead slammed into her son's face. The child woke up and started crying. The mother quickly pulled him to her chest and dragged him to the wall of the building. She crouched and protected him with her arms and knees. The terror in her black eyes was that of a cornered animal. She said a few words in Albanian which were drowned by the screaming of the infant.

Tobias turned towards Stefan. On his face there seemed to be a smile.

'The time has come to show what you're worth. Beat her up.'

Stefan clenched his fists and gritted his teeth but did not budge. Tobias insisted:

'It's an order! Beat her up!'

Stefan took two steps forward and looked at the woman. The mother managed to join her hands together in prayer and implored him not to hurt her son; her voice came out as a hoarse lowing. The child choked on his tears and was convulsed with violent coughing. Stefan was trembling and his tears fell. He turned slowly to Tobias and stared him in the eye.

'You fucking bastard.'

Tobias aimed a punch at his face, but Stefan sidestepped and at the same time elbowed him, catching his ear. Tobias was stunned, but Stefan had no time to continue beating him because three neo-Nazis hurled themselves on him and knocked him down. Stefan fell on his back on the stone floor. The other neo-Nazis kicked him and beat him with their truncheons. Stefan curled up like a hedgehog and only tried to protect his eyes. In a few seconds he had his facial bones, his teeth, his nose, an arm, and several ribs broken. His face was smashed into a bloody pulp and he could barely breathe. Jan watches the beating with a lump in his throat. The policeman leaning on the lamp-post lit another cigarette. The woman and her son had vanished.

At long last, Tobias shouted, 'Stop!'

STEFAN remained on the ground, unconscious. His body kept bleeding and getting colder. For nearly two hours nobody stopped to give him assistance. One man did stop and kneel down, but only to rob him. At last a prostitute who worked in the area played the Good Samaritan. Seeing that he could not stand, she felt sorry for him and went to a working telephone box to call an ambulance. The aid arrived half an hour later. The paramedics were drunk and argued about whether it was worth taking him to the hospital. The ambulance driver complained that he did not earn enough to be saving tramps. Only three hours after the beating was Stefan examined by a doctor. The latter suspected cerebral lesions and confided to a nurse that the patient could not survive. Stefan was in a coma for a month.

When he awoke the doctors told him that he was very lucky to have survived. He was paralyzed from the waist down, his face was deformed by the scars and broken jaws, he was deaf in one ear, and incontinent. From now on, his mother would have to take care of him.

During the time he was unconscious, Jan visited him twice – that was the only way he had the courage to ask for his forgiveness. He took his hand, knelt beside him, and begged for his pardon, but Stefan neither saw nor heard him. Months later, when Stefan returned home, Jan several times lurked around the street he lived in, approaching the entrance door, only to run away at once. He would never find the strength to face Stefan in a wheelchair. None of the books he had read had taught him how to expiate his guilt.

At the same time, Jan left the neo-Nazi group without giving them any explanation. He changed his way of dressing and let his hair grow. He knew that if they met him in the street they might beat him up and so he started avoiding the areas patrolled by his old comrades. One day, though, as he was leaving work, he came face to face with Tobias. The leader of the neo-Nazis was waiting for him on the other side of the street. Jan shuddered. It was dark and no one was about. All the same, although he knew he would not be capable of beating Tobias, he did not try to run or call his friend who was still inside the butcher's shop. He faced Tobias turning up as a well-deserved punishment that might, maybe, make him feel less guilty about what had happened. If Stefan could no longer beat him up, then someone else could take his turn and thrash him. This twisted logic calmed him. Slowly, he walked over to Tobias, ready to receive the punishment that would redeem him. Tobias had let his hair grow too, but still wore his usual black. Jan was nearly as tall as he was, but less broad-shouldered. Jan stopped a single step away from him, looked at him, and awaited the first blow. But nothing happened. Jan's surprise, more than from not being attacked, was caused by the unfamiliar expression on Tobias's face.

His blue eyes were not gleaming with hatred, his facial muscles were not tense, and his lips were searching for a smile. His tone of voice was soft.

'I heard that the boy hasn't got well,' Tobias said.

'He's ended up paralyzed,' said Jan.

Tobias raised his hand to his forehead. 'That wasn't what I wanted…'

Jan raised his voice. 'But it's what happened and now there's nothing to be done about it. We're both guilty.'

Tobias spoke more softly. 'No, I'm the only guilty one, and I'd like to help him.'

'Help him? And how would you like to help him?'

Tobias put his hand inside his leather jacket and took out an envelope. 'Take it. It's a thousand dollars. Give it to him, but don't tell him it was me who gave it to you, or he'll refuse it. Make up some story. You're the intellectual and you're good at that sort of thing.'

Jan took the envelope, speechless. Tobias slapped his arm and left at a quick pace. Jan watched his silhouette dissolving in the dark and heard his footsteps diminishing into silence.

The next day he asked for time off work and placed himself at Stefan's door to wait for his mother to come out. He was wearing his best clothes, had brushed his hair, and had put on aftershave. After three hours, the door opened and out came a tall, thin woman with grey hair. She was wearing jeans and a white shirt. Jan guessed that she was not much above forty. He went up to her and the woman looked at him with mistrust. Jan saw a lined face and hollow eyes that made her look older than he had thought, now.

'Ma'am,' he said, 'I'm a friend of your son's and I have something to give him.'

The woman took a step back. 'Who are you? If my son had any friends, they would have come to visit him. Get away from me right now or I'll call the police.'

Stefan held out the envelope to her. 'Please accept this contribution on behalf of his friends at the gym where he used to train. It's not a lot of money, but each of us gave what he could. If no one has come to visit yet, it's because we didn't want to disturb him. Tell him that, it's a gift from his boxing friends. Tell him we're expecting to see him again too.'

No sooner had the woman taken the envelope and started to open it, than Stefan made a kind of bow, and broke into a run.

Never again would he set foot in that street.

✠

Tobias

TOBIAS lived alone on the top floor of a ten storey building on the outskirts of the city. It was a flat of a hundred square meters with modern furniture, equipped with two televisions, a video apparatus, and a hi-fi system. There were no books, and no pictures on the walls, except for a poster of Maradona, in his bedroom. The fridge was full of food and beer. There was a closet which held two pistols, five knives, and a truncheon. There was a safe with ten thousand dollars. The front door was bulletproof. No neo-Nazi had ever been inside.

The Persian blinds of the apartment filtered the three o'clock sunlight. Tobias was lying on the sofa, drowsing. The bell rang twice, stopped, and rang twice more. It was the agreed signal. Tobias stood up, went to fetch the money from the safe, and a pistol from the closet. Then he put on his boots and a leather jacket and left home. When he reached the street he put on sunglasses and walked towards the black Mercedes parked in front of the building. Two men were in the car. He opened the door and got in the back seat without greeting them.

'Have you brought the money?' the driver asked.

'Do you think I'd be here if I hadn't brought the money?'

'Calm down, mate,' said the other man. 'Or you won't live to a ripe old age.'

The car set off and neither of the men spoke to Tobias again until they reached their destination. The driver switched on the radio and put on a Scorpions cassette at high volume. The other man sang along with the song 'I'm Still Loving You.' As Tobias had expected, presently the man who was singing turned around and handed him a blindfold.

'Put it on and lie down on the seat. If you raise your head, you'll be shot.'

Tobias followed the order and the man went back to singing. After a half hour drive, the car joined a minor road lined with trees and came to a walled house. From the street only the black roof could be seen. There were no other buildings in that area at the foot of a mountain. Two men in camouflage, carrying machine-guns, peeped from the top of the wall. A third man came to open the gate. The car went in and parked in the shade of a tree which had a shooting target stuck to it. There was a fresh smell of pines and wild plants. As on the previous occasions when Tobias had visited, the house was still unfinished, with bare brick walls, the garden full of weeds, and bags of cement in a corner.

'You can take off the blindfold,' said the man who had been singing.

Tobias went ahead with the usual procedure. He waited for one of the three men to open the door for him, got out, handed over his gun and allowed himself to be searched. With the confidence of an ex-Special Forces soldier, the man patted down his body and signaled to the others that the visitor was unarmed. Only then did they lower their machine-guns. Then the man who had been singing told Tobias to follow him. They walked through the weeds, climbed two cement steps, crossed a porch full of dry leaves, and he knocked on an iron door. The noise scared birds out of a nearby tree. Tobias turned his head, but he could no longer see them. Silence fell once more. The mountain embraced and hid the house.

The door opened.

Another bodyguard appeared, wearing a suit and tie, and with gel in his hair. Without uttering a word, he turned and started walking along a corridor. Tobias walked between the two men. Inside, the light was dim and the house was even more unfinished than on the outside. Bricks, cement, and steel bars were visible in the walls, and gravel on the floor. The smell of the building materials was strong. Tobias was led to a different room. Light came through the windows and there was another comfort: the floor was tiled, the walls were painted white, and there was a sofa with a table. On it was seated a man of middle age with grey hair and yellowish eyes, wearing a grey suit. He was smoking a cigar and drinking whisky. It was Pietr Huss, the old Chief Guard at the Akha concentration camp. Tobias greeted him and lowered his head.

'Have you brought the money?'

'Yes, Mr. Huss,' Tobias said, showing him the envelope.

The bodyguard took it from his hands, opened it, and started counting the money. He made a signal with his head to Huss.

'Good lad. It seems you have a knack for business.'

From a corner of the room the bodyguard went to fetch a case full of heroin, cocaine, and synthetic drugs, and put it beside Tobias' feet. The latter knew he should not inspect the contents, so that he did not offend the dealer. He had to trust, he had to accept that sometimes it might be a few grams short, he had to keep quiet to avoid problems. However, there was something in his face that was not consistent with his words.

'Thank you, Mr. Huss. I'm sure the goods are high quality.'

The dealer blew a puff of bluish smoke in Tobias' direction.

'Very good, lad, that's the right answer. Still, you're not sure at all, and you'd like to be able to bargain over the price of the merchandise. But you can't because you're an insignificant customer and we don't need you for anything. And if you died, no one would go to your funeral, would they? Do you know what you need to do? Work harder and earn a lot of money. You need to come in here with a hundred thousand dollars, and then we'll start treating you like a man. Get it?'

Tobias' face was red and his eyes were wide. But he knew that the conversation was over. Once again he dropped his head to show he had got the message, and picked up the case with the drugs. The bodyguard pointed the way out to him.

Pietr Huss took off his jacket and shoes. He was savoring the cigar and whisky, without haste. He knocked the ash on the floor and spun the ice cubes in his glass. The day had not gone badly for him. It was the third delivery of merchandise he had made and no one had caused any trouble. Although he had not made any huge deal, he had made a profit of forty thousand dollars. If he went on this way, he might be able to rise in the hierarchy. After all, he was one of the few who could say a few words in English. Within an hour, when he went to deliver the profits from the drug deals, he might just dare to put the question to his boss, Ivan Fiorov.

Helena, Hans and Guro

IT WAS three in the afternoon when the director of the orphanage was informed that there was a woman in the corridor who wanted to speak to her. Irina sighed. She was already getting ready to leave, to go to the gym, and here was some nuisance who wanted to annoy her. She decided that it would easier to get rid of her if she did not let her into her office. She stood up, smoothed down her skirt and jacket, touched her hair, and went to meet the visitor.

It was a tall, thin woman with white hair and grey eyes. She was wearing an old-fashioned black dress and boots that looked like a man's. Irina supposed she was an elderly woman whose pension was insufficient for feeding her. She probably wanted a job as a cook or cleaning woman, or perhaps some left-overs from the kitchen.

'Good afternoon, madam. My name is Irina and I am the director of this home. How may I help you?'

'Good afternoon. My name is Helena, and I'd like to consult some files.'

Irina wrinkled her brow. Yet another one who wanted to rummage through the papers of the orphanage? How the hell could that crap be of any interest to a normal person? She carefully assessed the woman in front of her and decided that this time she would not give in an inch to the caprices of a silly old woman. She had already had enough of the impertinence of the workers, who argued with her orders more and more.

'You'll have to excuse me, dear lady, but that request is against the internal rules...'

The woman took a step towards Irina. 'In the first place, don't call me "dear lady". I was responsible for this institution and for the whole system of child care in the last regime. I appointed and fired directors. I brought the previous president here. I know the rules and I'm quite certain that if it was possible to consult the files back then, it should be even easier now. So fulfil the duties of the post you occupy and take me to the archives room. I don't need your help or anyone else's to find what I'm looking for.'

Irina blanched. She had no idea whether the woman was telling the truth or was in fact crazy. She looked like a homeless woman, but the way she spoke was that of an educated person. It seemed risky to her to call the police, besides the fact that her boyfriend would not like to receive such news, and there might be a scandal in the event that the woman was telling the truth. Irina decided not to run the risk. After all, if the other woman had consulted the files and nothing had happened, then this one might do the same. This time, however, she would apply a rule that was indeed in the regulations.

'Well, if you insist, come with me. But you'll have to leave your ID in the office.'

As soon as the rule was observed, Irina took her to the archives room, opened the door, turned on the light, made a hand gesture indicating that she could begin her search, and left her alone.

Helena Yava looked around to assess what awaited her and put on a pair of glasses she was carrying in her pocket. Then she murmured to herself, 'Ruth, we'll finish him off.'

Only after half an hour of fumbling through papers, at times climbing the ladder, at times kneeling down, wiping cobwebs from her hair and sneezing because of the dust, did Helena begin to find her way around the archives. If it was in 1978 that Ruth accused

Zdanhov of molesting children of eight and nine years of age, then her search into the records of admittance to the orphanage would have to take in the years 1969 and 1970. On top of a cabinet Helena found two tattered files titled *Records* with the respective dates written in pencil. When she opened them, she found dozens of loose leaves that, yet again, contained information as varied as invoices for work done, memoranda, personal notes, minutes of meetings, and just a dozen or so records of admittance of children to the orphanage. She took a piece of a paper and a fountain pen and began to copy down the names of those children. Half an hour later she left the orphanage.

An hour after that, Helena went into a police station. It was an old building, with cracks in the walls and worm-eaten furniture. Under the old regime, political dissidents had been beaten in its cells. Under the present one, it was vandals, alcoholics and drug addicts who suffered the violence. Helena went up to the desk and asked to speak to Hans Ross. By now he was a man of thirty who had recently been promoted to inspector. When he saw Helena seated on a bench, he barely recognized her. Her white hair, wrinkled face, and withered body made her look a very different woman from the vigorous People's Commissar for Education who had long ago helped his mother. She herself, Mariana, was better preserved than Helena. Hans guessed that she had come to call to account some old debt. But it would probably be something easy to deal with, some problem common to all old women like neighborhood burglars or a missing cat. He smiled and went up to her.

'Doctor Helena Yava, how are you getting along?'

He remembers me, which is a good sign.

'Fine, thanks. How's your mother?'

'She's well too, thanks. How can I help you? Have you been mugged?'

'No, I've come here for a different reason...'

'Yes...'

'I've come to ask you for a favor.'

'If it's in my power…'

Helena handed him the list of children she had copied in the orphanage archives.

'I'd like you to help me find these people.'

Hans looked at it, intrigued. Besides being illegal, this was the kind of request made at times by people nothing like this lady to police officers, in exchange for bribes. And the result of such information was usually the appearance of corpses floating in the river, or dropped in the rubbish. On the other hand, he could not refuse her.

'Dr. Helena, if these people are alive, I'll find them. Let me have your contact information. Within a week I'll give you some news.'

Helena's eyes shone. 'I'm very grateful to you, Hans.'

On the way home, sitting on the seat of a bus full of smelly, noisy people, Helena thought that the values and ethics of the New Man she had tried to create had persisted in Hans. The ideology had not survived the changes of *Perestroika*, but the moral education she had wanted to inculcate in the youth of Slavia were still present in that man. *He could easily have said that he didn't remember me or that he didn't recall me interceding on behalf of his mother. He could have turned his back on me or sent some junior to throw me out without the least regret. A man who deals with violence, corruption and injustice every day only manages to stand it if he's hard-hearted. Sentimentality is taboo to a policeman. But Hans was able to show that he was grateful and he seemed genuinely moved to see me. After all, not everything is lost. My legacy shines in him and will be transmitted to his children.*

Helena shut her eyes and smiled. For many years she had not felt proud of herself.

After the fall of the regime, Helena had had to leave her flat, and was living now on the outskirts of the city in a modest home. The pension the new government had awarded her forced her to move to an old house without heating, which leaked when it rained. Most of her neighbors did not recognize her and those who did remember her former post did not bother her. Just one man, whose son had died in a concentration camp, always spat when he crossed her path.

Three days later, Helena was peeling potatoes for the soup that would do her for lunch and dinner when she heard the telephone ringing. She put down the knife and ran as fast as she could. When she picked up the receiver she heard the voice she was hoping for.

'Dr. Helena?'

'Hans?'

'Yes, I've got the information you wanted. I'll be expecting you at the station.'

'Thanks, I'll be there within an hour.'

Helena took off her apron, put on her old boots and a jacket, and left home.

When she arrived at the station and asked for Hans Ross, this time an officer led her to a room on the upper floor. The officer knocked on the door and opened it. Hans got up from his table and went to greet her. After doing so, he asked her to sit down and handed her a sheet of paper. 'Here's the information you asked me for.'

Helena's heart beat wildly, her eyes kept blinking, and her lips trembled. She blurted:

'Good work, comrade, I'm going to nominate you for a medal...'

At once she realized what she was saying and clammed up. Hans was more embarrassed than she was. Then Helena shook her head and started laughing.

'I'm sorry, I really am a silly old woman.'

'Don't worry about it...'

'Sometimes I wake up in the middle of the night and think I'm still the People's Commissar for Education. I switch on the light and start taking notes for some reform or other. I talk to myself. Then I recover my lucidity, feel ashamed of my pathetic appearance, and go back to bed with my feet frozen. Well, that's enough of idiocy. Let me see what you've brought me.'

Helena put on her glasses and started reading.

Mario Stanz died two years ago in a barroom brawl. Sandor Bronsky died two years ago when he was run over. Laszlo Volta died four years ago of an unknown disease. Vladimir Otto died five years ago of an overdose. Elias Roth died by suicide eight years ago. Daniel Sax is serving a prison sentence for drug dealing. Dario Avo is serving a prison sentence for pimping. Hector Dim emigrated to England a month ago. Petr Skoff emigrated to Holland two months ago. Guro Nuria lives in Freedom District, number 3, second floor on the right, and works as a travelling salesman. Tobias Munt lives in Red District, number 23, flat 14, and has no known occupation, but is suspected of dealing drugs.

Helena scratched her head and breathed deeply. This was not the information she had been hoping for. Apparently, of that group of twelve men she could count on no more than two.

Hans's face was no less somber than Helena's. He sat down as if he had just put a gun in the hands of a child.

'Dr. Helena, it's none of my business what you intend to do with this information. As your friend and as a police officer it's my duty to warn you that these men are outlaws, including the travelling salesman, and they could take advantage of you, even the ones who are in prison, if you go and visit them. I also found out that they were orphans or rejected by their mothers and were brought up in the boys' orphanage in the city. I'm not surprised that they've had violent deaths, committed suicide, or been sent to prison. Allow me to give you the following advice: don't try to communicate with them, even if you want to help them in some way, because it will only bring you trouble and suffering. You're not to blame. The ones to blame for the fate of these men have been tried. No one can do any more for them now.'

Helena smiled as if she had just been warned not to play with matches. Her eyes regarded Hans with tenderness. She took his right hand.

'You have a good heart. But don't forget that during my life I worked with people far more dangerous than these wretches. True murderers, whom I socialized with, and in a way, I helped them…'

'Don't say that, Dr. Helena, you're nothing like those people.'

'Hans, I was one of those people. I served a criminal regime. I escaped the trials, it's true, but my conscience is the most severe judge there is. I am guilty too. However, despite having done a lot of bad things, I have the opportunity to do some good now. Justice. As you know, the justice of the courts is imperfect, and that of God doesn't exist. I can't say any more, but I'm sure that if you only knew, you would be on my side.'

Hans' eyes dilated. 'Dr. Helena, I'm worried about your safety. Think carefully about what you mean to do. I may not be able to protect you. As you know, things have changed…'

Helena stood up and caressed his cheek. 'I can take care of myself. Thank you for everything, and give my love to your mother.'

On the way home, Helena reviewed the information she had got, and tried to decide which man she would contact first. Guro or Tobias? Hans described both as dangerous outlaws, but he had not given her any information about their personalities, their physical abilities or their habits. What could she do with a man without courage, with some physical handicap, or drug addiction? She needed someone who had received the highest acclaim in the Pioneers' physical tests. She needed a man with the hearing of a hare, the eyes of a lynx, the cunning of a fox and the teeth of a wolf. She needed a strong, intelligent man who had made his mark in the streets. Above all, she needed hatred. Ignorant as she was of the qualities and faults of the two survivors of the orphanage, Helena decided to approach the one who lived closest to her: Guro Nuria. Nevertheless, she knew that digging up a past of sexual abuse was as risky as fiddling with the wires of a time-bomb. The hate might explode in her face.

The next day, in the overcast morning, she left home and took a bus to an area near Freedom District. It was an apartment complex in the city suburbs built by Ionescu twenty years earlier, on which political prisoners had worked as slaves. Inspired by

Soviet architecture, at the time it was seen as a model of modernity in the service of the people. Now, though, it was nothing more than a desolate grey area. The pavements had holes, the streetlights were broken, there were rubbish bags everywhere and rats around them; the walls of the buildings were cracked, the blinds broken, and there was washing drying on the balconies. Since the fall of the regime, the police had ceased to patrol the area, and when they made a search they came with the support of armored cars. The gangs were in control. Drug deals took place everywhere, at night there were frequent gunfights, and there was a kind of popular justice for thieves and rapists. Two days earlier, a boy who had robbed a grocery was punished by one of the gangs, who broke two fingers on his right hand.

When any strangers came into the quarter, they were quickly detected by the younger gang members, and faced with armed groups who appeared suddenly, the intruders had to justify their presence here. If there was any suspicion of them being police informers they were attacked, and might be knee-capped. But that day no one seemed to care that an elderly, ill-dressed woman was wandering about the quarter. Helena did not fit the definition of a suspicious person. Probably they took her for a homeless person who was rifling through the rubbish for things she might be able to take home. Helena knew this was her natural disguise and tried to make herself look still more wretched, limping, twisting her head to one side, and simulating a crazed expression. As an excuse for wanting to know Guro's address, she would say, drawling and with a half-witted smile, that a cousin needed help. It all came out so naturally when she started to question people that she herself was amazed by her ability to play the dopey old woman. *Maybe you really are losing your mind.* Even so, only at the fourth attempt did she find anyone willing to give her the information she was seeking.

It was a woman of thirty, short and fat, wearing a yellow tracksuit, and leading a dirty child by the hand. Like the residents she had spoken to before, she looked mistrustfully at the old woman who addressed strangers in the middle of the street. Helena's sincere smile at the five year old daughter disarmed her. She paused, willing to give her a few seconds' attention.

'What do you want?'

'Good morning. I'm Guro Nuria's cousin. Do you know where I can find him?'

The woman looked stunned. 'Guro? You want to know where Guro is?'

'Yes.'

'Well, Guro must be at the market, selling his stuff. You know where the market is? No, of course you don't. It's in the park.' The woman pointed towards the end of the street. 'Go that way and at the end turn left, then right. It's a ten minute walk, or maybe twenty minutes for you. In the park they buy and sell anything you can imagine. Guro's bound to be there, but don't buy him anything. Watch out, you can't trust him.'

Helena thanked her, stroked the dirty face of the girl and set off. She was so excited at being about to meet one of Zdanhov's victims that she forgot to limp and pretend she was backward. She took long strides, with her head erect and a penetrating gaze. Once again she had the self-assurance and pride of a People's Commissar leaving her office to visit a school or Pioneers' camp.

She soon reached the park. It was a space with trees that used to have lawns and a fish pond. Now, on the beaten earth or inside the dry pond, dozens of hawkers squeezed together, with stalls, or displaying their products on the ground. Hundreds of people wandered about, looking at the merchandise. Flies buzzed. Stray dogs sniffed at food. The traders hawked their wares, people haggled over prices, and animals whimpered when kicked. The noise was deafening. The market smelled of fried food, grilled meat, bread, sweets, fruit, leather products, petrol, and chemicals. Mixed together, it all made a nauseating stench. For a few minutes Helena stopped to observe the market. She herself had bought and sold food and other things in street markets, but she had never been in such a chaotic place as this. There was not a single policeman, or inspector, no one in authority – the dread of the law of the gangs was enough to keep order. For the first time since she had come into the quarter, she did not know how to proceed.

The dark clouds in the sky were motionless.

A boy with a shaven head and tattoos on his arms came up to her and offered her pills to 'put her to sleep and take away aches and pains.' Helena moved away and was swept along by the crowd. For a while she wandered aimlessly. At length she decided to ask the traders about Guro. However, when they realized she did not want to buy anything, they turned their backs on her or insulted her; others pushed her or told her to get lost. Helena realized questions had a price. She approached a man with a white beard who was selling cheese, sausages and vodka, bought a spicy sausage from him, and only then questioned him. The man did not seem surprised. He looked around, pointed, and told her that Guro was near the lake, giving her a description of him. Helena struggled in the middle of the crowd, getting pushed, and having her toes trodden on, and took several minutes to get near the lake. There she found a number of traders: four were women and two were men. The sketch of Guro she had heard left her in no doubts about his identity: short and stocky, with curly black hair, brown eyes, a bent nose and a scar from his ear to his chin. He was missing a finger on his right hand. He was wearing jeans and a lilac hoodie.

Helena felt repugnance for the man. She tried to imagine him as a child, lost in the orphanage, but she could not picture him as a cute boy either. Ruth had told her that Zdanhov always chose the most beautiful children. But how could she guess what fetishes that pervert had? Whether or not he had been one of Zdanhov's victims, Guro knew what the former commissar had done to his fellow orphans, and he could be the instrument of her vengeance.

Helena moved towards him.

Guro had spread a cloth on the ground, on which he displayed second-hand goods: radios, sunglasses, bifocal spectacles, belts, shoes, clothes, hats, brushes, knives, and a vacuum cleaner of Russian manufacture. His voice was hoarse, and yet he could hardly make himself heard in the midst of all the yelling. Nor did the quality of his goods persuade people to inquire about the price. That morning he still had not sold a thing. Guro did not give up, though. He picked up some clothes and practically rubbed them in the faces of whoever was passing by. In the corners of his mouth a foamy spittle was forming.

Helena decided not to approach him there, but rather to stay and watch him until the market ended. Maybe on the way back to the quarter, if he went alone, she could talk to him. Or perhaps it might be better to start by buying a piece of the junk he was selling to gain his confidence. The first part of the plan struck her as even harder and riskier than she had supposed. The only thing she was sure about was that the man's reaction would not be pleasant. After all, what would she do herself if a stranger came and invaded her privacy? She had come ready to be insulted and attacked, but now she started to fear for her life.

Then it struck her that, in her longing to have revenge on Zdanhov, she was using his victims, disdaining their feelings. In a way, she was violating them again. Having convinced herself that they would want to join her in her settling of scores was just a projection of her wishes. *And what if what they want above all is to forget the abuse? What right do I have to reopen their wounds?* Helena no longer heard the racket of the market. In her conscience a battle was raging: her guilt was in revolt and was about to annihilate the plan for vengeance. Helena tried to avail herself of all her weapons at her disposal to silence it. However, the guilt kept fighting. Ethics did not tolerate dirty games. *A decent person does not take advantage of the suffering of another for his own benefit. That's disgusting.* Helena started sweating, and her hands trembled. It was then, facing imminent defeat, that her instinct acted. Why did she have to be a crusader for decency in a corrupt, immoral country? Why did she have to give up the only thing that had given her life meaning? Why did she have to want to redeem the world? After all, who could assure her that Zdanhov's victims really did not want revenge? She would just make a choice possible for them, and the decision would be theirs. If she denied them that option, then certainly she would be treating them like children incapable of making a choice. Justice had a price.

Helena no longer sweated nor trembled. Now she looked upon Guro as an ally.

Meanwhile she saw Guro take a little bottle out of his jacket and take a few swigs. Then he opened his mouth as if it had burned his throat and belched. Helena frowned, but did her best to dismiss the fact – in her country all men drank, and nothing proved that he was an alcoholic. She was thinking this when a couple turned up with a television and put it down next to Guro's goods. Both the man and the woman had coarse features, and wore grey tracksuits. Guro tried to pretend he had not seen them by hawking his wares in a louder voice. The woman grabbed him by the cuff and shook him.

'Conman, you sold us a TV that doesn't work.'

'We opened it and there's only stones inside,' said the man.

Guro pulled an expression of surprise and freed himself from the woman's grasp.

'That's a lie, when I sold you the apparatus it was in good condition. I've got the factory guarantee here,' he said, taking a piece of paper from his pocket.

The woman snatched the paper and tore it up. 'Think you can trick us again? We want our money back.'

'Yes, give us back the twenty dollars we paid you,' said her husband.

'Get lost, you're driving my customers away,' said Guro, pushing them.

The man pushed him back and Guro grabbed him by the throat. The woman came to her husband's aid and threw herself at Guro's legs. The three of them fell on the sheet and rolled on top of the merchandise, breaking glasses and radios. A crowd formed around them, laughing and egging on the combatants. Although he was facing two opponents, Guro did not admit defeat. The three bodies became so entangled that it was hard to tell who was fighting whom. Guro and the man were lying side by side and the woman seized Guro's legs, in a kneeling position, her backside in the air; Guro and the woman were lying on top of the man; Guro had the man and the woman on top of him; Guro and the man turned a somersault, forcing the woman to twist around and bang her back against the Russian vacuum cleaner. At last Guro managed to get free of the woman by giving her a kick in the chest, and climbed on top of the man, punching him in the face. The man kept taking the punches until his wife stood up, grabbed the broken television, and smashed it down on Guro's head. The crash was tremendous. Guro was knocked out and the fight ended. The couple opened a pocket in his jacket, took out twenty dollars, and showed them to everyone to prove they were only making amends for the fraud, and then left.

Helena watched, stupefied. She saw Guro lying beside what was left of his wares, with blood on the nape of his neck and his mouth open, and hesitated over whether to help him. Among the crowd no one seemed concerned about the state he was in. Opinions were divided: some thought it cowardly for two to fight against one, others thought Guro had got what he deserved, while others still were sorry the fight had been so short. From among the crowd a mongrel with grey fur appeared and began to lick his face. Helena felt pity: Guro no longer seemed repellent to her, but a poor abandoned child. She took advantage of the thinning of the crowd to kneel beside him and caress his face. Guro started to come around. Helena helped him up, took him to a water fountain and washed the wound on his head. Whether because he was stunned, or because no one had ever helped him before, Guro could not even manage to thank her. All he was capable of was a sad smile. Helena understood that she should not speak either; any word would break the brief spell that had been cast over both. Then she looked at him for the last time and hugged him as she had never hugged anyone, not even Ruth, nor any child; pity, remorse and tenderness were all mixed up in the long embrace that suffocated him until Helena's arms wilted. Guro had never felt so embarrassed. He could only think of one way to escape the situation.

'Don't you want to buy anything? I'll give you a special discount, just for friends.'

Helena smiled at him, turned around, and went away.

❧

Helena, Tobias and Jan

WITH Guro out of the running, Helena focused on approaching Tobias. Her most solid knowledge, as well as her toughest manners, had been acquired in the old regime. So she tried to remember something she could do to take advantage of the situation. During the period of the dictatorship, using various threats, the secret services had recruited pretty women to seduce foreign diplomats and businessmen. Many secrets had been obtained that way, and even a few desertions. However, she was no longer attractive, and nor did she have money to offer Tobias. On the other hand, she recalled that there had also been English and American intellectuals who leaked information to the Soviet Union for ideological reasons. A deep conviction had led them to betray their countries, or, put another way, a blind hatred of the capitalist system. Hatred was perhaps the strongest force that could motivate a human being, leading him to risk his own life. However many times she went over it in her mind, she could only count on the hatred of Zdanhov's victim to persuade him to kill the old commissar. On the other hand, assuming she did not find another poor devil like Guro, assuming she found the strong, violent men that Hans had described, it would not be wise to approach him tentatively but then suddenly let the mask fall and reveal her true intentions. With brutalized men, who were unused to the subtlety of diplomacy or the rules of etiquette, such tactics might be dangerous. People like that appreciated frankness, however harsh. If Tobias were the right man, she would at once dig her claws into his childhood wounds. And then, with a howl of rage, provided she did not become the victim, Zdanhov would be dead.

The day had dawned with white clouds which the sun broke through now and then. The temperature was rising. Helena took a shower and left home, heading for the Red District. This time she would not limp, nor pretend she was a daft old woman. She still wore the same old clothes and the same broken boots, for lack of any better, and her hair was badly brushed and her face without makeup, but she would be herself. When she got on the bus she could not find a seat. There were two tall, strong boys on a seat near her, but they did not so much as glance at her. They spoke loudly and used obscenities. But Helena did not blame them for their lack of courtesy towards an older person, or their coarseness. In fact their aggressiveness and selfishness interested her. Such characteristics, which up till now she had considered one of the main faults of young people, typical of personalities who had been badly brought up, now struck her as the most powerful weapons for survival. How could the children from the orphanage have survived otherwise? Would kind feelings have been any use to them?

Meanwhile the bus stopped and the two boys got up and pushed through the people until they reached the exit. One man protested and they insulted him. The other passengers looked away and the driver kept quiet. Helena went to sit in one of their places, and watched them through the window as they got more distant. The bus pulled away in a cloud of black smoke. Helena shut her eyes. She only hoped that Tobias was not the kind of man who would offer his seat to a lady on public transportation.

The Red District was very similar to the area where Guro lived. The same urban planning, the same state of decay and neglect, the absence of police officers and the proliferation of gangs. However, in the sun the worn out materials and the rubbish spread everywhere were even more apparent. The people Helena met in the street were equally hostile or indifferent when she spoke to them. When they did not avert their heads, it was to say they did not know who Tobias was. So Helena went to the address Hans had given her, and rang the doorbell.

Wearing pajamas and slippers, Tobias had turned on the television and put a recording of one of Mike Tyson's best fights in the video player. Next, he sat at the table to do his work: putting single doses of heroin, cocaine and synthetic drugs in little bags, which he would later resell to smaller dealers who would sell them on the streets. Apart from going and coming from the place where Koba's man supplied him with the material, Tobias never risked selling drugs outside his flat. The small dealers who came to buy them always ended up in jail or dead, only to be replaced by others, but so far, the police had never bothered Tobias. Apart from never opening the door to anyone who did not know the code of agreed rings, Tobias also enjoyed the protection of being Koba's client. Even so, he lived in a state of permanent anxiety about being arrested or found out by his neo-Nazi friends. More than once, he had barely managed to prevent them from beating up one of his dealers.

When the bell rang, Tobias jumped and five grams of heroin were scattered over the table. No one had ever rung at that time in the morning, and whoever it was, it was neither a customer nor a supplier. Tobias did not move; he focused his emotions and tensed his muscles as if he were about to face Tyson. The white dust glinted on the brown table. After ten seconds the bell rang again. Tobias stood up and went to fetch his revolver. He looked at the drugs and got ready to flush those thousands of dollars down the toilet, if they tried to break down the door. The bell rang again, longer and more annoyingly. With his hands shaking, Tobias put all the drugs in a rubbish bag and took it to the bathroom – at the first sign of them trying to force their way in, he would throw it all down the drain. He was sweating and his heart beat wildly. He had often practiced for this, but never thought he would really have to do it. He was waiting for the first thump on the door. Time seemed to stand still. Now Tobias only wanted it to be over. The agony endured, with no more ringing of the bell, or any attempt at breaking down the door.

Finally, Tobias decided to start Time up again: revolver in hand, he ran to the door and peeped through the spyhole. The corridor was empty. No steps were heard on the stairs. The bell had been silent for several minutes. Tobias remained tense. The silence was a soap bubble which might burst at any moment. He went to a window to look out, even though he knew he could not see anyone ringing at the entrance to the building. He returned to the door and pressed his ear against the wood. Apparently the soap bubble would last. Tobias breathed deeply. He went to the sofa and let himself drop on to it, one slipper falling off his foot. For a while he was in a stupor, unable to resume his work. On the television, Mike Tyson raised his arms in triumph after defeating Frank Bruno.

Meanwhile, Helena decided to stay in the quarter and began to look for a place where she might rest, eat, and maybe find out more about Tobias. As at the market where she had found Guro, here too the hawkers might be willing to talk to their customers. A banknote could loosen their tongues.

After some wandering, she found a bar. At the entrance there was a yellow awning with the logo of a brand of beer, and the door was hung with strips of various colors. A group of lads with a Pitbull were talking outside. They were wearing jeans, trainers, and imitation leather jackets. When Helena came closer, one of them called her an old wino and the others started laughing. The dog growled. Helena checked that the animal was tied up, passed without looking at them, and went into the bar. It was a dark room with five tables and a counter. On the walls were posters of nude women. On the ceiling was a machine for electrocuting flies. The floor was wet and her shoes stuck to it. A bitter smell clung in the air.

From out of the shadows a man appeared, dressed in white and holding a scrubbing-brush. He was short, with grey hair and a reddish face. His hands had prominent veins and black fingernails. He did not seem happy to see Helena.

'What do you want?'

'I'd like to eat, if possible.'

'Eat? This is a bar, not a restaurant, but maybe we can find something. Maria,' he shouted in the direction of the kitchen. 'Fry an egg.'

Helena took the chance to sit down. 'To drink, I'd like a Coca-Cola.'

The man twisted his nose. 'We only serve men's drinks here.'

'In that case, a beer.'

'Ah.'

The man turned and went back inside the bar. She heard orders given to the cook, drawers opening, and bins being dragged. Helena was alone for several minutes. She was not sure she had chosen the best place to get information on Tobias. The blue flash of a fly being electrocuted lit up the darkness.

Ten minutes later, the man came back with a scrambled egg and a bottle of stout. His face looked friendlier. 'Here you are. Hope you enjoy it.'

'Thank you.'

Helena ate her egg beneath the attentive gaze of the owner of the bar, who seemed to be expecting compliments. The egg was salty, but she said nothing. When she finished, she took out a banknote and placed it on the table.

'May I have another egg?'

The eyes of the owner of the bar widened, and his face opened up in a smile. He got up and went quickly back into the kitchen. Helena heard voices and noises again. In a few minutes the man, with a black apron and a blue cloth over his arm, returned with a steak and chips. Helena looked at the plate and saw a slice of dark meat and half a dozen greenish chips. Nor was the smell of the food very pleasant. She cut a piece of steak, put it in her mouth, and seemed to be chewing the sole of a shoe.

'Very good.'

'Ah.'

The café owner smiled, proud that his professional competence was recognized. He began to see Helena as a good customer, and she did not even have to ask him questions.

'I see you're not from around here…'

'Yes, I live in another district. I've come to look for a nephew I haven't seen since he was a child…'

'Ah.'

'His name's Tobias Munt. Do you know him?'

Once again the bar owner's face was somber. He sat beside Helena and cleared his throat. 'And you're Tobias's aunt?'

'Yes.'

'And you don't know anything about him?'

'I haven't seen him for fifteen years. I doubt that I'd recognize him.'

'Right, right…'

'I rang his doorbell, but no one answered. If I wanted to meet him in the street, could you tell me what he's like now?'

The bar owner scratched an ear. 'You won't tell him you spoke to me, will you?'

'Oh, of course not.'

'Well, he always wears black, his head is shaven, he has blue eyes, and he's tall and well-built, so it's not hard to recognize him.'

'Thanks.' Helena handed him the banknote and stood up.

The owner of the bar put his hand on her arm. 'You know, he's not a bad person. My wife helped him when he arrived her and now he protects us. The robberies and disturbances stopped at once. We shouldn't judge anyone. It was bad company, it was all these quick political changes, it was the devil, how should I know? He's not a bad person.'

Helena felt his hand trembling and saw sweat running down his face. 'Don't worry. He'll never know I spoke to you. I know better than anyone that he's not a bad person.'

The owner of the bar accompanied her to the exit, parted the colored ribbons for her to go out, took his leave of her with a nod and then stared at the group of lads. The message was clear. The boys were speaking in loud voices and they fell silent. The dog growled again, but none of them dared insult her this time.

Helena took a few more turns around the quarter. The rising

wind shook her and made her walk ever more slowly. Dust stuck to her sweaty face. Her body could hardly bear the effort. She had blisters on her feet and her legs ached. Her mouth was dry and her head felt as if it were bursting. Worn out, she went to sit on a bench near Tobias's building to wait for him. Her physical fatigue weakened the strength of her ideas. She began to doubt her plan and wondered if she were not really a silly old woman; then she asked herself again whether Ruth would have approved of her vengefulness, and whether the love she, Helena, had felt for her, had been replaced by this hatred for Zdanhov she was feeding. Once more her instincts erased the uncomfortable questions, and she convinced herself that she was only seeking justice. *Justice for Ruth, justice for the children, justice and nothing else.*

Two hours later, when she gad almost given up hope, was when Tobias left his building. He was on his way to the city center to meet the neo-Nazis for another nocturnal hunt. At first Helena was puzzled because she expected to see him entering rather than leaving. But she soon realized that the corpulent man dressed in black could only be him. She mustered whatever strength she still had, got up, and taking faltering steps, followed him.

'Tobias, I'd like to speak to you.'

Tobias kept walking without taking any notice of her.

'We have an enemy in common, Zut Zdanhov.'

The name struck Tobias like a wasp sting. His eyes goggled and his lips twisted. He stopped and turned round. He grabbed Helena by her jacket, lifted her into the air and shook her. 'You crazy old woman, get lost or I'll smash you to pieces. I won't warn you again.'

Tobias dropped her and Helena fell on her back. The pain was intense but she got up and followed him again. 'Ruth Meyer, the director of the orphanage. Do you remember her?'

Tobias stopped again. Ruth's name worked like a balsam that assuaged his fury. He turned towards Helena and stared at her, trying to recognize in her aged face the young features of one of the former auxiliary workers at the orphanage. However, he was unable to reconcile those facial characteristics with anyone he could recall.

'Who are you?'

'I'm Helena Yava. I was the People's Commissar for Education under the old regime. It was I who appointed Ruth to direct the orphanage. I loved her and Zdanhov killed her.'

Tobias stroked his shaven head as he began to return to the past. 'And what do you want from me?'

Helena took a deep breath. 'Ruth told me that Zdanhov abused the children from the orphanage.'

Tobias was pale and kept blinking. For a few seconds he was silent. Images from his childhood spun in his mind: the first time he saw Zdanhov at the orphanage, his smile, the way he had held his hand and led him to his car, the trip when he had given him chocolates, entering the enormous house, Zdanhov caressing his head, telling him they were going to play a game, starting to undress him, and his own attempt to resist him and Zdanhov's first slap, and falling to the floor with Zdanhov on top of him and then the yells, the yells which still terrified him and made him awaken from nightmares which repeated without end. Tobias had a knot in his throat and spoke in a distorted voice: 'It was years and years ago… I don't remember…'

Helena weighed her words carefully. 'Ruth told me there were a number of victims and she spoke with them.'

Tobias shook like a scared child. He had not yet come back from the trip in the time machine. 'He never tried anything with me… if he had, I'd kill him…'

Helena paused while Tobias pulled himself together. Then she risked everything.

'I want to kill him and I need your help. Help me avenge Ruth, who was your friend, and the children he raped.'

The idea of revenge ejected Tobias from the past: the helpless orphan became a brutal man again. He returned with such rage that he had an urge to bite his own flesh. His jaws flexed and his eyes looked like glass. All his muscles tensed. Tobias twisted his neck with a nervous tic. 'Let's talk somewhere else. Come with me.'

Before long, Helena was inside Tobias' flat. She was surprised by these rooms belonging to someone she had supposed to be poor. There was no luxury or ostentation, but the size of the size of the place and the quality of the furniture were beyond the reach of most of the population. Tobias invited her to sit down on a brown leather sofa and told her he was going to get something to eat. Helena answered that she was not hungry, but he was already on his way to the kitchen. He soon appeared with a plate of smoked salmon tempered with lemon, and a glass of white wine. Helena looked with astonishment at the salmon: since her time as a People's Commissar she had tasted nothing like it. Shyly, she cut a piece and put it in her mouth. She shut her eyes and licked her lips. Then, without holding back, she ate and drank with delight, almost forgetting what she had come here for. Tobias sat on the other sofa and watched her. His expression of rage softened. He waited for Helena to finish eating before he spoke to her.

'I want to help you finish that animal off, but it won't be easy. He's protected by a very powerful guy named Ivan Fiorov. He must have paid him a lot of money because he never leaves home without calling a bodyguard. It won't be easy for us to get near him, and for business reasons, I can't sort out the problem with Fiorov.'

Helena's eyes shone. 'I've got a different plan. Let's lure him into a trap.'

Tobias scratched his chin. 'Trap?'

'Yes, let's give him what he likes: children.'

Tobias frowned; he was starting to doubt Helena's sanity. 'Are you serious? I don't like that plan.'

'Wait, let me explain. He's not going to touch the children. They're just bait for him to open the door.'

'Go on.'

'First of all, we have to awaken his lust by offering him children.'

'And how are we going to do that? Are you thinking of going to an orphanage and asking to borrow their children?'

'No, the streets are full of children exploited by foreign gangs.

They're orphans. The women who go about with them are not their mothers. If we pay them, it won't be hard to get them to rent for a few hours.'

Tobias looked at her, perplexed, but he was beginning to realize that the woman was determined to eliminate Zdanhov and would do so with or without his aid.

'What then?'

'He usually walks in the park in the city center and sits on one of the benches to enjoy the sun. It's the perfect place. Just then, someone will show him the children and make him an offer. A high price, so as not to arouse suspicion. He won't be able to resist. His perversion will be stronger than his fears.'

'Maybe…'

'Then there will be some bargaining about the price of the children and the place where he can rape them. He'll probably want to take them home, since old habits die hard. And then, when he opens the door, it'll be the time to attack him. You could play this role from the start because he's not going to be able to recognize you. And the bodyguard won't be there because Zdanhov has no interest in revealing his secrets.'

Tobias stood and paced about the room. 'It's a risky plan. A lot could go wrong. For instance, he might not even be interested in the kids.'

'That's true, that could happen. But with the resources at our disposal, it's the only way we can catch him. I've been thinking about this for years and I don't see another way. Are you willing to try it?'

Tobias went to the window. He took deep breaths while he gazed into the distance.

'All right. I, or someone I trust, can tempt Zdanhov with the children, but it would be better if you bargain with the beggars who go about with the kids in the streets. I'm no good at that sort of thing.'

The next day Helena started looking for beggars with children. She found them sitting on the ground with barefoot children, holding bowls for alms. Their dirty, famished, sad faces and their ragged, smelly clothes made her feel pity and revulsion at the same time. She banished both feelings. As she spoke a little Albanian and Romanian she managed to gain a certain amount of trust with the women. She found out that the children were the property of other people, and these women were guards, in a way, like the girls who take the village headman's sheep out to graze. Although she offered them the same amount for two hours as they would get for a full day's work, the women were afraid of disobeying their bosses. One of them showed her scars from beatings and cigarette burns on the arm of a child. Helena trembled. She was almost on the point of leaving and giving up her merciless plan.

In the middle of the afternoon, on the edge of a bench, she found a middle-aged woman with a child of six. The woman had sooty skin, and wore a headscarf and a black skirt and blouse; the boy was dark with grey eyes and wore brown trousers and a black jacket with worn-out elbows. The woman's face was an inexpressive mask with a wart on the chin. The child wore a sad smile and his nose ran. Helena realized this beggar was more experienced than the others, a veteran of mendacity who knew all the tricks of the trade. She approached her the same way, giving a coin to the boy and asking where they came from and if they needed anything, but the woman did not look as though she felt like chatting. The boy continued begging like a programmed machine.

Helena went straight to the heart of the matter. She took out a twenty-dollar bill and showed it to the woman. Her eyes widened and she tried to grab the note. Helena withdrew it.

'I'll give this money to you if you lend me the child for two hours.'

The woman struggled to her feet. Her putrid breath struck Helena. 'Let me see it.'

She took the bill and examined it like an expert in forgeries. 'When do you want to take him?'

'You're here every day, aren't you?'

'Yes.'

'So I could drop by at any time.'

'Twenty dollars.'

'You needn't worry, no one will harm the child.'

'Bring back alive.' The woman made a gesture of irritation and sat down again.

Helena looked at the boy and saw him receiving more coins. His angelic face inspired pity and guilt in the passers-by. The metal clinked in the bowl. The boy lowered his head in thanks. The woman pulled him by the arm, examined the quantity of coins and decided to empty the bowl into her pocket.

A few minutes later, Helena entered the city park. After a few turns around it, she saw Tobias leaning against a tree. His face did not presage good news. He invited her to sit on a bench with him.

'He didn't turn up, and honestly, I'm not going to be capable of speaking to him. I'm not a good actor, I can't pretend emotions. It would go badly.'

Helena put her hand on his shoulder. 'Don't say that, Tobias, we can't give up now.'

'Of course not. I know someone who could play the role better than me. He's a kind of diplomat…'

Helena raised her voice. 'But that's a big risk. He could inform on us…'

'Don't worry. He won't inform on us because I could put him in jail too. I know his history. Let me speak to him and then we'll see.'

Helena's hand passed over her grey hair until it reached the flaccid skin of her neck.

'I hope you know what you're doing.'

'Trust me.'

The sun was beginning to set and the shadows were lengthening across the park. A cold wind shook the leaves of the trees. Few people were out walking. In the distance a dog barked. Helena stayed there in silence for some time, chewing over ideas. Suddenly, she got up without a word and left. Her plan seemed ever less likely to succeed. Again she wondered if she were not getting senile and losing the power of reason.

Half an hour later, Tobias reached the road where Jan worked. The butcher's was open and carcasses were being unloaded from a lorry into the storeroom. The smell of the meat was strong. Two men in red overalls carried the animals on their shoulders. They looked as if they had been flayed too. When the work was done, the lights of the butcher's went out and Jan appeared. He had long hair and wore light-colored clothes. Seeing Tobias did not scare him; he thought he had come to bring more money for Stefan. Tobias went up to him and told him he had a favor to ask of him. His tone of voice made Jan realize that the neo-Nazi leader did not wish to order steaks; it was the meat of a human being that, with his help, he wanted to carve up. They went to a bar nearby and sat in a deserted corner. Tobias ordered two beers from the waiter and began to sketch out his plan to his friend.

Jan listened for some time, but suddenly interrupted him. 'Are you nuts? You want me to help you sell a child to an old pervert who will then take it home and abuse it?'

'The kid won't be abused. As soon as he opens the door, you cover his mouth with your hand, and I go in. It shouldn't be hard for you. The rest is up to me.'

'No, no. It's a really dangerous plan. We'll both end up arrested.'

'Before you left the group, you did more dangerous things.'

'I'm not proud of that time.'

'I'll give you five hundred dollars.'

Jan was quiet. He drank a little beer. 'What did this guy do?'

'I told you, he owes money to someone.'

'And why do you need me? Why don't you ask your mates for help or do everything on your own?'

'He knows me, I can't be seen. Also I don't like to mix politics and business.'

Jan shook his head, smiling. 'Tobias, you really are useless at making up stories.'

Tobias clenched his fists. 'Who cares what the motive is? The guy's a piece of shit and he deserves a lesson.'

Jan looked at Tobias, who lowered his eyes. For some moments both were silent.

'There's an old guy who's into children and you want to fuck him up. This has nothing to do with money, or politics…'

'No.'

'And the old guy knows you…'

Tobias did not answer, but began to blush.

'This old guy must have abused a lot of children in his lifetime…'

Tobias raised his eyes and lowered them again. His eyelids were leaden.

Jan was enjoying the game of cat and mouse. The fearsome neo-Nazi leader was at the mercy of his claws, and he was going to roll him from one side to another until he was tired of toying with him.

'I can imagine what would have happened in the old regime, when there was total impunity for certain people…'

Tobias tightened his grip on his beer glass.

'This old guy raped dozens of innocent children. Poor little things, whatever happened to them? They can't be normal people. Either they killed themselves or became violent adults. Psychopaths, sociopaths, at least that's what the books say…'

Tobias was ready to smash the glass in his face.

'He really is a total piece of shit. He's unforgivable. If he'd touched me, I'd kill him.'

Tobias raised his eyes towards Jan again. They were injected with blood.

Jan felt his desperation and decided he was satisfied. The cat withdrew his claws and ended the game. The mouse was in bad shape, but accepted the torment he had been through.

'Will you help me or not?'

'You can count on me. You don't have to pay me a thing.'

Jan held out his hand to Tobias, who had to rein himself in so as not to sob. They got up and hugged.

That night, at home, once again Tobias drew Zdanhov as a monstrous creature with a cigarette in his mouth. Although he no longer remembered the drawings he had done long ago in the orphanage, the resemblance between those and these was startling. The main difference was that there were no other characters burying iron stakes in the creature. After he had done four drawings, he himself picked up a knife and cut out Zdanhov's face. Then he went to bed and slept without nightmares.

The next day, when they met in the park again, Helena listened to Tobias's news with an expression similar to that of the Albanian beggars. A third person involved in the plan to kill Zdanhov, and what was more, he could only take part at the weekend? Seated on a bench with some rotten planks, the sun burning her head and the wind scratching her neck, her spirits were too low for her to put up any objection. She was indifferent to the small change that Tobias gave her as alms. The responsibility for what was happening was not his – a young man she hardly knew – but her own. In the end, a plan to kill someone was a lot more complex than an educational reform. Still, she would have to see it through to the end now.

She was distracted, watching a pair of sweethearts passing by, when she felt Tobias's strong hand squeezing her arm. She looked at his face and saw the same feral expression he had had when he threatened her. Tobias was staring at the entrance to the park.

'It's him. Look discreetly.'

Helena looked to her right and fifty meters away saw an old, bald, fat man, limping, and a tall, well-built man following a few paces behind. She hardly recognized him. As Zdanhov got closer, his stained, swollen face with bags under his eyes grew clearer. She smiled. Never had the former People's Commissar for Culture and Propaganda looked so fragile to her.

'He might recognize you,' Tobias said. 'You'd better get up and go for a walk.'

Zdanhov was wearing a blue suit and a white shirt of elegant cut, and highly-polished brown shoes. He passed Tobias with a shuffling gait, not looking at him. He had heard the shouts of a group of children playing in a grassy area and headed in that direction. When he saw them he started walking faster, which made his shoulders and head sway. The bodyguard looked as if he were used to such scenes, and without disguising an expression of disgust, he loitered behind. Zdanhov liked privacy and had retained an air of shyness, which led him to dismiss the bodyguard whenever he managed to meet up with young rent-boys. He sat on a bench nearby, lit a cigarette, and watched the lads. The sight of the children running and turning somersaults on the grass excited him. He ran his tongue over his upper lip, caressed his arms and squeezed his thighs together.

♛

Zdanhov and Fiorov

WHEN the regime fell, after escaping a prison sentence, Zdanhov tried to find protection from his old enemies. Among the victims of his sexual abuse, those he had sent to concentration camps, and others whose lives he had ruined, there were plenty of people who wanted their revenge on him. His head had a price on it. Even so, the biggest threat was the most powerful man in the country, Fiorov. If he decided to settle scores, it would be better to commit suicide first. Others linked to the old regime, or business competitors, had turned up floating in the river, or hanging from bridges; the bodies were mutilated and showed signs of torture. Although it meant laying his life on the line, he decided to take the initiative. Despite Schwartz's extortion, he still had half a million dollars in a Swiss bank. He would grovel at the feet of the victor and pay the required tribute, in the hope of receiving a pardon.

Fiorov seemed to be expecting Zdanhov, since on his first attempt to speak to him, the guards at the mansion let him in. Escorted by two men, Zdanhov was taken to a room decorated with works of art and antique furniture. No sooner had he entered than he discovered the painting. The electric colors and elongated bodies struck him like a whiplash. Between stupefaction and rage, he contemplated El Greco's *Christ Driving the Moneylenders Out of the Temple*. That painting, hanging there, was the ultimate expression of his defeat, of the victory of capitalism over communism, and of the absolute power of Ivan Fiorov. The moneylenders might have been driven out in the time of Christ, but they had returned more powerful than ever, and now it was they who drove out their enemies and demolished regimes. Worse still, they got hold of the art. Money was the new religion, the market was the Bible with its commandments, and the moneylenders had become prophets. Resurrected from the concentration camp, Fiorov had become the lord of the temple, and he promised miracles.

Minutes later, the master of the house appeared. He was in a good mood: he had just signed a contract to distribute Coca-Cola in the country. His business empire had gained a new branch and a profit of millions was assured.

Fiorov wasted no time on Zdanhov's attempt to justify sending him to a concentration camp, by blaming the dictatorship.

'As you know, I was just a pawn of the regime's…'

'Be quiet. What have you got to offer me?'

'Two hundred thousand…'

'Don't be an idiot, you stole far more than that.'

'I've suffered blackmail and extortion. I don't have much left any more…'

'How much?'

'Four hundred thousand, and if possible, I'd like some protection.'

Fiorov wanted more, but did not feel like haggling. He decided it was better to take the money than kill the old man who had fallen into disgrace. Living in humiliation would be a sufficient punishment. He nodded and made a gesture for Zdanhov to leave. He wanted to be alone to relish a vision that delighted him: manna fallen from heaven in the form of bottles of Coca-Cola.

Helena and Micho

ONE sunny, windless Saturday, impeccably dressed in a beige suit, with a felt hat on, Zdanhov returned to the park, after lunch. Tobias, Jan, and Helena were waiting for him. If everything went as they expected, Zdanhov would stay at least an hour in the park, enchanted by the sight of the children playing – who appeared by the dozen at weekends. That would give Helena time to go and rent the boy from the beggar and hand him over to Jan so he could spring the trap. Provided Zdanhov bit the bait and wanted to take the child home – dismissing his bodyguard in the meantime – then Jan, as the legitimate owner of the boy, would insist on accompanying him to the entrance so that, when Zdanhov opened the door, he would push him inside and handcuff him. Then Tobias would appear and take vengeance.

Helena no longer wondered whether the plan would work or not, she simply wanted it to be done with for once and for all, for good or ill. She had unleashed something that was no longer under her control. She felt as if she had got hold of a weapon, but a stranger would take aim and decide when to pull the trigger. In forty minutes she had done the deal of hiring the child and handed him over to Jan. The ammunition was about to be fired.

On the way back, the child gave her his hand and told her that his name was Micho. Helena felt her chest tighten. She realized the child had a name, like any other human being. She was determined not to speak to him, but she failed. Once she had taken his hot, soft little hand, she found herself saying that he was very handsome, that they were going to play a kind of game and he should not be scared, that one day he would be very happy, and whatever other kind, pathetic phrases occurred to her. Micho smiled and called her aunt. Helena stopped at an ice-cream stall and let him choose the biggest one. Seeing the joy of the boy as he devoured the chocolate and vanilla ice-cream, clicking his tongue and giving little leaps, she was touched. She stroked his hair, capered about too, and almost hugged him. An idea began to germinate. A light breaking through the darkness. Zdanhov's fate concerned her less and less.

Zdanhov was sitting on a bench, watching two children accompanied by their mothers, when Micho appeared in front of him. The vision of the child with dark hair and grey eyes, so lovely, was as if an angel had descended from heaven. His mouth opened and his heart accelerated. Instinctively, he looked around to make sure the boy was alone. No one was protecting him. He could thrust his claws into the prey.

'Sit down, my darling.'

Micho did not understand the language, but understood the invitation. He climbed on to the bench and sat with his bare feet swinging. Zdanhov stroked one of his legs.

'Where are you from? Where are your parents?'

Micho said something in Albanian and Zdanhov smiled. He guessed the boy must have run away from whoever was exploiting him, and was lost. He could hardly believe his luck. He could do whatever liked with him and no one would mind. He was thinking of the best way to take him home when Jan, wearing his brother's wedding suit, sat on the bench too.

'He's cute, isn't he?'

Zdanhov trembled. 'Who are you? What are you talking about?'

Jan answered sweetly. 'I'm his owner and I noticed you are interested.'

'I'm sorry, but you're mistaken.'

'A hundred dollars for two hours. You can take him wherever you want. I won't ask any questions, as long as you hand him back to me alive.'

Zdanhov was getting up, but he sat down again. He looked at the bodyguard, who had noticed the approach of the stranger, and made a signal for him to leave. Jan smiled.

'Allow me to introduce myself. My name's Marko and I'm a businessman who works with very important people in this country.

We have the best children and our clients are entrepreneurs, film stars, politicians, judges, and even the police. We guarantee security and secrecy. As you know, these children are illegal immigrants who don't have any rights. Our clients are always protected by the law. If there's any problem, the children are deported and no one asks any questions. I noticed that you are a refined gentleman and that's the only reason I let Micho approach you. The scum don't touch these children. These are luxury goods for high society people. Do you have any other question to ask me?'

Zdanhov looked at him with mistrust. One devil told him there was something fishy, while another told him not to waste the opportunity.

Jan continued. 'What's more, as you must have noticed, this boy's a virgin. If he were not, he wouldn't be so smiling and cheerful. He has no idea what's going to happen to him.'

Zdanhov threw his cigarette on the ground. 'And why, if your clients are really such important people, don't you take such a valuable boy to them? What are you doing here with him?'

'My dear sir, he arrived two days ago, along with thirty-seven children. The others have already been requested, and he's the only one left. He was the oldest, that's the reason. Our clients only appreciate tender meat. And do you want to know why I'm with him? Because it's the best place to earn my commission. Money, it all comes down to money.'

Zdanhov scratched an ear and bit his lips. He had not touched such a young child for a long time. At a signal from Jan, Micho got up from the bench and went to play with another boy. The two rolled on the grass, amid shouts and laughter. Zdanhov twisted his neck like a snake before a hopping bird. One of the devils told him that the little angel was escaping him.

'I suppose you aren't interested, then?'

Zdanhov fidgeted on the bench and straightened his jacket, his leg shaking.

'Wait a minute, let me think.'

'Take your time.'

Zdanhov was sweating. He raised his hat and wiped his forehead with a handkerchief. Once again he looked around in every direction in search of anything suspicious. He only saw couples, adolescents, and old people. They were strolling without taking any notice of him.

Jan was aware of his fears. 'Don't worry, there are no police here. And as you know, you can buy any of them with a few dollars.'

Zdanhov took a deep breath, then looked at his watch. 'I'll take him. Two hours.'

'Agreed, but I'll accompany the boy. I never let my precious, defenseless merchandise out of my sight.'

Zdanhov regarded him with distrust again. 'I don't allow strangers in my house.'

'My dear sir, I never go inside the home of my clients, unless they ask me to help them get the child ready. We have tranquilizer pills, ropes, handcuffs, whips…'

Zdanhov raised a hand. 'Speak quietly. I don't need any of those things.'

'Fine, I'll wait outside for you to return the boy to me and make the payment. You won't regret it, you'll see.'

Zdanhov lived in a new house with a small garden on a housing estate built after the fall of the regime. High walls, painted white, and an iron gate, guaranteed him privacy. He had no contact with his neighbors and most of them did not know who he was.

The sun was starting to go down and the temperature was dropping when he reached the entrance of the house, accompanied by what he thought was his victim, and a pedophile's pimp. Micho was eating a sandwich and drinking a Coca-Cola: he was beaming. Jan was smiling. The other houses had their curtains drawn and only a couple of adolescents were playing football at the end of the street. A trace of suspicion led Zdanhov not to open the door in front of Jan. With a solemn air, he tried to make him leave.

'Mr. Marko, in two hours you can come and pick him up.'

Jan took the knife out of his pocket at that moment and pushed it against Zdanhov's belly, shielding the weapon with his body. 'Open the door or I'll kill you right here.'

Zdanhov's eyes started and his mouth twisted. 'I'll give you any money you want, don't kill me.'

Jan head-butted his eyebrow, which started to bleed. Micho was surprised, but not scared because he had seen similar scenes of violence. The blood that ran down Zdanhov's face and on to his shirt did not scare him either. He just stepped back a few paces.

'The door!' said Jan.

Bloody-faced, Zdanhov took the key from his pocket, put it in the lock, taking some time because his hand was shaking, until finally he was able to open the door. At that moment, at a run, Tobias appeared. He had a pack on his back and a pistol in his hand. He pushed Zdanhov inside the house, entered, and shut the door. On the outside, Jan went up to Micho and told him in Albanian not to be scared. Micho shrugged his shoulders and Jan gave him his hand. Anyone who did not hit him or shout at him was a friend. When they went by the boys who were playing football, they joined in with a few kicks and headers.

WHEN Jan and Micho got back to the park, it was already dark. Helena was waiting by a bench. She kept sitting down and standing up, over and over again. Her head turned in every direction, but all she could see were pairs of sweethearts, drug-addicts and alcoholics on the grass. No sooner did she see Micho, than she ran to him and hugged him. She was laughing and weeping at the same time. She kept kissing him, saying, 'My boy, my boy, I'm sorry, I'm sorry.' Micho hugged her too and called her aunt. Jan felt embarrassed.

'Right, it all went fine, the boy's here, and if you don't need me I'll be off.'

Since he got no reply, he turned and left the park at a run.

Presently, Helena went to buy clothes and shoes for Micho and then took him home. She gave him a bath, cooked him a meal, offered him chocolate, put him to sleep in the only bed she owned, and told him stories until he fell asleep. Before the night was over, she called a friend of hers who was a lawyer to start the process of adoption of a foreign child.

♛

Tobias and Zdanhov

THE CURTAINS in Zdanhov's dining room were drawn and only a little light entered through a skylight. Zdanhov lay on a Persian carpet, bound and gagged. For the first few minutes Tobias had beaten him with punches and kicks, with no explanations. Zdanhov's face looked like a steak tenderized by a mallet. He had a broken nose and several broken teeth, a dislocated jaw, a split eardrum, and both eyes were swollen shut. Few of his ribs had resisted the kicks and a vertebra had snapped. Zdanhov was coughing and struggling to breathe. Tobias had unleashed his fury without calculating the consequences. Suddenly he realized he was ruining his plan. If he continued beating him, he would not be able to relish the slow, agonizing death he had dreamt of for his rapist for years. He needed to keep him alive to make him suffer, and just as importantly, so that he understood the reason he was being punished.

Tobias was sweaty and panting. The knuckles of his right hand were raw and he had torn his black shirt. He sat on the sofa and looked at his victim. He was alive, but an old man that age could not survive much longer. Before Tobias began the torture, he would have to confront him with his abuse. He had to make him relive all the violence he had wreaked on the defenseless child Tobias had been, and on all the other boys at the orphanage he had raped. This was the moment Tobias had most longed for, but also the one he had most feared. He was going to recall and translate into words the images of the nightmares that had tormented him for years. He was going to enter a time machine of horrors. Voluntarily. In a way, he would be raped again. He was afraid of not being capable of what he had planned, of losing control of his feelings, and worst of all, of crying once more in front of his rapist. If that happened, he would kill him at once.

He got up, looked for the kitchen and filled a glass of water. He came back to the dining room and emptied it on Zdanhov's face, washing off the blood. Zdanhov moaned, fearing that the beating was going to start again. Tobias realized he was capable of listening.

'I was nine years old when you came to the orphanage the first time. I remember as if it were yesterday. It was a summer's morning and Elias and I were playing during one of the breaks. We were almost happy. With the new director, things were changing. We were being treated like children for the first time in our lives. But in the midst of dozens of other abandoned children, you sniffed me out like a hunting dog. We were the prettiest and the most tender, right?'

Tobias paused. His jaws quivered and tears started to his eyes. He held them back and went on. 'Elias was the first to be taken. When he came back, he couldn't speak, he just cried. We all knew that something bad had happened. Two days later, it was me…'

Tobias fell silent and moved away from Zdanhov for a few seconds. 'Two days later you took me to your house. And then…then you did what you wanted with me, remember? And afterwards, you gave me chocolates and told me this was our secret and I shouldn't tell anyone. That was the first time. Then… it was so many times. I wanted to die. I wanted to kill myself. But I held on. Elias couldn't bear it. You killed him. But I survived. It's just that I'm not a person any more. I'm an animal. I have no feelings. I have no pity. All I have inside me is hate. And here we are, just the two of us, and I'm going to make you pay for what you did to us.'

Tobias took out a knife, opened the blade, and knelt down beside Zdanhov. The latter sensed his nearness and groaned more loudly. Tobias looked at Zdanhov's stomach. His hand shook. He had planned to castrate him, but now he could not do it. Having to touch his sex again was beyond his strength. However, the knife would not go unused. Tobias altered his plan. His gaze fell on

Zdanhov's head. He turned him over, pressed a knee into his neck, grabbed an ear and began to cut it off. Zdanhov let out smothered yells, writhed, and kicked out. However, Tobias had tamed him. The blade went through the cartilage and the blood ran. Suddenly, Tobias had the ear in his hand and he raised it like a trophy. Then he flung it away. Slicing Zdanhov up nauseated him. He had thought of cutting up his face and piercing his eyes, but he decided not to do it. Unlike Jan, he was not a butcher.

Then he stood up, went to the table where he had put his backpack, and opened it. He took out a can of petrol and a box of matches. He unscrewed the top of the can, went back to Zdanhov and poured the petrol over him. The smell filled the room. Zdanhov screamed again. Tobias sat down on the sofa to enjoy his desperation. He was in no hurry. However, the sight of his suffering brought a strange idea to light.

Tobias stroked his shaved head and raised his eyes. To fit that thought in his mind he would have to drive out others that had long been installed there. It was not easy to shift them; deep roots sustained them. He went through a struggle. His head nodded from one side to the other, his nails scratched his beard. Fighting ideas was harder than a brawl in the street. Ideas did not bleed, or give up – they had to be pulled out by the roots. Victory appeared, but if felt like a defeat to him.

All my life I've been taking revenge on the wrong people, poor wretches just like I was as a kid. Immigrants, gypsies, drug-addicts, everyone I beat up, I mixed up with Zdanhov.

Regret, though, had no smell, unlike the petrol. He got up and kicked Zdanhov's back for the last time.

'You've guessed what's going to happen to you by now, haven't you? I'm going to burn you like a pig. You'll never rape anyone again.'

Tobias spread more petrol around the room and returned to the table. He picked up the matchbox and approached Zdanhov. He opened it, took out a match, and struck it.

Fiorov

WITH just one month to go before the first free elections in Slavia to elect a democratic government, the polls indicated a draw between the Freedom Party and the Party of Democracy. The Freedom Party was the only one that had campaign offices in every city and town in the country. Fiorov had invested five million dollars in the electoral campaign, which had provided temporary employment to two thousand people. His strategy consisted of a nationwide tour in which, apart from rallies, parties were held with free food and drink, and vital household and kitchen goods were given out to the poor – who made up half of the population. In response to opponents and journalists who accused him of buying the votes of the needy, he answered that they were insulting the dignity of the lower classes, and that they, his opponents, had never done anything for them. He went on to affirm that there were forces in the country who wanted to keep the poor in poverty so that they could continue to manipulate them. Some journalists who attempted to enter low-income housing projects where Fiorov had offered free gifts, were assaulted and expelled. Fiorov, on the other hand, appeared in photographs in new posters hoisted on the shoulders of the inhabitants of those projects, with the legend, *The Friend of the People.*

With fewer resources, the other parties organized clarification meetings and a few rallies. The lack of experience and organization of these forces resulted in inefficient campaigns. Posters were printed with spelling mistakes, contradictory declarations were made by leaders of the same party, and rallies were scheduled at which the main speakers failed to turn up. To make the situation worse, the leaders were constantly attacked on the television station owned by Fiorov with accusations ranging from marital infidelity to international espionage. Used as they were to the control of information by the old regime, the majority of viewers did not question the truth of the news given on the television; moreover, the penalties for libel anticipated by the law rewarded the wearing down of opponents with fake news.

One Sunday, at nine in the evening, the Democracy Party held a rally in the central square of Tiers. The weather was mild and the sky was starry. Thousands of people, most of them young, waved green flags; the older ones, who were still unused to freedom, seemed like people at a ball who don't know how to dance. There was a stage with spotlights and a sound system relaying music. Two electricians were making the final checks on the equipment. The plan was that after four speakers, Adam Jacek would close the rally.

Presently a tall, thin man ran on to the stage, dressed in a blue suit and a red shirt. The spotlights illuminated him. He was a sports journalist who had volunteered to act as presenter. In an exalted tone, as if he were commentating on a football match, he greeted the crowd, saying the Democracy Party rally was about to begin. At once, making theatrical gestures with his right hand, he introduced the first speaker, Jacob Levi, as 'a man of culture' who had been a victim of the dictatorship and had had all his goods confiscated. From the wings, Jacob Levi, with white hair and a white beard, thin and bent over, appeared in a wheelchair. Although he was not a party member, the leaders had invited him to speak because they thought a handicapped person would evoke sympathy among the crowd. As a party that had been formed on the basis of the Solidarity resistance movement, they also hoped, by showing a man who had been imprisoned and tortured, to wipe out the memory of the public that in the past some of its members had resorted to violent methods that had led to the death of a woman. To them, Jacob Levi seemed the right public figure to make everyone forget Leonidas Vall.

In his turn, Levi accepted the invitation to be a speaker at the rally as he would have accepted an invitation from any other party. Ingenuously he hoped to make his contribution to enlighten the electors about the importance of democratic values. He had prepared a speech in which, by his own example, he would try to show that diversity of thought enriches a country, and that restricting opinions is an assault on the rights of the citizens and impedes the development of the nation. Knowing that the people had been trained to obedience to power, and associated politics with might, Levi hoped to prevent the electoral campaign from polarizing the people and degenerating into violence. On seeing the crowd he was to address from his platform for the first time, he was amazed. There was enthusiasm, joy and civility. Fear belonged to the past. Those people waving flags and smiling truly seemed to be in communion with the democratic values he hoped to transmit to them. If his participation could contribute to there being no incidents between the members of the different parties, he would consider that he had served his country well.

As soon as his introduction was over, he received a microphone and prepared to speak. The spotlights that illuminated him were too bright for his tired eyes, but before that applauding crowd, everything seemed bearable to him. He took a deep breath, raised a hand to request silence and began his speech. 'My friends, thank you for coming...'

At that moment a Molotov cocktail exploded near him and the stage began to burn. Chaos ensued: people shouting, trying to put out the fire, and bumping into each other. One of the spotlights blew up and the broken glass struck a woman's face. A man pushed Levi's wheelchair to a stair, but no one appeared to take him off the stage. Although he was handicapped, Levi was the only one to remain calm. In the crowd, some people began fighting. Firecrackers went off and raised a cloud of smoke. The crowd ran in all directions and anyone who fell was trampled. The yelling rose in volume. Shop windows were broken. Police car sirens increased the confusion.

Half an hour later, the square was empty, with green flags and shoes scattered on the ground. It smelled of burning. Thirty people, among them Levi, were taken to hospital. No one was arrested.

The following day, on Fiorov's television channel, they showed pictures of the rally and a journalist analyzed the incident, declaring that for a political party known for its violent methods, it was no surprise that disturbances should occur; those responsible belonged to the party itself and it had all been nothing but an internal struggle for power; so peaceful citizens should keep away from the Democracy Party, since it was probable that more acts of violence would occur. It was regrettable, they concluded, that there were political parties who did not respect the rules of democracy.

A week later, the Freedom Party held a rally in the same place at the same hour. It was a cold, cloudy night. The square was full of demonstrators, more old people than young ones, waving blue flags. Stalls offered free food, drinks, and cigarettes. On an enormous stage colored lights shone, and pop music blasted. Six female dancers in mini-skirts carried out an erotic choreography. The speakers were an actress, a TV presenter, a footballer and Ivan Fiorov himself. To assure security at the event, forty armed guards under the command of Pietr Huss were spread throughout the crowd.

The first three speakers – who had each received two hundred dollars – did not speak about politics, but about Fiorov's human qualities. The actress had been in two films during Ionescu's regime and was now the star of the first soap-opera produced in Slavia. She was blonde, had green eyes, and wore a black dress and a gold necklace. As well as the money, she had received five doses of cocaine. Beginning with a smile and ending almost in tears, she told the crowd how Fiorov had supported her career and helped her family under the dictatorship, without asking anything in return.

The television presenter had a program with a large audience in which citizens appeared and told their hard luck stories, and then received advice and material help. He was bald and had a black moustache, and wore a grey chalk-striped suit. As well as the money, that night he had been offered a night in a hotel with three prostitutes. He spoke of the social work Fiorov was developing for the benefit of orphans and the elderly, giving the vulnerable a dignified existence, and declared he had never known such a good man.

The footballer was the captain of the national team, and enjoyed great popularity. He had brown hair and eyes, and wore a track suit. As well as his fee, he had been given the same offer as the TV presenter. He said that thanks to Fiorov sports, and especially football, would soon reach a level comparable to that of the great European powers, and he ended his speech with a few flips and headers with a football.

The crowd gave them ovations, thankful for the simple language, the touching stories, and the forecast of future sporting success.

At last, a presenter announced that Ivan Fiorov, 'the savior of the nation', would speak. To the sound of the national anthem and illuminated by spotlights, he ran on to the stage, wearing a black suit and a red tie. The crowd reacted with applause and yells. Fiorov made the victory sign with both hands raised, shaking his head, and at times jumping about. He went on like that for some minutes, tweaking the crowd as if they were puppets connected by strings, until at last he lowered his arms and everyone fell still and silent.

'I have a dream. A dream that every man and woman in this country will be prosperous and happy. Successful in life. Wealthy. If I have succeeded, you can succeed too. Because you are the best people in the world. Yes, each one of you can have everything you have dreamed of, and guarantee the future of your children. Yes, it's true, the sky's the limit. But be warned, your dreams can only be fulfilled if the country is well governed. If there's a strategic vision for the future. That's why you need to choose the best leader. And I'm the only person capable of turning Slavia into a rich, developed country. With your support, of course, because you will be my ministers. My government will be the government of the people.'

Fiorov paused to listen to the crowd's applause. Then, finger pointed, he went on:

'Our opponents have no experience whatever in economic affairs. Their world is one of philosophical theories, literary debates and an elite culture that interests no one. Not one of them has ever got his hands dirty, used a screwdriver, or created any jobs. They don't know what ill-paid, hard work is. They don't know what it is not to have food or clothes to give to their children. They don't know you or respect you. All they can do is talk and make promises they can't keep. They want to create a country where there's no room for the working classes and the old. Is that what you want?'

'Noooo!' thundered back the crowd.

'Shall we stop them harming the people?'

'Yeeees!'

'Shall we win the election and turn this country into a model for the world?'

'Yeeees!'

For another ten minutes Fiorov went on making promises to improve the lives of the citizens and prolonging the call-and-response with the crowd, asking questions in which he wanted to get their approval of his qualities and reveal the perversity of his opponents. Excited by this direct participation in the rally, the ordinary people shouted ever louder, convinced that they really were Fiorov's ministers and were taking part in vital decisions about the future of the country.

Two weeks later on an independent television channel there was a debate between Ivan Fiorov and Adam Jacek. Fiorov appeared in a black suit, a white shirt and blue tie – all by an Italian label. Jacek was wearing a grey suit and white shirt – of Slavian manufacture. Fiorov was tanned and in good shape. Jacek was pale and had bags under his eyes. Besides the questions asked by the moderator, the rules of the debate allowed for the two candidates to question one another freely. During the first half hour, the candidates presented their well-known plans for government. In a monotonous tone, Jacek explained in detail, with calculations and projected figures, what his aspirations were for the country. In a lively fashion, Fiorov outlined a similar program, substituting figures for promises. From then on, with the moderator powerless to prevent it, the political debate gave way to a personal attack.

Jacek began the offensive. 'It's important for the electorate to know that Ivan Fiorov, also known as Koba, devoted himself to smuggling during the dictatorship, and other illicit activities that involved the elite of the regime. He got rich and helped enrich many People's Commissars. Worse still, he guaranteed the survival of the dictatorship. This man has no scruples and doesn't consider the means to attain his ends. He should be tried for complicity in the crimes of the former regime. How can anyone with such a past govern the country?'

Fiorov smiled and shook his head as if Jacek were talking nonsense. 'What my opponent means is that during a period when everything was scarce, I brought vital goods into the country. At times circumstances forced me to deal with the authorities. There was no alternative. I don't regret that, in fact I'm proud of having fulfilled some of the people's needs, and having given jobs to a lot of people. What's more, it's probable that my opponent or his family benefited from my business. Can you deny that you bought food or medicine on the black market during the time of the dictatorship? Rice, beans, vegetables, aspirin…'

Jacek shook his head too, pulling a disgusted face, but hesitated, and Koba took advantage to keep provoking him:

'Besides, it's strange that my opponent speaks of crimes when his old organization launched terrorist attacks that killed innocent people.'

Jacek flushed with fury. 'That's a lie. I never approved of violent methods to topple the regime. They were dissidents who acted on their own behalf…'

'Dissidents? Their own behalf? Then you're admitting that you lacked the power of leadership, and couldn't even control your own men. How can you expect to govern a country if you were not capable of leading a group of half a dozen people?'

Jacek thumped the table. 'Controlling criminals is your specialty. I only know how to work with honest, peaceful people.'

'Apart from being a weak leader, you're not even capable of admitting that your organization was responsible for the attack on the Witten factory in which the manager was killed, and which impoverished the country still more. That shows serious lack of character, Mr. Jacek.'

'How dare you, you bastard? If I'd been to blame at all, they would have executed me when they arrested me. But I was freed, weeks later.'

The moderator interrupted. 'Calm down, gentlemen...'

Fiorov smiled. 'Yes, you need to calm down, Mr. Jacek. You're cutting a poor figure before the viewers.'

Jacek clenched his fists. 'Your tactics won't work. Everyone knows what kind of person you are. A gangster, a gangster.'

'Unlike you, I'm a man who doesn't hide his past and cares about the people.'

'I'm also proud of my history of peaceful resistance to the regime, and of having fought for freedom. It was my actions, not yours, that toppled the dictatorship.'

'What do you have to say to Luda Schwartz's family?'

'What? You really are a lowlife.'

'How much is a human life worth to you?'

'Scum!'

Once again the moderator appealed for respect.

Jacek kept fidgeting in his chair. Koba pointed at him and spoke to the camera.

'This is what you can expect from this man. An inability to admit mistakes, a lack of leadership, a lack of self-control, and an absence of compassion. Is this the president you want for our country? Is this what we toppled the dictatorship for? Any one of you has better qualities than Mr Jacek.'

Jacek addressed the camera too. He raised his finger as he spoke, almost shouting:

'My dear fellow citizens, don't let yourselves be fooled by this criminal. He doesn't believe in democracy and he's a danger to our country. Ivan Fiorov represents a return to the dictatorship and its repressive measures. If he is elected, Slavia will become a kind of Sicily and no country or financial organization will trust us. We have to stop this man seizing power. I appeal to all of you who want to live in freedom and democracy to vote for me, because

I'm the only candidate who can prevent him from winning the election. I appeal also to the citizens this man tried to buy, offering them tools and food. Don't sell yourselves for a mess of pottage. He's exploiting your poverty for his own advantage, but if he attains power, you'll be forgotten at once. Social concerns are not part of his ideology, that is if he has any ideology apart from that of banditry. His friends are, and always have been, the powerful. Vote for me to avoid the takeover of the country by this gangster.'

Fiorov applauded with a sarcastic smile. 'Congratulations, Mr. Jacek, you're a talented comedian. You're declared that I represent a return to the dictatorship, you've spoken of moral principles and a takeover. Once more you've repeated that I was a friend of the powerful in the regime. So how do you explain that I was in a concentration camp, and not you, the self-proclaimed opponent of the dictatorship?'

Fiorov paused, but Jacek did nothing but shrug his shoulders.

'Dear viewers, Mr. Jacek doesn't want to answer my question because he's hiding something. The time has come to unmask him. Please give me your full attention, all of you, because I'm going to give you proof that Jacek was an informer of the previous regime.'

Fiorov pulled a serious face, and carefully took out of an inside pocket of his suit the document forged by Olin. Then he showed it to the cameras.

'I also have here an affidavit made by foreign experts who declare that this is a genuine document produced by Ionescu's regime for their accounts. In other words, Mr. Jacek was paid to inform on citizens. Indeed, he is responsible for the imprisonment, torture, and deaths of thousands of people.'

At that moment Jacek got out of his chair and advanced on Fiorov. The latter could have taken him on, but he let Jacek punch him, threw himself on the floor, and pretended to be unconscious. The moderator waved his arms and ordered the cameramen to turn off their cameras.

The next day, all the newspapers reported on the front page the story that the legendary opponent of the communist regime,

Adam Jacek, might after all have been an informer. On Fiorov's TV channel, as well this news, they highlighted the aggression that Jacek subjected him to. Jacek's campaign managers released a statement swearing that the accusation was false, and appealing to the supporters of the Democracy Party to demonstrate in the streets against the maneuver. However, instead of the tens of thousands of people they expected, just a few hundred gathered before the party headquarters for an hour, but ended up leaving crestfallen. At the same time, the Freedom Party made an appeal to its supporters to keep calm and not get involved with Jacek's supporters. The other parties decided not to comment on the scandal.

Two days later the Freedom Party won the elections with sixty per cent of the votes. The Democracy Party was in second place with twenty per cent of the votes and the other parties had the remainder. Fifty per cent of registered voters abstained from voting. The electoral commission and foreign observers declared that the election had gone off without incidents and there had been no irregularities.

Flanked by drunk supporters, Fiorov appeared on television declaring that the people had won the election and given a lesson to the world; he promised to begin working the next day and announced that it was a time for reconciliation, inviting his opponents to present their proposals for the benefit of the nation; he spoke of rigor, transparency and honesty, and said he was going to sell his businesses in order to devote himself exclusively to government.

Right after they took power, as if they had been preparing it in advance, the government of the Freedom Party approved two laws in parliament which the opposition and journalists classified as antidemocratic. The Law of National Security punished with ten years in prison any individuals who attacked the interests or safety of Slavia. In practice, a number of the activities of the opposition parties, such as demonstrations or vigils which lacked authorization, were now criminalized. The Libel Law punished with seven years in prison written or oral statements considered false or injurious. In practice, journalists and the opposition lost the right to freedom of speech. In order to enforce these laws, the government appointed a new Attorney-General with wider powers, who in his turn informed the judges that any failure to apply the laws might result in mandatory retirement. As a result of these measures, within six months twenty journalists had been arrested, along with seven opposition members of parliament, five university professors, and two hundred citizens. With the practices of the old regime as their benchmark, the majority of people thought that, since there were no longer concentration camps or death sentences, the new repressive measures represented democratic progress, compared to the dictatorship. One had to respect the government, and whoever went too far deserved their punishment.

However, there were some who could not resign themselves.

Ana Kull

ANA Kull was a twenty-six year old journalist whose father had been in a concentration camp for four years, and was unable to work when he returned. At the time Ana was ten and for a long time she bore the label of daughter of an enemy of the people. She had even had difficulty getting into the Department of Journalism at university, and had faced the hostility of a number of classmates and professors. For her the advent of *Perestroika* had meant, apart from the toppling of the dictatorship, a settling of scores with the past. Ana took part in demonstrations, believing that after the fall of the regime the people would choose a democratic government, and at last she would be able to freely exercise her profession and narrate the tragedies of the dictatorship.

The founding of Koba's Freedom Party frightened her, but even so, she believed that in the end the voters would not let themselves be tricked by Fiorov's populist maneuvers. After all, it was an educated population and everyone knew his reputation. The rage she felt when she heard the result of the election made her decide to follow her father's example. She would have to fight the new dictatorship. Making use of fictional characters and allegories in order to get round the libel law, she had managed to publish some satirical stories in *Europa* magazine, in which she revealed the road to tyranny that the regime was following. The editor of the magazine trembled whenever she presented him with a new story, but never refused to publish her. 'You have more courage than all of us,' he told her once. The regime's police had her under surveillance, and would have already arrested her if Fiorov himself had not given instructions to the contrary: 'Nobody reads her, apart from half a dozen intellectuals. She still hasn't crossed the line. Leave her alone for the time being.' That did not stop Ana from getting threatening telephone calls, nor did it prevent her car from being torched.

Ana was working on a new text called *The Corrupt Man*, in which she hoped to expose the web of shady businesses which benefitted the prime minister, Ivan Fiorov. This time she knew that she would cross the line that had protected her from his rage until now, but she decided not to give in to fear. She sat down at her work desk, picked up a pencil, and read what she had written.

Once upon a time, a black knight appeared in a kingdom, killed the king, and took power. The knight brought about big changes in the governance of the realm, guaranteeing the people's lives would be better. However, the result was disastrous. If the people had not lived well formerly, from now on their lives became even worse. Their misery and hunger increased. Nonetheless, the knight's army patrolled the streets and did not allow anyone to criticize him; those who did were arrested and forced to labor as slaves. They might also be hanged or decapitated.

This tyranny lasted many years.

One day the people revolted and drove out the black knight and his army. They launched fireworks and held celebrations that lasted a week. Then the people assembled in the main square and everyone was consulted on the choice of who would rule the country. They did not want any more monarchs or despotic rulers. From now on, they would live in democracy.

Everything was going so well that nobody thought it mattered that the richest man in the country was starting to give presents and wine to people. And that is why they, who had never been given anything, chose him to rule, convinced that he would be their friend. They preferred to forget that this man had been a business partner of the black knight, and thus had supported his tyranny. The presents and the wine spoke louder than moral principles.

As for him, the rich man promised that once he were elected he would govern for the good of the people, and so that there would be no conflict of interests, he would sell his businesses, of stud farms, munitions factories, and leather and fur goods.

The people were so happy that they did not find it strange it was poor people, who had no experience in these fields, who bought the businesses of the rich man. The man who bought the stud farm was a shoemaker who had never even owned a donkey. The man who ended up with the munitions factory was a fisherman whose only possessions made of iron were his hooks. The man who took over the leather and fur business was a mason whose only skill was in breaking rocks. None of them could read, write, or do sums that involved multiplication or division. All the same, there were people in the realm who bred animals, worked in iron, and did business abroad. Even so, the rich man did not choose them to provide continuity for his enterprises. No one thought this contradiction strange, either.

One day, a sly old man invited the new owners of the stud farm, the munitions factory and the leather and fur emporium to have a drink with him in a pub. They accepted, and after an hour, they were quite drunk. Then the old man started asking them questions about their activities. At first, they just laughed. But they soon told him the whole truth. Not one of them knew a damn thing about the subject, and to tell the truth, they had not taken a single decision. The real owner was still the rich man who paid them to pretend they had bought the businesses.

In this way, the rich man was able to rule the country and look after his own interests at the same time, which brought him nothing but benefits. Just weeks after he was elected as ruler, he passed a law to stimulate the economy. Part of the revenue from taxes would be devoted to help animal breeders, merchants, and manufacturers. The people were overjoyed because they thought many families would be supported. However, the ruler decided that only three businesses would receive the subsidy: exactly those that still belonged to him.

About this time, one very hot day, a fire swept through the mountains and burned half the forested land. Thousands of trees were destroyed and hundreds of animals died. A black cloud hovered over the town for five days. An old woman died of the fumes. Never before had such a tragedy been known in the land. It became known that the burned area belonged to a shepherd who seldom descended to the town. What was more, the shepherd had taken out a fire insurance policy of very high value, and as a result, would become rich.

This time the people were suspicious, and a group of four men, armed with clubs, climbed the mountain to meet the shepherd and demand an explanation. The shepherd tried to escape into a cave, but they caught him. Instead of offering him wine, the working men threatened to tie him to a tree and burn him alive. The man revealed everything. It was he who had set fire to the mountain. He also confessed that he had only possessed half a dozen goats, no more. The land that had burned had in fact been in his name, but the real owner was the ruler who had paid him to play the role of landowner, set fire to the trees and claim the insurance.

That same day, the church bell rang to summon the population. The peasants dropped their hoes, craftsmen stopped their work, and mothers brought their children in their arms. In under ten minutes, the village square was full. The men who had climbed the mountain were on a stage. They asked for quiet and told what they had heard from the shepherd. The crowd murmured. They were all furious. In the meantime, the sly old man asked people to help him up on to the stage, and also exposed the rich man's scheme for the sale of his businesses. The people started to insult the ruler and someone spoke of taking up arms to topple him.

The ruler was taken by surprise. His guard had no time to prepare

for the attack. Soon after, half of his guards, on learning about his
frauds, deserted him and joined the people. The palace was surrounded
by working people with swords, axes, and torches. They demanded that
he surrender, or the same would befall him as had befallen the forest he
had had burned down. The guards who had remained loyal to him fled
from the palace. The ruler appeared at the window with a white flag.
The people derided him and laughed at him. The ruler begged them to
spare his life. One of the men who had spoken on the stage shouted that
no one would do him any harm, and everyone seemed to agree. In a
few minutes, the doors of the palace opened and the ruler surrendered.
Some people spat on him, but no one struck him. Then the people put
him on a mule, took him to the town gates, and drove him out forever.

Ana put down her pencil. She would not edit anything; the
story was ready for publication. Anyone could understand who the
target of the satire was.

Fiorov, Remus and Huss

AFTER rewriting his play *Hope*, Remus's life became hell. He was
arrested on the charge of denigrating the values of the regime and
sent for a year to a concentration camp where the guards broke
his fingers as an additional punishment. After the installation of
democracy, he was accused of collaborating with the dictatorship
and no director would touch his plays. In the world of the arts,
no one would talk to him. He had become a leper. He gained
redemption when Fiorov invited him to become his advisor on
cultural matters. Although he was seldom consulted, he received
a salary that kept penury at bay. At the same time, those who
had rejected him became cordial again. When Fiorov's secretary
contacted him, he hurried to the government headquarters. At last
the powerful prime minister would wish to hear his opinion.

A bodyguard escorted him to Ivan Fiorov's office. The latter
told him to sit down at a table on which Anna Kull's story was

lying.

'Read this text and comment on it. Take all the time you need.'

Remus put on his glasses and concentrated on reading. 'In literary terms...'

Fiorov raised his hand. 'I don't give a shit about literary terms! What I want to know is whether there's an incitement to revolt here, quite apart from libelous insinuations.'

'Well the metaphorical language is subjective and open to various interpretations.'

'What? Speak plainly, man.'

'I mean some people could read an incitement to revolt in this text, while others could read it simply as a harmless story.'

'So where does that leave us? Do we have grounds to accuse this journalist of undermining the security of the nation, or of libel?'

'In my opinion, legally, you can't do much, since it deals with a story that takes place in an imaginary setting, with fictional characters. If she denies the link with your government or with you, no one can prove the opposite. The girl did her job well.'

Fiorov thumped the table. 'Shithead!'

Remus shook. 'Me?'

'Her, stupid. It seems the metaphors have confused you. You can leave.'

As soon as Remus had gone, Fiorov called Pietr Huss.

'I've got a mission for you. A journalist who's writing things that challenge me.'

'If you'd let me take action at the start, we could have avoided these problems.'

'You were right. From now on I won't be tolerant with people like this.'

'Should I shut her up for good?'

'Yes, forever. But be careful, journalists from abroad are going to ask questions. It's a dangerous profession.'

'Don't worry. We've already got rid of plenty, and nobody's discovered a thing.'

'Yes, but they weren't journalists.'

'Damn them. In the old days they were serious professionals who knew their place, but now…

'Will you deal with her?'

'Trust me. Even if the secret services of other countries come to investigate, they won't be able to find any evidence against you.'

'I know, but don't make it easy for them.'

'Would you prefer me to make her disappear, or that she commit suicide?'

'Suicide her. She looks crazy, it'll be more plausible.'

'Yes, boss.'

Jan, Ana and Szut

JAN was sitting at a table in the library with his friend Nina, a primary school teacher he had met not long ago. It was six in the evening and there were few people in the reading room. Two lamps with white light illuminated the newspaper *Europa,* which Jan was reading, and *Time,* which was in front of Nina. When he finished reading Ana Kull's story 'The Corrupt Man', Jan turned to his friend and asked her to read it too.

Five minutes later, Nina gave her opinion. 'This journalist is really brave. She's not fooling anyone. Our prime minister is unmasked as a gangster who still controls his old interests, and uses public money to finance them. I also liked the ending, where the working people revolted and deposed the corrupt ruler. That's exactly what our people should do.'

Jan shook his head. 'The denunciation of corruption is important, but the incitement to violent revolt is risky. It could degenerate into civil war. There are plenty of examples in European history.'

'Maybe, but through democratic means he'll be able to remain in power as long as he likes. All he has to do is redistribute money.

Raise the salaries of civil servants and old age pensions and he's got the vote guaranteed. That's what you call the perfect dictatorship.'

'Our country has a long history of violence and we need to put an end to it. The dictatorship taught us to hate and attack. That's why we get involved in so many senseless acts of violence. Our youth is lost, and they vent their frustrations on people who aren't to blame for anything. They believe you have to beat someone before you're respected. They think they're defending some principle but in fact they're just becoming troublemakers.'

Nina frowned. 'I've never been involved in any violent act. I might have pulled my sister's hair when we were little, but as an adult I've never hit anyone. My siblings and my friends are all peaceful. What do you mean? The football hooligans?'

Jan blushed. 'Yes, that kind of thing.'

'Did you use to get into fights, Jan?'

Jan swallowed hard and took his time to answer. 'A while back I used to run around with guys who liked getting into fights… lads' stuff… not any more, though…'

'I hope you've come to your senses, Jan.'

'As you see, I'm in revolt against the use of force. But you seem to be in favor of it.'

Nina laughed. 'OK, you win. What do you want to do? Write a letter to the editor?'

'I'm going to go there and talk to Ana Kull in person. It's my civic duty to warn her about the danger of inciting violence. Journalists should be responsible because they influence their readers. Do you want to come with me?'

'Now?'

'Yes.'

'I can't, it's really late. Anyway, I think what you're going to do is daft. They may not even talk to you. And if they do, they'll talk about freedom of expression. Get it?'

Jan had a gleam in his eye. Although he disagreed with the appeal to violence, he was beginning to feel a certain fascination for the journalist and wanted to get to know her. It was not for the pleasure of violence, nor to avenge herself, but for the future of the nation that she was risking her life. He said goodbye to his friend, turned off his lamp, and headed for the newspaper offices.

Like the rest of the free press, *Europa* had been founded after the fall of Ionescu's regime. The owners were two brothers whose parents had been imprisoned under the dictatorship. *Europa* claimed to follow an independent editorial line, giving a platform to columnists from both the Right and the Left – and yet excluding communists. Its section on culture was considered the fullest in the national press, with pages devoted to the cinema, to art, the theatre, to religion, and wines, all of which attracted a wide-ranging audience. The satirical stories of Ana Kull and others appeared in a special supplement on Sundays.

Europa was edited in a three storey building in an old quarter of the city, in a street which had borne the name of Che Guevara and which since the fall of the regime had been called Father Ivo Karlovic Street. When Jan got there and saw all the lights on in the windows, it reminded him of a party. He found a doorman at the entrance and told him he would like to speak to Ana Kull. The man picked up a telephone, spoke to someone, and asked Jan to wait. Minutes later Ana appeared looking tired, a sheaf of papers in her hand. She was wearing black slacks and a green sweater. Her hair was unbrushed and her face lacked makeup. Jan realized her work was no fun. He tried to smile as she approached, but her face remained grave.

'Ana, I came to tell you that I admired your story, "The Corrupt Man". You have to have a lot of courage to reveal the dishonesty of our prime minister like that. Everyone who reads it is going to know that he's the target.'

'Thank you...'

'But if you don't mind me making a criticism, I think the end of the story could be misinterpreted...'

'Misinterpreted how?'

'I mean people might be led to think that we can only rid ourselves of this man through violence.'

'But that's exactly what I want them to think. That's how Ionescu was toppled and that's how Fiorov will have his political career ended too.'

'The truth is, the last regime only fell with the protests because it was already decrepit. Attempting to topple a man like Fiorov by force would only lead to a bloodbath. Are you willing to accept the responsibility for that?'

Ana looked at him strangely. 'Pardon me, but I don't see what your point is. My story only intends to wake the citizens up and show them that they have the power to change what's wrong. I don't have the power to unleash a coup d'état. Do you know of any writer or journalist who's managed to pull off a feat like that?'

'All I know is that in our country violence lurks on every corner. There are plenty of desperate people who have nothing to lose. Things could easily get out of control and any one of us could be a victim.'

Ana's eyes widened. 'Are you threatening me? Who sent you?'

Jan raised both hands and shook his head. 'No, you've misunderstood me…'

Ana pointed a finger at his face. 'Listen, you can tell your boss that I'm not afraid of him and I won't shut up.'

Then she turned her back on him and returned to the office. When she got there, she sat at her desk and threw the papers she was carrying into the air. The noise of the typewriters ceased. Her colleagues looked at her, but said nothing. In the opposite corner of the office, the editor got up. There was no sound but of his footsteps. He came up to Ana.

'Have they threatened you again?'

'Yes.'

'You must be careful. If they're no longer afraid to show their faces, it's because they're protected.'

'It was different this time. The guy was subtle. He began by praising the story for unmasking Fiorov's businesses, but in the end he tried to put the blame on me if there's a coup d'état.'

'That's weird. Are you sure it wasn't some nut with nothing

better to do?'

'No, he knew what he was saying. He was calm and his speech was coherent.'

'Fiorov's men are not that subtle. They make direct threats. They break your legs, cut your ears off, throw acid in your face. This guy must have acted on his own behalf.'

'Yes, maybe it was just someone who's angry with life.'

'Whatever, you need to be doubly careful. If you want to you can stay in my house for a while.'

'Thanks, but I'm not going to let them beat me. I'm going to go on living my normal life. I'm taking self-defense classes.'

The editor lowered his head and bit his lip. 'All right, as I said before, you're braver than all of us. But don't make it easy for them. Stay alert. Without a gun, your self-defense lessons are useless. To tell the truth, against those people you'd need an army.'

Ana smiled. 'I can take care of myself without guns or bodyguards. The threats just give me the strength to go on satirizing the creature. Culture is more powerful than force. In the end we'll bring him down.'

Just then the sound of the typewriters filled the office. All of Ana's colleagues were working on something: local news, foreign news, the economy, a gossip column, sports, film reviews, travel; some used a literary style with long sentences, while others had a more objective style and used short sentences; some were rigorous in their presentation of the facts, while others let their imaginations carry them away; none, however, was writing about Ivan Fiorov.

As usual, Ana got out at four o'clock in the morning after 'putting the paper to bed'. The night was cold and the sky overcast. Wearing a jacket and a woolen hat, she was walking towards where her car was parked. A colleague had offered to accompany her, but she had refused. She walked in a state of high alert, eyes and ears peeled, turning her head at the slightest sound or shape in the dark. She would switch to the opposite pavement if anyone came in her direction or if she heard footsteps behind her. Although she had said she had no need of weapons, she carried a kitchen knife in her pocket. In the small hours the streets were deserted, which made her relax her vigilance somewhat. Presently, on entering another street, she saw a body lying on the pavement. A wino who had fallen asleep. Before she started getting threats, she would have gone to his aid. Now, in place of wretchedness, she saw traps everywhere. That prostrate man might jump up the moment she got near and put his hands on her neck. Even after she had checked that he was an old drunk, she passed by him without pausing. Unlike the characters in her story who were unafraid of the ruler's power, she did feel fear, although the claimed she did not. In real life, Ana had become a terror-stricken person stuck in a plot that was no longer under her control. Besides, she was alone. In her story, the revelations of corruption had led the people to rise up. In real life, her revelations had led the people to shrug their shoulders. Now a cat mewed on a rooftop. Ana's hair stood on end and she unsheathed her claws: the blade of the kitchen knife gleamed in the light of a streetlamp. When she realized it was just an animal, she put the knife away, paused a few moments, and did not know whether to laugh or cry. The corners of her lips rose, but a cord pressed against her throat.

A little further on was a pedestrian crossing which led to her parking spot. Ana carefully looked each way before crossing over. The road was deserted. Ana stepped on to the crossing. A cold wind froze her cheeks. She wanted to get to the other side fast, but her feet seemed leaden. The contrast between the white stripes and the black asphalt caught her eye. All of a sudden, coming from a crossroads, a car appeared at high speed, with its headlights on full beam. Ana turned her head, and like a dazzled animal, was paralyzed. She stopped seeing the car and only heard the engine's roar. The car was closer and closer and she could not move. Five meters from the crossing, the driver hit the brakes. The tires squealed and the rubber burned. The car stopped centimeters from Ana. The windows opened.

'Get out of the way, you moron.'

'Next time we'll run you over.'

'Go home and sleep.'

Then laughter. A bunch of university students coming back from a party.

Ana took a deep breath, looked ahead and made it to the pavement. As soon as she sat behind the wheel, she locked the doors. Only then did she notice she was shaking and her back was wet with sweat. The key fell out of her hand when she tried to put it in the ignition, and she took her time finding it again.

After a trip of twelve minutes, driving at high speed and not stopping for red lights, she reached home. She lived by herself on the sixth floor of a building in a new part of the city. She left the car in the residents' car park. Before getting out, she looked all around her. The lighting was dim. There were only two lights and one had a burnt-out bulb. The shadow of a tree looked like a monster's claw. With the knife in her hand, she ran to the entrance of the building and quickly opened the door. She was panting. She went to the lift and pressed the button for her floor.

Seconds later, she entered her flat. She locked and bolted the door and turned on the light. Only then did she calm down. She took off her jacket and woolen hat and went to the kitchen to drink a glass of milk. After using the commode and brushing her teeth, she went to bed. She took her shoes off, undressed, got in bed and turned off the lamp. She only got to sleep half an hour later.

When he heard her snoring, the man sent by Huss waited a few more minutes before he acted. His name was Szut and he had belonged to the old regime's secret police. Now he was one of Fiorov's security men. His specialty was simulating accidental deaths. Two hours before Ana's arrival, he had opened her door with a picklock, and researched the best way to go about his business. As a rule he attacked his victims as soon as they got home, but the design of the flat did not allow for ways to hide himself as he would have liked. So he would run the risk of the neighbors hearing her screams and calling the police, who might be suspicious that it was not an accidental death. Then he thought that the wardrobe in the bedroom would be the best place to ambush her. Most people used it in the morning when they woke up to choose their clothes. The journalist might have different habits, and in that case, he would have to stab her the moment she opened the door and alter his plans for the removal of the body. Such a hitch would force him to give explanations to his boss, and mean further hours of work.

Szut was wearing gloves and rubber-soled shoes. He switched on a torch and came out of the closet where he had been hiding. He moved slowly towards the bed. Ana was lying on her stomach with her face turned to the left. Szut observed her for a few moments.

So young and pretty. Why didn't she enjoy her life like the rest? Why did she have to get mixed up with the powerful? These youngsters are so stupid, they never learn anything. She could have been happy and she's ruined her life. She's lucky at least that she won't suffer.

He placed himself to her right. In his left hand he had a cloth soaked in chloroform. He put the torch on the bed and brought the cloth up to Ana's face. He let her breathe the liquid for a few seconds and then covered her mouth and nose with the cloth. Ana shuddered slightly, but then her body was inert. Szut turned on the lamp, knelt on the bed and turned her over on her back. Next from a pocket in his jacket he took a syringe, put it in Ana's right hand, made her insert the needle in a vein in her left elbow, and injected the liquid. It was a dose of heroin strong enough to kill a horse.

Ana began to breathe slowly, her blood pressure dropped, and her heart raced. Ten minutes later, she died.

Her body was only found two days later, when the editor called the police. The doctor who performed the autopsy ruled that the cause of death was suicide with an overdose of heroin. At the *Europa* editorial offices, the owners, the editor, and the journalists had a meeting to discuss Ana's death. They all agreed she had been killed on Ivan Fiorov's orders. There were yells, people thumping the table, and insults. The prime-minister was called a murderer, a monster, and a psychopath. Some journalists swore they would reveal the truth of the case, others said they would continue to write Ana's satires on the government. It was the duty of journalists, they said, to pick up the torch she had lit and carry it until the government was toppled. The owners and the editor supported the decision: the country and the rest of the world would know that a journalist had been murdered by the prime minister of Slavia. However, in Ana Kull's obituary the following day, not even the causes of her death were mentioned. Nor did any of her colleagues raise the suspicion that she had been assassinated, nor write any satirical story like hers. The flame of the torch went out before anyone else could be burned.

The same thing happened in the rest of the independent media. Although the journalists knew Ana had been killed for political reasons, no one dared touch the subject. Furthermore, on the TV channel controlled by Fiorov the news was given that the death of the journalist Ana Kull was related to her past of dependence on drugs and alcohol, as well as to her links with the world of international prostitution.

Olin and Aliocha

AFTER the fall of the regime, Igor Olin lived with Aliocha in a small house in the city suburbs. Most of his neighbors showed more indifference than hostility to him and there was even an elderly couple who showed their esteem for him, calling him 'the only honest man in the country.' Olin had managed to find a job as an accountant in a Russian used car company that had recently set up in the country, and thanks to his salary and a few thousand dollars he had managed to embezzle while he was Commissar for the Economy, he managed to pay a nurse to take care of Aliocha while he was at work. Aliocha no longer had the attention and comfort of former times, but even so, he had a reasonable quality of life. As for Olin, he had learned to change nappies, and to wash and feed his son almost as well as the nurse. He spoke to him every day too, and hugged him before he went to sleep. However, the embezzled money was running out, and if he could not find a better job, he would be forced to send his son to a home for the disabled.

It was midnight when he sat at his desk and put a sheet of paper in his old typewriter.

Ivan Fiorov,

I decided to wait until the electoral campaign was over to write you this letter. This way you cannot pretend you did not have time to read it or to reply. In other words, you can have no excuses.

I made an agreement with you when I was People's Commissar for the Economy. I delivered two million dollars to you, whose provenance was the state coffers, to invest in your businesses, and in return you promised to pay me interest of half a million dollars. At the time there was also the matter of returning to the state the money taken from it, but as the regime which I belonged to no longer exists, and currently you are the ruler, I consider that matter closed.

As I see in the streets the number of clients consuming the products in which you invested the money (and which I suppose you must have reinvested several times over), I am sure this business has brought you a considerable income. It may even have been the best business deal you have done up until now. I must admit that, leaving aside all questions of ethics, your instinct for earning money is extraordinary. Probably you even set up the rehab clinics you mentioned to me, or perhaps an undertaker's.

However, there is a problem: you still have not paid me the half million dollars that belongs to me. I have tried to contact you several times, by telephone, and by visiting your house, but whoever answered the telephone or spoke to me on the intercom always said the same thing: Mr. Fiorov was not at home.

The time has come now for you to make yourself available.

As I am sure you are a man of your word, I know that in the next few days you will meet me so your debt to me can be liquidated. I will give you two good reasons to do so. As I am certain you know, I have a severely disabled son whose care requires very considerable expense. As my present means will not permit me to keep him at home much longer, I will have no choice but to place him in a home for the disabled. In one of those dens, where he will be subjected to ill-treatment and malnutrition, he will not last long. However odd it may sound to you, there was a humanitarian reason for me to make the proposal to you for the investment of the two million dollars.

The other good reason for you not to refuse to see me is the following: I have in my possession documents that prove the transfer of funds made to you, which I would like to hand to you in person.

I trust I have clearly outlined the reasons why I urgently need to speak to you.

Finally, I wish to clarify that you should not consider this letter a threat, since as you know, that was never my way of solving problems. Civilized people like us reach an agreement through dialogue. Therefore within a maximum of eight days from the receipt of this letter, I shall expect you to be in contact with me.

Yours sincerely,
Igor Olin

OLGA was a redhead with light eyes, long legs and firm breasts. She was nineteen years old. Her literary qualifications consisted of her high school diploma. Before she was hired as a personal secretary, she did modelling jobs or played volleyball. Three other girls with similar physical attributes had filled the post and had been fired shortly afterwards because their performance had not reached the desired standard. Olga knew the demands of the position were high and every day tried to outdo herself. She was never late, always had a smile on her face, and threw herself into her work passionately. This was her greatest professional challenge.

At eleven o'clock in the morning, Olga was on her knees on the carpet in the prime minister's office, with her head stuck between Ivan Fiorov's legs. The prime minister was seated with his eyes closed and his trousers around his ankles. For the sexual favors he received, he rewarded her with fifty-dollar bills. Despite Olga's performance, though, Fiorov was not feeling much pleasure. The distribution of the Coca-Cola was proving less profitable than he had expected. Beer was still the beverage of highest consumption in the country, and Fiorov was hatching a plan to force the owners of the main factory to sell it.

Suddenly, someone knocked the door.

Olga carried on with her task since, besides knowing that nobody would dare enter without the prime minister's authorization, he had instructed her not to stop for any reason. To her amazement, he tapped her head and said, 'That's enough, go and see who it is.' Olga got up, reapplied her lipstick, tidied her hair and waited for Fiorov to pull up his trousers. Then she went to the door and opened it. The other secretary winked at her and gave her a box with the post delivered, already sorted into official and private matters. That day, there were fifteen letters from government departments, a letter from an embassy and six private letters – Olin's and five from business partners. Fiorov always began by opening his private correspondence. He noted the senders of the letters, and on finding Olin's name among them, sent Olga away with a gesture.

He opened the letter, read it, screwed it into a ball, and threw it in the rubbish bin. Then he picked up his telephone and told the other secretary to summon Pietr Huss to his office.

Ten minutes later, wearing a suit and with a haircut copying Fiorov's style, but wearing dirty old shoes, Huss entered the office. As usual, he remained on his feet, a pace away from the desk. He knew he would be ordered to solve something by illegal means, but waited for Fiorov to speak.

'I've got a problem.'

'A problem similar to the one with the journalist?'

'Kind of. A guy is blackmailing me and I want you to deal with him.'

'Who is it?'

'Olin, the former People's Commissar for the Economy.'

Huss scratched his neck. His jacket sleeve was too short and a worn shirt cuff showed.

Fiorov laughed. 'Are you scared? Have you forgotten that communism is finished and he's just a poor devil with no power at all?'

Huss forced a laugh, showing a gold tooth. 'You're right. These changes have been so quick that even I forget they aren't in charge anymore.'

'You'll never stop thinking like the old regime, will you? The project of the New Man failed with young people, but seems to have worked with you.'

Huss fidgeted with his hands as if he did not know what to do with them. 'I don't understand these things very well. Sometimes I wake up in the middle of the night and I don't know for sure if I'm in the past or the present. I have to turn on a light to figure it out.'

Fiorov shook his head. 'Do you miss being a camp guard?'

'No, not at all. I'm very grateful to you for giving me this chance to work for you.'

'The last regime stopped Time, and I'm going to accelerate it. Working for me, you're basically removing some defective parts from the clock. Get it?'

Huss was puzzled and took his time answering. 'I reckon so…'

Fiorov raised his right hand. 'Well, enough jawing. You know who he is. All you have to do is send one of your men to shut his mouth. If a former People's Commissar vanishes, no one will miss him. People will say justice has been done at last.'

'You're right, don't worry. We'll find out where he lives and works and within a few days the problem will be solved.'

Fiorov nodded and Huss left.

The following morning, Szut arrived at the used car stand where Olin worked. He was wearing sunglasses, jeans, a white shirt patterned with blue cornucopias, and Adidas trainers. He hoped to be taken for one of the thousands of citizens who bought imported clothes and tried to copy the lifestyle of the European democracies. Owning a car of German manufacture, even if it were an old Mercedes, was one of the signs of prosperity that everyone tried to show off.

The stand was a glassed-in salon with a marble floor and a wood ceiling. Three Mercedes and three BMWs were displayed in two rows. Each car was a meter from the next, and the rows were three meters apart. Powerful lighting made their red, grey and white paintjobs gleam, giving the impression they were brand new. Two salesmen wearing blue suits and black ties welcomed customers and tried to convince them that here were the best cars in the world, at bargain prices. What they omitted to say, however, was that most of the cars came from Russia, that each milometer had been recalibrated so that the mileage was halved, that some of the engine parts were not original and that even the new seats of certain cars had replaced old ones which were removed because they were stained with the blood of people murdered. Olin worked at the back of the stand in a space reserved for employees. Among other tasks, he was supposed to fool the taxman with false declarations about the firm's profits.

Szut was looking at the cars when a smiling salesman appeared. The sound of his patent leather shoes echoed in the salon. Szut simulated interest in a red BMW. The salesman opened a door and began his usual spiel about the car's qualities. Szut got in, sat at the wheel, and nodded his head. However, he was not listening.

He must be in the office. He works here to give the impression that he earns a salary. I bet he's got one of these cars, he must have stolen enough for that. Honest people drive Ladas or use public transport. Yes, this one really deserves to die.

Meanwhile, in came a middle-aged man, fat, with grey hair and beard, wearing a grey suit but no tie. The salesmen greeted him but he did not even look at them. Isaak Miron, the owner of the stand, had arrived. Of Russian birth, before the Soviet *Perestroika* he had belonged to the Central Committee of the Communist Party. Miron had hired Olin for his professional competence, but also because he saw him as a former comrade fallen on hard times. Unlike himself, Olin had been unable to adapt to the new times. 'This is my revenge, that capitalism tried to destroy me and now I'm sucking its blood,' Miron used to say. Whenever he could, Miron invited him to have lunch with him and reminisce about old times.

Miron entered the offices and a few minutes later came out, accompanied by Olin. Miron talked nonstop and Olin kept quiet. They walked by Szut and he was surprised at how much the old People's Commissar for the Economy had aged. The photograph Huss had given him corresponded to a man of about fifty, but this white-haired man with a wrinkled face and a bent back looked twenty years older. Nor did the old suit he was wearing look right for a wealthy man. Szut almost felt sorry for him. Without taking leave of the salesman, he got out of the car and followed the two men.

He trailed them for several minutes until they went into a pizzeria called Vesuvius. Szut went in too and sat at a table some distance away from them. The restaurant was decorated with pictures of St. Mark's Square in Venice, the Coliseum in Rome and the Leaning Tower of Pisa. There was a counter behind with wines and Italian sausages. The tablecloths and napkins were red, checkered with white. The waiters wore a similar uniform and greeted customers with a comically pronounced *Buon' Giorno*. In the meantime a young waitress approached the two men's table and handed them a menu. Miron looked her up and down from head to foot, whistled and made a flirtatious remark. The girl blushed. Miron ordered two pizzas and a bottle of champagne. Szut kept his eyes on Olin, who seemed distanced from everything. Miron started telling yet another story of when he had belonged to the Central Committee of the Communist Party: a party at the Embassy of German Democratic Republic for which twenty prostitutes had been hired, two of whom he had taken with him to a luxury hotel in Moscow. These stories, which nearly always involved orgies, drunken excesses, and at times the spanking of women, ended in laments for the collapse of the Soviet Union and insults for Gorbachev. Miron spoke loudly, laughed uproariously, and drank the champagne as if it were beer; Olin still had not touched his glass and listened in silence to his boss's story.

When a waiter appeared at Szut's side, it struck him that he might not have enough cash to have lunch in such a restaurant – he usually resorted to food stalls in the street when he was working. He studied the prices on the menu carefully and ordered the cheapest dish and a beer. The waiter withdrew and Szut took out his wallet and counted his money. He would have to do without dessert and coffee. Minutes later, a very thin pizza was put in front of him: on a scant covering of cheese were two slices of salami. Szut stuffed his napkin around his neck, picked up his knife and fork, and began to cut the pizza. He devoured it, chewing with his mouth open. He had never tasted such a delicious pizza. Presently, he put down his knife and fork and started using his hands to break it up and bring it to his mouth. For a few moments, he forgot to watch Olin.

Meanwhile, Miron, having forced Olin to toast the success of business, wealth, health, and women, raised his hand, snapped his fingers, and ordered the girl to bring another bottle of champagne. The moment she heard him, the girl fled to the kitchen and refused to serve him. Presently an older waiter appeared, who tried to put a second bottle of champagne in the bucket filled with ice. Miron pushed him, thumped the table, and demanded that the girl serve him. At the counter, the manager realized there was a problem and hastened to intervene. He appeared smiling, regretted what had happened, and said the girl was feeling unwell. Miron shook his head and uttered a few swear-words in Russian. Embarrassed, Olin started gulping from his champagne glass. The manager blushed and stammered excuses. Miron took out a fifty-dollar bill, flung it on the table, and swore that if the girl did not come back he would never return to the Vesuvius again.

Like the rest of the customers, Szut watched the scene. He gripped his beer glass and gritted his teeth. If they had been outside, he would have got up to punch Miron. He was sorry his boss had not given him orders to kill that man instead of Olin. Then Szut saw the manager pick up the fifty dollar bill, bow to Miron, and head to the kitchen. Shouts were heard, and a plate breaking on the floor. Shortly after, with her head lowered, her eyes half-shut and her nostrils dilated, the girl returned to the table. Miron clapped his hands, called her a good girl, and slapped her thigh. Without a word, the girl opened the bottle of champagne, serving Olin first, and then Miron. She stayed there, waiting for another order, but Miron started telling another story, this time about the Cuban Ambassador's wife, and he forgot her. The girl looked at the manager and he made a signal to her to leave.

Szut asked a waiter for his bill. He had already given sufficient attention to the man he was going to kill. With the information he had got from Huss, he decided he would do it the next weekend when the nurse who looked after the handicapped child was not there. Now he would have to discover Olin's habits and pick the best way to eliminate him.

Szut was watching Olin and did not realize that someone had placed a saucer with a slip of paper in front of him. He heard a childish voice say, 'Sir.' He turned his head and saw the girl Miron had harassed. Seen up close, with the flesh of her face so smooth, her lips so pink and her hands so delicate, she seemed still younger to him; maybe she was not even eighteen yet. He saw in her glance that rage had given way to sadness, which made her look more vulnerable. The girl exhaled a sweet aroma in which scent was mixed with sweat. Szut tried to smile at her, but she avoided eye contact. Szut saw the total he had to pay, got out his walled and put all his money – two notes and five coins – on top of the bill. The girl did not even realize that this customer was trying to give her a tip. She quickly took away the saucer with the bill, as if she feared that Szut might seize her wrist, and turned and headed for the counter. While the manager was giving the change, Szut stood up and left the Vesuvius.

SUNDAY dawned with a clear sky and low temperatures. There was no wind and a mist meandered through the streets. At seven in the morning, the first beams of sunlight struck the façade of the district where Olin lived. Soon after, in a street still shrouded in shadow, Szut parked an old Lada in front of the home of the former People's Commissar. He was wearing black clothes, rubbersoled shoes, gloves and dark glasses. He sucked a mint. In a backpack on the passenger seat, he had a pistol with a silencer, a knife, a flask of chloroform, a handkerchief and syringe with another dose of heroin strong enough to kill a horse. Szut opened the misted window a little, and fixed his eyes on Olin's door. He knew he would soon come out into the street; the light entering the windows was like the smoke that makes an animal leave its den.

An hour and a half later, the door opened. Wearing a grey overcoat, Olin descended one step and headed for the pavement. The sun struck his eyes and made him raise his arm in front of his face. He walked with his back bent and had coughing fits. Olin had already given Aliocha some porridge for breakfast and now he was going to buy bread and the newspaper. Szut had studied the area and knew there was no shop, café or bakery nearby. So he had close to ten minutes to get inside the house and prepare the attack. When Olin reached the end of the block and turned left, Szut picked up the backpack and got out of the car. He waited for an elderly couple to pass, headed to the door, inserted a picklock, and after several tries, opened the door.

Szut found himself in an entrance hall with a brown carpet and two hooks on a white wall stained by humidity. He walked slowly to a room with linoleum on the floor, a neon light on the ceiling, a pine table with two chairs, a sofa of tanned sheepskin, and an armoire with a television set. He went through the room and into a kitchen. He could smell fried oil. There were dirty plates and glasses in the sink, a small fridge and a gas cooker. From the kitchen he moved into a narrow corridor which led to two bedrooms. He entered the closest one and saw a bed with a mattress visible and the sheets thrown back. There was a bedside table with a reading lamp and a wardrobe with a mirror. Shoes, boots and slippers were lined up in a corner.

Then Szut went into the other bedroom.

In a bed with bars, he discovered Aliocha. Wearing white pajamas, he was lying on his back with his head turned to one side. His yellowish eyes were staring at something and his mouth was open. On the pink skin of his face was sprouting a red fluff similar to a moustache, and tufts of beard on his chin. His body was thin, his neck had purple veins, his wrists were twisted and his fingers curved like claws. He gave off an acrid smell. He breathed with difficulty.

Szut came up to him slowly, as if Aliocha were a threat. He put his hands on the bars and whistled. He watched him for some time. Then he stroked his hair and sang a lullaby his mother had put him to sleep with. Aliocha accepted the caress and the unfamiliar voice without showing anxiety. Szut began to talk to him.

'Poor thing. And they insist that God exists. What were you born for? What are you doing in this world? You just make work for others. And who's going to look after you, once your dad is dead? Maybe the best thing for you would be for me to wring your neck. It would be an act of mercy. You'd suffer less than if you go to a lunatic asylum. Yes, but you're out of luck. You weren't included in the service and I'm not going to risk my life for your sake.'

All of a sudden he heard the noise of a lock opening. Had Olin come back earlier than he had expected, or could it be the nurse or someone else? Szut took out his revolver and hid behind the bedroom door. He heard footsteps in the entrance hall going to the living-room and then the kitchen, he heard bags being placed on the table, and footsteps again, very close, in the corridor. Someone came into the room. Szut pressed the gun into his neck.

'On your knees, hands behind your head.'

Olin obeyed. 'I knew this would happen.'

Szut kneed him in the kidneys. 'Shut up.'

Olin stopped himself from shouting, but could not help a coughing fit. His trunk doubled over, his knees flexed, and his face ended up close to the floor.

Szut let him recover. 'Don't speak, obey me and it will be over quickly.'

With difficulty, Olin returned to his former position. 'Listen, if I'm going to die, don't I have the right to some last words?'

Szut took a step and stood in front of Olin. The colorless face of the man, deeply furrowed and with baggy eyes, already looked like the face of a dead man. 'Quick.'

Olin saw the barrel of the gun in front of his face, but felt no fear. He raised his neck toward Szut. He thought he had seen this man dressed in black somewhere.

'Finish my son off too, a shot in the nape. Without me his life will be hell.'

Szut took a deep breath, looked at Aliocha and realized he was agitated. He was silent for a few moments. 'This is what we'll do. I've got a syringe which you're going to inject in a vein in your arm. Then I'll inject an equal dose in your son. It will look like you killed him and then committed suicide. Neither of you will suffer.'

Olin twisted his lips. 'What guarantee do I have that you'll keep your word?'

Szut laughed. 'In your position, you have no guarantees at all. If you don't agree, I'll kill you anyway, and abandon your son. Is that what you'd prefer?'

Olin took his hands from behind his head and brought them up to his cheeks until they met at his nose. 'So why don't you inject him right now?'

Szut brought his gun up to Olin's eye, forcing him to close it. 'All right, give me the syringe and tell me how to do it.'

Without losing his aim with the gun, Szut took a step back, slipped the backpack off his shoulder, put it on the floor, and took out the syringe. 'Take off your jacket and roll up your left shirtsleeve.'

Olin obeyed.

'Very good. Now stretch out your arm and with the tip of a finger on your right hand find the most salient vein in the area of your elbow joint. Do you understand?'

'Yes.' Olin prodded his thin white arm, which seemed to have had all the blood sucked out of it long ago. His finger slid to the left and the right, up and down, as if it did not know what it was supposed to be looking for. Olin went faster, which only made him feel more lost still. He cursed. The vein was an eel that had dived into deep waters. Presently he turned towards Szut to seek his help.

'I don't understand this very well…'

Szut almost laughed. Then he approached again. 'Wait. Take your finger off your arm.' Szut picked up the handkerchief he had in the bag and made a tourniquet for Olin's arm. The eel emerged and showed its purplish back. Szut pointed with his finger.

'Can you see that vein there?'

'This one here? Will it do?' Olin looked happy, as if he had found a treasure.

'Yes, you don't have a better one.'

Szut handed him the syringe and once again Olin's hands fumbled.

'Pay attention now. You're going to insert the needle into the vein and press down the plunger of the syringe very slowly. We aren't going to bother with disinfection or other precautions. Don't be afraid, it won't hurt. In fact, you're actually going to feel pretty wonderful. Then you'll go to sleep and… it'll all be over.'

Without hesitation, Olin pierced the vein and began to inject himself.

'That's right, go on, don't hurry.'

Olin began to feel his head spinning, his muscles relaxing, his jaw slack and his tongue still; he breathed slowly and felt cold; his pupils contracted, his lips and hands turned blue. He fell to the floor, his body convulsing, and vomited.

Szut observed the scene. He was not watching the slow death of a human being caused by a heroin overdose, but a successful procedure that would render him eight hundred dollars. Olin's spasms and rolling eyes, instead of horrifying him, made him think of a car with a powerful engine and strong headlights. A BMW. Szut imagined the new car he would buy, perhaps in the stand where Olin worked. Yes, it was just one of those cars that he wanted and deserved. When at last it seemed that his victim had stopped breathing, he knelt beside the body and put a finger on the carotid artery; then, so there could not be the slightest doubt, he took his pulse. Olin was dead. Szut clenched his fists as if he were celebrating a victory. The BMW was already on its way to him.

Only then did he realize he had forgotten about Aliocha. That poor wretch would not even be worth a tank full of petrol to him.

He got up and went back to the bars of the bed once more. Aliocha seemed calm again. His gaze was vacant and his mouth was open. His breathing was slow and heavy. Szut stroked his face. 'I'm sorry, little monster, I had to kill your father and I can't kill you. You're really going to have to stay on your own in any old hole. But don't worry, you won't last long, they'll soon do you in. Either with beatings, or a pillow, or maybe they'll forget to feed you. Right, I'm leaving now. The nurse will find you tomorrow and try to find a place for you. Bye.'

Two days later, Fiorov's newspaper published an obituary on the former People's Commissar Igor Olin.

Igor Olin
1918 – 1990
Like all the leaders of the communist regime, Igor Olin had a nebulous past. Little is known about his family origins or his own career until he appears as a professor of Statistics at a university without prestige. During the German invasion he collaborated with the Nazis and informed on several colleagues who were then executed. He rose in rank. After the revolution, he came home and joined the communists. He rose in rank. Olin was always on the side of victors and this was the only reason for his success.

In 1950, the dictator Alfred Ionescu invited him to be People's Commissar for the Economy. Thus began a new existence for this ambitious man. Olin became the mainstay of the regime and the confidant of the dictator. Since he guaranteed the economic survival of the regime, he was one of the greatest culprits for its barbarities and the crimes it committed. His private life was punctuated by excesses and violence. He loved beating young prostitutes and enjoyed setting fire to animals. After the fall of the regime, he was tried and sentenced, but benefitted from a juridically dubious amnesty. He never showed remorse for anything.

Igor Olin was a man without morals or scruples, who was capable of the greatest infamy. As he was unable to bear the loss of his privileges after the fall of the regime, he committed suicide. Olin was not made to live in democracy and freedom. Terror fascinated him. He served Nazism and Communism with the same fanaticism. However, he did not wish to leave this world without committing a final filthy trick: he left his severely disabled son an orphan, and he will now have to be taken to a state care home.

Readers are invited to contribute to lessening the suffering of this innocent victim by making donations to account number 667773400 in the National Bank.

Roman

THEY called it Drugville.

It was situated on the outskirts of Tiers in an old timber warehouse abandoned after *Perestroika*. All kinds of drugs could be bought and sold there, sexual services were on sale too, and those who did not pay their debts to the dealers were beaten and sometimes executed. It was a brick building with a zinc roof, six meters high, forty meters long and twenty wide. The floor was of cement, the walls were windowless, and the only light entered through a side door that had been forced open. In the summer, temperatures could reach thirty Celsius, and in the winter fell to freezing.

Dozens of addicts lived in Drugville in tents, cardboard huts, or simply leaning against a wall. Every day hundreds of other drug addicts visited, as well as clients seeking cheap prostitutes, and minor dealers and gangsters hired to collect debts or liquidate whoever did not pay. The space was also colonized by mice, cockroaches and spiders. Whoever came in had to walk carefully so as not to tread on the bodies lying on the floor, the syringes or lost preservatives, the puddles of vomit, the blood and excrement scattered everywhere. In spite of the bonfires they lit in the winter, and the smell of the timber which never vanished, the stink of the filth was nauseating. Noise was incessant owing to the moans of those in withdrawal, the shouts of the delirious, and constant wrangles. There were often thefts and fights between addicts, scenes of oral sex in full view of everyone, deaths by overdose and beatings carried out by debt collectors. When they decided to kill someone, they dragged him outside and shot him. The same happened to those who died of an overdose: like sacks of rubbish, they were thrown by the inhabitants behind the building. Twice a week, a van that picked up dogs came to pick up the bodies and bury them in a common grave. The police never intervened because there were officers who dealt in drugs or extorted money from those who sold them, or who used the youngest addicts as free prostitutes. Besides, politicians and the majority of the population opposed the demolition of Drugville because they thought it preferable for a ghetto of addicts and criminals to be far away from the city.

In short, Drugville was a place that pleased everyone.

Roman Schwartz was pale and shaking, his eyes were red and his lips cracked. In the last few weeks he had lost eleven pounds. He had not taken a shower for four days. Dressed in a grey tracksuit, and with a rucksack on his back, he entered the building at noon, covered his nose and leaned against a wall near the entrance. Although he had been coming here for months, he had never been able to get accustomed to the filth. The day before, he had arranged with his heroin dealer to meet him there at one in the afternoon. The pains he was starting to feel from withdrawal had led him to arrive early, even though he knew he would not find anyone before the scheduled time. There were other dealers there who could sell him the drug at the same price, or even cheaper, but Roman did not trust them. Most of them adulterated the heroin with substances that could cause the death of the user. At least two girls he knew had died that way.

Presently, Roman saw a girl he knew coming in. She was tall and thin, with her face covered with blemishes and spiky black hair. She wore a denim jacket and jeans and carried a black shoulder bag. The girl passed him with quick steps, avoiding the prostrate bodies but not minding what filth she stepped in, until she reached a cardboard shelter where her friend lived. He was sitting at the entrance with his head between his knees. As soon as he saw her, he got up and grabbed her by the arm. He shouted at her and tried to take her handbag from her. The girl resisted and shouted too. They fought. He gave her a punch that knocked her down. While the girl lay stretched out on the floor, her friend snatched her bag, opened it and took out a wad of banknotes. Then he went in search of a dealer who could sell him a dose of heroin. Meanwhile the girl got up without anyone's help. Her face was bloody and her clothes dirty. She looked all around until her gaze seized on something. Then she wiped her face, tidied her hair, took lipstick from her bag and painted her lips. She turned back towards a short, fat man with dark glasses who had just arrived. They spoke to one another. The man nodded and the two went into a deserted corner. The man leaned against the wall and dropped his trousers; the girl got on her knees and started to blow him. Some people passed nearby, but did not even look. The act lasted no more than five minutes; the man let out a yell and the girl took his member out of her mouth; the man gave her two notes and she left.

Soon after, three men with an Alsatian came in. One was an old man with white hair who carried a walking stick, and the other two were younger. Roman watched them, intrigued: it was obvious they had come in search of someone, but the group looked nothing like a drug gang; they were dressed as peasants and it seemed to be the first time they had ever been in a place like this. The dog handler ordered it to search, the old man struck anyone within reach with his stick, and the other man insulted the addicts. Everyone moved out of their way. Whenever they passed a tent or shelter they knocked it down and forced its occupants to show their faces. Those who protested were assaulted or bitten by the dog. Suddenly, in the middle of the building, a boy stood up and tried to run; however, he was swaying and he ended up falling flat on his face. One of the men saw him and shouted. The group rushed in pursuit of the fugitive. The old man was left behind, but the two younger men and the dog quickly reached him. They picked him up off the floor and started punching and injuring him. The old man hit him across the back with his stick. The dog, though, did him no harm. Then they took him out of the building. The boy was handcuffed, and he lowered his head. He was crying. The dog tried to lick his face. As they passed by Roman, he heard the old man say the boy was a disgrace to the family. The group vanished and Drugville went back to normal.

When he saw his dealer arrive, Roman was so excited that he salivated, and ran to meet him. He too had turned into a dog when his owner came near with food. The dealer had put a collar around his neck. He depended on him and he placed himself at his feet, obediently, awaiting his meal. However, he had to pay for it. It was not enough to wag his tail and lick the hands of his owner. The latter neither desired tricks, nor affection, nor did he want to show his pet to his friends, or enter him in a contest. He only wanted dollars.

The dealer was a man known as Pi, a little older than Roman. Like all the minor dealers, he bought the drugs from Pietr Huss. Although he was beginning to earn hundreds of dollars a month, he always wore a tracksuit and old shoes to hide the signs of wealth. He did not use drugs, or drink alcohol. He was in good shape and had already beaten up other dealers who tried to steal his clients. Although he was feared for his strength, he always carried a handgun in his pocket. Pi's business flourished because he had managed to create a reputation for nearly pure drugs, or at least not too badly adulterated. However, Pi also yearned to drive a BMW; in order to get his hands on the steering wheel of one, he needed to break some of the rules of drug-dealing.

'Got the money?'

'Yeah, here you are.' Roman held out a hand with banknotes he had got from selling a watch left him by his mother, Luda. Pi counted them slowly then handed him a bag of heroin.

'Is it the usual?'

'You know my gear is the best around.'

'Sure.'

Pi left and Roman looked for a corner. He rolled up the sleeve of his left arm, put his backpack on the floor, and took out all the gear he needed to shoot up: a syringe, a lighter, a spoon, and half a lemon. He looked all around to make sure no one was about to rob him, and started the process. He put a few drops of lemon juice and the powdered heroin on the spoon, lit the lighter and waited for the drug to dissolve. When he managed to obtain a liquid, he put the spoon on the ground, stirred with the needle, and pulled back the plunger of the syringe. Then, in a thin white arm pocked with track marks and bruises, he inserted the needle in the fattest vein and shot up.

Roman shut his eyes and felt himself free of gravity. His anxiety was over, his body no longer hurt, and he felt better and better. Colored lights shone. Melodies played. Perfumes spread around him. He was in paradise. Then, like an angel, Lia appeared. She was wearing a white dress and was prettier than ever. She smiled at him. She wanted to return to him, she regretted having swapped him for another man, and what's more a terrorist suspected of murdering his mother, she asked for forgiveness for having destroyed his life and promised she would never leave him again, she wanted to make up for the suffering she had caused him. She loved him. Roman saw her before him as clearly as if she were flesh and blood. The same blue eyes and red mouth, firm breasts and long legs. He was moving his lips to kiss her and making gestures to caress her. He wanted to make love with her right there. Then suddenly Lia vanished. Everything went dark. And from paradise, Roman returned to hell. Pleasure became pain. Roman could not breathe and he felt his chest tearing apart. He began to convulse and vomit.

He fainted.

♛

Schwartz and Roman

UNLIKE his old comrades, Schwartz had not gone to Fiorov to ask his forgiveness in exchange for money. His professional experience in dealing with criminals had taught him that with men like Koba no deal would be respected if the other party had no power. Even if he gave him all the money he had, Fiorov might at any moment change his mind and decide to kill him. He was above the law and nothing would happen to him. Besides, as he only respected power, any show of weakness or self-abasement could only make things worse. So he decided he would not go down on his knees before the new owner of the country. Thus, although he could have emigrated, he went to live in an old quarter of Tiers with Roman.

The change from a luxury flat with five rooms to a house with two bedrooms and plumbing problems and damp ceilings was not easy. Of course the money he had extorted from Zdanhov could have enabled him to live in more comfort. However, Schwartz preferred for others to think he had become a victim. He wore old clothes, simulated a bent-over gait, and put on an expression of suffering. Even so, he was the target of more insults, threats in the street and by anonymous letters, refusals to be served in shops and expulsions from bars, attempts to run him over and other aggressions, than Olin or Zdanhov. His only consolation was that Roman had been spared. Except for a few problems at school, Roman had never been bothered elsewhere.

All the same, Roman was not himself.

To begin with, Schwartz attributed the change in his son's behavior to the reality that he was unprepared for, to his own trial and the accusations that he had committed crimes, to the fact that he had not got over the trauma of his mother's death, and, maybe, some disappointment in love. Roman had stopped speaking to him, had bad marks in school, he came home late, had become irritable, lost a lot of weight and looked ill. He no longer socialized with his friends, but went about on his own or in the company of misfits. Attempts to talk to him had resulted in evasive answers or hasty exits from the house. Meanwhile, when he realized that valuables were disappearing, and banknotes from his own wallet, Schwartz understood at last that his son had more serious problems. As he no longer had the power to order anyone to follow him, he took on the task himself.

One morning, after Roman had left without saying a word, he went after him. It was easy to follow him through the streets, but when he ended up at a bus stop, Schwartz could not go on. The attempt to discover Roman's destination was unsuccessful too because the bus stopped at ten stations before it reached its final one on the outskirts of the city. So Schwartz had to follow the bus in his car. By then he suspected where his son was going, and unsurprised, when Roman got off at the last stop, he followed him on foot for ten minutes until they reached Drugville. Although he knew it was a place where drugs were sold and consumed, and knew all about human degradation from the prisons and concentration camps, although he had come across several addicts on the way, and had seen a girl prostituting herself at the entrance to the building, the shock of seeing that circus of zombies horrified him. As if he bore no responsibility for what had happened, Schwartz cursed *Perestroika*, Democracy, Capitalism, and above all, Fiorov, the main culprit of all the ruin. On the other hand the victims did not deserve any more of his pity than the opponents of the old regime. If his son had not been inside he would have gone in search of a can of petrol to burn the building down.

That very day, he decided to have Roman committed. To persuade him to accept treatment, he had rehearsed a talk with his son in which he would make him see the risks he was running and the fact that there was no other solution for drug addiction. He convinced himself that he would expound solid arguments and that the result could be nothing less than his son's full agreement. After all, he did not want to die and he wanted to be free of that misery. However, when Roman came home with his white face and purple bags under his eyes, dirty clothes and a fetid smell, Schwartz was struck dumb, lacking the courage even to tell him he had discovered the truth. He greeted him, lowered his head, and allowed him to shut himself in his room. With that specter his son had become it would not be possible to have any kind of conversation. Now Roman was a creature from another world, whose language Schwartz did not know. First he would have to manage to bring him back and regain his confidence before he brought up the subject.

Nevertheless, the reestablishment of trust was not what Roman needed to satisfy his addiction. Nor did stealing from his father, denying the theft, or insulting him help the relationship. Schwartz was preparing to commit him by force when one night Roman did not come home at dinner time. Schwartz kept pacing up and down, peeping constantly out of the window, opening the door although no one had rung, kicking the furniture, cursing, pulling out his hair, scratching his neck, and drinking vodka from the bottle, until at eleven o'clock at night, he picked up a torch, left home at a run, got into his car and headed for the world of ghosts and zombies.

Minutes later he arrived at Drugville.

Schwartz entered the building with his torch on and pointed its beam frenetically in every direction. He fought against the darkness, cutting it up with luminous strokes. His adversary, however, recomposed himself without giving up Roman. Schwartz realized he would have to change his tactics. He lowered his light sabre, returned to his point of departure, and slowly began to illuminate each square meter of the space and each face he found. The chaotic incursion gave way to surgical assaults. He saw startled faces, raving faces, lifeless faces. As he moved on without finding Roman, he began kicking the addicts lying on the floor. When at last he completed the circuit of the building, he seized a boy leaning against a wall and asked him about Roman; the boy shook his head and Schwartz threw him to the ground.

Then he ran to his car and tore off towards the public hospital.

It was an old building that lacked sufficient doctors, nurses and equipment to take care of the people in the emergency room or treat the hospitalized patients. For that reason, and because elderly people had been abandoned there, patients were in beds in the corridors, or in places like the warehouses for cleaning products. Infections with super-resistant bacteria and food poisoning were all too frequent.

Schwartz parked his car in one of the places marked for ambulances, entered the building at a run, jumped in front of a queue of people waiting for the receptionists to register them, and shouted out his son's name.

'Roman Schwartz! Is there anyone here with that name?'

The receptionists told him he would have to wait his turn, the people in the queue protested, Schwartz threatened everyone and a security guard appeared who tried to throw him out of the hospital. Schwartz yelled and threw himself on the floor. The rumpus attracted more people, among whom was a doctor, Dr. Max Steiner.

Faced with such a scene, he was in two minds. As he recognized Schwartz, he wanted him thrown into the street; on the other hand, he saw a desperate man begging to find out about his son. Steiner went into action. 'Leave him alone. You can't brutalize this man like that. We're in a hospital. Can't you see he's worried about his son? I'm asking the ladies working here to give him the information he wants.'

The guard released him, those who had been protesting sat down, ashamed, and Schwartz himself was embarrassed. A nurse helped him to get up. Schwartz was disheveled, with his shirt-tails out of his trousers, and panting for breath. He turned towards Dr. Steiner to thank him but the doctor turned his face away and left. Two women whispered about what had happened. Meanwhile a receptionist called him.

'You want to know if we have a patient here named Roman Schwartz?'

'Yes, please.'

The girl typed the name into her computer. The system took its time processing the data. Schwartz was shaking. At last the information appeared.

'I'm sorry. I can't find anyone with that name.'

Schwartz leaned over the counter until his face was close to the girl's.

'He might have been hospitalized without any ID. Let me see the patients in intensive care. Please.'

The nurse intervenes. 'Come with me.'

She led Schwartz to a lift where they ascended to the third floor. The nurse took him along a corridor with neon lights to the far end of the building. She found a doctor and explained the situation to her. Then she opened a door and let him into a ward with twelve beds in which patients were hooked up to machines. A mixture of smells sickened Schwartz: body odor, iodine tincture, and cleaning products.

'You can see for yourself,' the nurse told him.

Schwartz had already seen them and was nearly sure none of them was Roman. Even so, he got closer to the beds in which men were lying and observed their faces. He only found people older than his son. He turned towards the nurse.

'Isn't there anywhere else he might be?'

The nurse shrugged her shoulders. 'Only the morgue.'

'Take me there, please.'

The nurse led him to a lift again and they went down to a basement.

It was a grey space with concrete walls and a cement floor. It smelled of bleach. The temperature was around 10 degrees Celsius. It contained eleven refrigerated compartments, each one with the capacity to hold five corpses. The lighting was weak and the doors of the refrigerators were tinged with the surrounding grey. To Schwartz it felt as if he had come into a garage. In the room was an attendant in a blue overall, whom the nurse asked if he could show them the corpses. The attendant made a gesture with his fingers and Schwartz understood what he wanted. He took out a five dollar bill and handed it to him. The man put away the money and opened the first refrigerated compartment. He pulled out the tray on which lay the corpse, raised the sheet covering it with a jerk, and showed it off smiling as if he had performed a conjuring trick. It was a girl who had drowned; if not for the bluish color of her face, she might have been asleep. Schwartz shook his head and the attendant put her back in the refrigerated compartment. Then he repeated the motion with the other four corpses. None of the deceased was Roman. In the next refrigerated compartment, Schwartz encountered men and women who had been run over, died in falls, had heart attacks, cancer, and other diseases. Some had disfigured faces, others were swollen, while yet others looked like mummies reduced to skin and bone. His son was not among them. The expression on Schwartz's face had not altered. The nurse touched his arm and led him to the exit. The morgue attendant seemed disappointed. The show he had given of revealing the corpses, however well paid, had not pleased the spectator.

Schwartz left the hospital but did not return home. Nor did he try to find Roman in the new private hospital, where he knew they would not have admitted his son because he had no credit card. Schwartz headed for the cemetery. At that hour the gates were closed and there was no one there, but he could not bring himself to go anywhere else. He left the car in the empty car park and got out. The night was cold and the sky dark. The wind whistled and the leaves rustled. An owl fluttered by, crying, and somewhere a dog howled. Schwartz walked to the cemetery's entrance gates and stayed there stuck to the iron bars, looking at the graves.

At half past six in the morning, the day began to dawn. Behind Schwartz, the horizon was a magic lantern: it projected a black light that became purple, then turned orange and next yellow, and finally exploded in a white glare. Schwartz watched the transformation of the cemetery, but the light, instead of modelling life, announced its end.

At half past seven the man who looked after the cemetery

arrived. He had a reddish face, brown hair, and a red moustache. He wore blue overalls too wide for him, and bunched boots. His father had had the same profession and he had inherited the position thirty-seven years before. Apart from burying the dead, it was his job to look after the graves, pull up weeds and make any necessary repairs. He was proud of his work and he used to say that his clients never complained. Perhaps for that reason, he was wont to urinate on the ground or against the walls. Even so, before entering the land of the dead, he would arm himself with a bottle of vodka.

On seeing Schwartz beside the entrance gate at such an hour, he took him for a lunatic. From time to time people like that appeared, saying they wanted to die, that they had come back from the dead, or muttering meaningless phrases. In his own manner, he tried to console them. He took a bottle out of his pocket and took a swig from it before accosting him. His voice was a hoarse drawl. 'Don't worry, it's not your turn yet.'

Schwartz evaluated the man before him. He was not worth more than two dollars.

'Take it.'

The man's eyes widened and he took the note. 'I'll warn you that if you mean to rob a corpse, I won't help you. It's dangerous at this hour.'

Schwartz shook his head. 'Listen carefully, I want you to open the grave where the corpses brought by the city council are buried.'

'Ah, the tramps in the common grave. I buried two yesterday. Our country hasn't got the money to keep them in fridges and I think it's better not to waste any time with people like that. It's doing a favor to their families, because no one cares about them. Let's take a look, they won't smell yet.'

Schwartz shut his eyes and took a deep breath. 'Hurry up, before anyone comes.'

The gravedigger opened the gate and led Schwartz to the far end of the cemetery. They walked in silence for the five minutes it took to get there. The sun was higher and it illuminated an area of dark soil with dozens of wooden crosses identified by numbers. Everywhere there were yellow flowers whose sweet scent attracted insects. It was the so-called 'Beggars' Plot.' A new law passed by Fiorov's government, with the justification of fiscal economy and better public health, had decreed that the dead who had no identification should be buried the same day. However, in practice the measure aimed at cleaning out corpses from Drugville so the narcotics traffic could work more efficiently.

The gravedigger went to a nearby hut, dragging his heels. He came back with a rusty spade on his shoulder that bent his back over. Before the grave, he looked at the earth and bit his red moustache. He put down his spade, took out his vodka, and gulped. Only then did he start working. Very slowly, as if he had the weight of a headstone in his hands, he stuck the spade in the soil and began to throw hillocks of earth to one side. Schwartz restrained the urge to shout at him to work faster. He took a step and stood before him with his hands behind his back. The gravedigger felt the pressure and tried to work more quickly. His face turned mauve and he started to gasp for breath. Presently he put down his spade, caught his breath and wiped the sweat off his brow with his blue sleeve.

'Don't stop,' said Schwartz. 'You were paid to do this job.'

'Let's take it easy, or the dead man will be me.'

When the gravedigger took the bottle out of his pocket to have another swig, Schwartz could not contain himself. He snatched the spade out of his hands, pushed him aside, and began digging with all his might. Far from taking offence, the gravedigger was relieved. Schwartz was soon uncovering an ever deeper hole. The spade strokes made a dull sound. The earth flew everywhere. Insects fled. Suddenly the sound was different. The spade had struck something harder. Schwartz dug carefully and saw a white thing emerge from the dark earth. A finger that seemed to point at him. He was stupefied. The gravedigger sniffed, cleared his throat, and pulled his overalls straight before he made his excuses.

'They didn't bring coffins. It's not my fault.'

Then Schwartz flung himself at the earth and began scraping

at it like a dog looking for a bone. He cut his fingers and broke his nails. He opened up the hole. First the hand appeared, then the arm, and finally the face of the corpse. It was dirty, its eyes were shut and its mouth was full of dirt. It smelled bad. Roman had died of an overdose eighteen hours earlier. Schwartz took his face in his hands and kissed his cheek. The only moment when Schwartz repressed a sob was when his lips touched the cold skin. Then he picked up a handkerchief and started to clean Roman's face. His chin, his lips, his teeth, his cheeks, his nose, his eyes and his forehead. His dull skin extinguished the light of the sun.

'Call someone responsible. I want to get my son out of here,' he told the gravedigger.

EVEN before Roman had been buried, Schwartz could think of nothing but revenge. Someone was guilty of the death of his son, and he had to kill him. Nothing but doing justice with his own hands would satisfy him. He had allowed Luda's murderers to escape, but he would not leave the man who killed Roman unpunished. Ivan Fiorov was going to die. How, when, and in what manner, these were the questions that occupied him. That night he went back to analyzing the information he had gathered on Fiorov under the old regime. A criminal responsible for the death of dozens, who did business with several People's Commissars and liked young girls – nothing he did not know already, with the difference that now he ruled the country. This astute, implacable man had been in a concentration camp and had known how to win the people's vote. He seemed indestructible and capable of anything. All the same, if it were possible to kill a guy like JFK, it was possible to kill a guy like Fiorov. He remembered the maxim of the old comrade Mao Tse Tung: *Power is at the end of a rifle barrel.* His own little pistol guaranteed him the power to do justice, even if he perished in the act. Lee Harvey Oswald shot JFK in the head knowing that he would die too; Schwartz was equally prepared to carry out his suicide mission. He would just have to be patient and wait for his target to expose himself, in Fiorov's convertible.

Schwartz put away his file and stared at his nails, which were black from the earth at the cemetery. He had been unable to clean them. It was all that was left of Roman. Dirt become purity. He joined his hands delicately, pressed them to his heart, and shut his eyes. He would have given his life, he would have given anything, to have Roman come back to life. He thought of the hundreds of men and women whose deaths he had decided, he thought of Father Karlovic, and even of Luda's murderers. Apart from them, he had perhaps also robbed those who loved them of their lives. One never died alone. If he could have gone back, if he could have started again, he swore to himself, he would not have killed anyone. Life was… Tears ran down his cheeks. He sobbed. And then, emerging from a forgotten corner of his memory, as if it had been waiting for this stimulus to awaken, as if it had been called, as if it could not have been any other way, the music resounded in his head:

'We were born to be alive…'

Aliocha

THE STATE asylum was twelve kilometers from the city, in an old church property. Ionescu's government had created it during the sixties during a campaign for building new hospitals and clinics. Called the Mental Health Center of Tiers, its aim was to demonstrate that, unlike the capitalist system, whose mental patients were outcasts, under the socialist system they were treated as citizens with full rights. The regime's propaganda had presented it as the most advanced asylum in Europe: innovative scientific methods, contact with nature and devoted staff guaranteed a peaceful stay and good chances of recovery.

It was a yellow building of three storeys, designed for two

hundred patients. At present, it held twice that, which made it necessary to install bunks in the wards, and which had made the canteen into a labyrinth. It had a park with fruit trees and a kitchen garden where some of the patients worked. Hens and sheep roamed freely. A barbed wire fence sealed it off from the outside world. Those interned there included the mentally handicapped, schizophrenics, manic-depressives, patients with Alzheimer's and cerebral palsy, amnesiacs and criminals. Under the old regime, political opponents had also been imprisoned there, and subjected to treatment meant for violent lunatics, such as electric shock therapy, excessive medication, and solitary confinement in cells with straitjackets. The staff consisted of five psychiatrists, thirty nurses, ten cleaning ladies and two gardeners. In a cage were two German Shepherds that were used when there were attacks on the staff or fights between the lunatics. The patients were forced to get up at eight in the morning and go to bed at eight in the evening. They were served four meals a day. The building had not been repaired for many years: the paint was cracking on the walls, the floor tiles were cracked, there were leaks when it rained, the doors stuck and squeaked, the kitchen had broken equipment, was infested with cockroaches and gave off an acrid smell, and the heating in the wards did not work. In addition there was a constant shortage of medicine and other vital materials used by the nurses. Hot water showers were only available in the winter and visits were not possible outside the weekends. After the installation of democracy, there were strikes, thefts, and absenteeism from work.

Aliocha had been placed in the asylum a month before. He was given a bed on the third floor, where there were other sufferers from cerebral palsy, Alzheimer's patients and people with severe depression. It was the quietest area of the asylum, as long as the rest of the patients did not enter there. Two nurses had the task of taking care of the helpless patients like Aliocha, feeding, washing and dressing them. However, Aliocha had become thin, he stank, he had developed scabs, and spent the day groaning. When he was upset, the nurses either ignored him or sedated him or beat him.

Two weeks after his arrival, a lunatic from the first floor attacked him and broke one of his teeth. The doctor who supervised him commented to a colleague that it would have been better if Aliocha had died.

However, there was a patient with Alzheimer's who took an interest in Aliocha, and at times, tried to be kind to him. He was an old man whose illness had begun to erase his memories; he barely remembered who he was and was incapable of understanding where he was. Dots formed in his head, but when he tried to join them up, he could not find the pattern that made up the picture. The past was a gallery of abstract paintings. Even so, Aliocha's presence succeeded in igniting brief sparks in the darkness of his memory. By some caprice of the illness, the process of destruction in his brain that had made him amnesiac had spared, paradoxically, a distant memory of meetings with a child who had cerebral palsy. He had visited him at his house, seen him in his bed with bars, and had held him on his lap. Years later, he had seen how the child had grown into an adolescent just as incapable of surviving alone; that day, he had whistled the song of a bird to him, and he had seemed to enjoy it.

Alfred Ionescu remembered Aliocha.

After the trial, Ionescu had begun to show cognitive disturbances, and the provisional government had set up a medical commission to evaluate his mental state. Comprised of three psychiatrists, two of whom had undergone threats and coercion under the old regime, the commission concluded that Ionescu was suffering from irreversible dementia and advised that he be committed as he was incapable of looking after himself. Most of the members of the provisional government considered that it would be a form of justice to sentence him to an asylum that he himself had created. Thus, against his will, Ionescu was confined to the Center for Mental Health in Tiers.

His disgust at being held prisoner, the inadequate medical care, the poor nutrition, the cold, the contact with the insane, the forced work in the kitchen garden and the beatings he suffered from nurses and cleaning ladies whose families had been victims of the regime, all accelerated the process of mental decline in Ionescu. Six months after being committed, Alzheimer's disease had conquered part of his brain. The staff called him 'boss' and often asked him questions about the government of the country:

'What measures have you taken to develop the economy? Are you going to lower taxes? Where are you going to build the new airport? When are you going to welcome the President of the United States?'

At first, he understood the mockery and fell into a fury; little by little, though, the questions ceased to have any meaning; in the end he could not even understand what they were asking him about. Even so, the staff continued to have fun at his expense, shouting in his ears, slapping his head, or tripping him up when he did not react. The doctors ignored the abuse and the only inhabitants of the asylum who showed him any affection were the German Shepherds, to whom he gave hunks of bread.

One afternoon, after walking in the asylum's gardens and spending hours peering out through the barbed wire fence, Ionescu went back to the ward. He did so neither from fatigue nor any other reason, since his legs carried him at a slow ambling pace from one place to another without any purpose. Instead of taking orders from his brain, his muscles seemed to be animated by their own fathomless, iron will. Wearing the suit he had had on when he was tried, now buttonless and worn at the elbows, and rubber slippers, he passed by a doctor and two nurses, none of whom paid him the slightest attention. As he climbed the stairs, a schizophrenic tried to tell him something, and it was his turn to ignore him. Ionescu had his hair buzzcut because he had had fleas, his face was unshaven and he had not taken a shower for six days. His countenance was a gaunt, wrinkled mask, with a twisted mouth and two glass marbles for eyes. The blemishes on his hands had darkened and grown, so they seemed like cockroaches bursting through his skin. He breathed as if he were wearing a gas mask.

The door of the ward was open and Ionescu went in. In a

corner, a female nurse was shouting at Aliocha for having vomited in his bed.

'You pig, they don't pay me enough to look after freaks like you.'

To Ionescu the shouts of the nurse sounded like an unfamiliar language, but when he saw her stooped over the bed, smacking Aliocha, the spark lit up again. His muscles lost control of his body, and what was left of his conscious mind took over again. He moved towards the nurse, shuffling in his slippers. She was a woman of forty, short and fat, whose father had been a concentration camp guard. She was unaware of his approach and turned in surprise when she felt Ionescu's frozen hand grabbing her arm. Her surprise turned into astonishment when she saw the transformation of the old man's face: the moribund eyes gave off sparks, the flaccid face had tensed, and the gaping mouth revealed menacing teeth. His putrid breath struck her.

'Leave him alone, or I'll have you shot,' said Ionescu, raising his arms as if he had a rifle in them.

The nurse was paralyzed. Her face was livid, her pupils dilated and her lips tight. Her shoulders fell and her back slumped. Her hands trembled. The man she had been taught to fear, the father of the people who had made thousands disappear, was before her, threatening her. She had never forgotten being taken to listen to a speech of President Ionescu, or of his authoritarian voice, which had frightened her so much. And it was the same voice, albeit weaker, that she was hearing now. For a few moments, the nurse's pinafore was changed into the pink dress in which her parents had taken her to Ionescu's rally, and the hair that was held in place with a grip became two pig-tails. The nurse picked up the cloth she had been using to clean up Aliocha's vomit, lowered her head, and left.

Ionescu came closer to Aliocha, who had not stopped moaning. He was wearing white pyjamas too big for him, a black sock on one foot, and a blue one on the other. His head was resting against the bars of the bed, his mouth was open and his eyes were red; a crimson boil was erupting on his neck. Ionescu took a handkerchief from his pocket and cleaned the rest of the vomit on his chin, his pyjamas, and the sheets. Then he held one of his hands and caressed his face. He spoke childish words and tried to whistle birdsong. Minutes passed. The sunlight disappeared. Aliocha began to calm down, shut his eyes, and not long after, he fell asleep.

⚜

Maria, Lia and Leonidas

MARIA Kirchner went inside her house with two bags full of food. Her hair was white, she walked bent over, and was nearly blind in her left eyes because of a cataract. She went to the kitchen where Lia was waiting for her to start breakfast. She put the shopping on a table with a blue cloth and sat down next to her daughter. Lia smiled at her and poured her a cup of coffee.

'I've brought bread, fruit, jam and butter. You've got to eat properly.'

'Thanks, mum, but you could have let me go to the shop.'

'Why? Don't you think I'm capable?'

Lia smiled. 'I think you're very stubborn.'

Maria pulled a face and drank a little coffee. 'Look, I'm going to ask you once more: are you sure you know what you're doing? Wouldn't it be better to wait a bit longer and let the government carry out those investigations?'

Lia stopped chewing a hunk of bread and only then did she answer. 'Mum, the government isn't interested in digging up the past. The creature who's in charge would end up spattered with mud. But I will only be at peace when I find out what happened. It's the only way I can get over the calamity that struck us.'

'Lia, you ought to know that it's dangerous to interfere with the people in charge. What's more, in your condition, three months pregnant, it's hardly the right time...'

'I'm not afraid of them and I'm ready for anything.'

'I'm not.'

'I know, mum.'

'I'd like to find your father too, but…' Maria sobbed.

Lia took her hand. 'Mum, don't cry. Dad's been dead for many years, but we survived. It's our duty to discover the truth and reveal the crimes of the dictatorship. And that's what I'm going to do.'

'You want to make the world spin the other way round, but you only have the strength of your own arms, because mine aren't much good anymore.'

'Mum, since *Perestroika* the world has changed direction. I've only got two arms among the millions that brought about the change, but I have to continue the struggle. I'm going to find dad and discover what they did to him. I'm going to restore his reputation and recover the paintings they stole from him. The world will know there was a painter who resisted the dictatorship and paid for it with his life. That's where my duty lies.'

Maria was looking into space and did not seem to be listening to her. 'If it were not for you, I think I would have…'

Lia interrupted her. 'Don't say anything.'

'I'm sorry.'

'Mum, just think of your grandchild who's about to be born. Think how he'll have a better life than ours. He'll live in freedom and enjoy rights we never had, even if it has to be in another country.'

Maria shrugged her shoulders. 'Freedom… I still haven't got used to that word. Nor can I get used to the idea of you having a child when you're unmarried. Is that freedom too?'

Lia smiled again. 'If we're responsible for our actions, yes, that's freedom.'

Maria picked up an apple and started peeling it with brusque knife-strokes. 'This is all too much for me. I don't know whether I'm happy or sad. Go on then, go ahead and find your father. Maybe then I'll be able to live in freedom at last. Freedom, for me, is peace. And I've never had that.'

Lia remembered her father's paintings again. Such colorful men and women, with such intense expressions and gestures so dramatic they were frightening. They seemed alive, they seemed to be speaking to you, they required your attention. However, none of them was at peace. What they were, on the contrary, was anxious, when they were not in intense pain. Why? What might have happened to those people, since you never saw any threat nearby? The dictatorial regime was not a sufficient explanation. Back then she had not been able to answer the question, but now she thought she had found the answer. Hadn't her father, with the mysterious foresight of artists, begun to unveil the future reserved for them? Then, in the dozens of girls he had painted and drawn, which she had supposed imaginary creations without the least resemblance to anyone she knew, like the composer who conjures up variations on the same theme, after all, he had been projecting *her* face. The anguish of his daughter after he had been sent to a concentration camp.

The next day, a Saturday, at seven in the morning, Lia and Leonidas began a five-hour train journey, with changes at two stations, which would take them to the town of Akha, four kilometers from the former concentration camp where Ludwig Kirchner had died. They started the trip in a train full of passengers with comfortable carriages, and ended it in an old one with half a dozen travelers seated on wooden benches. They were served a hot meal at the beginning, and cold water later. They left in a mild temperature and arrived in a cold place. Lia spoke to Leonidas about various subjects, never mentioning the purpose of the trip, as if they were going on a holiday. Leonidas was keen on the idea of exposing the crimes of the Ionescu regime, but as the train progressed on its journey and he discovered that Lia did not want to speak about her father, he began to feel embarrassed. He pattered around the subject and looked out of the window, where he saw the same scenery of fields and mountains. His memory of having killed a woman came back to haunt him. Everything he was saying seemed besides the point and ridiculous. Lia noticed this tension and fell silent. It was as though the silence of Kirchner and Luda were the only way of establishing a connection on their journey. The noise of the train and the conversations of the other passengers collided with an invisible barrier raised by those two ghosts. When they were already near their destination, and a pall of fog hid the hills and fields, it was not so much space, as time, which seemed to have changed. They were travelling into the past. Their destination was the same, but each was searching for something different. Lia hoped to find her lost father. In Kirchner's grave Leonidas hoped to encounter the ultimate justification for having killed Luda. Lia remembered the moment she had arrived home and found her mother crying. Leonidas remembered the moment he had learned that the terrorist attack had caused a victim's death.

The town of Akha had a population of two thousand inhabitants who were engaged in farming and business. There was just one school and one health clinic. The station was a halt at which three trains a day arrived and left. The appearance of outsiders caused curiosity and suspicion. The couple found themselves on a cement platform with a zinc roof. From there they went through a white ticket office and came out into a square. It had an earthen floor, in the center of which was a tree and a wooden bench, bordered by stones. The square led to a narrow street which split into two more that did not appear to lead anywhere. They saw no one. There were just two stray dogs and a beige Lada parked a few meters away from them.

A gust of wind raised the dust and made them fasten their jackets.

They approached the car in the hope that the owner would appear. On looking through the driver's window they discovered someone lying on the rear seat. A newspaper covered his face and he was snoring. They walked around the car and peeped in through the back windows. There was also a bottle of vodka and pornographic magazine on the seat. Leonidas knocked on the window, once, twice, three times. A middle-aged man wearing a black suit and a white shirt threw the newspaper into the air, got up suddenly, and opened the door. The couple stepped back. The man was bald, with dark eyes and a hooked nose. He clenched a fist and shouted:

'Can't a guy have a rest anymore? What do you want?'

Lia held Leonidas' arm. 'I'm sorry if we woke you. We've just arrived and we're looking for a taxi.'

The man took a deep breath. Then he took a pack of cigarettes from his pocket and lit one. 'I'm not a taxi driver. There isn't one in this place.'

'Sorry…'

'I'm a farmer and my wife runs a grocery. I'm no pauper. I'm only here because my son has gone off to study. I can take you wherever you want to go. Have you got money?'

Leonidas interrupted. 'Can you take us to the old concentration camp?'

The man threw his cigarette on the ground, shut his eyes and gritted his teeth.

'Again? Has this become a pilgrimage? What are you going to do there? Snap photographs and take some souvenirs home with you? Do you think a concentration camp is Disneyland? I was there two years. I had to eat mice and cockroaches to survive. I saw a lot of men die there. They died frozen, or for lack of medical attention, or beaten. They died of fear. You wouldn't have lasted a week if you'd been sent there. Go home and wise up.'

Lia took a step forward and glared at the man. 'My father died in the camp.'

Enjoying himself firing arrows at the easy target of the outsiders, the man had not counted on them being protected by a shield. One of the arrows bounced off and struck him. The man twisted his mouth in astonishment and was silent a few moments. Then he scratched his neck and cleared his throat. His tone of voice was no longer aggressive.

'What was his name? In what year was he sentenced?'

'Ludwig Kirchner. He was a painter, and he was sentenced in 1978.'

'I was sentenced in 1980 because a neighbor had a grudge and informed on me. In my time, he was no longer there.'

Leonidas butted in the conversation. 'As you see, we aren't tourists looking for entertainment. This search is very important for us. Will you take us to the camp?'

'Ten dollars.'

Lia gave him the note, the man inspected it for several seconds, analyzing its texture, and only then did he open the door of the car for them. Lia and Leonidas got in and sat on a seat with torn upholstery and broken springs. The smell of alcohol, sweat, and women's perfume nauseated them. The man sat at the wheel and turned on the stereo. On an old cassette, Demis Roussos was singing 'Goodbye My Love, Goodbye'. The car started, went round the square and continued along the road to the right. The engine rumbled and the suspension shook. Inside, the vibrations set off noises. With no seat-belts, Lia and Leonidas held tight to the seats to avoid banging into one another. As the route moved further away from the station, cultivated fields and small homes appeared. The smell of tilled earth came in through the open window of the driver. They encountered farmers driving carts and grazing sheep. Suddenly, out of nowhere, a band of dirty, ragged children began running behind the car and hurling stones at them. The driver stuck his head out of the window and insulted them. Then he started speaking again.

'Some of those poor wretches are orphans whose parents died in the camp, others are the children of the guards or other people who worked there. They all get along well. That's what I call a national reconciliation.'

Lia risked a question. 'What about you? Have you forgiven the guards who maltreated you in the camp?'

The man turned his head around and showed a smile with broken teeth. 'I gave one of them a good thrashing with a stick, I cracked his skull and broke a few ribs, and then I forgave him. That's how things work around here. That's our justice. An eye for an eye, and a tooth for a tooth, and in the end, we're all friends. Do you get it?'

Leonidas joined the conversation. 'It's a good method, for sure, but only for those who survive.'

Once again the man turned his head round. 'It's the same thing with the dead, the family tries to find the people who were to blame, gives them a few cudgel blows or a bullet in the head, and then forgives them. One way or another, the hatred is buried and life goes on. They can all rest in peace.'

Lia realized he was speaking to her. 'So is that what you recommend I do? Kill my father's murderers so I can forgive them later?'

The man slowed the car down while he pondered his response. 'You came here for some reason, right? Do you think that if you start imagining the tortures your father suffered you'll feel better? Do you think you'll feel peace when you tread the ground where he's buried? In any case, if you think you're going to find him, you've got a disappointment coming. The dead were buried in random places by the other inmates, who the guards forced to dig the graves. The only rule was to bury them far away from the camp. They're everywhere. It's impossible to discover all of them. I'm sorry to be so frank, but maybe you shouldn't have come.'

Lia felt Leonidas stroking her hand. She did not answer; she had no desire to continue the conversation. None of the three spoke again. The driver accelerated the car and turned up the volume of the music. He was happy. This time he felt he had hit the bull's eye.

A few minutes later, the arable lands gave way to trees, the human beings disappeared, and the car entered a forested area. The road became a winding track. The air got cooler and was laden with aromas. The journey went on for another twenty minutes. The driver had to swerve to avoid holes and boulders, coax the car up steep slopes, and stand on his brakes to avoid running over a wild boar. Then, after a long bend, the forest opened up into a plain. A hundred meters or so ahead, like a lost temple, was the old concentration camp. Surrounded by a barbed wire fence three meters tall, there stood the four wooden barracks that had sheltered the prisoners, the hut that had served as a kitchen, the two-storey building that had belonged to the guards, the Commandant's house and the four watchtowers. The entrance gate was wide open, and everything of value had been pillaged.

The driver stopped the car and turned to the passengers again.

'I'm staying here. In a couple of hours it will start getting dark. Don't get lost and if anyone turns up, don't be scared. They're all good people.'

White clouds covered the blue of the sky in tatters. The sun filled them with light, only to empty them like balloons afterwards. The wind lost its breath. They heard the chirping of birds and the humming of insects. The couple got out of the car and walked towards the camp. The barbed wire fence was a serpent that hypnotized them. In the lacerating metal threads he finds the tip of the tangled threads of redemption. She was lost in a labyrinth of horror. Each of them forgot the other's presence; they had never been so alone in their lives.

When they reached the entrance gate, Lia stopped as if she were standing before the maws of a monster. The camp was going to swallow and dismember her. However, she was equally incapable of turning back. She had successive visions of her father, cadaverous and wearing a grey uniform, shaking with fever in a bunk, being beaten by the guards, and raped by other inmates; shouts, screams and groans intensified the horror of the images; and these were all mixed up in an osmosis of violence and suffering where the body of Ludwig Kirchner was tortured without respite. Lia shivered and shook her head, muttering senseless phrases to herself. Leonidas embraced her.

'We'd better leave. It wasn't a good idea to come here.'

Lia pushed him away. 'No! No!'

Leonidas moved off. 'Take it easy, I only want to...'

'Shut up.'

For some time they stood in silence. Lia swept the camp with her gaze. She began to speak again with her eyes riveted to the top of one of the watchtowers. 'If I ran away, I'd never have peace again. They would have won.'

Lia went into the camp and Leonidas followed at a distance. The soil was thick with weeds and little bushes. Insects and lizards darted in the undergrowth. The sun cast long shadows on the buildings, that escaped on the other side of the fence. Lia walked towards one of the barracks. The wood was rotten and broken, and the door and windows were missing. Lia reached the entrance: there was nothing inside and part of the floor had disappeared. Only a musty smell was left. She had hoped to find something: a cot, a table, a tool, any object that might give her a clue about what her father's life had been like in the concentration camp. That emptiness prevented her from picturing the everyday life of a prisoner. She had found a book with blank pages.

Presently, they heard a shuffling behind them. It was a tall man, with white hair, a ruddy face and vacant eyes. He came towards them at a doddering pace with bent back. The two turned towards the stranger, not knowing he was Stanislau Yovic, the former Commandant of the camp.

After the fall of the regime, he had been arrested, tried, sentenced to ten years in prison, and finally pardoned. His alcoholism had worsened and he had never been able to find another job. Since he had no family, he had become a beggar. Lost, he had decided to return to the only place where he had had a stable life and had been respected. It had struck him that he could become a sort of guide for visitors interested in the horrors of the old regime – if there was tourism in Nazi camps, there would be in Communist camps, too. When he returned there he was attacked by ordinary people, among them the taxi driver. He was hospitalized for two months, and ended up lame in his right leg, deaf in his left ear, and with half his teeth broken, but he survived. And with time the locals ended up tolerating the presence of the drunk who had neither hearth nor home. In a more merciful version of an eye for an eye and a tooth for a tooth, they had forgiven him. Thus, at weekends, Yovic spent the afternoons at the camp, waiting for someone who might pay for his booze. He had prepared a simple story and it was nearly always successful.

Smiling, he approached the visitors. 'I have been watching you for a while and I thought it was about time I introduced myself.'

'Who are you?' Leonidas asked.

'I worked here as an assistant in the kitchen and now I'm the guide who gives information to visitors. I don't charge anything. You can give me whatever you see fit.'

Leonidas glanced at Lia and saw a trace of suspicion on her lips. Could this man write a single line of any kind in the blank book of the concentration camp? She decided to question him. 'So how long did you work in the kitchen here?'

Yovic answered in a soft, submissive voice. 'I came here very young. You might say I worked as an assistant from the time the camp opened.'

'So long working as an assistant, yet you were never promoted to chief cook? You must have been a terrible assistant.'

Yovic was unprepared for questions like that. He blinked and sniffed. 'Well, as you know, in those days there were lots of injustices…'

Lia glanced at Leonidas, who shrugged his shoulders, meaning she should not waste her time questioning the man. Lia took a dollar bill out of her pocket and the eyes of Yovic gleamed. There was a bottle of vodka right there.

'Listen carefully. I'm going to ask you some questions and it's very important that you give me exact answers.'

'Of course, of course…'

'Do you remember a prisoner called Ludwig Kirchner who came here in 1978?'

Yovic turned pale. Memories of talks he had had with Kirchner came tumbling down, of the pictures he had shown him, of the punishment he had given him, of his illness, the doctor's visit and his death. However, his remorse evaporated faster than alcohol fumes.

'Kirchner… yes, I remember… He was a painter, wasn't he?'

'He was my father.'

'Ah…'

'What happened to him?'

Yovic lowered his head. He had to come up with a plausible story quickly. 'It was awful. There were common criminals here, violent men, murderers, and one day… a criminal stabbed him…'

Lia interrupted him. 'Stabbed him? For what reason? My father was the most peaceful man in the world and he never got involved in quarrels, especially with people like that.'

Yovic passed his hand over his hair. 'Yes, your father was a very quiet man, certainly. It wasn't his fault. The other guy tried to rob him and he protested. That was all it took for the criminal to kill him. These things happen fast in prisons, you can die over a trifle.'

Lia glanced at Leonidas again, who shrugged his shoulders once more. The story was poorly told, but not implausible.

'And do you know where they buried him? Can you take us there?'

Yovic had got his confidence back. 'Sadly, I can't help you. No one spoke about the subject.'

Lia closed her eyes and remained silent. Leonidas was about to take her arm and lead her away when she went back to questioning Yovic.

'Just one more question. Do you remember if he painted anything in the camp?'

'No... I don't remember... I don't pay much attention to that sort of thing...'

'Maybe he might have given a drawing to someone?'

Yovic pretended he was trying to remember. 'I don't know, but if he really painted anything, someone must have stolen it...'

No one said anything else. Lia clenched her jaws. Leonidas took a deep breath. Yovic held out his hand to take the dollar bill.

When they got back to the car, the sun had vanished. Lia looked at the sky. The pink balloons of the clouds had burst. She felt lost, unable even to remember her father's face. That drunk had made everything up, the taxi driver might have been lying too, no one was trustworthy, and the truth – that she might never find. Her mother was right, her arms were not strong enough to stop the world and set it spinning the other way. They would only live in freedom when they found peace. Where?

Leonidas, on the other hand, was serene. He had freed men from that camp and prevented others from dying there. The price had been the life, not of an innocent victim as people said, but of a collaborator of a criminal regime. Luda's ghost was left in the camp, to dissolve somewhere with Kirchner's corpse. His world was starting to turn in the direction he wanted it to.

They got into the car in silence, determined not to speak to the driver again. Nor did he ask them any question, having little interest, apparently, in taking up the conversation once more. However, the car did not move. They looked at one another and in the end Leonidas spoke to the driver. 'What are we waiting for? We want to leave.'

The driver hacked. 'If you don't mind, I'm going to give someone a lift…'

'Who?'

'The camp guide.'

Lia jumped out of her seat. 'What? Are you kidding us?'

'Don't take offence, miss. Life is really tough in this town and we have to help each other. I bring him here and take him back and he gives me half of what he earns.'

Leonidas thumped the seat. 'Then why did you make that drama of indignation about us wanting to visit the camp? There was no need for all the play-acting, was there?'

Finally the driver turned his face to the passengers. 'You may not understand it, but I meant what I said. I can't stand seeing people doing tourism at my expense and the expense of so many others who died in the camp. If they were journalists or doing research, I might understand it. But the only people who turn up are young lads with their girlfriends who start taking selfies, all happy, and that turns my stomach. As I told you, I have to earn a living.'

As he finished, Yovic opened the front door and got in as if it were public transport. The driver picked up a bottle of vodka hidden under the carpet and offered it. Lia spat to the side. The only voice heard during the trip back was that of Demis Roussos.

♛

Helena, Schwartz, Lia and Fiorov

THE EXHIBITION was called *Oppression, Resistance, Freedom* and it had been organized by Fiorov's government in the Palace of the Arts. The curators were the writer Albert Remus and the painter Hector Lott. Comprised of photographs, paintings, sculptures and videos, it aimed to show the relationship between art and history in the country over the past two decades. *Oppression* exhibited works of art created during Ionescu's regime, accompanied by an introductory text which explained that the regime had used art as propaganda. *Resistance* exhibited works by artists who were victims of the dictatorship, whether by censorship, or by the imposition of aesthetic rules, or indeed internment in a concentration camp; the introductory text explained that by refusing to conform to the official canons of taste and adopting Modernism, these artists had used their art to condemn the violence perpetrated against citizens. *Freedom* exhibited works of art created during and after *Perestroika* by young artists; the introductory text declared that even when they resorted to abstract motifs or others that were hard to decode, they were celebrating the new era of democracy and freedom.

The exhibition's gala opening was at three in the afternoon on Saturday, 2 July, 1990. Twenty young women chosen by a modelling agency had been hired to serve the visitors. Wearing white blouses, tight black skirts and high heels, and instructed to smile constantly, they offered vodka, champagne and French wines, as well as caviar, lobster and smoked salmon. Thirty agents from Fiorov's personal bodyguard, in civilian clothes, among them Szut, had the task of ensuring the security of the event. Three Art Historians, duly identified with a lapel badge, one in each salon, were ready to answer questions from the visitors.

It was a sunny day, with high temperatures. The beams struck the neoclassical building, highlighting the revolutionary scenes sculpted in the marble pediment, which was supported by Doric columns. Gleaming, the Communist heroes looked as if they were about to escape from the façade and descend the flight of twenty steps to start another revolution. However, it was the people who had beaten them who climbed up the stairs to visit the exhibition that celebrated the fall of the regime.

In the adjacent square, kept at a distance by a line of policemen, were dozens of hawkers who were vying for the best spots with each other. Their awnings and sunshades formed a mosaic of many colors. The aromas from their food were as intense as at any other fair. One of them had managed to get closer than the rest to the area where those invited to the exhibition passed by, without anyone daring to approach him. Beside his cart where he kept his potato hamburgers, Chef Kristoff was constantly busy serving his customers.

HELENA Yava had come to the exhibition with Micho. Apart from her own interest, she wanted to teach Micho something about the contemporary history of his new country. As she suspected that the exhibition would denigrate part of her work as People's Commissar for Education, she was prepared to clarify the distortions, mistakes and lies she expected to find. After they had gone through the metal detector at the entrance, and passed by the four armed policemen who had orders to prevent the entrance of suspicious visitors, they went into a corridor with a red carpet that led to the three salons. Like the majority of the visitors, Helena chose to start at the beginning, in the salon that had the works of art created during the regime she had served, the works that were now classified as *Oppression*. Helena began reading the introductory text displayed on one of the walls, but did not get beyond the first paragraph.

Just as the Catholic Church used the sensuality of Baroque art to seduce the faithful, Ionescu's regime used photography and realism in painting and sculpture to convince the citizens that they lived in a sort of paradise on earth. Both promised an illusion meant to distract the people from the hardships they lived with.

With a grimace of anger, she tugged Micho's hand and moved towards the works of art. The first on display to the visitors was a photograph of Pioneers, a meter long by sixty centimeters wide. A group of forty boys and girls, between the ages of twelve and fifteen, dressed in blue trousers and skirts and white shirts, with red scarves at their throats, were lined up in four ranks at attention, as if at a military parade. The sunlight struck them diagonally, illuminating the left side of their faces but leaving the right side in semi-darkness. In the second rank, in the third place, stiff and serious, was Roman Schwartz. Helena recognized the photograph and paused to gaze at it. The Pioneers were part of her project. She had often been beside them, embracing them and giving them good advice. The declaration that they had been oppressed outraged her. Suddenly, she turned to Micho.

'Look carefully at these boys and girls. Do they strike you as unhappy?'

Micho looked at the image, intrigued, but was unable to say anything.

Helena went on as if she were talking to herself. 'No, a lot of them are actually smiling. Those young people had the best education available at the time, they mixed with hundreds of other adolescents and children, had contact with nature, and practiced sports. We kept them away from vices and taught them fundamental principles like discipline, honesty and solidarity. I'm sure these boys and girls are successful adults today. Maybe in a different way from how I planned it, but they're the new men and women. The world belongs to them.'

Micho nodded and Helena kept gazing at the photograph for some time.

Next, they proceeded through the salon, looking without interest at statues of Ionescu, and some paintings. Only the picture of the factory that Kirchner had been forced to paint aroused their interest. Helena remembered this image too, of the gigantic industrial complex, with its chimneys spewing black smoke, which seemed to swallow up the tiny workers who came in through the main gate. The background of a yellowish plain that merged with the horizon was the only pleasant feature of the painting. She was unable to explain to Micho that the people who worked in this factory were as happy as the Pioneers and were not oppressed.

They were coming out of the salon, Helena at a quick pace and Micho almost being dragged, when they came across Jan, who had chosen to start with the 'Freedom' section. The adults were embarrassed, but the child smiled and would have hugged the friend he had played with one day, if his mother had not pulled him away. Helena and Jan neither spoke nor nodded by way of greeting, but in the brief eye contact between them, in that intense gaze, anxious and grateful, they established the greatest act of complicity of their lives.

Now Helena and Micho went into the salon in which were exhibited the works that symbolized the Resistance. Helena began to read the introductory text, but once again was unable to get beyond the first paragraph.

Faced with a brutal dictatorship that aimed to regulate all the citizens' activities and control their thoughts in order to prevent turns that might endanger the foundations of the regime, artists like Ludwig Kirchner wielded their paintbrushes as an act of resistance.

Helena and Micho began looking at the twenty paintings by Kirchner hanging there. They were portraits of naked and dressed women, dancers, everyday scenes and landscapes painted in intense, contrasting colors; the influence was from primitive art, where the artist sought the vital forces of nature and the animal side of the human being. They had belonged to Ivan Fiorov since the agreement he had made with Jacob Levi to call a doctor who would try to save the painter's life. Although she did not agree with the political interpretation given to the works, seeing them instead as the free expression of the artist, Helena gazed at the paintings with fascination. She did not associate the suffering she found in some of the characters' faces with a condemnation of the conditions of life under the dictatorship, but instead with an exorcism of the demons of the creator, reminiscent of what Edvard Munch had done with *The Scream*. Unaware of aesthetic or sociological matters, Micho was only interested in the nude women.

After looking at Kirchner's work, they went to a closed partition within one of the salons whose entrance was controlled by a worker who asked the youngest visitors for their identity cards. Apparently, only people over the age of eighteen could go in. There was a long queue. Intrigued, Helena went to read the text which explained the reserved admission work.

After the loss of the Greco-Roman tradition of nudity as a symbol of virtue and of sex as one of life's pleasures, and its replacement by the Judeo-Christian concept of the body as a cause of shame, and of pleasure as a sin, the totalitarian regimes of the twentieth century made use of the repression of sexuality – especially of women – to achieve the complete submission of the individual. The intrusion into the citizens' private life was meant to destroy the last free act which remained to them. It was the total castration of the human being. This is why the videos of the French director Mathieux Foucault (especially Perestroika in Bed*), which have wrongly been considered pornographic by the lay audience, constituted a form of resistance to Ionescu's regime. Managing to evade police surveillance, Foucault used the body as a weapon of protest, and sex as an act of rebellion. Thus, in the brutal copulations of these anonymous men and women, the orgasm they reach may be called FREEDOM.*

Helena laughed and turned towards Micho. 'This stuff is in the wrong place. They should have put it in the salon reserved for comedy or the paintings of lunatics. I hope you never see it, my son.'

Micho, who had lost interest in the exhibition after the nude women, shrugged his shoulders. 'Can we leave now, mummy?'

Meanwhile, in a corner of the salon, an old man in a wheelchair whose face was scarred and who had lost one ear, had been observing the two of them for some minutes. His chin trembled and his eyes were bleary. At first he wanted to shout, to be able to stand up, to have a gun in his hand. Gradually, though, his rage gave way to confusion. From the moment he saw them, Zdanhov understood everything: the man who had almost burned him alive and the former People's Commissar had conspired to get their revenge on him. However, if that was obvious, what followed did not make sense. Zdanhov was trying to feel his way in a dark room in which he could not find the light switch. He did not understand why they had not killed him. Unable to understand the trauma of rape, he had concluded that that man had not had sufficient motive to kill him. On the other hand, he considered it inevitable that Helena would want to kill him to avenge the death of Ruth. In the past he had never seen the former People's Commissar showing the least compassion for the regime's enemies. So why should she show any compassion for him now? Besides, if they had only wanted to beat him up, why had they used the child in such a risky plan? These questions would remain engraved like the scars on his face, and finding the answers would prove as impossible as finding his missing ear.

PIETR Schwartz had picked the day of the opening of the exhibition to kill Ivan Fiorov. He had reached the conclusion that he would never be able to get close enough in the street when Fiorov got in and out of his car, and he could not risk a long-range shot, because if he missed, the bodyguards would eliminate him at once. His only chance of killing him would be a public event where Fiorov was forced to mingle with the people, exposing him a little more. In fact the exhibition united a number of conditions that made him vulnerable – as did JFK's last trip in Dallas. However, as there would be metal detector at the entrance, and guards to inspect suspicious visitors, Schwartz would have to make use of a weapon other than a pistol or a knife. Recalling the methods that the secret police used to eliminate opponents of the regime, Schwartz decided that a sharpened pencil would be the most efficient method. Unfortunately he did not have at his disposal the deadly poison the Bulgarian secret services had used to execute the dissident Georgi Markov, in London, on the tip of an umbrella. But once he had evaded the weapons check at the entrance, he could kill him with a blow to his throat. It was a suicidal plan and there were many factors that might prevent him from carrying it out, such as not having the necessary training or the dexterity, but Schwartz could not hope for more. On that day, he would risk everything.

With the pencil in the pocket of his jacket, he went through security without being patted down, and entered the Palace of the Arts. He gripped his weapon in his right hand and never let it go. The wooden object had become a battery that permitted him to move. If he let go of it, he would be deprived of his source of energy, and would be unable to take another step. The works of art and the three salons were as if non-existent, concentrated as he was solely on killing Fiorov. Nevertheless, when he remarked, as he had expected, that the prime minister had still not arrived, he wound up noticing the images offered to his view. At first, he saw only colors and shapes without any meaning. However, having gone through the salons with works devoted to *Freedom* and *Resistance*, and staying put in the salon devoted to *Oppression*, the images began speaking to him. The photograph of the Pioneers appealed to him. With a hesitant step, Schwartz approached the picture. It was just like looking at an old family photograph. He began to analyze the faces of each of those boys. When he found Roman, the twelve-year-old child being educated to serve his country, he let go of his pencil. He remembered having taken his son to the Pioneers' headquarters that day, and having hugged him when they parted, and he remembered the pride he felt on seeing his son taking his role so seriously. Schwartz opened his mouth and made guttural noises. The visitors moved away from him and he was soon alone. Schwartz touched the photograph with both hands, as if he could grab Roman, rescue him from the paper and bring him back to life.

Then a murmur began at the entrance of the palace and spread through the three salons, in agitated of voices. The sounds of the crowd became the true nexus that unified *Oppression, Resistance,* and *Freedom.* Suddenly, silence. The guests halted their conversations and the young women serving them did not dare to take a step.

Ivan Fiorov had arrived.

Schwartz woke from his trance. He looked for the last time at his son's face, kissed it, and turned around. He brought his hand to his jacket pocket to grip the pencil and moved with swift steps to entrance hallway. Then, ten paces away, he saw Fiorov. He was surrounded by people offering him their hands and smiling. For a few seconds Schwartz paused to look at him. The navy blue suit, the white shirt and red tie; the tanned face, the dark eyes, and teeth that were too white. He gripped the pencil with all his might. Abruptly, his stare riveted on Fiorov's throat, he shot towards his target. He advanced five steps without any obstacle, then pushed away a woman who did not move aside, took two more paces, and when he judged he was close enough to throw himself on Fiorov, he raised the arm with the sharpened pencil in his hand. At once Szut barred his way, another guard grabbed his wrist and disarmed him, and two more men threw him to the floor and immobilized him. Schwartz still managed to shout, 'Assassi…' but someone covered his mouth and gave him a blow to the head, knocking him out. The other guards led Fiorov to one side, while Szut and his men picked up Schwartz and carried him outside the building.

A hubbub started in the hallway, a girl dropped a tray with glasses of champagne, and an old couple left the exhibition, but soon everything was back to normal. The visitors in the salons had not noticed anything. Fiorov was calm. He had expected something similar, just as he had expected the neutralization of the threat by his bodyguards. He knew his popularity would grow when the media broke the news that someone had tried to assassinate him.

LIA had been unable to persuade her mother to visit the exhibition which was going to show the works of Ludwig Kirchner. 'See the paintings they stole from us? Don't ask me to do that. I couldn't stand it.' In that event, organized by the government of the man who had seized the spoils of her husband's work, she could find neither freedom nor resistance, but only oppression. Lia shared her mother's feelings concerning the exhibition of something that belonged to her, but unlike her mother, she longed to see the paintings once again. 'I must go. I have received the challenge and I cannot fail in the fight. It's the final battle. Afterwards, I will be free.' On the other hand, Leonidas feared that being confronted with yet another profanation of the memory of her father would only add another link to her chains. It was a battle she could never win. However, he did not manage to develop his argument, because Lia, squeezing his arm, closed the discussion. 'Trust me.' There was nothing else to say or ask. He would accompany her in this new leap in the dark, where art could not be more harmful than a concentration camp. Anyway, he had never seen any of Kirchner's paintings.

During the trip by car to the Palace of the Arts, Lia never once mentioned her father's works of art which they were about to see. Just as when they had made the train trip, any other subject seemed more interesting or appropriate to the situation. Leonidas was no longer surprised. She was saving his strength for the battle. In this way he was complicit in the farce of pretending that it was just a weekend jaunt like any other. If that were the fighter's strategy, he would respect it. All the same, when they reached the building the façade was so imposing and freighted with symbols that it gave them both pause. It was as if a part of the dictatorship remained present, resisting and challenging democracy. Even though inside the exhibitions celebrated freedom, the façade endured as a warning that totalitarian forces continued to keep them under surveillance, lying in wait for the accident that would occur in the course of history when fear made people run towards the claws where they expected to find protection. Nor would it be of any benefit to demolish the building or destroy the façade with a bomb, since the germ of totalitarianism had already found a new host.

Lia roused Leonidas from his trance by tugging at his arm. 'Come on, you're the one who seems as if he's scared to go in.'

Having passed through the security checks at the entrance, under the suspicious eyes of two guards, Leonidas allowed himself to be led by Lia's warm hand. He expected her to head straight for Ludwig Kirchner's works, but to his amazement Lia went into the *Oppression* salon. There were over twenty visitors there; the older ones contemplated part of their past in silence, while the younger ones talked nonsense. Lia looked around everywhere, paying no attention to the works of art, her head turning like a radar scanner searching for an object. The photograph of the Pioneers and the painting of the Witten factory – which she did not consider a true picture of her father's – did not merit more than a quick glance. Leonidas, on the other hand, could not take his eyes off the factory he had had blown up. He saw it just as it was portrayed: as a devourer of human beings, that had to be destroyed. Presently, Lia took his hand again and they left the salon. They crossed the corridor, ignored a smiling young woman's offer of champagne, and went into the area devoted to *Resistance*.

In this salon there were three times as many visitors. There was a smell of perfume, sweat and tobacco. Some of the men were drunk, and telling dirty jokes. A group of women were laughing and talking in loud voices as if they were in a bar. Two children were tearing about wildly. Few of the visitors were looking at the pictures. Once again Lia began to scrutinize the space, her gaze pausing on the each person's face, and when their backs were turned, moving so she could see them from the front. Only then did she look at her father's paintings. She remembered them all as though she had only seen them last a few weeks ago. However, the change from the gaze of the child to the gaze of the adult had transformed the works. The paintings no longer frightened her. The anxiety of the characters and the disturbance of nature were still apparent, but it was as if she were observing a storm moving away. The emotional turbulence of the work belonged to a past era, a time of terror that no longer existed. She no longer had a face like these sad girls; they were a kind of distant relative that she wanted to get away from. Lia had taken one foot out of that epoch and was ready to take the next step with the other.

Seeing her so absorbed in the contemplation of the paintings, her expression serene, with a trace of a smile, Leonidas supposed he had been wrong, and wondered about their effect on Lia. *Might it be that these fiery colors, the reds and oranges that sear the skies and burn the faces of the figures – was all this the red hot iron bar that cauterized the wound?*

Suddenly Lia turned, without taking his hand or saying a word, and disappeared into the crowd. Leonidas struggled to follow her among the visitors, and had to weave past some and push others aside, but he knew where she was going. Shortly, he found her by the entrance to the salon which represented *Freedom*. There was a similar number of visitors to those who had been in *Resistance*, but here there was no noise. The drunks restrained themselves, no one spoke loudly, and the children seemed like Pioneers in their movements. Lia stared at a group at the far end of the room and her lips drew back in a smile that showed her canine teeth. Leonidas understood what she was going to do, but said nothing. In this battle his role was the spectator compelled to silence. He awaited the outcome. But Lia was in no hurry. Controlling the exit gave her an advantage over his opponent. Her glare remained fixed, but her smile had vanished. She was taking deep breaths, releasing the air through her mouth. As she seemed undecided about moving forward, Leonidas read the introductory text to the works of art displayed on the wall.

Following years of Resistance to Oppression, artists were able to express themselves in Freedom. Figurative and abstract, explicit and enigmatic, highbrow or lowbrow, the present grouping of works of art is like a shout bellowed at last from the throat.

'Ivan Fiorov, you thief! Give back the paintings you stole from my father!'

Everyone stared at Lia: some open-mouthed, others frowning, and one girl covered her mouth to stifle a laugh. Fiorov was petrified; here was something he had not foreseen. The guards raised their hands to their guns. Szut was going to move towards Lia, but an order from his chief stopped him.

'Leave her alone.'

So Lia began to walk and a corridor opened wherever she passed. People fell back in silence. The only sound was her shoes drumming the wooden floor. At the end of the corridor Ivan Fiorov awaited her. At the start of it, watching her walk away, was Leonidas. With every step Lia took, the viewers' suspense grew. The air seemed ionized by electrical charges. From a sculpture made from objects found in the rubbish, a piece was hanging off. Lia was seven paces from Fiorov and had already made eye contact with him. Two black spheres stuck on a white background, aimed at her. In them she saw neither anger, nor fear, nor any emotion. However, it was not the gaze of a dead doll, but of a reptile in a state of alert. Her eyes did not waver, but his closeness made her slacken her pace. In another three steps she would be near enough to slap him. Quickly, Fiorov forestalled her. He stepped forward and stopped Lia in her tracks. He was more than a hand's breadth taller than she was and nearly twice as broad in the shoulders. A smile appeared like a sudden crack in his face.

'I see there's a misunderstanding. I'll be happy to explain things to you in my office.'

Lia smiled too, her canines ready to bite; she took another step and pointed at his face.

'There's no misunderstanding. I demand that you return Ludwig Kirchner's paintings, which you stole from my house. You're a thief, Ivan Fiorov.'

LIA and Leonidas were thrown out of the exhibition by Fiorov's guards, accompanied by jeers and insults from the majority of the visitors. He let himself be led out without resisting, while she protested when they grabbed her arm. However, they were not assaulted, or arrested, nor was any kind of complaint lodged against Lia. At the time, the cold air of the late afternoon appeared to be the only punishment for the incident.

Lia

AFTER the confrontation, Fiorov ordered Huss and Remus to be present at his house at ten o'clock in the evening. Dressed in their best clothes, they arrived ten minutes early, but only rang the doorbell at the exact time. They were checked by the security guards just like any other visitors, and received with grumbles by the housekeeper, Irina. Then they went into a large salon with windows, decorated with antique and modern furniture, oriental vases, African carpets, leopard skins, silver salvers and maps. Fiorov sat in a black leather armchair in a corner of the salon and, for the first time, he ordered them to sit on the sofa. Huss and Remus obeyed, without leaning back on the cushions. Fiorov went straight to the point.

'You saw what happened at the exhibition. I want to hear your opinion.'

Huss and Remus exchanged looks as if to decide who should speak first. Remus lowered his gaze.

'Boss, you know what I think about such cases,' said Huss. 'What's more, that woman's ungrateful. You tried to help her father and did you see how she thanked you? What she did is no different from an assassination attempt. Don't let her try anything like that again. Because that's exactly what she'll do, since she interpreted your kindness as a sign of weakness. Democracy invites people to disrespect authority, in the belief that nothing will happen to them. Just give the order and the problem will disappear. I know she's pregnant, and if that's any impediment, we can wait until she has the child.'

Fiorov took a deep breath and looked at Remus. He straightened his back still more before he spoke.

'Boss, dozens of people heard the accusations of the painter's daughter. If anything happens to her, your image as Prime Minister will be affected. Here at home we can limit the damage, but abroad there will be grave repercussions. With the Chinese and the Arabs there won't be any problems, but the Europeans and the Americans are a real pain about all these human rights. I understand that you must be disgusted at her ingratitude, which doubtless is unforgivable, but my advice to you is to solve the problem another way. The best way to be free of that woman is to exile her. Send her far away. In the first few days the foreign newspapers will give her some attention, but within a week she'll be forgotten. The art thefts of the Nazis is the subject that interests global public opinion.'

Huss interrupted him. 'Then do what Stalin did with Trotsky. Send her to Mexico and I'll go there and deal with her.'

Remus shook his head. 'No, that would be even worse. If Trotsky had died of natural causes, he would never have attained the fame he has now.'

'If you let her get away, she'll keep making trouble. Journalists are your enemies too.'

'There's no perfect solution…'

'The old methods are always the best,' said Huss.

'Unless… don't be offended by what I'm about to say, boss… unless to shut her up, we give her what she wants…'

Fiorov raised his eyebrows then made a hand gesture to signal that the meeting was over. Huss and Remus stood up, said goodbye to him and left. When they went out, Fiorov lit a cigar and blew out a long grey puff. His dogs were barking at the visitors, but he did not hear them. The smoke spreading through the room reminded him of the fog that used to wrap the concentration camp in the dusk. At once the cold and the smells of the barracks were present again. Fiorov saw Jacob Levi begging him to find a doctor to come and save Kirchner. *We made a fair deal, in the circumstances. It would be fair in any circumstances. Yes. Isn't life worth more than art? It's not your fault he died. You didn't send him to a concentration camp, or make him chop wood. And who made him defy that idiot Yovic? If he had been smarter, he'd still be alive. No, you owe absolutely nothing to that ungrateful family.* Fiorov sucked in more smoke from the cigar and blew it out slowly. The matter was settled. He started thinking about his businesses, but Lia's blue eyes emerged in the smoke.

✦

TWO days later, Maria Kirchner, Lia and Leonidas were having lunch when they heard the doorbell ring. The metallic buzz made them stop moving their cutlery. Pieces of chicken, potatoes and beetroot hung suspended between their plates and their mouths. The smell of the cooking disappeared. Lia and Leonidas stared at one another. Maria got up to open the door. She came face to face with a well-built man with greying hair and yellowish eyes, accompanied by a thin man with white hair and green eyes. The latter smiled and introduced himself.

'Hello, my name is Albert Remus and this gentleman is Piotr Huss. We've come to speak to your daughter, Lia Kirchner. And we have a parcel to deliver to you too.'

Maria had no time to say anything, because at once another two men in overalls appeared who asked her to stand aside and came inside her house, carrying a big box.

'Where shall we put this?' one of the men asked.

Coming from the kitchen, Lia barred their way.

'Who are you and what are you doing?'

'Ask the bosses there,' said the other man.

Lia watched Remus and Huss passing her mother as if they owned the house, and advancing towards her. The hallway was cramped for so many people. The delivery men put the box in a corner and leaned against the wall to let them pass. Leonidas put his hand on her shoulder.

'Lia Kircher, we need to talk,' said Remus.

'There's nothing to talk about. Get out! If you don't…'

'You'll call the police?' Huss asked.

Meanwhile Maria came up behind the visitors. She remembered that years ago a group of four men had invaded the home the same way, threatened her with guns to show them where her husband's paintings were, and had at once stolen them. At least that day Lia had been at school. Her voice came out wrenched, as if from a dying person.

'Daughter, I'm tired of all this. I've had enough of strangers entering our home. Let's hear what they have to say so we can put an end to this matter for once and for all.'

Huss turned towards her. 'Lady, very important business brings us here. It would be a big mistake to send us away. I suggest you receive us in a more appropriate place.'

Soon the five were sitting in the living room. Remus and Huss sat on a sofa without asking permission, Leonidas chose a chair far away from them, and the two women remained on their feet. Lia crossed her arms and tapped her foot on the carpet.

'We're waiting. Speak.'

Remus crossed his legs and began. 'First of all, I apologize for the intrusion, but the matter couldn't be dealt with in the street. We were sent by the Prime Minister, Mr. Ivan Fiorov, with two missions. The first is to offer you five pictures by the painter Ludwig Kirchner…'

Lia raised an arm and cut him off. 'You aren't offering us anything because those paintings were stolen from this house. What's more, we demand the return of the twenty works of art Fiorov appropriated. So…'

Remus did not allow her to finish. 'I'm sorry, but you're ill-informed. The pictures are in the possession of the Prime Minister owing to an agreement made when your father was a prisoner. He was ill and…'

Lia glanced at her mother, who shook her head.

'We never heard that. When they came to steal the pictures they didn't give us any explanation. This story is another of your lies. You can leave.'

Remus took a deep breath, leaned his head on the upholstery of the sofa and shut his eyes. Huss straightened his back and leaned forward. His voice came out like thunder.

'Listen, we don't give a damn whether you believe us or not. The paintings are here, and if you don't want them, we'll take them back. As far as I'm concerned, it can all go on the rubbish heap, which is the right place for shit like that. Now listen carefully to what I'm about to tell you. Two days ago you seriously slandered the Prime Minister which, in other circumstances, would cost you dearly. However, our Prime Minister has decided to be merciful because he understood that you, like your dad, act without thinking of the consequences. That's why, so that everything ends well and no one gets hurt, I'm inviting you to make a journey abroad and remain living there…'

Lia took a step in Huss's direction. 'You can tell the Prime Minister we reject his proposal. He's the one who should be exiled to a desert island and rot away there alone.'

Huss stood up. 'It seems I didn't make myself understood. The proposal that you leave the country is not one you can refuse. Put your hand on your belly and ask your child if he wants to live.'

Maria let out a shout and Leonidas rose at once. They both stood in front of Lia, forming a barrier.

'If you do anything to her, I'll kill you both,' said Leonidas, clenching his fist.

Huss laughed. 'Yes, if you remained alive, I'm sure you'd try to kill us. You have the experience, don't you? But you won't remain alive. No one in this family will.'

Remus got up too then and opened his arms wide. His face was pale.

'Calm down. The conversation has got out of control. I'm asking you, Lia Kirchner, to reflect on what I'm about to say. For reasons it's not worth discussing right now, this country treated your father badly, and it will treat you, your child, and your mother badly. I don't want that to happen. Look at me. Once I was an independent creator too, maybe even a better-known one than your father. I had thousands of readers, I was studied in the universities, they compared me to the best European writers. My life was perfect. But the gods sometimes punish those who rise too high. When the regime changed I realized that if I wanted to survive I had to make a difficult choice.' Remus' voice shook as he went on: 'They say I sold my soul to the devil, that I betrayed myself, and even unkinder things. And it's true, I stopped being who I was. The price I paid was high. I lost my friends and nobody respects me today. But I'm alive.' Remus paused and looked up. 'Your choice is easier than mine. You don't have to abdicate your dignity, betray your ideals, or inform on anyone. All you have to do is choose to live and save your family. I'd give everything I have if someone could have made the offer to me a few years ago that I'm making you now. Please accept it. Accept it for yourself, for those you love, and even if it's a matter of indifference to you, so that I can have something to feel proud of.'

Everyone was silent. Lia, Maria and Leonidas exchanged perplexed looks. Huss felt like beating him. Remus took an envelope from his jacket pocket and held it out to Lia.

'Here are three tickets to Paris. You will leave within five days. On arrival you will find an official from the embassy who will take you to your house. The government will pay your expenses for a year, no questions asked. There won't be any retaliation if you give an interview to the newspapers or make any kind of public protest. That was the best I was able to do for you. Accept the offer, Lia.'

Lia

IT WAS one o'clock in the morning and Lia could not sleep. She put her hand on her belly and felt the baby kicking. She smiled. It was not the discomforts of pregnancy that kept her awake. The exile in Paris had turned out more difficult than she supposed. Her mother took antidepressants and spent the day in bed, Leonidas had been unable to find a job and had started drinking too much, and she had done the same as Remus – saved her life, but lost her honor. If living in freedom meant finding peace, then the three of them had gone to a prison. The lodgings might be comfortable and the views stunning, but they were still prisoners.

Lia went to the window that overlooked the rue Marie Tibault and gazed out for a few seconds. The coming and going of the white and red lights of the cars, the yellow streetlight flickering, a prostitute smoking a cigarette, a poster of the man who did not like immigrants – the squint-eyed gargoyle who had become her new enemy. An idea slid like a curtain that hid the view. For weeks it had stirred in her. She turned her head towards the desk. She hesitated. She bit her lip. She was afraid she would not be capable. She was afraid of opening the wound even more. She was afraid of invoking the devils and not being able to tame them. Worse still, she was afraid of being ridiculous. How would her mother react? What would Leonidas say? And the others, whose permission she had not asked? Lia went back to gazing at the street. The curtain would not open. Until, finally, she turned around, sat down, and switched on the computer. It would not be in Paris, nor London, nor anywhere that she would find what she sought. The key to the prison was not hidden in the Eiffel Tower. In truth, it no longer even existed. She would have to create it. The computer was the forge where she would hammer it into existence and the key was a story.

It was a story that would tell the tragedy of her country and fill in the blank book of her father's death. An epic book with many villains, but no hero, that began before her birth and continued until the present moment. One part would be real, another part she would have to invent, but was not that how History had been written throughout the centuries? *What is truth?* Pilate had asked Jesus. The truth was what the majority decided it would be, at any particular moment. Pilate had found Jesus innocent, but the crowd considered him guilty. That was the truth on which Christianity had been founded.

Now it was her turn to play Pilate, and in contrast to him, she had decided that Ionescu's regime was guilty. Next, she would present her verdict to the crowd and it would be them, the readers, who would choose the truth. No new religion would be born, naturally, but a utopian belief with roots in the myth of the Garden of Eden promising paradise on earth would attract even more disbelief. Besides, the democracy that had allowed Fiorov's rise to power would not come out with much dignity. Even so, in the midst of filth, flowers would spring up: love and solidarity.

That was the truth that Lia hoped for in *Perestroika*.

Then she remembered the taxi driver who had taken her to the concentration camp, and his bizarre concept of Biblical justice. Would she be killing her father's murderers that way, only to forgive them afterwards?

At once she thought that she would not, she would never forgive them. But then she realized that if she continued to feed her hatred she would never find peace. The key would open the door to another cell. Growing from an adolescent to a woman, she would carry on incarnating the anguished characters of her father, whether alone at home or wandering the streets. Worse yet, she would imprison her child in the past. The taxi-driver may have been a liar, but he had supplied her with the master-key for escaping from that concentration camp. Jesus had been able to forgive and turn the other cheek, but other men did not have that ability. Like Herod, dictatorships killed the innocent at birth. To perfect the justice of the Old Testament was the solution. Forgiveness had a price for the executioner: some demanded one of his eyes, others a tooth; *I* will be satisfied with writing the truth.

Lia Kirchner, Paris, 1992

The End

ABOUT THE AUTHOR

JOÃO CERQUEIRA holds a PhD in Art History from the University of Porto, is the author of nine books and is published in eight countries. His novel, "Jesus and Magdalene" won the *2020 Indie Reader Awards*, the *Silver Medal* for *2017 Global Ebook Award*, and was nominated for the *Latino Book Award 2015*. His recent novel "The Tragedy of Fidel Castro" won the *USA Best Book Award 2013*, the *Beverly Hills Book Award 2014* and the *Global Ebook Award 2014*. His latest novel "PERESTROIKA - An Eye for an Eye and a Tooth for a Tooth" was a finalist for the *2021 Eyland Awards*, a finalist for *Fiction Factory Chapter Novel Competition 2012*, finalist in the *2023 Latino Book Awards*, and winner of the *HFC 2023 European Book of the Year Award*. He was born in Viana do Castelo, Portugal where he currently resides.

Find out more at: www.joaocerqueira.com

www.ingramcontent.com/pod-product-compliance
Lightning Source LLC
Chambersburg PA
CBHW030031030726
47500CB00001B/46